DAVID WILLIAM PEARCE

IN THE SERVICE OF OTHERS

A MONK BUTTMAN MYSTERY

Black Rose Writing | Texas

First printing

ISBN: 978-1-68433-777-4
PUBLISHED BY BLACK ROSE WRITING
www.blackrosewriting.com

Printed in the United States of America
Suggested Retail Price (SRP) $19.95

In the Service of Others is printed in Chaparral Pro

*As a planet-friendly publisher, Black Rose Writing does its best to eliminate unnecessary waste to reduce paper usage and energy costs, while never compromising the reading experience. As a result, the final word count vs. page count may not meet common expectations.

To the many readers who have helped me continue on with these characters and this series.

IN THE SERVICE
OF OTHERS

PROLOGUE

He found it in a pocket. A folded article, written the year before and cutout from a copy of the San Diego Union Tribune. A short piece about two marines killed in Afghanistan. Detective Mallory thought it an odd thing to find. Who still reads the newspaper?

The two men were in their twenties. A couple of troublemakers the old guy called them. Two former Marines, homeless and dead. Both died from a single shot to the heart. Both had Semper Fi tattooed on their biceps.

Those Mallory talked to weren't surprised. There had been trouble between the two and the others in the makeshift camp. The old guy, a Vietnam vet, lamented having to live through this nightmare again.

"But what do you expect? Nobody gives a fuck about you when you live in a ditch in the land of movie stars and dilettantes," he said, kicking the dirt at his feet. "People don't care. Why should they, their kids aren't dying."

Mallory listened to the man's rant as he picked through the mix of trash and personal effects in what passed for a place to live. It was the contents of a small box that caught him by surprise. Two dog tags tied together with two purple hearts. He suddenly wanted to be somewhere, anywhere else.

Four men lost.

Two in a faraway land; two in La-La-land.

1

It was all gone.

The courtyard with the art déco fountain. The quaint little bungalows. All bulldozed and hauled away along with the remains of the six other blocks. What was left was an enormous expanse of debris, surrounded by a chain-link fence, and fronted by a picture of the fabulous business and residential community set to rise from the forlorn moonscape in front of me.

It was in this dance with the past, when I felt the gun being pushed into my ribs.

"I want the money, *Buttman*."

I looked at the scrawny kid on the other end of the gun. "Get in line."

Apparently, times had been tough. He stunk. I wondered how long it had been since he last showered. His dingy brown hair clung to his head as it ran to his shoulders. Tattoos of dragons covered his arms as well as one running along his neck. His clothes were threadbare and didn't appear to be any cleaner than he did.

"I'm not kidding," he informed me.

"I got a hundred on me." I reached in my pocket.

"I want the money you took from Gene and Frankie, Buttman, or should I say *Sunshine*?"

I laughed.

"I don't think that's funny, Buttman!"

"I'm sure you don't." I was trying to figure out who he was, and how he'd know about Frankie and Gene.

His face tightened. "I'm not afraid to shoot. I've killed before, Buttman."

I wasn't impressed. "I'll take that into consideration."

A yellow haze was obscuring the sun, marring an otherwise pleasant day. I looked past the strung-out punk. Two large men, one white, one black, eased up behind him. Anton put his gun into the punk's side, while Mr. Jones reached around and took the 9mm out of the punk's hands.

He stood there. No Plan B.

I got close to the punk. "Alright killer, who are you and what makes you think you can just hold me up and demand money?"

The punk looked at the three of us. He might have believed he could take me, but not my two companions. "My name is Manny," he mumbled softly.

"And what's your connection to Frankie and Gene? Those two were dead long before you were born."

Manny looked at me as though I should be intimately familiar with such things. "They were my uncles."

That made me smile. "So, you're Holly's boy?"

The punk curled his nose at the name Holly, but nodded just the same.

Holly Pronto was the mousy product of Maybin and Garla Pronto; the proud parents of the town's notoriously murdered bullies, Franklin and Eugene. My memories of the Prontos were thin. All I remembered of Holly, was of an unusually small girl, certainly when compared with her idiot parents and delinquent brothers who towered over her. Her son didn't carry much of the Pronto's genetic material either.

I stood there taking him in, unhappily transported to a rural road surrounded by laughing gunmen and a dying friend being dragged off, tied to the back of a truck. "Your uncles murdered my friend you little fucker, so unless you want to find yourself charged with armed robbery, you'll need a better reason for this botched stickup than wanting a pile of fool's gold."

Holly's boy didn't have an answer and I could see Mr. Jones was disinclined to spend the afternoon standing in the hot California sun.

"What are we going to do here, Buttman?" he demanded. Anton, a man of few words, merely smiled.

I directed my ire at the punk. "What's it going to be, Manny?"

Turns out Plan B was pushing me out of the way and running down the street. We watched as he lost his balance, fell down, screamed a few choice obscenities, looked back to see if we were following, and continued his haphazard escape. Anton laughed and Mr. Jones shook his head. I brushed off my jacket and directed my companions to the diner I used to habituate in the days before wealth corrupted me.

The plump waitress with the colored hair led us to our booth and handed out menus with a half-hearted smile. I don't know why I dragged them here. It was Jones I wanted to talk to, but Anton liked to tag along. He knew food was part of the deal and he liked to eat on someone else's dime, my dime.

I had a lot of dimes these days; more than I could possibly count.

It had been a year since Judith dumped her fortune on me. A year since she took her life. Cancer was killing her and she wanted the final say. I still had that beautiful house on the hill, but like all things, it was now different.

As we ate, I kept drifting back to my life before Judith, before Agnes, to the small bungalow nestled within the Moonlight Arms. It was a good life I reminded myself; easy going, inexpensive, and unobtrusive. All gone. Joanie was gone too. She needed time to think, needed to get away. That was more than half a year ago. I gave her a lot of money to help "facilitate" the sale of the Moonlight Arms to the Ipcis Group.

I'm a soft touch.

"Who was the kid?" Anton asked. "Was it good to let him run off like that?"

"Not to worry," I said. "Like all bad pennies, he'll turn up again."

"We'll need more than that, Buttman," Jones interjected. We were supposed to be discussing our new joint venture, fostering young musical talent rather than the distant past.

I shrugged. "It's not important. We can head over to the club after lunch, see how you're spending my money."

Jones cracked a big smile. The erstwhile Mr. Jones, known by family and friends as Orville Riley, liked to make fun of my antipathy towards being rich.

"Will the poor little rich boy be complaining about his hard times? All those burdens that weigh him down, and how life was so much better when he was a nobody running errands for rich lawyers?" he asked.

Both he and Anton thought this supremely funny.

"Be nice or I'll take my money and go elsewhere," I huffed.

Jones shrugged. "My business is booming; it won't hurt me. But Anna and Mikal, and all the kids that got their hearts set on using the place, might be. I'm sure Agnes wouldn't mind you pulling the rug from under her daughter after all the promises you made." He had to point that out.

"Fuck you, Orville."

Orville and Anton roared with laughter.

It was a hard life!

∙   ∙   ∙   ∙   ∙

The performance space was in Echo Park. It was a property Xavier Dunkle owned and was willing to lease as a loss leader for tax purposes. Originally, it was supposed to be a place where musicians could get together to rehearse and collaborate. Simple enough. That was the plan, but plans change, and it's not like LA lacked a vibrant music scene to begin with. But bright-eyed dreamers were always looking for places to play. Another venue was always welcome and for those like Mr. Jones, whose preference was jazz, blues, and soul, opportunity knocked.

Mikal was the first to greet us. "Hey, look who's here!"

Mikal Thorvaldsen was Joanie's ex. That's what we assumed. She didn't actually say they were through, and Mikal wasn't terribly concerned. He was a good-looking musician, who probably never had a lonely night in his life. When he heard about the project, he had the thought that it would also be ideal for those itinerant instructors who needed a space to teach.

"Hey Mike," I said.

He smiled and shook my hand. "Mr. Jones, are you keeping our benefactor safe?" He winked at Orville and Anton.

"Depends on my mood." The big black guy slapped me on the back. "Are we still on to open next month?"

"We are," Mikal cheerfully offered. "The contractor says the theater is ready, and the teaching spaces opened a couple of days ago. We've got quite a few seminars set up already. The only thing that's still a little iffy schedule-wise is Anna's kitchen. I don't know all the particulars, but it's coming along. Should be sweet, man, sweet."

He pointed me towards the entrance to the theater, "Why don't we check it out?"

"I'd love to." I was lying.

"The sound is fucking outrageous," Mikal continued. "Had a few friends come over for a jam last night, and the board kicked ass. I can't tell you how

4

much everybody loves this place." I didn't know what he was talking about. He must have noticed. "I got a couple of kids down the hall working on a duet. I'll bring them in. You'll be blown away, man." Mikal jogged down the hall as Jones and I went in the theater. Anton, ever the professional, kept a lookout at the door.

I shook my head. "You know, I'm still fairly anonymous. Does he have to do that?"

Jones looked back towards Anton. "I suppose you're right. The rest of us fairly anonymous types have people sticking us up and asking about money all the time too."

"I don't need the condescension."

Mr. Jones took off his dark sunglasses. "Maybe not, but I know a number of people, people who know you, who would disagree."

"Is this another Agnes thing?" I harrumphed.

He laughed. "Everything is an Agnes issue with you, motherfucker."

The dear Mr. Jones had evolved into my Agnes nag. He was the traditional type, or more precisely, Orville was. His alter ego, Mr. Jones; the badassed security dude who kept morons like me safe, allowed him to be more distanced and occasionally profane. But Orville was never far away, and Orville, as channeled by Jones, was not happy I hadn't gotten my shit together and married not only a good-hearted woman who loved me, but one who continued to put up with my idiotic personal bullshit.

Which made me think of Judith.

I didn't intend to find myself in love with two different women, and I did a wonderful job of bullshitting my way through most of it, even if I was the only one buying it. Judith loved me just as Agnes did, though in her own way. It was supposed to end in a perfectly reasonable and organized way. No cancer. No suffering. No dying. Judith would tire of me and I would marry Agnes. It would all be good.

The two young performers hopped on the stage. The theater was intimate, seating about two hundred, and just enough rise in the seating so the people in the back could see more than the back of the heads in front of them. A woman sat at the grand piano and a man stood behind his acoustic bass. She counted off, and he started walking the fingerboard. She joined in and soon the normally stoic Mr. Jones was snapping his fingers, keeping time with his toes, and smiling to the beautiful music reverberating throughout the theater. Mikal too was grooving. Bastard was right, the room sounded wonderful.

As the duo played, I drifted into the past. Had it really been a year since Judith died? The calendar said it had. I didn't want to dwell on that any more than I wanted to dwell on my problems with Agnes, but they were inseparable. To resolve one, I had to resolve the other. It didn't help that the duo had slowed things down with a ballad that was insinuating itself into my idiotic personal bullshit. Agnes continued to hold on to me despite my equivocations about marriage. Yet it was everywhere. Barron was going to marry his girlfriend, Gerta. Rebekah and Fidel were planning their wedding now that their daughter, Elizabeth, had arrived. Even Calista and Andrea were getting married this weekend at the old man's farm. As Orville would say, it was getting time for me to do the right thing.

The players finished their short set. We thanked them and Mikal introduced me to the two guys running the boards; one for sound, one for lights. They happily pointed out all the amazing things they could do from live sound and recordings, to a mind-boggling number of visual effects. They were very excited. I assured them I was excited too.

Jones and I collected Anton. In the dining hall, we found Anna huddled with the contractor. It was her idea to use the venue not only for music, but food too. A place to try new things. From her years at the culinary institute and her time up north, she knew plenty of people who were interested. With her brother back in California, and my giving her mother some stability in the boyfriend department, she was ready to move back to LA. Agnes was thrilled. Simon not so much. But between Eric arguing on her behalf, and Agnes volunteering Judith's money, he grudgingly said it was up to her. I let her live in the big house with Fidel and Rebekah.

As I said, I'm an easy touch.

"Mr. Sunshine!" Anna exclaimed. She had picked up that less than adorable affectation from Emily, who often came to LA to hang out at the pool at the big house.

"Please don't call me that," I groaned.

"Oh, lighten up, Sunshine," intoned Mr. Jones.

"Is a nice name, no?" This from Anton, who until then had been nice and quiet.

"It's ok, I'll be good," Anna said. "Let me show you how it's going." She glanced at the contractor. "I've been assured we'll be up and running soon..."

She led us to the three serving areas artfully designed like food trucks. It was an idea a confederate of those planning the place thought was cute. Each "truck" was outfitted with the necessary tools of the trade. Anna bounced from spot to spot, clearly excited about everything that was going on. I wondered how they would ever make a dime, but I'd been admonished about my gloominess and I had money to spend. Besides, Xavier needed a tax dodge.

Mr. Jones was ready to go. "I got things to do, Buttman." He looked over at Anton.

"Then you've got things to do. I'll be fine. Tell Coretta I say hello."

He wasn't buying it. "Anton can stay, keep an eye on you."

"Why?"

"Cuz a guy just tried to stick you up, that's why." He seemed amazed I'd even ask.

"Manny? I'm not worried about him. Get going, I'll be fine and Anton doesn't need to stay either." I found my surety comforting.

"I better not get any calls about you gone missing," he grumbled. He motioned to Anton. There was real business to attend to.

Anna and I watched the two of them leave. Her phone rang. It was her mother. She waited six rings before answering.

"Yes, mommy dear..." She looked at me with a smirk on her face. "Yes, he's here." She put the phone on speaker.

"You *forgot* your phone again didn't you, Monk?" Agnes was trying to be mad at me.

"I didn't forget, I used my no phone card today."

"Very funny! You know I don't like it when I can't get a hold of you."

"Yes, you've mentioned it a time or two. What's so important that you had to track me down, and don't say the wedding this weekend because I haven't forgotten." I returned the smirk to a knowing Anna.

"Then I won't say it, Mr. Smarty-pants. However, I wanted you to know that I'm up at the big house with the baby. If you need me, that's where I am. I know you don't believe me, but I don't want you to worry if you find I'm not at home."

"Why would I worry about you, Beautiful?"

We could hear her sigh through the phone. "You're a jerk, Buttman!"

I laughed. "Some things never change. See you soon."

Agnes said something else, but I wasn't listening, too many things around me were changing.

2

Anna hugged me and sent me on my way. It was the kind of hug that made me pause, not because I didn't appreciate it, but whether I deserved it to begin with. Anna had been careful around me from the moment I'd met her three years before. A byproduct of her mother's disastrous relationship with a man named Jordan. I was by comparison fairly decent, so maybe that was it. Still, it was long and firm and filled with a heartfelt sureness that stirred the lifelong sense within me of being a fraud.

The drive, crisscrossing the neighborhoods of LA, was pleasant. What had once been a quiet house inhabited by one, was now boisterous and occupied by many; another something I vacillated about. I missed the quiet, but the quiet made me think of Judith, and I was tired of missing her. At first, I thought about selling the house; I was amazed at what it cost to keep it up; amazed at the taxes, and more amazed that it was Agnes who persuaded me to keep it.

"What, you don't have enough money?" Her typical response to my whine about costs.

"You said you didn't want to stay in Judith's house." My rejoinder.

"Judith is dead, you told me that, remember? It's your house now and houses go through many owners."

I grumbled at having my own ill thought out logic thrown back in my face.

"Besides, there's lots of room and it's a popular place. Are you going to tell Zach and Emily and Mr. Jones they're no longer welcome because it's a burden to you even though it's not?"

"I don't think I like you much right now!" It was all I could think of.

"Nonsense, you're still madly in love with me!" She kissed me, which didn't help.

The house had five full-time occupants and any number of part-timers. Rebekah and Fidel moved in after that heartless bastard Monk Buttman sold the Moonlight Arms to those heartless bastards at Ipcis Corporation, forcing Rebekah to find new accommodations. Fidel's little apartment, she claimed, was too small for him, her, Zachary, and a baby on the way. Since they worked in Hollywood, she reasoned, the house was a good way station till they got more established in their new business, which they bought with financial assistance from that bastard Buttman.

Anna was the other full-time resident. Her being there was based on the same faulty reasoning employed by my daughter and her expanding family. The part-timers were Agnes, her son, Barron, and his bride to be, Gerta. Either or all of us could have lived there full time; there was certainly room, but Barron was stationed at the Army base in San Luis Obispo, and preferred his own place, owing, I think, to Agnes' complaining that they weren't coming around enough. I told her it was because they were young, had their own lives, and given that Gerta was transfixed by California, a stronger desire to explore, rather than waste their time hanging out with his mother.

"You're a jerk, Buttman," was how these conversations usually ended.

My preference was to live at the house Agnes and I shared in West Covina. It was close to where Agnes worked and it was a nice size for the two of us. I had put a lot of effort into cleaning up and organizing the place, and was loathe to just up and leave simply because I suddenly had more money than I needed or deserved. That nerve grew more sensitive after that bastard Buttman sold the Arms, and my beloved bungalow was demolished.

"And you think I need therapy," Agnes would say when I foolishly opened up to her with my feelings.

"You know I'm not sensing a lot of sympathy here," I would complain.

"Not to worry," she said smiling. "Should you ever actually need some sympathy, I'm sure there's a shoulder out there willing to lend itself to you for a reasonable fee."

"I hope you remember that when you have to sign the pre-nup!" I huffed.

Agnes merely shrugged.

●　　●　　●　　●　　●

My grandson was the first to greet me.

"Gamps!" he shouted as he ran towards me.

"Dude!" I swept him into my arms and kissed him behind the ear. I then nuzzled the ear, to which he responded with squeals of delight.

"Monk, don't do that the baby's trying to sleep." Zach and I looked over at the agitated woman named Agnes Duquesne. Elizabeth was sleeping in her arms.

Elizabeth did not seem terribly bothered by the racket coming from her brother and grandfather.

"What, we can't have any fun?"

"No!" the agitated woman replied.

"Wow, seems like the wrong person is taking the nap, huh Zach?"

Zach was in complete agreement.

Agnes was having none of it, so the boy and I crept stealthily past the agitated Agnes and the sleeping Elizabeth to the great outdoors. There we put our feet in the water and ruminated about how crazy life can be. After a few minutes, the agitated Agnes could take no more of it, and placed the sleeping child in the bassinet and joined us by the pool.

"We're supposed to be serious caretakers, Buttman. I promised Becky we'd make sure Lizzy got her nap in today. You know she's been fussy lately—"

"Becky just wanted to get back to work, and if she was worried, she could have made other arrangements or not gotten pregnant in the first place," I said.

"You're some father figure, Sunshine." Agnes put her head on my shoulder and her arm around my waist. She was tired. Motherhood was a lot more exhausting now that she was twenty-some years older. Zach too needed a nap.

"I'm the best of the best," I said to the two sleepy-heads leaning on me. "Looks like it's naptime for Aggie and Zach." Agnes pinched me and Zach turned when I jumped, "Let's be careful with those fingers, Ag," Ag mumbled something incomprehensible.

I directed Agnes to the loveseat and put Zach in his pen by the pool. I joined Agnes, and she curled up next to me, our feet stretched out across the ottoman.

It was the kind of shimmering southern California day that made all my complaining and navel gazing utterly ridiculous. A soft ocean breeze was keeping the smog at bay. The sun, lightly filtered by high clouds, lolled above us, and the view of the city to the ocean extended from one end of the yard to the other. I was surrounded by my beautiful grandkids and a woman who foolishly loved me and I was having a hard time getting with the program.

Therapy wasn't sounding so bad.

"Your *assistant* called." Agnes muttered in the midst of my reverie. "If you'd had your phone, I wouldn't have to take your calls on top of caring for your grandchildren." She snuggled closer to me.

"Stop with the nagging, you love every minute you get with the kids. What did my *assistant* want?" Agnes didn't care for Natalya. She had the bizarre idea that I was grooming Natalya to replace Judith and ultimately her.

"She doesn't like to talk to me," Agnes whined.

"Maybe that's because you're always a prickly pear when she calls."

"You shouldn't be fucking around with a twenty-year-old, it's unseemly."

I opened my mouth but decided there was no point in stating the obvious, no matter how many times I'd stated it before. There was no sexual interest on my part, even if no one else believed me. Natalya wasn't even the problem. It was the other women who had learned of my ill-gotten gains. I don't know how the word got out; I wasn't broadcasting it, but they began approaching me, mostly at the galleries Natalya would drag me to. I expected her to run interference for me as part of her job as assistant, but she had no interest in that, and I'd come to find that Natalya Constantinescu was a hard-headed single-minded twenty-year-old.

"I don't care if you want to fuck them," she would say in the most matter-of-fact voice. "Men do what they want and these women do too."

Natalya Constantinescu had become my assistant by happenstance, like most of what had come to pass in the last three years. When pressed, she said her father sold her as a domestic when she was eleven, after her mother died. In truth, she was brought here to whore, as Big Mike so nonchalantly put it. Big Mike Kovalenko somehow decided Natalya was his true love, never mind that he was forty years older, and bought her from the Russian gang that abducted her. True love apparently made it ok to rape a twelve-year-old girl. I crossed paths with her after I learned Judith was sick. Big Mike had set up a scheme where he promised Natalya a lot of money, but not really, with a dunderhead named Desmond, who called himself Link Deal; a guy I was foolishly running errands for through A and A. What she actually had were shares in a land deal run by the family business of Xavier Dunkle II, another character I came across as I was dealing with Judith dying.

Natalya thought she had half a million dollars. When it came to light she did not, the proverbial shit hit the fan, and she outed the despicable Big Mike. I offered to buy the options for far more than they were worth, but Natalya had other ideas when I met her at my lawyer's office to seal the deal. I knew something was amiss when I noted the smile on Ms. Lagenfelder's face as opposed to the serious face of Ms. Constantinescu.

"Alright, what's up?" I asked.

Ms. Lagenfelder spoke first. "Your friend here had a few questions about you and Mrs. Delashay's art philanthropy. I informed her you were overseeing those grants." While maintaining a professional demeanor, I could tell Ms. Lagenfelder was eating this up.

Natalya entered the fray.

"I want to know if you would be willing to change your mind about the money and instead let me work for you. I love art and believe you might need someone to help you. Ms. Lagenfelder said that Mrs. Delashay took care of the grants, but didn't know if you would, and suggested I ask you about them." Ms. Lagenfelder's smile continued to grow.

"Uh-huh..." was my response.

Natalya went on. "I know you think I'm too young and don't know how to do this, but I've been studying art for the last five years and I know many of the gallery owners. I'm sure if you told them, they would help me and show me how everything works."

"Uh-huh..."

She went on about how it was important for her to work for her money, and that maybe this would be a good way for both of us, seeing as I don't have any idea what I'm doing, and it's very easy to be duped by charlatans and con artists. I was to infer that she would not be duped as I so obviously would be.

"What do you think of my proposal, Mr. Monk?" Mr. Monk?

Mr. Monk wasn't so sure.

Somehow, I got talked into it, and the ever-helpful Ms. Lagenfelder, with some backing from Mr. Macklgrew, my money guy, facilitated the position of assistant to Monk Buttman, Esquire. A woman named Brigitte DuBare, who owned several galleries, as well as other real estate, agreed to take on Natalya after a fairly intensive interview process, and my willingness to pony up the dough for an office to house my erstwhile assistant. Brigitte knew the game inside and out and found a younger version of herself in Ms. Constantinescu.

Like I said, I'm an easy touch.

"I don't have my phone on me," I said to my sleepy companion.

Agnes shifted and pulled *my* phone out of *her* back pocket.

"Thanks," I said after she plopped it on my chest. I tapped the icon associated with the number of my assistant. It was easy to tell that Agnes was paying close attention.

"Mr. Monk, I wanted to tell you that Ms. DuBare has invited you to a showing next weekend, and I just wanted to confirm that you'll be there."

"Tell her I want to go too," Agnes piped in without asking.

"Sounds like a great time. Will you let Brigitte know I'll be bringing a guest? Yes, Aggie would like to go as well," Aggie tried to pinch me, but I quickly grabbed her free hand.

"I will inform Ms. DuBare. Thanks, Mr. Monk."

The call ended with Aggie giving me the eye.

"So, you want to go now, huh?" Agnes had turned down all of my previous offers to take her along. She was certain the people there would spend the night judging her, and that was something she could do without.

"I think I should get some culture," she said. "Plus, I want to make sure you're not lying to me about all these women."

"Suit yourself."

"That means you have to take me shopping so I'm not an embarrassment to you in front of all your rich friends."

"I look forward to it."

Aggie pinched me, which made me flinch.

•   •   •   •   •

Fidel and Rebekah came home around six. Agnes decided we would take off for the old man's farm from here rather than meet at the house in West Covina. She had thoughtfully packed for me while I was out being important. They all played with the baby while I was cooking dinner. Some things never change. Fidel and Zach came over. Zach sat in his highchair. Fidel and I had a beer while the food cooked.

"How's the biz?" I inquired. As majority owner, I felt the need to know.

"So far, so good. We had a series of production meetings today for the filming that's supposed to start on Tuesday. I warned Becks this might be her last free weekend for a while. We've got contracts for at least the next six months, and maybe more if the shows get picked up or extended. That's good for business, but I wonder if she's ready for that."

Rebekah had returned from their trip to Hawaii both thrilled and a little tired from the work schedule. Fidel had told her it could be hectic or boring or both. Pregnancy, mixed with the anxiety of getting the company up and running, had taxed her stamina.

Their company, *We Got This LLC*, which provided production support for all the technical equipment used by the film crews, originally belonged to the man Fidel had previously worked for, but he wanted to retire and Fidel, along with the three other guys who worked there, thought it was a great opportunity if only they could figure out how to finance it.

Enter the lobbying daughter.

It wasn't just that she thought it was a good idea, there was also the not so insignificant fact that she decided she'd found true love and was, oh by the way, pregnant.

"What?" was her response when I questioned her sanity.

"Zach's only a year old! You couldn't wait a little while?" I was flabbergasted.

"Well, it wasn't plan planned, but we're ok with it." *They were ok with it.* They were also ok with Agnes and me providing a lot of free daycare. Agnes didn't seem to mind, even when I pointed out that at this rate, we'd be raising more than just a few grandkids. I wondered how she felt about that now that Lizzy was here and wearing her out.

To make things more exciting, it was happening at a time when I was completely overwhelmed by everything going on with Judith's trusts and the many, many people and organizations asking for money. People with the kind of money I had fallen into had flacks to deal with this sort of thing. *My* flack was the irrepressible Carson Macklgrew and his company that aided wealthy idiots like me. Not only did he supervise the holdings within the trust, but also disbursements and grants and acquisitions. I didn't mind financing Rebekah and Fidel's dream, but I didn't want to throw away good money, if such a thing exists, simply because they thought it a fantastic idea. So, I did what any good father would do; I dumped it in Carson's lap.

This proved fortuitous, as he had in a previous life worked in the accounting division of a major studio and knew more about the biz than I ever would. He researched the company Rebekah and Fidel wanted to buy, sat the five of them down, demanded they lay out their plans and organizational charts, and reviewed their prospects within the film industry. On the plus side, the company had a firm foot in the biz, and other than Rebekah, the guys had expertise in the field and a good feel for landing contracts and future business. On the downside, none of them had any real tangible assets, so if the company tanked, that bastard Buttman would be on the hook. Carson Macklgrew then dumped it in my lap.

"I don't know that I personally would back this, but I do think they have a good sense of what they want to accomplish, and it wouldn't be money wasted."

I gave them the money and took, grudgingly, a sixty percent ownership stake in the company. Technically, they were to pay me back on a prearranged schedule, but Agnes assured them I would not pull a Scrooge and toss them out on the street. I casually mentioned that I didn't agree to that, to which Agnes smacked me.

Did I mention I'm an easy touch?

3

We loaded everyone into the Mercedes and headed north to the farm. With Anna in LA, there was no reason to stop in San Francisco and therefore no reason to take the coast highway. Instead, we barreled up the interstate, at least where the interstate wasn't packed with other vehicles impeding our journey. Since the car only sat five, we decided to let Lizzy enjoy the trip in the laps of, in descending order, Rebekah, Fidel, Agnes, and me when we swapped drivers in San Jose. I don't know if technically we were breaking the law, but with the tinted windows no one would know unless we were pulled over.

Agnes whined about Anna and Barron not joining us and then called me a jerk when I pointed out that they didn't know either Calista or Andrea, and were more interested in going to Joshua Tree National Park than hanging with their nosy mother.

"Why do I talk to you?" she harrumphed.

"I haven't the slightest idea."

"Do you avoid your mother?" she pestered Fidel. It was his turn on the hot seat.

Rebekah started laughing.

"What?" Agnes didn't get the joke.

"His mother lives in Arizona with her new man. She's been kinda busy with him," Rebekah told her. Fidel just smiled and nodded.

"Oh." Agnes was stymied.

"I don't spend a lot of time with my mother," I offered.

"Oh, shut up, Buttman!" Agnes sank into her seat while I stifled a laugh.

The rest of the drive was uneventful.

The farm was dressed for the wedding. The first of two. Rebekah and Fidel were planning on marrying here in the next month.

Most of the faces I recognized, some I didn't. The ones I didn't turned out to be the family; at least those of Calista's willing to come, and Andrea's friends. Andrea had no interest in inviting her family as they disowned her years before.

A stiff-looking Marine was standing in the back observing the rest of us.

That was Jacob, the youngest of my stepbrothers, and the one I'd never met. He was born after I lit out for Virginia and had already joined the Marines when I finally returned. He was tall, sturdy, and looked deeply uncomfortable. I thought that odd considering he'd grown up here. Whatever their history here on Moses Bohrman's commune, few ever returned feeling uncomfortable. My mother and I being the known exceptions.

Bored with the pre-festivities and eager to avoid any talk of weddings with Agnes, I went over and introduced myself. He seemed surprised.

"Not what you expected?" I offered my hand.

"Not exactly..." He shook it.

"What? Too tall, too good looking?"

He smiled. "Something like that. I heard a lot of stories about my long-lost older brother." Jacob was maybe an inch taller than I was. I attributed this to his excellent posture, and my feeling the mighty weight of having no real problems.

"Well, don't feel bad, most people are disappointed when they first meet me." Agnes and Judith were exceptions, but that was an exceptional day for a variety of reasons. "So, you came back for the wedding?"

He smiled at that. "No. Moses didn't mention there'd be a wedding. I'm just trying to stay out of the way." It was nice to know I wasn't the only son who called him Moses rather than dad.

"Yeah, me too."

I saw Emily milling about, bouncing between her relatives, Agnes, and Meredith. She noticed the two of us in the corner and came over.

"Mr. Sunshine!" She wrapped her arms around me. I hugged her back.

Emily had grown at least five inches in the last year and was exhibiting all the outward signs that she would not be a carbon copy of her mother, Calista; at least not physically. She was tall and curvy rather than short and slender. She'd become interested in boys and men and those sorts of things. Her garden was still important, but no longer the focal point of her life. She'd also developed a strong attachment to the house on the hill and the life it intimated. Calista was not thrilled by this development.

"Can I go back with you tomorrow?" Emily asked.

"That depends on what your mom says and where you are in your school work." I was being evasive. I didn't want to be stuck in the middle of one of their continuing arguments over this. The school thing was a dodge, and she knew it. Every time she came down, she brought her school work and got up bright and early to finish it by the pool. That freed her to devote her day to hanging with Zach, swimming, or most blasphemously, wondering how she could talk her mother into letting her move to LA so she could go to a regular school with regular kids, or what she believed regular kids to be.

"She and Andrea are going to San Francisco for the week. I don't want to be here all by myself," she groused.

"You live on a commune. You're never by yourself," I countered.

Jacob stiffed a grin.

"You know what I mean," she huffed. Emily looked at Jacob as she let go of me. If I remembered correctly, he was about twenty-five and I imagine, from a young girl's perspective, quite attractive. "Hi Jacob." She smiled and leaned against me as she took him in.

"Emily." He smiled at her. "You look very pretty today."

Emily crinkled her nose. "Thanks. I don't really like this dress, but I have to be part of the wedding party," she said, slightly arching her back.

Jacob continued smiling.

Sadly, her flirting was interrupted by Meredith calling to her. It was time to begin the show. She slinked off, and Jacob and I went to where Agnes was standing. I introduced them. Agnes, too, found the young man to be quite attractive. That made me smile a mile wide, which she immediately noticed.

"It's not the same thing, Buttman!"

I laughed. "So you say, but I'm not convinced."

Jacob was confused, but I didn't want to bore him with the trivialities of my problems. Agnes elbowed me in the ribs, to which I made an overly theatrical *oof*. With that, we sat down with the rest of the Bohrman clan; Moses, Meredith, brother Sterling, his wife, Felicia, and their three kids. They came up a day early to hang with Jacob, Meredith, and Moses.

The wedding was a breezy affair, light on religion and long on personal statements of love and promised fealty. Calista and Andrea clearly had a good time, and that always helps with the crowd. I noticed a few in Calista's group tighten up when they were up there smooching. Agnes mostly kept her eyes on the festivities, but she looked my way more than a few times and took my hand early in the ceremony and held on tight till it was time to stand and watch the happy couple walk down the aisle. I expected as much and didn't complain.

The spread following the ceremony was quite tasty, with a large number of vegetarian and vegan dishes. The omnivores were shuttled off to one side, but there was enough animal protein to satisfy the Mackinaw brothers and their ilk, including me. Wine, naturally, was the beverage of choice. The farm was mostly vineyards at this point.

Agnes had more than a few glasses.

There was singing and dancing, and I made a point of hitting up as many of the women in Calista's family as I could. A few were reticent, but it's tough to turn down a man in a good-looking suit, so most grudgingly went along when Agnes wasn't horning in. I could tell she was lapsing into a down period and by getting her up and moving, whether through jealousy or not, I was hoping to keep her from sliding down too far. The evening ended with our sending the lovebirds off to San Fran and their respective family and friends to wherever they were staying.

After helping to clean up, I found Agnes in our room sitting at the edge of the bed wearing just her blouse and underwear. She was fiddling with her bra. I sat down next to her and brushed the hair away from her neck. She looked at me with an alarming amount of sadness and resignation in her eyes. I kissed her forehead and then rested her head on my shoulder.

"You're kinda glum on such a happy day."

"I guess." A tear or two rolled down her cheek.

It had been an up and down year for us since Judith died. The first three months were difficult, mostly because of my inability to own up about how I felt about Judith, and there was everything I was expected to do because Judith, in a fit of idiocy, dumped her prodigious wealth on me. It made getting over her just that much harder.

Agnes bounced from being certain I belonged to her, to being certain she was getting fat and old and it was only a matter of time before I was off living the good life with my new younger girlfriend, Natalya, or Monika, or some other hot babe who would surely lure me away. It made my head hurt.

Then there were all the good vibes coming from Rebekah and Fidel, Barron and Gerta, Calista and Andrea. Even Anna had a new guy, although she was frustratingly coy about him. Most were getting married, or planning to, and excited, and then there was me and Agnes. Technically engaged, but no talk, no planning...

There were good times, too. Times when the two of us cast off our particular stupidities and simply enjoyed being together. I was hoping this would be one of them. Agnes put her arms around me as I leaned back, causing us to fall on the bed. I brushed the hair out of her face and kissed her. She was warm and soft, and it was impossible not to want to pull her closer. I started kissing her neck with the intention of moving to her wonderful breasts. I never got there.

"Do you still love me, Monk?" She lifted my chin, so I was staring at her wet eyes.

"I believe I mentioned it earlier today." I didn't want to get into some serious discussion of our feelings.

"I'm serious, Monk. Do you still love me?"

I lowered my head and groaned. "Please don't say I'm only here because I feel obligated, or that you're getting old and fat and how could I love you when there are so many other beautiful women out there, because I'm not in the mood. I know you're in one of your anxious periods and I don't want to make things worse, but not tonight. If sex isn't on the menu, that's fine. But I really don't want to get into all that." I rolled off of her. "And yes, I still love you."

"Then why won't you marry me?"

"Fine, we'll get married when we get back on Monday."

Agnes smacked me lightly on the arm before taking my hand and putting it on her breast. "You know I want a wedding, not some trip down to the courthouse." She moved closer to me, running her hand along my leg and unzipping my fly.

"I know, but we can't just jump the line in front of Rebekah and Barron..." With her breast in my hand, I was no longer interested in talking. I didn't think she was either as she put her hand down my pants.

"I don't even have a ring..."

True, but the ring was in my coat pocket, had been for nine months. I bought it on one of those beautiful days when everything in the world felt right and I happened upon a jeweler with a small store in Beverly Hills. I had planned on a candlelight dinner later that day, but Agnes had different ideas. Ideas about how I didn't love her anymore...

Her hand was on my cock, slowly moving up and down. My hand found that delightful spot between her legs as my mouth found hers. The ring could wait. We went at each other, driven by conflicting desires that pushed us until we were worn out. Agnes tucked herself under my arm as we lay there.

"What was she like?" Agnes was running her hand along my chest.

"Who?"

"Judith. I'd like to know. Did she do things I don't do? Things you'd like me to do?"

"Like what?" I regretted the words as soon as they came out of my mouth. Always think before you speak, fool.

"Did you fuck her in the ass?" I rolled my eyes and pulled the pillow over my head. "Did you?" She poked me in the ribs.

"All the time. It was all she wanted to do."

She poked me again. "I'm serious."

I moved the pillow just enough so I could see her face. Damn, she was serious. "Where is this coming from?"

Agnes fidgeted a bit. "I heard a lot of people are doing it, that's all."

"Uh-huh, people like who?" I knew who. Only one of her friends would bring up stuff like this.

"MaryAnn said it's popular now..." She half smiled as she confessed the name.

"MaryAnn. Is MaryAnn getting fucked in the ass?"

Another sheepish smile. "She thinks it's ok to try new things..."

I shook my head. "I'm sure she does, and if that's what you want to do, we can give it a try, but I think there's more to this than whether Judith and I engaged in anal sex. I'm also, and I can't stress this enough, really not interested in talking about it."

Agnes' serious face returned. "I want to know about her. I want to know why you stayed with her so long." She poked me again.

"Stop doing that!"

Agnes retreated to the other side of the bed. Tears forming in her eyes. "I just want to know, that's all," she whispered.

I let out a deep sigh. After not asking for a year, after giving me hope I could forget about this, she asks. And what do I do? Act like an ass. That bastard Buttman!

"If I tell you, will you promise to let this go? Judith is gone. It's been more than a year. I haven't been with anyone else. I like being with you, just you. Only you, ok!"

She turned to me, the tears streaming down her face. "Ok." She reached out and took my hand, which I found deeply disconcerting. "Did you love her, really love her?"

I took a deep breath. "Yes, I loved her, and yes, to anticipate more of your questions, the sex was good, but it wasn't better than ours. We never talked about living together or getting married or anything like that. I kept going because there was something about her, a combination of her looks and the way she thought about things that I was drawn to."

I tried not to picture Judith, but that was like trying not to breathe. "I know she loved me because she said she did when she had no reason to lie. That's all there was to it. I never really thought about why I continued to see her other than I wanted to. I know I should have stopped and I've apologized many times, but it over, she's gone. I'm still here, not because I feel obligated to be here, but because I want to be here, because I love you and care about you." I reached over and wiped the tears from her face, "Please stop crying, it's done."

"Why won't you marry me?"

"I already told you I would." She leaned in and I kissed her salty lips.

"I still want a wedding and a ring," she said between kisses.

"I haven't forgotten." We continued kissing and I casually inserted my finger into her anus. She flinched before pulling away with a rather surprised expression.

"Remember," I reminded her, "MaryAnn said lots of people are doing it." She smiled, and we went back to kissing each other.

4

I got up first, said a small prayer for a nice quiet uneventful day, and left the ring on the counter in the bathroom. She found it as I was making the bed.

"This is for me?"

I looked around as if she were talking to somebody else. "Of course, it is." I resisted the urge to be a smartass at the obviousness of the question.

"It's beautiful!"

"Then it fits the person wearing it."

She smiled and rushed over to hug me, kissed me, and whispered something rather salacious in my ear. I laughed and recommended we remember to pick up some personal lube if she was serious. We kissed some more before I mentioned that Meredith and the others were waiting for her in the kitchen. I watched her bounce out of the room. I let out a huge sigh of relief before looking for something to do.

Apparently, Jacob had the same problem.

We sat on the porch waiting to be told what to do. After a few minutes, we gave up and helped the kids set the tables. Sterling wandered in and said hello. He didn't seem to know what to say. Fidel had Lizzy in his arms with Zach wandering beside him. Moses rode to the rescue, gathered us up, and pointed to the head of the table. The food was brought out, and the rest of the clan came to sit down. The Mackinaw brothers joined us. Agnes frowned when she realized the prized seat beside me was taken. I shrugged and she sat by Meredith, Rebekah, and Emily. Fidel handed the kids to their mother before reluctantly joining us men.

The conversations started with many a question for Jacob. About life in the Marines, being deployed, staying in the Marines, being home, and then returned to the normalcy of vineyards and wine after he said little and demurred on much. Apparently, he had no interest in detailing his life to his family, or the rest of us here at the farm. Moses had that look of deep concern, but didn't pursue his questions, thus allowing the Mackinaw brothers to grill Sterling on how the distribution of the farm's grapes was going. Fidel happily answered a few questions about his new business in Hollywood and which actors were total jerks. All while we stuffed our faces. Sunday mornings meant pancakes and sausage.

God bless Sundays.

Once the meal was over, Fidel mentioned he had to run into town for a few things, and I invited Jacob along. He didn't want to go, but Moses insisted. "Go see how things have changed."

"I haven't been gone that long, and it's a small town," Jacob objected.

"Sorry, dude, looks like you're screwed," I said.

"Alright, I'll go."

I patted him on the shoulder.

Sterling, at the last possible moment, jumped in the car with us. We all looked at him. "What, I can't hang with my bros?"

Nobody said no.

.   .   .   .   .

Our mission, well technically Fidel's, was diapers. They were running low. Sterling, who was a bit of a babbler, went on about his trips in the night to get baby stuff, and how there were so many choices it became confusing. That made me chuckle.

"What?" He was also overly self-defensive around me.

"Nothing. I just think it's interesting that you can deal with a thousand labels of wine, but struggle with four or five brands of diapers, that's all."

"Well," he responded, "diapers really aren't my thing!"

It was while arguing about diapers, that I saw Holly Pronto out of the corner of my eye. In passing, I noted to the group that I saw her son in LA.

"You saw Manny?" Jacob asked, surprised.

"Yeah, he wanted money." Nobody got the reference. "You know him?"

"A little. We enlisted together. He went into vehicle maintenance after boot camp, and did a tour in Iraq, but that's about all." I wondered what he'd think of Manny now if he saw him.

"Given his appearance, I don't think he's still a Marine."

"A lot of us get out. I know a couple of guys down at Pendleton who are from here. They're still in, and a few in LA who are out. I thought about going down to see them." His eyes seemed to lose focus as he said this.

"You're welcome to stay with us if you'd like."

His eyes refocused. "Thanks."

Jacob followed Fidel to the register while Sterling wandered over to the tabloid magazines. I kept looking at Holly, deciding to say hello. I was curious if she knew Manny was in LA.

She didn't recognize me. Maybe it was the name. "You're Monk who?"

I thought her suspicion was cute.

"Buttman, Monk Buttman, I used to live up here. I saw your son, Manny, the other day. Thought I'd say hello."

Her face tightened at the name. Like mother, like son. "You know Manny?"

"No, but he thought he knew me even though I left before he was born. I knew your brothers, Frankie and Gene."

Holly didn't seem very impressed. "A lot of people knew Frankie and Gene. What was Manny doing with you, Mr. Buttman?"

It was my turn to smile. "Asking about money."

It was then her beady little eyes widened. She was a short chubby woman with a deep distrustful streak and an old story tucked in her head. An old story kept alive by her idiot parents.

"Who are you, mister?"

"Sunshine Bohrman, but I don't go by that name anymore."

She suddenly understood. "I shoulda known. I heard stories about that. Daddy said there was money, but I never believed it. It just made everybody crazy thinking it was out there. Money that was ours..." Holly's face tightened again. I was just more bad memories tied to her dead brothers and idiot parents.

"There wasn't any money, just a bad deal, and that died with James and your brothers."

Holly Pronto, or whatever her name was now, stared off in the distance. "Where is Manny?"

"He's in LA."

She took stock of her hands. "I guess I should be glad he's not dead." Holly wiped her eyes, hoping there were tears. "I did what I could for him..." She shook her head and looked the other way.

I watched as she walked off.

•　　•　　•　　•　　•

Moses found me on my crate, staring at the garden that Emily tended. She had come round earlier, looking over the plants and begging me to intercede on her behalf to Meredith about coming down.

"I'll see what I can do," I said.

She noted my lack of enthusiasm. "I'm really good with Zach and Lizzy, you know..." Emily had gotten better at working her arguments. The petulant, irritated twelve-year-old had morphed into a wily duplicitous thirteen-year-old playing on what she thought were my weaknesses.

"I promise I'll talk to her." I did my best to sound like I was on the team. I don't think she was convinced. "Meanwhile, you can go help Rebekah with the kids. It'll help prop up your case."

Emily gave me the eye, but smiled and was on her way.

Moses stood there. I looked up at him. He was stroking his thick white beard. I wondered how much white was in my beard now? Didn't matter, I had no plans to grow it back. I knew he was here to talk to me rather than just happening upon me in a moment of splendid stupor. He moved to the edge of the garden and sat down on the four by fours framing it. He seemed tired and agitated.

"I'm worried about Jacob," he said at last.

"Jacob? Worried about what?" I was genuinely surprised.

"I'm certain something is bothering him, but he keeps blowing me off, saying he's fine. Sound familiar?" Boy, you have one terrible year and no one lets you forget it.

"Nope." That got a smile out of him. "Maybe he *is* fine, just different now. Life changes a man. I think you said that once, and I imagine being a Marine these last five years has affected him."

"Ordinarily, I'd agree with that, but I know he's not sleeping. I found him wandering around the vineyards in the middle of the night. I flashed my light, so he'd see me, yet he was still startled when I approached him."

"What were you doing up in the middle of the night?"

He didn't care for the question. "Worrying about you boys and Jacob in particular." Poor Moses, all he really wanted was us four boys to stay here and commune with the earth. Instead, we all ran off. "I don't know what's happened to him in that goddamned war, but something changed this last time out. He's different, closed up, careful, and anxious. He wasn't like that the last two times he came home. Maybe it's PTSD... I don't know. I just know he's not the same. I've tried to talk to him, tried to be helpful, and don't know what to do about it."

"And when you ask, he tells you it's ok, that he's fine."

He tried to smile. "Yes, just like you."

I laughed. "Must be a genetic defect we all carry." I stood up; my back was getting stiff. "I assume you want me, the brother he doesn't know; other than whatever wild-eyed stories have been floating around, to see if I can find out what's wrong."

Moses stood. "Yes. He mentioned going down to see some of his buddies, said he might stay with you. Maybe he'll say something. If he needs help, maybe you can get him to see someone..." His eyes were watering up. "I worry. I... I don't want him to do something terrible to himself."

"I don't think he'd harm himself." Now I was worried.

"I hope he doesn't, but war is a terrible thing, does terrible things to people..."

"A lot of men go to war and come out of it ok."

"But many don't. I knew a lot of guys who went to Vietnam. They survived, but they did not come back ok. And I don't want him going back again and again. I... I want him to get out, finish up, and come home."

The young Moses Bohrman, the man who hated capitalist warmongers chewing up young men in pointless wars, was struggling with the older Moses, whose favorite son was changing in another pointless war. His very own flesh and blood caught in the system, soon to be torn apart by the faceless machinery of The Man.

"I'll see what I can do." I gave him a hug, and we headed back to the others.

· · · · · ·

We loaded up the cars. It was decided, reluctantly, that Emily could come down while her mother and Andrea were in San Fran, but this would not become a routine occurrence, even if no one believed that. This was worked out through a teleconference between Calista, gently prodded by Andrea, Meredith, Rebekah, Agnes, and Emily. I appreciated being left out of it. Since seven in the Benz wasn't going to work, Moses cajoled Jacob into motoring down with us in his jeep. Emily volunteered herself and yours truly to keep Jacob Company.

While it was tempting to dive right in with whether Moses was right about Jacob, I chose instead to let Emily flirt as we made our way south to the environs of greater Los Angeles. It was harmless fun. He was on to her and it allowed the hours to pass. She asked about life in the Marines, said she like the dress uniforms, but not the camo. He told her stories about how different the Middle East was. There was the climate to begin with, hot and dry. The religion; everybody was a Muslim. The people and their customs; how it was a different world for boys and girls.

"What do you mean?" Emily asked.

"Girls can't do whatever they want. Well, maybe they can try, but there's a lot of social pressure, and they face disgracing their families if they're not careful. They can be married off early if their families decide they've found a good match."

Emily considered this. "I read about that once. I don't think I could do that..." Emily struggled to process that thought. "Did they like you over there?"

Jacob didn't say anything at first. "Some do. Some don't. We're just trying to help, keep the peace, protect American interests."

Oh, if only the young Moses was riding along with us. I could hear him now. "American interests are corporatist interests. You're just cannon fodder for imperialist western demagogues, who have no concern for your well-being other than how they can make money off your corpse! Wake up! Fight back! America's poor shouldn't be killing Asia's poor so some fat cat a half a world away can profit from it!"

Jacob saw me smiling in the rear-view mirror. "What?"

"Sorry, I couldn't get Moses out of my head. He preached a lot when I was little about the perils of American interests."

Jacob nodded in agreement. "I had a hard time explaining my decision to join."

"I can hear him going on and on about being nothing more than a tool of the imperialists..." Weren't we all tools of the imperialists? "If you don't mind my asking, why did you join?"

"Because I thought it was important; because I wanted to get away; because I believed there's a kind of nobility in serving others, even if they didn't understand or wouldn't do it themselves. It was something we all agreed to do."

"Do you still believe that?" I asked.

He looked at Emily.

"Yes, and no. I think now it's what's important to me, what I think I should do. I don't know so much anymore what other people believe, people who have no idea what it's like, what it means. Service to your country isn't what it used to be. I get thanked a lot, but I wonder if they even know what they're thanking me for. There are times when it seems like I'm in two different worlds that only cross paths every once in a while."

He thought some more and shrugged his shoulders. Emily asked a few more questions before we settled into the comfort of the tires whining as we motored on.

I forgot to ask what he meant by *we* all agreed to.

·　　·　　·　　·　　·

We got to the big house late, ordered pizza, watched as Jacob was dazzled by the opulence of his surroundings, and put the kids to bed. Fidel and Rebekah said goodnight. As we sat out by the pool, I tried to explain to Jacob how I, Monk Buttman, came to own such a place, which necessitated bringing up Judith, which led to her painting in the library/kid's playroom, which led to an uncomfortable silence as he, Agnes, and I stood there. Neither Agnes or I wanted to talk about the dead woman on the canvas. We got him to his room and said goodnight. Agnes wanted to go home, but we had to watch the babies, because Fidel and Rebekah had to get going early the next day and we, or I should say Agnes, had foolishly agreed to watch the babies. We were staying.

"I have to go to work tomorrow," she muttered.

"Then go, we'll be fine. I have Emily to help," I said with a smirk.

"I don't want to go by myself and it's a long drive," she fumed.

"Hey, you wanted to keep working." Wait for it...

"Hey, not all of us are rich like you, Buttman," she said in her faux-outraged voice.

"Not my problem."

"You're a jerk, Buttman!"

I smiled. "I hope you remember that when it's time to sign the pre-nup."

Agnes groaned, left me and my smirk, and got ready for bed.

5

I rousted the still peeved Ms. Duquesne and prepared for another delightful day. Fidel and Rebekah were trying to get ready while dealing with Zach running around and Lizzy crying. Emily wandered out of her room and picked up Zach before he could get away, Rebekah sat on the couch to breastfeed Lizzy, Fidel collected what they needed for work, and I prepared breakfast. Agnes moped out in time to eat. Jacob surfaced just as everyone with a job was about to leave. I handed him a cup of coffee. He stood with me, Emily, Zach, and Lizzy as we bid them a good day.

"We're staying at the other house tonight, Buttman," Agnes grunted.

"We'll talk about that later, Honey-bunny." Lizzy was sucking on her pacifier as I helped her wave to the grumpy woman. "Say bye-bye, Lizzy." Lizzy spit out her pacifier.

Agnes shook her head and closed the door.

"How'd you sleep?" I asked Jacob as I retrieved the pacifier.

"Ok. It's a really comfortable bed." I took his word for it.

"Yeah, Judith had a rule about buying crappy stuff. Don't." I motioned to Emily and Zach, who was trying to get away from Emily's iron grip, "Alright, you two, time for morning chores and homework."

Emily frowned. "You're as bad as mom, Mr. Sunshine." Zach laughed at that. "You be quiet," she said. He just kept laughing.

We made the beds, and Emily got her homework out. I handed Lizzy to Jacob, who stared at me like I was nuts.

"Let me know if she goes off." It took him a minute to figure that out before taking a sniff.

We gathered by the pool. Zach was not allowed in until Emily was finished. He tossed a ball with Jacob, who handed Lizzy to me and was relieved the baby was no longer his responsibility. Lizzy was hungry again, so I fed her and set her down for a nap. Emily rushed through her homework, pouted when I pointed out her errors, made the corrections, and then jumped in the pool. She was already in her bathing suit. Zach tried bypassing protocol by jumping in with a regular diaper but was apprehended at the pool's edge and forced to wear the appropriate swim diaper. Jacob availed himself of a suit after I told him they were in the cabana.

"I'm probably going to take off after lunch, see if I can find my friends... I have an address here somewhere..." Jacob was assisting Emily in teaching Zach how to swim.

"And leave me here alone with these kids?" I stammered.

"Oh, put your man pants on, Mr. Sunshine!" demanded Emily. "We can take care of these little kids."

"Uh-huh. Is that how we talk to grown-ups, Emily?"

Emily was undeterred. "That's what Agnes says."

"Agnes has personal issues," I said.

"That's what she says about you, Mr. Sunshine!"

"Yeah!" shouted Zach. Jacob was struggling to keep a straight face.

"You see what I have to put up with! I doubt you put up with this kind of insubordination in the Marines."

"You'd think," was all he said. Zach and Emily had the temerity to laugh at me.

"That's it," I bellowed. "Do I have to invoke the master of the pool rules?"

Emily and Zach both frowned.

As master of the pool, I had the absolute right to be arbitrary and capricious when it came to pool time, thus the master of the pool rules. One of the few perks of actually owning the place. Other perks included rules on the proper care of the home, including disturbing the flow and design of the house, not putting stuff away, thereby abusing Theresa's good nature when it came to keeping the house clean. I didn't technically need a cleaning person, but it was a big house, she needed the money, and I already had to keep the house in West Covina clean. It all worked out. My somewhat disorganized daughter and fiancée bitched about the rules, but Rebekah didn't have money for her own place; unless she didn't mind commuting three or more hours a day, and Agnes was certain if I barred her from this house, I'd stop going to the house in West Covina. So, they caved.

So did Emily.

"Alright, I'll behave." She returned her attention to letting Zach splash Jacob.

Having won the battle for house supremacy, I sauntered off to the kitchen to make lunch. While we were eating, Jacob looked up his friend's address and asked if I had any advice for the best route. I tried to think of something that wouldn't defame driving in LA. I drew a blank.

"Use the traffic app. It's supposed to know the best route based on traffic conditions," I offered. I didn't have the heart to tell him conditions were terrible everywhere, but why spoil the adventure of learning that on your own.

"Ok." He didn't seem so sure.

Once we finished lunch, life slowed down. Jacob took off after I gave him the code to get back in, and the lowdown on dealing with the fuzz should he be stopped here in beautiful Beverly Hills. Zach and Lizzy napped, while Emily read a book by the pool. I used the time to go over the earnings reports the delightful Mr. Macklgrew sent over. I did what I could to be interested, but it was all the same thing. This investment experienced this growth, these annuities had this value, and here's how much cash is on hand. Emily came over, and pored over the reports with me, asking questions I didn't know the answers to.

"Ask Macklgrew," I said.

As we sat there, Anna wandered in. Apparently, none of us noticed she hadn't been home the night before. A sheepish grin covered her face.

"It's not what you think." She looked around. "Is mom here?"

"She's at work, remember? Mondays, Wednesdays, and half of Thursday. What's not what I think it is?" My grin was smarmier.

"Nothing. How are you, Emily? Hanging out with Mr. Sunshine, huh?" She was definitely her mother's daughter.

"Just seeing how rich Mr. Sunshine is," she said.

"I'm just the executor of the trust," I said.

"I think that only has to do with wills," countered Anna.

"Technically," I stammered, "but I am following the instructions of the will to its, um, intended intentions."

Anna laughed at me, which caused Emily to laugh at me. "So why is Mom still working if you have discretion over all this money?"

"Because we're not married and if I dump her, she's going to need to make some money. Also, if she continues working for Johnny, even if it's not full time, she can say she has her own money and isn't living off the estate of her boyfriend's dead girlfriend. You know your mother and her rationalizations."

Anna nodded. "I do. She still complains about *Ms.* Constantinescu. I told her if you were going to leave you would have by now, but you know Mom."

"I know Mom. So where were you last night, young lady?" I gave Anna my most stern parental expression. "And you know if I don't ask, I'll be asked why I didn't ask."

"Nothing, really. It was a late night. Besides, I can do what I want. I'm not a teenager anymore," she demurred. "And it was purely platonic, if you must know."

"I'm not the one who must know and you know that." Emily was absorbed in our silly back and forth.

"Well, let you-know-who know there's a show tonight at our new venue. I've even gotten a provisional ok to cater the event. The health department came by and seemed happy." Anna opened the refrigerator and took out the leftovers from lunch.

"Can we go, Mr. Sunshine?" asked Emily.

"I suppose. We'll see what you-know-who thinks."

"Maybe Jacob can go," she mused.

"Whose Jacob?" It was Anna's turn.

"My younger brother, he's in town looking up some friends."

"He's cute," added Emily.

"Is he?" Anna asked. Emily nodded. "Then maybe you should invite him?"

I nodded. What else could I do?

·   ·   ·   ·   ·

Agnes made her joyless return at approximately six-ten, demanding we stay at the other house, to which I reminded her that she was off the next day and there was still the matter of watching the babies, so if we went back to the other house, we'd have to get up extra early and sit in traffic to get back here. She didn't care for that.

"Is Anna here?" she asked.

"Nope, she left about two hours ago. They're having a show tonight and she got the ok to cater the event. We're all invited." We were out by the pool living the good life. Emily and Zach in the pool, Lizzy and me sitting comfortably nearby in the shade. The oppressed working woman was deeply envious, or so I presumed. "We're going." I pointed to Emily. "You're welcome to come along."

Agnes stood there with her hands on her hips. "I'm going to need my kisses first, Buttman."

I made a big show of having to get up, with a baby in my arms no less, and saunter the five feet before offering myself to her. She considered smacking me, but I had a baby in my arms.

"You're an ass, Buttman." This before she kissed me.

"I gotta be me."

"Yes," she kissed me again. "You keep telling me that."

I handed her Lizzy, which seemed to lighten the put-upon woman's disposition. Lizzy was in a good mood, laughing and smiling as Agnes offered her fingers and then pulled them away. Zach climbed on the chaise to play too. He wasn't overly jealous of his sister, always interested, always helpful. He offered his fingers too, which delighted Lizzy. I made a little something to eat, something to tide us over till we got to the theater and whatever Anna had in store. Emily changed for the evening. Tight pants and a tight shirt which oddly alarmed me. Then again, it may have been the makeup she put on.

"Agnes showed me how to do it," she said when I pressed her on it.

Agnes wasn't any more concerned than Emily. "She'll be with us, grandpa. Lighten up for christsakes." The four of them sat on the couch looking at me like I was a moron. All I could think of was Natalya being hauled off at that age to be prostituted to creepy old men.

"I'm just asking," I said, not wanting to be overly moronic.

Rebekah and Fidel came home and took their shift watching the kids. The two hot babes with the moron headed to the theater. I sent Jacob a text just in case he had any interest in joining us.

The performance center, named the Manifesto, was full. Agnes went to find Anna, while Emily and I wandered around. The show was organized as an open mic format where each band or performer would get to showcase three songs. The first act, a trio featuring piano, bass, and a singer, was completing a sound check. It didn't look like there were any open seats. We wandered down the aisle, checking out all the different characters in the audience. It was while wandering that Mikal found us.

"Monk!" Every time he saw me it was as if the sea was parting. "I was hoping you'd make it. We got seats for you right up front." I didn't occur to me I'd have my own seats.

"Thanks, this is Emily." Emily, awestruck, just stood there.

"It's great to meet you, Emily. My name's Mikal. Do you like music?" Mikal offered his hand; Emily took it.

"Uh-huh." Like I said, awestruck, and yet Joanie needed a break from the guy. I didn't get it.

I saw Agnes by the theater doors and waved to her, and together we took our seats. Emily saved the seat next to her for Jacob. Mikal stayed for a moment to say a few words to Agnes and then bounded onto the stage to introduce the opening act.

"Alright, let's get the show going, but first I'd like to thank all of you for coming tonight. It's a big deal for our performers to have a crowded house to play to; really gets the juices flowing. And I'd especially like to thank our benefactor, Mr. Monk Buttman, for his generous support in getting this hive of activity going." He pointed my way. I lowered my head, not wanting to be fingered as the generous donor, but Agnes, ever faithful Agnes, elbowed me in the ribs and I reluctantly, very reluctantly, stood briefly for the smattering of applause that accompanied my embarrassment.

"I specifically wanted to remain anonymous," I whined to Agnes under my breath.

"Oh, buck up, Moneybags, no one wants to hear you complain about your good fortune."

"That's not very helpful, you know—"

Agnes shrugged. "Then my work here is done."

The show turned out to be a rollicking affair, not just for the music, but also for the cameos Mikal had finagled from a number of well-known musicians, who happened to be in town. Everyone in the place seemed to be having a good time, though I didn't canvas the entire audience. Anna's goodies were well received, and nothing in the kitchen blew up or broke, making the evening an even greater success. Mikal introduced the people who played, well-known or not, as we stood in the lobby after the show was over. I was also introduced to several of the music teachers making use of our new teaching spaces, and, naturally, those smartasses who had to make a comment on my idiotic name.

Live and learn.

Mr. Jones came by to give me more grief. This after Agnes informed him of my discomfort with being outed as the guy wasting Judith's money.

"Man, it's a good thing I like you, Buttman, cuz sometimes your act gets a little thin."

"You're not helping either," I harrumphed.

"I'm not here to help, Buttman." He then turned serious, which caught me off guard. "Your friend is hanging out in front of the building. Manny. Isn't that what he said his name was?"

"Manny? Interesting. I ran into his mother the other day. Not a lot of love lost either way. Think he's tailing me?"

Jones groaned. "What do you think?"

I thought of a joke but held my tongue. "Let's go find out," I suggested.

Jones frowned and shook his head.

Manny was out front, standing to the left of the door. He stiffened when he saw me and Mr. Jones. I expected him to take off, but he didn't run.

"You should have come in for the show," I said.

"Music's too loud. I can't do loud music anymore. It hurts my head."

I thought about that and Jacob's comment that Manny had been a Marine once. "That's too bad, the music was good. Maybe the VA can help with your head?" His expression, such as it was, soured at the term VA.

"They won't help." He looked past me to the towering Mr. Jones. "I know you have the money, Buttman. You can hide behind your friend here, but the money belongs to me."

I laughed. "How the fuck does it belong to you? Your mother doesn't even believe that story, and at least she was alive when all that stupid shit was going down."

He didn't like my bringing his mother into this. "How do you know what my mother thinks?" Manny was beginning to fidget.

"Ran into her over the weekend, she sends her regards."

"I bet she does," he sneered. "I won't let you get away with this, *Buttman*, I won't." He turned and walked away. I could feel Jones looking down at me.

I looked at him. "No problem."

"I think you're full of shit, *Buttman*. Care to explain what he's talking about?"

"It's not important. Shouldn't he be able to go to the VA if he was in the Marines and has a problem? You were in the Army, right?"

Jones put his hand on my shoulder; something he rarely did. "Yeah, but more than likely he didn't get out honorably, and that matters when you need help. Probably not right, but that's life."

We went back into the building.

6

After the funfest with Manny, I collected Agnes and Emily and we headed back to the big house. It was getting late and I was tired. I was trying to connect the dots with Manny, and how he knew where I was, and it was making my head hurt. Emily went to bed and Agnes waited for Anna, who floated in about an hour after we did. I found a glass, ice, whiskey, and a comfortable seat by the pool. The light from the city below danced in the wispy breeze that moved about my aching head. It occurred to me that I spent an inordinate amount of time drinking whiskey by this pool. There were other locations within the house that I should use more often, such as the library or the entertainment room, but the library had the painting of Judith that sent me into a funk; no need for that, I was already in a funk, and the entertainment room lacked the view I'd grown accustomed to. Agnes came and ushered me to bed. She wrapped me around her as we lay in the dark.

"Was Anna here last night?" she asked as I was trying to fall into a fitful sleep.

"What did she say?" was my non-answer.

"She didn't say..."

"Then why do you ask?"

Agnes burrowed in deeper. "I'm certain something is going on with her, but she doesn't want to talk about it and that worries me."

"Why?"

"Because I think it involves your old girlfriend's boyfriend, Mikal, that's why!"

"Mikal? What makes you say that?" I didn't want to know.

"It was when he came over while I was talking to her. You were outside with Mr. Jones—"

"And?"

"*And* it was the way they looked at each other. The way she looked at him. I could tell."

"Well, he is good looking."

"He's also your age!" Her indignation was palpable.

"You're my age."

"I'm younger" —*a whole three years*— "than you. I don't want her seeing some old guy. I don't care how good looking he is."

"You're seeing some old guy?" It was like shooting fish in a barrel.

"Why do I talk to you? This is important!" she groaned.

"I don't know why you talk to me, but it might be your unwillingness to dump me for reasons unrelated to money and sex, but whether it's important, I don't know." I waited to be pinched. Surprisingly, it didn't happen. "What I do know is that Anna wasn't here last night, but that wherever she was, it was purely platonic. That's what she told me."

"And you believed that?"

"I saw no reason not to. She is a grown woman, you know."

Another groan from Ms. Duquesne, "That doesn't help, and what do you mean my unwillingness to dump you? What's on your mind, Buttman?"

That made me smile. "It's not important. Get some sleep." I kissed her and fondled her breasts.

"Monk?"

"Goodnight, Beautiful."

. . . . . .

My fitful sleep lasted three hours. It was at that point that Agnes woke me saying there was a noise by the pool and I should go see what's going on. I should have asked what she thought was going on. Reluctantly, I left the warm bed and the equally warm woman and ventured outside. There I found Jacob sitting at the edge of the pool where if you didn't know better you might think he'd fall into the city below. He looked up for a moment before returning his gaze to the city lights.

"You alright?" It was a stupid question, he looked anything but alright.

He didn't answer right away, but eventually asked, "Is this a Moses' question?"

"Yes, and no. He said he was worried about you; that you weren't sleeping, and it *is* the middle of the night, but it's more the look on your face. You're obviously upset." I sat down next to him not knowing what else to say, wondering if I should say anything more. Jacob stared at his hands. "Did you find your friends?" popped into my head.

"No, they weren't there. The guy said he threw them out; said they were trouble, and didn't care where they were."

"Did he say what kind of trouble?"

Jacob turned to me with a half-smile, but only for a moment, then the smile disappeared. "No, but... but I'm pretty sure I know what." He didn't elaborate.

"What about the guys down at Pendleton, maybe they've heard something?"

Jacob was back to examining his hands. "He didn't know where they were, he was worried about Lewis—"

"What about Lewis, is he missing too?" I asked, wondering who *he* was.

"Lewis is AWOL," he corrected me. I assumed that was bad.

"Then what's the plan?"

He laughed in an unfunny voice. "There's no plan, just lots of questions." The exhaustion was becoming obvious.

"Who wants the answers?"

Jacob wiped his eyes. "No one wants the answers." He was crying.

That shocked me. Marines don't cry. Marines are too tough for that. Crying was for fools like me.

I put my arm around him. "You need to rest. Come on."

He got up with me and I got him back to his room. I slipped him some of Agnes' magic sleeping pills. Wrong, maybe, but he had to get some sleep. I stayed a few minutes before leaving him.

Now I couldn't sleep.

•   •   •   •   •

I got up early, took a shower and made a pot of coffee, or more accurately, I pushed the button on the expensive coffee/espresso/cappuccino machine and it brewed a pot of coffee. For reasons unknown, I didn't feel too bad, despite being tired and stressed, and decided it was a good morning for pancakes. Blueberry pancakes. The gang started filtering in as the aroma of bacon and pancakes filled the air. The worker bees were up first, followed by the mother and daughter combo, who had the teenager and the kids with them. I didn't expect the Marine, but he wandered in too. Blurry-eyed and half asleep, no doubt aroused by the delightful smells filling the house. I passed out cups and plates and directed the hungry masses to the grub. There's nothing like seeing one's family filling up on homemade delights to make you feel reasonably useful.

Anna and the Marine cleaned the dishes as the worker bees got themselves out the door for another punishing day in the film industry. Agnes and Emily kept Zach and Lizzy in line while I had a second cup of coffee. Jacob thanked me for breakfast, then retreated to his room. Made me wonder if he'd eaten anything since yesterday's lunch. Anna deflected her mother's entreaties into her personal life, preferring to hold Lizzy instead. Zach, Emily, and I headed to the bedrooms to complete our morning chores, Zach didn't actually do much, but I believe his heart was in the right place. Emily tried to get out of doing her homework, but the master of the pool rules said no homework, no pool.

"You're a jerk, Mr. Sunshine."

"It gives me a reason to wake up each day. Now get to it."

With Emily focused on her homework, and Anna, with an assist from Zach, focused on feeding Lizzy, Agnes pulled me into the kitchen. She had something on her mind.

"I want to know what you meant last night." Last night?

"Nothing, just that you should have a little faith in your daughter, that's all." The market was open.

"Not that!" Her eyes narrowed as she stood next to me. Apparently, she wasn't buying today.

"What?" I never learn to keep my idiot mouth shut.

"I mean the thing about me dumping you. It was all I could think about last night."

"It's not important," I sat at the counter. Agnes sat next to me.

"I want to know what you meant'" She put her hand on mine.

"It's nothing,"

Agnes squeezed my hand. "I don't believe you, tell me?" I leaned in and kissed her. "I still want to know what you meant." I kissed her again.

"You won't like it and I see no reason to spoil the day."

"And making me worry will be better?"

I shook my head. You set the trap, dumbass. You can be angry when you step in it!

"Alright, I meant that you should have left me when I was seeing Judith, but you couldn't do that, just as you couldn't leave Simon, or even Jordan. I mean you knew Simon was gay yet you stayed. He was the one who left. Jordan nearly killed you, yet it took Johnny to finally get him away from you, and I kept coming up here, but you never left or even threatened to."

She rolled her eyes, cupped my face with her hands, and kissed me.

"You're right, I should have left you and Simon and Jordan, but I didn't and I've explained why to you a number of times, so it's not like you don't already know." Agnes continued caressing my face. "Why is this coming up now?"

"I don't know," I said, but I was lying. "That's not true, I know why, it just seems petty and narcissistic compared to what's going on with Jacob or the kids—"

"Which is what?"

"They have real problems, real concerns. I don't, but I don't feel like I have any control over what's going on around me, and yes, I know how that sounds."

Agnes smiled and let go of my face. "Ah, your big crisis over Judith's money, Judith's house, Judith's legacy. Monk just wants to be a poor boy living in a tiny bungalow, working odd jobs, and spending his free time hanging out at the beach in his stylish hand-me-downs."

I grimaced at my deep philosophical leanings being so concisely belittled. "Something like that," I mumbled.

"So, give it away. We still have our little house, and the kids will be alright on their own. Have a little faith. Isn't that what you tell me when I whine about things?"

I grimaced some more for effect. "Something like that."

"Exactly." Agnes got up then pulled me up. "It's a nice day. Let's go to the beach."

That used to be my line.

Everyone was thrilled at the news. Well, the kids certainly were; the adults needed some cajoling, Jacob in particular. But with Anna on board, at least till she had to go to the Manifesto, he reluctantly agreed. Emily thought that was a good thing too, so much so that she talked her way into riding with Anna and Jacob rather than the fogies and the babies. Agnes used the time on the road to pepper me with questions about Jacob.

"He seems like a nice guy, about the right age..." she mused.

"He's also in the Marines and that means long deployments to dangerous places."

"I spose, but he doesn't have to do that forever. Does he have a girlfriend?"

"I didn't ask."

"You're not being very helpful here, Buttman."

"You're welcome."

"Seriously?" she huffed. I didn't care. We were cruising along in the Falcon, the top down with that cool ocean breeze caressing our heads. "I think he's a better match than Mikal."

"Possibly, but he's not here to keep Anna out of the arms of her ancient paramour and besides, I don't think there's anything going on between Mikal and Anna. It's more likely he's simply taking her under his wing, more as a mentor than a lover. I'm pretty sure he's waiting for Joanie to come to her senses and return to him."

Agnes harrumphed at that. "You said she ran off with that Brian guy after you sold the bungalows out from under the geezers."

"Ouch! I did not sell them out! They were all taken care of—"

"Except now there's no place for other low-income seniors to go," Agnes snorted.

"Whose side are you on?"

"The geezers." The wind was blowing her hair into her face, which she compulsively tried to brush away. A futile gesture to say the least. Like my trying to rationalize selling out the geezers. Monk Buttman, you heartless bastard.

"*We're* almost geezers, my love!"

Another harrumph. "Speak for yourself, Buttman. I'm still young and vibrant," she said with an unusual amount of brio.

"Uh-huh." It was my turn to harrumph. "Nice as it might be to play matchmaker between Anna and Jacob, I don't think either has time for a budding romance. Anna is already busy with her food thing at the Manifesto and Jacob is having his own troubles."

"What do you mean troubles?"

"I don't know exactly, but I think it has something to do with his platoon, or unit, or whatever they call the group of guys he served with. Apparently, a lot of them have gone missing and he's worried and isn't sleeping. That's what you heard last night. It was Jacob out by the pool. He was in tears. That's how bad it is."

"Yeah, that's not good."

"Thank you, Dr. Feelgood."

Agnes feigned mock indignance. "You know what I mean."

"I know what you mean, so for the time being let's not put too much energy into fairy tale romances, ok?"

"I promise nothing," she purred while I sighed.

It's hard work trying to have a bad time at the beach unless you're some kind of anal fussbudget. The sun's out; the water is just the right temperature; the waves lap rather than pound, and you're only minutes from food and libations. Booze was probably a bad idea at this time of the day, but other than that, not much to complain about.

Emily and Zach played in the sand between bouts of running into the surf. Agnes and I played with Lizzy under the beach umbrella, while Anna and Jacob made small talk. It never occurred to me he might be shy around women, but it looked that way from where I was sitting. Agnes was surreptitiously watching them and smacked me on the arm when they went for a walk down the beach, as if I hadn't noticed. Emily was a little annoyed when she discovered they'd taken off without her, but Zach took her hand and they went for their own walk.

I wondered about the separation Jacob must feel coming back after so many years in the service. This wasn't like when I was a kid. There were a lot of veterans in those days due to the draft from World War II to Vietnam. Everyone knew someone who served. Did they now, or were they just sympathetic figures put in front of us at ball games? The disconnect between a life of patrols in a place like Afghanistan and a life of modern consumerism here in SoCal, especially Beverly Hills, must be almost otherworldly at times, and yet we expect them to simply adjust from one to the other. It was just a line of work, maybe like the fuzz or firefighters, except you're doing it on someone else's turf for reasons that may or may not make sense. Something was going on, but I knew nothing about that life, that calling, and Moses thought I could help.

Me, Monk Buttman, that heartless bastard.

Moses helped me after James was murdered...

I needed that help...

Badly...

Maybe that could be my thing?

7

Anna took off at noon. Jacob and I were responsible for provisioning the group's lunch.

"We don't provision. We simply load up before we head out on patrol." Apparently, my attempt to bond over commonalities was failing, "Nice try, though."

"Thanks," I sighed. On to the next subject on my list.

"You like Anna?" I was required by Agnes to reconnoiter Jacob as to his feelings.

He merely raised an eyebrow. "Are you trying to set me up?"

I raised mine. "I'm not, but Agnes is convinced that Anna is involved with an older man, which Agnes finds objectionable, and well, you are an attractive young man."

He smiled in a sad sort of way. "How do you know I don't already have a girlfriend?"

"I don't." I tried to act as lackadaisically as I could. "But I assumed if you did, you'd point that out. Do you?"

Jacob shook his head. "Not anymore." He fumbled with his phone before producing an image of a young woman standing next to him in uniform. "I was away too long..."

"Sorry."

He just shrugged, "That's the way it goes." It was probably time to move on to other uncomfortable subjects.

"Any idea what you want to do about your friends?" We stopped at a food truck and bought hotdogs and chips of the hip cuisine kind found here in foodie mad LA.

"I'd like to find out if they're ok."

That made me smile. Monk Buttman, hard-boiled private dick!

"I can help with that. Believe it or not, I've had some recent experience in such matters and I know people who can help if the need arises."

He looked at me, the wheels spinning. "I'd like that," he said.

"Alright, after lunch we'll get to it."

After lunch it was time to head back. Zach and Lizzy faded in the car, while Emily pestered Jacob about whether it was good or bad that they didn't or hadn't gone to a regular school.

"It's different, I guess, but I thought it was ok," he told her, which wasn't what she wanted to hear.

"Yeah..."

"You don't like being schooled at the farm?" I asked.

"It's all right, but there are no kids my age. I just wonder what it would be like to be around other kids my age. You went to public school, didn't you, Agnes?"

Agnes was in her own little world and had to be drawn back in to the conversation. "Um, yeah, I went to public school. I liked it for the most part, I mean sometimes it was boring and sometimes people were mean, or ignored you, but I had my friends and I did ok." Agnes noticed me snickering, "What?"

"Oh, nothing..."

Aggie smacked me in the arm. "What's so funny, Sunshine?" she demanded.

"It's not exactly a ringing endorsement, that's all," A reasoned point I thought.

"Why do I talk to you?"

"I don't know, it's convenient?" I laughed as she smacked me again.

"You're a jerk, Buttman."

"Some things never change." She tried to look mad, but it didn't work. Advantage, Buttman.

The afternoon came and went with little in the way of concrete action. I, as master of my domain, was obligated to discuss the minutiae of our domestic affairs with Theresa, the young woman who kept the house clean, and Wilmer, whose company kept the yard in the lovely conditions suited for such an exalted neighborhood. My job was to ask idiotic questions and nod my head like I knew what I was talking about. They were both good natured towards me, which I took as a favor not to be taken lightly. On the plus side, I paid them well, which salved my sense of being a fraud and an interloper.

Agnes was in the library with Lizzy, although Lizzy was sleeping. Agnes had lately developed an alarming interest in Judith and her likes and dislikes. I found her contemplating the painting of Judith up on the wall. I could see Emily through the door to the pool faithfully completing her homework. Zach was sitting at the table with her. I assumed Jacob was in his room. I sat next to Agnes and looked at Judith standing there.

I tried not to miss her.

Agnes nudged me. "Did she like it?"

"Like what?"

Agnes turned and winked. "You know, what we talked about."

I let out a deep sigh. "Didn't we talk about this already?"

It was Agnes' turn to sigh. "You think we did, but really we didn't. You say a few things and think that's it, or you blow it off, or change the subject. Did she?"

"If I tell you, will you stop bringing this up?"

"You say that too." I didn't care for the knowing smile plastered across her face. "A lot."

I fell back on the tried and true. "Why is this so important to you and why are you bringing this up now?"

She patted my hand in a smug, condescending manner. "You've asked that almost as many times as the others. You're like a broken record." I made an unpleasant face as she turned to the painting lording over us. "I want to know because I don't want her memory standing between us. If I understand why, then she won't be this unknown thing that haunts our relationship, and yes, MaryAnn suggested we talk about this if you feel the need to blame someone. I don't want her to be some mystery that I don't understand."

"And knowing whether she liked anal sex will make you feel better?"

"Odd as that sounds, yes. It makes her more of a regular person. Did she?"

I considered my options and evasions. What the hell. "Yes, she did."

"Did she orgasm when you did it?"

Images began dancing before me, erotic images of me and Judith. "Sometimes..."

Agnes got up and went to the painting. "What did you like best about her?"

"Her neck, she had the most graceful, elegant neck."

"Not her boobs?" Agnes was baiting me, she knew how much I liked her boobs.

"No. She had nice boobs, but you know yours are my favorite."

She grinned and came back to the couch. "Why don't you ask me to do it?"

I put my hand on her knee. "I don't know. It was something she initiated. To be honest, I don't know that I would have asked if she hadn't asked first. Same with you. I won't say I didn't enjoy it, but I'd feel kinda like a pervert asking you to do it."

Agnes smiled and nodded. "Yeah, that sounds like you."

"I'm surprised you haven't tried it yourself." I threw the ball in her court.

She acted shocked. "You mean like did Simon practice on me?"

"You ask. I ask." It was nice to see her embarrassed for a change.

"No, sex with Simon didn't include that. The others I foolishly hooked up with were only interested in hand jobs or blowjobs, because as one of them so nicely put it, 'I don't know where that pussy's been.'" She pondered me for a moment. "It doesn't say much for my choices that you're the only one who liked returning the favor down there." Agnes scrunched in next to me, her eyes alight with mischief.

"Their loss. Are we done?" I leaned in for a kiss.

"For now." She leaned in too.

Lizzy was waking up.

The rest of the day evolved as it usually did. The kids came home to take care of their kids. I made dinner, which was seared chops with a salad, and later there was ice cream for dessert. Jacob came out for dinner but said little. At this point, I think everyone felt his sense of unease. We ended the day with a Disney movie out by the pool.

I offered to talk.

"I'm alright, just tired," he said, which made me cringe.

Isn't that what I told everyone a year ago after Judith had died? I knew I was lying, but I didn't want anyone to worry. "Even if you don't think I'd understand, it's good to let it out."

Jacob stared at me with the faintest of smiles. "Thanks, maybe another time."

"Would you like some of Agnes' magic sleepy time pills?"

"Sure."

I retrieved them and left him out by the pool.

Agnes, titillated by the salacious talk earlier in the day, and aided by two glasses of wine, had romance of a certain variety on her mind. I, sadly, did not. Still, it was difficult not to be aroused finding her on her stomach, her head resting on her hands, a broad smile on her face, a circular pillow under her hips, and her underwear pulled down to her knees. On the table was a bottle of love lube.

"Something on your mind?" I asked, not entirely oblivious to the obviousness of the situation.

"Something..." She wriggled her behind for effect. I sat down beside her, running my fingers ever so lightly on said behind.

"Is this something you want to do or something you think you should do for my benefit?"

"A little of both."

My fingers were becoming more adventurous. "Then heaven forbid that I should be the one to deny you your pleasures."

She pulled me close. "Heaven forbid."

• • • • • • •

Darkness covered us as we laid there, arm in arm; our lasciviousness sated, our bodies cleaned, clinging to one another before we fell to our slumbers.

"Was it everything you'd hoped it would be?" I asked. Time for the postmortem.

"It was certainly different. Is it bad manners for me to mention that you didn't seem very excited?"

Oh, for the days when nothing interfered with an erection.

"It wasn't you or the sex or anything like that. It's this thing with Jacob. He sounded just like I did a year ago. Something is eating him up, but he's ok, no worries." I sensed the righteousness welling in the woman next to me.

"It's incredible frustrating, isn't it, *Mr. Sunshine*?" She added an unwanted poke. "It just makes you worry more!"

"Yeah, yeah, no need to state the obvious. Any ideas, thoughts, about what to do?" I took hold of her free hand to prevent any more fingers to the torso. Instead, she simply pulled me in tighter.

"Hope and pray like I continue to do."

That didn't help.

·   ·   ·   ·   ·

The next day was just me, Emily, and the babies. Jacob took off without saying much of anything to anyone. Agnes grumbled about having to go to work but went all the same. Emily wanted to go to the mall to check out the beautiful people. Natalya called to remind me of Saturday's art gallery to-do, and Anna wandered out of her room. I'd forgotten about her. I was having a hard time keeping track of everyone's comings and goings.

"Is Jacob ok?" She sat on the rug by the couch where Lizzy was flapping her arms and legs, flailing at the toy swing hanging just beyond her reach.

"No, something's bothering him, but he won't say. Everything's just fine. Just fine." Anna had reached out to Lizzy and Lizzy began pulling on Anna's finger. "Did he say anything to you yesterday?"

"He didn't say much. I didn't know if that's just the way he is, or if he's quiet around people he doesn't know." Anna took hold of Lizzy's tiny hands. "He did say he felt lost at times and struggled with what to do with his life, whether to stay in or get out. And then he said something I didn't understand, something about honoring the oaths you take, or something like that. I asked him what he meant, but he just stared out at the ocean and said it didn't matter now. Is he in his room?"

"No, he left a while ago. He's trying to find his friends, guys he served with."

"Well, maybe they can help. They'd probably understand better than we would."

"I hope so." I watched as she absentmindedly played with Lizzy.

"We should take him with us Friday night. Barron and Gerta are going." Friday night? "Grand opening?" I offered.

She just laughed. "Um, yeah, didn't Mikal tell you?" Anna looked back at me.

I simply shrugged. "Probably, but I seem to miss things from time to time. Yeah, we should drag him along, might do him good. You got all your permits?"

"Yeah, it's all good. As a matter of fact, I should get going. There's a lot of prep I need to do for Friday." Anna picked up Lizzy, turned, took a step, turned again, and then sat down next to me on the couch. "I'd like to ask you something."

"Sure."

"A while back I heard you and mom talking and she said something about Jordan and me. I want to know what that was about." I had to think for a moment; I thought she was going to ask whether she should be dating Mikal, even though I didn't think there was anything there.

"Your mother was concerned that Jordan would come around, that he would somehow find out you were in LA. I told her not to worry, that he'd never be back."

Anna shifted towards me. "How would you know that?"

"After you said you'd like to be a part of our little adventure down at the Manifesto, and knowing your history with him, I wanted to make sure that there would be no problems. Money has certain advantages and one is getting information. So, I had some people I know look into what happened to him or where he might be."

"And?"

"Jordan is dead. They found his body in an alley in Reno a few years back. Someone cut his throat." The information, a favor from Bernie, was reluctantly confirmed by Detective Mallory. Anna didn't seem shocked or surprised, just unsure.

"Did Johnny do it?"

"Don't know, don't care. Either way, it's none of my business. All that matters to me is that neither you or your mother need to worry about him." I decided not to mention that he'd been beaten to a pulp before his throat was cut.

"Does mom know this?"

"No. I thought she'd ask, but it hasn't come up. Maybe she knows, maybe she doesn't. Either way is ok, I suppose."

Anna merely nodded before handing Lizzy to me. "I have to go. Thanks for telling me."

"Sure."

Lizzy grabbed my tie, as I watched Anna leave, and began playing with it. I pulled it away and waited for her to grab it. Emily and Zach wandered in from the pool. Zach was dripping. I pointed to him and then the door. Emily turned to where I was pointing. "You know the rules. No wet clothes in the house."

"Can we go after that?" she asked.

"After lunch," I said.

"We can eat at the mall," she suggested.

"We can eat here. Off you go with señor drippy pants." Zach laughed and tried to say drippy pants which came out 'zippy ants'. Emily groaned and took her charge by the hand.

During lunch the phone rang.

8

The first call was from Jacob, he'd gone to Pendleton to see Cameron, one of the guys he knew, the guy who told him Lewis had taken off.

"Cam told me Kurtis grew up in Watts. Maybe his family knows where he is, but he didn't know exactly where in Watts. Have you ever been there?" Watts?

"No, but I have a friend who probably has. I can ask him. Is there anyone there who can help find his home address?" I heard him murmuring to someone with him.

"I'll try to find out. I'll let you know." He hung up before I could even ask what Kurtis' last name was.

Emily and Zach were watching as I was talking to Jacob.

"Is Jacob ok?"

I wondered if I should be alarmed or comforted that so many of us were concerned about Jacob's welfare.

"Oh, I just think he has some things on his mind. He's worried about some of his friends and he's trying to find them, so I offered to help."

Emily cocked her head in a way that suggested she knew more. Zach noticed this and mimicked her response. "Is there anything I can do?"

"I don't know, but we'll do what we can. Us Bohrman men can be stubborn. You probably noticed that."

Emily smiled. "I noticed. Can we go now?" Zach nodded in agreement.

"We have to clean up first,"

Emily rolled her eyes. "Then let's get to it, Mr. Sunshine."

It was Mr. Sunshine's turn to smile.

The second call came as we were loading ourselves into the Falcon. It was Joanie!

"Buttman," I answered with as little interest as I could fake.

"It's Joanie, do you have a minute?" The voice on the other side sounded tentative, something I don't remember her being.

"We're heading out. Can you meet us or are you out of the country?" It's important to ask these things because you never know.

"Ha-ha, very funny. Meet you where?"

The big mall in Beverly Hills, Beverly Center, on the boulevard, you can't miss it."

I heard her groan through the phone. A lot of people were groaning lately, mostly at me. "I know where it is. I'll meet you at the food court. You know where that is, right?"

"I guess we'll find that out when we get there. Adios."

"Still the same... Bye."

Emily and the kids were ready to go. Emily's agitation was evident. "Can we please go now?"

At least she said please.

· · · · ·

Joanie wasn't prepared to deal with a well-dressed man and three children. I told Emily she could wander on her own, so long as wandering included Zach. More groaning which made Zach laugh. I gave Lizzy to Joanie. She was genuinely surprised I would do such a thing. I considered my day made.

"She doesn't bite, no teeth yet. Just cradle her in your arms," I helpfully offered.

"Ha-ha!"

I watched as she treated the child like fine crystal. "So, what's up? I didn't know if I'd ever see you again after you disappeared into the ether."

Joanie frowned at me. "Again, ha-ha." I shrugged. "I had things to do, that's all, and it was easier to do them on my own, that's all."

"You're repeating yourself."

"I'm just... I don't know. How's Mikal? Have you seen him?"

"I see him quite a bit. We're both a part of the Manifesto. Although I'm mostly providing the financing. Have you forgotten that?"

Joanie handed Lizzy back to me.

I sat Lizzy on my lap and looked at Joanie. "What's up?"

Joanie sat there, clasping, and unclasping her hands. "Brian and I are getting married."

"Congratulations." I believe that's the pro forma response.

Joanie shifted in her chair. "I know you don't like him, but he's a good guy."

"I never said he wasn't a good guy. My concern was that he wasn't the right guy, but you evidently believe differently, and if you're happy then that's all that matters. Am I to assume this little meeting is about how to tell Mikal?"

Joanie grimaced. "Something like that. Is he ok?"

"Seems to be. He's very excited about the performance center. As a matter of fact, the grand opening is Friday night. You should come and check it out. Bring Brian if you like. Does he enjoy music?" She didn't care for that option. "If not, then come by yourself. I don't know if that'll be the best time to tell him you're gone for good, but from what I can see, he's a pragmatist, and he'll probably congratulate you and ask if you're still singing. We all move on. That's life."

"Maybe you—"

"No! I can console him after the fact. After all I know what it's like to be told it's over, but I'm not going to deliver the news that you're cementing your new life with Brian through matrimony."

"Agnes is right, you are a jerk."

I smiled. "It's who I am." She didn't think that was funny.

"Speaking of Agnes, are you still with her or have you moved on with the teenager?"

"I'm still with Agnes, and as much fun as Natalya is, that doesn't include active sexual congress, and she not a teenager. As far as we know, she's like twenty or twenty-one."

"As far as you know?" she smirked.

"I didn't ask for her birth certificate. I guess if I asked, she'd tell me. What I do know is that she and I are not involved." There were more smirks from Mikal's ex.

"Shouldn't she be going back to wherever she's from?"

My turn to smirk. "I don't know what you have against her, but she's here legally. It took a little work, but if you have money and know the right people, things get done. Just look at you. If it weren't for the fact that I had some property that was coveted by your man's company, you'd still be eking out a living and worrying about your future. Instead, you've got money, security, and a new man to spend the rest of your days with. Hmmm?" I raised my eyebrows for effect.

"Yeah, yeah, yeah."

"What are you going to do about Mikal, anything?" It was obvious she didn't want to deal with this.

"He's not with anyone else?"

"If he is, he hasn't brought her around, and given how much time he's put in to the performance center, I'd be surprised if he did." I looked at her, thinking of our time together, short as it was, trying not to be smug, "It's up to you whether you tell him or not. I think you owe him that. Friday night's an option."

"I'll think about it. Where is this place?" I gave her the address. "And how are you, Monk Buttman? Has wealth totally corrupted you?"

"Absolutely." Lizzy was squirming. A sniff test confirmed my suspicions. "It's time to change the baby, and I should probably make sure Zach isn't driving Emily nuts." I got up and put Lizzy in her stroller for the short trip to the restroom. "I hope I see you Friday, but if not, it was good to see you and best of luck with Mr. Whalen."

She sat there looking at me. I knew the look. I'd seen it many times before, but this time she was on her own.

"Thanks," was all she said.

I left her to the cadences of the Beverly Center Mall.

•   •   •   •   •

I spent the rest of the afternoon processing Joanie's good news. It danced with the memories the two of us shared. Ten years is a long time to know a woman and maintain an idiotic crush, but I stilled loved her and worried she was fucking up her life for the formalities of "feeling secure." She was right that I didn't know Brian beyond his yen for my cluster of bungalows, but I still believed Mikal was the better man, and one day she'd miss him in that horrible way our surety fails us when we realize the foolishness of our choices.

Such is life.

Emily, with Zach trailing, gazed in wide wonder at the abundance of the mall and the shops inside it. I followed at a discreet distance with my granddaughter fast asleep in the stroller. Occasionally, Emily would signal for me to come closer, to check out a particular item in a window, or to let me know she was going in so she could check it out. Her way of saying I needed to keep Zach from becoming too much of a pest. Apparently, neither of her parents or their significant others let her window shop much. Thus, our forays allowed her to find out for herself what the rest of humanity, or those in LA, were up to. She found many things she liked and I would have happily bought them for her. I had, after all, money burning a hole in my pocket. But I'd been chastised by Calista earlier in the year when I thought nothing of buying Emily two dresses along with a pair of close-fitting jeans and a stylish tee that Emily had seen on a girl wandering the mall with her friends.

And shoes. Emily loved shopping for shoes.

This provoked a rather bitter exchange between mother and daughter, and I was the chump in the middle. I shrugged and promised to not be so profligate in the future. But it was hard. For once in my life, I could spend without concern, and was being stymied in my attempts to be a grand man, even if it was only in the eyes of a thirteen-year-old.

"It's not your place to spoil Emily, Sunshine," Agnes said when I tried to sway her to my side of the argument. "It's your place to spoil me and maybe our kids. Otherwise, you'll just continue to be in the trouble you find yourself in now."

"You know I was hoping for a little more support!" I protested.

"That's what your *girlfriend* is for."

I ignored that.

My daydreaming was interrupted by both the phone and my grandson. Zach needed to be changed and the phone was ringing or chiming or whatever that goddamned noise was. The caller was Jacob. He had a home address for Kurtis, or where Kurtis once lived. He asked if it was a good idea for him to go into a black neighborhood by himself. I didn't think it would be a problem, but said I would ask Mr. Jones. He asked who that was.

"He a good guy who finds me mildly irritating," I said.

Jacob laughed at that.

"I'll call Jones and see what he thinks." I put the phone away and commenced cleaning up Mr. Poopypants. Zach didn't like being changed anymore, but wasn't potty trained.

"If you don't like this, learn to go to the bathroom."

"NO!" was his response. I just laughed. "Ool!" he said, his word for the pool.

"You have to take a nap first."

"NO!"

I sighed. I used to spend my afternoons enjoying the quiet of my bungalow and a cold beer. I sighed again.

After cleaning Zach and collecting Emily, who did not wish to leave this consumer's paradise, we were back on the road to the house on the hill. Once there, I called the always delightful Mr. Jones to get his opinion on Jacob's foray into Watts.

"Watts? What business would you have in Watts? You and that Dunkle aren't buying up properties, are you? There's a lot of bad blood brewing over that kind of thing," he warned.

"No, nothing like that. My brother, Jacob, is trying to find a guy he served with in the Marines, and is hoping whoever lives there, I'm assuming his family, will know where he is. It's just that."

"Uh-huh. Where in Watts?"

"On Anzac, not far from the elementary school. I looked it up on my phone."

"Did you now?" I could hear the condescension through the phone.

"I really don't need the levity," I said.

"That's not what Agnes tells me," he snorted. "When are you planning this trip into my part of town?"

"You don't live in Watts and Agnes doesn't know what she's taking about."

It was his turn to sigh. "Work with me, Buttman. When?" Am I that bad?

"My guess is tomorrow. We haven't actually gotten that far yet."

Jones snorted again. "That's SOP with you, Buttman. Call me when you have the time and date."

"What, you don't think I can handle this on my own?"

"No," Jones laughed, "I don't." He continued laughing as I ended the call.

Emily commandeered the table by the pool while Zach napped. Lizzy was awake, so I fed her. Emily labored on the homework she just happened to forget earlier. I had a beer and called Ms. Lagenfelder down at Aeschylus and Associates. Remarkably, she answered my call.

"Yes, Mr. Buttman; what can I do for you?" Always polite.

"I'd like to move ahead with the prenup documents we discussed the other day." Technically, it was a couple of months ago.

"Are the payouts and property arrangements to remain the same as before?"

"Yes. We can review that when the document is ready."

"Certainly. When would you like this to be ready? Is there a rush on it?" she inquired.

"No rush. If you can get it ready in the next few weeks; whenever, that's good," I told her, wanting it done, but not this minute...

"We can do that. Anything else I can help you with?"

I thought about that. Drew a blank. "No, that should do it. Thanks for taking care of this..."

"My pleasure. Have a good day."

I promised I would.

·   ·   ·   ·   ·

My beloved tossed her meager possessions on the counter as I was preparing the evening meal. She did not appear particularly upbeat.

"Bad day, Beautiful?"

"I want to go home, Buttman!" she demanded.

"Is my love bunny unhappy with her commute, or is work wearing on you?"

Agnes smacked my arm. "Works fine. Rey asked about you since you haven't been by in some time." Rey was the bartender at Johnny D's dive, which was next door to his thriving gray market lending establishment.

"Yeah, I miss my long talks with Rey, but we have responsibilities that keep us here. Would you have me kick everybody out so we can go back to our simple little lives?" I got the stink-eye instead of an answer.

"I want my kisses, Buttman."

"We all do, Beautiful."

That didn't improve her mood. "I'm serious here, Buttman! There are some things I won't let you put off, so get your ass over here and kiss me!"

I smiled and pulled her close. "There's no need for that." I kissed her enough that she ventured a smile. Lizzy was fussing in her pen. "The baby needs you." I kissed her before sending her towards Lizzy.

"Are we ever going to go back to you and me?" She had retrieved the baby and was watching me sear the tuna.

"I don't know. Maybe I'm being too nice, too supportive. Maybe I should kick them out and make them fend for themselves."

Agnes grimaced as Lizzy's parents came through the door. I didn't think Anna would be back for dinner and had no idea when Jacob would show up. Rebekah took Lizzy and Zach ran in from the pool or tried to before Emily grabbed him.

"No wet suits in the house, dude." A helpful reminder from Fidel. I wondered if Rebekah would ever tell Zach of his biological father.

I turned to Rebekah, who was nuzzling her daughter. "Agnes wants me to kick you guys out so we can go back to our old life."

"MONK!" Agnes bellowed. I just laughed.

My daughter frowned. "Very funny, dad." Lizzy laughed.

"Who says I'm joking?"

The women were not pleased, but there was dinner to consume, so I let it slide. Instead of working out where they would live, the conversation consisted mainly of how the business was going, and the big show two nights hence.

"Barron and Gerta are coming. I don't know where they're going to stay, but I'm sure we'll find room for them," Agnes was rambling.

"No doubt." They could always sleep in Judith's room, like I did after she died. It was a room that often went unused. Jacob showed up later that evening and wanted to go to Watts the next day. I informed Jones, who seemed surprisingly supportive. We agreed to meet at his house at noon. Jacob said he hoped it would clear things up. I asked if Lewis had been heard from.

Jacob said no and left for his room.

9

The day did not go as planned.

Agnes was not amused when I informed her that we, Jacob and I, were leaving, but I said it was no big deal and we'd be back soon, after all we were simply going to talk to Kurtis' family.

"Simple as that?" she asked.

"No big deal," I assured her.

"You haven't forgotten about our plans for tonight, have you?" Of course, I had. She must have noted the lack of comprehension on my face. "Barron and Gerta will be here. We're going out. Anna's coming along. Big family get together. You remember, right?"

"I do now." That didn't help.

"I was expecting you to help me get ready," she pouted.

"We'll be back," I promised. I had the best of intensions.

Never promise anything.

Mr. Jones was waiting for us outside his house, amid the heat and smog, wearing black from neck to toe, which was how he did things. Jacob didn't know what to make of his companions, both in suit and tie, both of whom he considered way over-dressed. Neither I, nor Mr. Jones, conformed to the hip new styles. He was lost to the Seventies, and I to the Sixties. We piled into the Chrysler sedan, Mr. Jones' new ride, for the twenty-minute trip to our destination in Watts. Nobody seemed interested in conversation beyond the immediate desire for information on one Kurtis Santos. As we turned onto Anzac, Jones pulled over and turned to me and Jacob.

"Before we go in, I'd like to know a few things. How long have you known this man?"

"A little more than five years. We went to boot camp together and we were in the same platoon. Kurtis and Mason got out about a year ago," Jacob said.

"Anything out of the ordinary I should know about? Anything that might make this more than just a casual visit?" I didn't know where Jones was going with this.

"I don't think so, I'm just trying to find out how they are; how Kurtis is doing," Jacob answered.

Jones looked at me. "This Mason, just a friend?"

I looked at Jacob.

"Yeah, just a friend," Jacob reiterated.

He was lying. Jones knew it too. We got out and went to the front door, which was set in an open porch. Several blooming flower pots cluttered the entry. I knocked.

A woman's voice cried out, "Who's there?" A small woman with cinnamon skin and like colored hair peered at us through the screen door. She opened it just enough to take in Mr. Jones and the two white guys with him. "What you want? You and these two? And don't lie to me, I know liars when I hear 'em."

Jones smiled and removed his glasses.

"We're asking after a man named Kurtis Santos. This young man served with him in the Marines."

The woman eyed Jacob. "You know Kurtis?"

Jacob seemed hesitant to answer. "Yes, ma'am, I'm trying to find out if he's ok."

Her eyes grew tighter. "Ok? You want to know if Kurtis is ok? What's your name?"

"Jacob," he whispered.

"Jacob what?" she demanded.

"Jacob Bohrman."

The woman's eyes filled with tears and you could feel the anger shimmering off her. Jones' admonition in the car was knotting at my insides as I watched the color leave Jacob's face.

"You got nerve coming here, Jacob Bohrman. I know about you. I know what you did, you and those other boys. I know what you did to Kurtis and that no good Mason. You can't hide behind these two. It's in his book, the one the police gave me after they found him. You and those devils raped him, didn't you, out there in that goddamned desert? You knew he was different, and you raped him and abused him, and made his life a living hell, and you got the goddamned nerve to come to my house asking if he's ok. Well, you know what, Jacob Bohrman, Kurtis is not ok; Kurtis is dead! That crazy white boy he loved shot him down and then killed himself." Her body shook as she spoke, her face contorted with rage.

Jones and I turned to Jacob. It was in his eyes. What she was saying wasn't a lie.

His voice was barely audible. "That's not true, I didn't—"

"Don't you dare lie to me, I know what my boy was, but he was a decent man and what you did was an abomination. Now you get off my porch and off my property before I get my shotgun and give you what you deserve, all of you!"

Jacob was trying to speak, but Jones spoke first.

"Our apologies. We'll be on our way." He put his sunglasses back on and then took Jacob by the arm and led him back to the car. I followed, trying to make sense of what was roiling in my head. Jacob wouldn't look at me when I turned to him in the backseat.

"Jacob," was all that came out.

Jones reached over and put his hand on my sleeve. When I turned to him, he shook his head. We sat in silence as Jones drove out of Watts. Ten minutes later, in Huntington Park, Jacob jumped out of the car and took off running. I rolled down the window to shout, but Jones again stopped me.

"Let him go, Buttman. Hungry?"

"What?"

"Are you hungry?"

Hungry? "No!"

He rolled up the window from his side. "I am, and we should talk."

Minutes later, we were at the sandwich shop just down from the moonscape that was once the Moonlight Arms, sitting in a booth waiting for our lunch.

Jones cajoled me into ordering. "You need to eat."

I stared out the window. "I don't understand."

"You don't understand why you need to eat?"

"Why are you fucking with me?"

Jones merely shrugged. "Someone's a little sensitive today, aren't they? I mean she didn't accuse you of rape, did she?" He followed that with a swig of beer.

"You think this is a joke?"

Jones put the beer down. "You know I don't. But I also know when things ain't right, and things ain't right with your brother and whatever he's up to. I know. I still stay in touch with the guys I served with, I know how they act, how they feel. It's a constant, whether good or bad, and it was obvious by the way he was acting that this wasn't going to be good. That's why I asked what I did, and based on how he acted I wasn't surprised by what happened."

The sour pit in my stomach was reaching out and grabbing the rest of my insides. "You believe what she said? What she accused him of?"

"All kinds of things happen when you're out there. People do things they would never do back here. Nobody likes to talk about it. It's like a what happens in Vegas stays in Vegas kind of thing."

"Are you saying things like that happened with you?"

Jones shook his head. "Not to me directly, but things happen, things get said, rumors spread. Most of it gets ignored or swept under the rug. Maybe if it happens to you, if you're involved, then something gets done. But it's not always a priority. The culture has expectations and rules. That's the way it is. I don't know if everything she said was true, but I believe there's fire with that smoke, and I know you believe it too."

He was right.

I sat there, not wanting to believe my youngest brother participated in the gang rape of a fellow Marine. If he did, why was he looking for the people he raped? Was he coerced? The waitress brought the food, and I did my best to eat some of it. Agnes called. I knew what she would say before she said a thing.

"What's going on? Jacob raced in the house, grabbed his stuff and raced out. He didn't say a word. He looked terrible. What's going on, Monk?"

"Jacob's taking off," I said. "Maybe he's going home; he didn't say. I don't know exactly what's going on."

"What does that mean? Where are you?"

"I'm with Jones, I have to check on a few things then I'll be home. We can talk about this later." I could feel the phone shaking in my hand.

"I don't like this, Monk Buttman!"

"I don't either. I'll see you in a little while."

Jones was watching me. I said goodbye to Agnes. "What now?" he asked.

"Mallory, I'm going to call Mallory, find out what happened to Kurtis and Mason. See what the police know. Other than that, I have no idea what to do. Hope that Jacob will be willing to talk at some point."

Jones curled his lips. "You think he's going to open up about something like that to someone he doesn't really know?" He had to bring that up.

"You're not helping here."

"I'm just being honest. Now eat your lunch."

"No," I said, channeling my inner Zach. Jones shook his head and went back to eating his.

•   •   •   •

Mallory was in his office. He answered his phone and told me to come on down. We had an interesting relationship going back to Desiree Marshan and that mess, which was followed by the thing with Desmond or Stoiker or Link Deal, the guy playing all sides of a made-up scam. Natalya was suing Desmond just to make his life more miserable. I said it's like blood from a turnip; nothing there, but she wanted someone to pay and it wouldn't be Big Mike Kovalenko. He skipped to Eastern Europe to avoid the child rape charges sitting in the DA's office. Mallory had been a party to all of it, as had I. He sat back and smiled ruefully as I knocked on the door.

"Mr. Buttman, always a pleasure. Have a seat." I sat down in the steel chair with the worn cushion across from his desk. "You said you wanted to ask about a man named Kurtis Santos."

"I did, and a man named Mason. I don't know his last name, but was told they were dead, that they killed each other."

He sat up and tapped a file on his desk.

"Almost. Mason Saunders shot Kurtis Santos and then shot himself." His eyes turned to the folder in front of him before turning to me. "What's your interest in these two?"

"My youngest brother served with them in the Marine Corps and was looking for them. He was shocked to hear they were dead. We heard it from Kurtis' mother, or who I think is his mother."

"Small woman? Reddish-orange hair?" he asked.

"Yeah, lives in Watts."

"Her name is Aretha Harvin. She was Kurtis Santos' aunt. She told us both of Mr. Santos' parents were dead. Said she raised him. The two men were found in a homeless camp after reports of gunfire. It was a murder-suicide. What did your brother have to say about them?"

"Very little, only that they had gone to boot camp together and had served in the same company in Afghanistan."

"Did he mention they were gay?" Mallory was looking right at me.

"No." I got the distinct feeling that he was well aware of what Ms. Harvin had said was in Kurtis' book. "No, he actually said very little, and was quite upset to hear they were dead."

"Is he willing to talk about what he knows? There are some questions I have."

"I don't know, but I doubt it, at least for now. He took off, I assume to head back north. He did say that they had been kicked out of their apartment, that there had been trouble—"

"Yes, I know about that. The police responded to several domestic calls concerning the two men. The reports indicated they were probably PTSD episodes, and because there weren't any signs of physical violence and neither would talk or press charges, there wasn't much we could do other than refer them to VA services."

Mallory shuffled through the file on his desk and pulled out a sheet of paper, which was a copy of what looked like a newspaper article. The light went out of his eyes. "I don't know why this bothers me," he said at last. "I've seen these kinds of deaths before. Maybe it was the two purple hearts in the small box beside them..." We sat in the quiet of his office as the rest of the station buzzed with activity. I felt acutely out of place, wondering what he really knew about these young men, both dead and alive. At last, he handed the paper to me. "I don't suppose you know anything about this?"

It was a brief article about two Marines killed in the north of Afghanistan by the Taliban. They were from a company of Marines stationed at Camp Pendleton. Mallon Dezi and Raphael Lambert were their names.

"No, I don't know anything about it. Jacob never mentioned it. Do you think it means anything?"

Mallory shifted back in his chair. "That's what I'd like to know. It's odd to find a press clipping in the possession of someone so young. Most don't read an actual paper. They get their information off the internet and yet here it is. Maybe it's merely a token, but I think there's more to it. I contacted the Marines, and they said the two men killed in Afghanistan had served in the same company as Mr. Santos and Mr. Saunders, but that's all they would say."

"You want me to look into it?"

Mallory smiled. "I heard you've cultivated a few sources independent of the police and other legitimate law enforcement communities."

I smiled in return. "Is that a yes?"

"It's not a no. There's no place for me to go as a detective, but I would like to know if there's information out there that would provide some answers."

"There was no note explaining why Mason killed Kurtis and then himself or if it's part of something else?" I asked just to answer my own question. I think Mallory knew what I was after.

"Mr. Santos left a diary of sorts written as a book. It details certain events and his feelings, much of which he was ambivalent about, and he did mention your brother among others. But there was nothing in it to suggest violence between him and Mr. Saunders, or that he wanted to leave the relationship; the kinds of things you find between partners who are coming apart." He paused for a moment, as if remembering something. "There was a single reference to a pact, but no explanation or any other mention of it."

"What'd he say about Jacob?"

Mallory looked directly at me. "Only that he was a part of it." I decided not to ask a part of what.

I got up. "Thanks for your time, detective. If I hear or find anything, I'll let you know."

Mallory got up and walked me out of the station. We stood in the bright sunshine.

"We see a lot more of them these days. Lost vets. Homeless. Depressed. I know they make up a small part of the whole, but it bothers me. I come from a family that served in the military and I was taught to honor that service. We try to get them help, but it's not our job and there's only so much we can do," he said.

"I'll keep in touch. Thanks."

I walked to the car, looking up at the sky. Bright light for a black mood.

10

I sat in the Falcon with the top down, staring at my goddamned phone. I had to call Moses, but the knot in my stomach tightened as I thought about what I should say. Too little. Too much. Just the facts, man? I knew I couldn't *not* call. That wasn't an option. For the old Monk, the guy hiding in LA just a few years ago, not a problem. But not now. Moses answered on the third ring.

"Jacob's left LA. I think he's heading back home, but I don't know for sure," I blurted out. How's that for cryptic?

"What happened?"

I gave a brief thought to hanging up.

"His trip down here didn't go well. The people he wanted to see are either missing or dead, and he's pretty shaken up about it. He didn't say anything before he left, so I'm not a hundred percent certain that he's heading back home, but I wanted to give you a head's up, just in case."

"What do you mean dead?" I noted a small amount of alarm in his voice.

I also gave a brief thought to saying, "*Are there different kinds of dead?*" Might not be the right moment. "Murder-suicide. Jacob thought they were alive and well. Let me know if he shows up." I waited for Moses' diatribe.

"Then will you be bringing back Emily?" I didn't think of that. Apparently, the assumption was that Emily would go back with Jacob.

"Yeah, I can do that. It'll be on Sunday."

"Thanks." And that was that. I continued staring at the phone. The day was just getting weirder and weirder.

. . . . .

Agnes was happy to see me, small favors. I got a big hug and a kiss. It was then I saw Barron and Gerta on the couch. I winked at Agnes, who curled her nose at me.

"Barron, Gerta; it's good to see you. Was the drive down tolerable?"

They had come from San Luis Obispo, where he was stationed. Barron was a carbon copy of his father if you added some of Agnes' girth to him. Not that Agnes was fat, but her side of the family tended to be more stout than Simon's. Gerta matched up nicely to Barron, as she seemed to epitomize the old adage about good German stock, curvy and solid. He stood erect, no doubt from his military training, with his bright blue eyes shining; another gift from Agnes' side of the family. His hair was very nearly the same color as Gerta's, a light sandy brown, but much shorter. She was close to him in height and had a pleasant cheery face punctuated by big eyes not quite as blue as her soon to be husband's.

"No worse than usual." He put out his hand, and I reciprocated. Gerta smiled and nodded.

"Anybody hungry?" Agnes helpfully inquired.

"A little," replied Gerta.

"Great. Monk, why don't you fix us something," she demanded.

I was not amused or hungry! "I wonder how Natalya's doing?"

Agnes' turn to burn. "Nice try, Mr. Player."

I shrugged. "Fine, but I don't want to hear any complaining later."

I called to Emily and Zach, who were, surprise, surprise, out by the pool, and asked if they were hungry. Turns out everyone was. I put together some cheese and crackers, fruit, and drinks for the kids. Agnes was responsible for any beverages the adults might want. She smartly handed me a whiskey on the rocks. We waited patiently for Anna and the parents of Zach and Lizzy to return, making small talk about weddings and California and life in the Army. I thought about the day's events and whether I should say anything. I was curious about Baron's experiences, but given Agnes and Anna's history with sexual abuse, it probably wasn't the time or place to bring it up. Agnes changed that.

"What's going on with Jacob?" She turned to Barron and Gerta. "Jacob is Monk's younger brother. He's in the Marines."

"There was bad news, and it hit him pretty hard. I think he wanted some time alone."

"What bad news?"

"Two of his buddies were found dead and another is AWOL," I said.

"AWOL?"

"It means away without leave," Barron told his mother.

"Oh. How did the others die?" Agnes wouldn't let go.

"Murder-suicide. They were lovers." I don't know why I added that. So it made some kind of sense?

The three of them took this in. I noted Barron looking at me for a moment.

Agnes sat there with her mouth open. "Really? Oh, good lord..." My thoughts exactly. Agnes turned to Barron. "Are there lots of gay guys in the Army?"

Barron smiled slightly. "Not that I know of, but it's no longer a big deal. Some come out, some don't."

I wondered if their family history was percolating below the surface given Agnes' questions, prompting unwelcome thoughts.

Agnes opened her mouth, but I interrupted, "Did you show them your ring?"

"What?" She seemed lost before smiling. "Oh yeah." Agnes held out her hand. "Buttman's finally making good on his promises." Gerta examined the ring, Barron merely watched.

"When are you getting married?" Gerta asked, concerned that it might interfere with her and Barron's wedding.

"Right after she signs the prenup," I said. Agnes tried to elbow me in the ribs, but I anticipated that and moved out of range.

"Seriously, Buttman?" I could see she was disappointed in missing her mark.

"Sorry, baby, but that's the way it's got to be. As to the question of the ceremony, we'd probably wait till summer with Fidel and Rebekah getting married next month and you two next Spring. Don't want to pack everyone in too tightly."

Gerta nodded in approval. Agnes feigned agreement.

In due time, the rest of our menagerie made it home, and those of us destined for greater things piled into the Mercedes and headed into the warm LA night.

Our destination turned out to be a restaurant named Pilon, that a friend of Simon and Eric's had opened and Anna had promised to check out. It was designed in a retro-chic modernist styling that was in line with what all the other new restaurants were doing. I don't remember if the food was any good, my mind was drifting. The conversations were a blur as well, revolving around a family dynamic I was unfamiliar with; Barron and his effect upon his mother and sister. Like Gerta, I pretended to pay attention, all the while worried that I wasn't worried enough about Jacob. The problem was I didn't know what *I* could do. I didn't know him any better than I knew Barron. They were known unknowns or vice versa; relationships you were not consulted about prior to.

The evening dissolved into separate bedrooms, after too much food and drink; helped along, fortunately or unfortunately, based on how the day's events were viewed, with Barron and Gerta taking the room abandoned in haste by the youngest of the Bohrman brothers. No one had heard from him and I allowed Agnes to distract me from this worry with semi-drunken sex before the old wandering dreams of displacement, dreams that haunted me when I'd first returned to California, came back in all their elastic glory. I lasted till three in the morning before straggling to the panic room where the blackness engulfed me.

Morning brought a headache and a moody disposition in my beloved.

"I don't like it when you sneak off like that, Sunshine."

"No?" I tried to grin.

"NO!" Agnes did not.

"Couldn't sleep, that's all. No need to get all worked up."

Agnes, now disinclined to argue, merely shrugged and kissed me. There were plans afoot concerning the day's events and preparations had to be made. I sat on a stool sipping coffee as the women put their heads together in consideration of the best places to go to buy the proper attire for both the gig at the Manifesto and the art show the next day.

"I'm going to need some money, Honeybunny." Agnes was playing cute.

"You have a card and a limit," I said.

Another shrug from my beloved.

Emily, keen to the idea of more shopping, jumped onboard. I reiterated that homework comes first. Agnes told me to lighten up. I served them a delicious breakfast of yogurt, granola, and blueberries before seeing them out the door. Agnes wasn't thrilled with either the breakfast or my comment that it would allow her to still fit into her clothes.

"You're a jerk, Buttman."

"Just doing my job."

Barron seemed quite content to sit by the pool, collect some rays, and occasionally check his phone. The kids and I played in the pool. I could do with a quiet languorous day. Didn't last long. The phone rang, and I hoped it was good news from Jacob, but it was Ms. Lagenfelder instead. The prenup was ready to be reviewed and signed. I told her we'd be by next week and thanked her for her time and trouble. I dried off Lizzy, fed her, changed her diaper, and put her down for a nap. Zach splashed about with one of the pool toys while I retrieved a beer.

"Care for one?" I asked Barron.

"Sure."

I took one out for him and we enjoyed the sunshine and the sounds of Zach making war on the pool's glistening surface. Unlike his sister, Barron did not share his concerns or reservations about me, his mother, what happened in the past; actually about anything at all. I found this quite refreshing. Agnes tried in vain to change that, but we ignored her and she gave up. We were ok with one another as superficial figures and if it went no further, everyone would have to be happy with that. After lunch he played with Zach till it was Zach's naptime, while I got Lizzy up and took care of her. Barron seemed intrigued with the baby, so I handed Lizzy to him. He smiled uncomfortably as I did.

"Gerta's been talking about kids, so I might as well get in some practice."

"Sure. Just put her in the playpen when you're done."

I returned to my chair for a nice pleasant nap of my own. The phone woke me from bad dreams about untilled furrows.

It was Jacob. A text: *sorry about yesterday had to go take care*

He woke me up for that!

I tried to fall back asleep, but the kids were whining and the women were back. Anna stayed just long enough to drop off Agnes, Gerta, and Emily, before leaving for the Manifesto. Barron and I were encouraged to delight over what they had bought. We applauded their every purchase. Emily was the most excited. Agnes had disregarded Calista's edicts on spoiling Emily, allowing her to buy two dresses, two pairs of pants, two blouses, and, quite necessarily, two pairs of shoes. They were all beautiful in their new ensembles, and we men were smart enough to show our appreciation. Rebekah and Fidel returned in time to discuss what to do with the kids. I courageously offered to watch them, at which point Agnes told me, no. It fell to Fidel to watch the youngsters while the rest of us gussied up and left him behind.

• • • • •

The Manifesto was packed, and the shows were entertaining if a little uneven; most of the performers were not professionals. The food was excellent, and, as far as I know, no one got sick. All plusses in my book. Joanie made an awkward appearance while I was talking with Mikal. We made pleasantries before she asked to speak to Mikal alone. Natalya came with a few of her new art friends. I played it up for Agnes, who was unimpressed. I introduced Barron and Gerta to Mr. Jones, who was accompanied by his wife, Coretta, and his kids, Marcus and Ella. I mentioned that Mr. Jones had been in the Army during Desert Storm. That made Jones smile. Both Barron and Orville had spent time in Iraq. Both had ties to a fraternity I knew nothing about.

They made small talk about serving and how nothing really changes, even after a quarter century of involvement in a small Arab country. The rest of us pretended to understand. Jones pulled me aside just as we were making our way to the auditorium.

"Your friend Manny is outside."

"Is he? How interesting."

Jones didn't care for the answer. "Head in the game, Buttman, it's not interesting."

"He's just lost, that's all, probably hungry too. That gives me an idea." I turned towards the door.

"Where are you going?"

"I'm going to talk to him. Josef's here, I'll take him with me if you're worried." Jones turned as if going with me. "You can stay. I'll be alright."

"I don't like this, Buttman."

"Neither do I, but it won't go away on its own. I'll be back in a little bit."

Jones wasn't convinced but didn't stop me. I grabbed Josef, and we made our way to the scruffy young man standing across the street. Manny looked around to see if others were moving in on him too. I asked Josef to give us some room. His enthusiasm for my little adventure mirrored Jones'.

"He might have another gun, you never know with these guys," he said.

"I suppose, but it wouldn't help his cause. I'm no-good dead. No worries." I smiled at the tall man with the buzz cut. Josef shook his head as a sly smile came to him.

Manny was leaning against the window of the boutique shop across from the Manifesto. He visibly stiffened as I approached. If nothing else, he appeared to be cleaner than the last time I saw him.

"Waiting for me?" I asked.

"Just watching—"

"For what, clues, answers to the puzzle of the missing money?"

"I know you paid for this place. I know you have a lot of money, and it had to come from somewhere, and I know you didn't earn it because you used to be a broke-assed nobody," he sneered.

I wondered if he had any inkling of my desire to be a broke-assed nobody once more. "Serendipity paid for this, I'm simply the conduit. If you think I paid for this with whatever money your dead uncles might have had, you have no idea what things cost."

"You could've got a loan."

"You need a lot more than a couple hundred grand for that kind of loan."

I noticed his eyes began spastically blinking. He was aware of this and tried to shade his eyes with his hand.

"I need that money..." he muttered.

"To do what?" I demanded.

"What does anyone do with money, live!" Manny rubbed his eyes in a vain effort to stop the blinking.

"There's no money. Accept that."

"THEN THERE'S NOTHING!" he screamed. This caused Josef to step in, which only heightened Manny's tick.

"Nonsense," I said, "there's always something." I put my hand out to keep Josef at bay. "Why don't you come inside, listen to the performers, have something to eat. If the music is too loud, we'll get you some earplugs. If you have something honest to say, say it. But no more of this hanging around thinking it's going to make something happen. It won't." I knew I had to get back, there was only so much time to banter with a fool.

He hesitated, but followed Josef and I as we headed back to the Manifesto.

I watched our leery little companion carefully slide between the more comfortable and cosmopolitan people around him. He found a few things to eat, and after securing some sound attenuating plugs for his ears, a place to sit and listen. Whether he enjoyed it, I couldn't say, but he was still there when the final performer was finished. I thought to say something, but he was long gone by the time I completed the glad handing and congratulations; as if I did anything important. Mikal was subdued, processing whatever Joanie had said to him. My happy little band was running out of gas. Anna had to close up, but promised to come back to the house as soon as she could. Agnes was sure she had other plans.

"She's allowed to have her own life," Barron told her. Agnes grumbled, but admitted he was right. I laughed and got poked for my efforts.

Manny was waiting by the door. The entourage gathered around me, as did Mr. Jones. Other than Jones, I think they were mostly curious about this scraggly haired dude. The dude was obviously nervous with everyone watching him.

"Thanks for the food, but I haven't changed my mind," he whispered.

"You're welcome, but I'll need more." I handed him a card with a number where he could reach me. "We can talk when you're ready."

Manny put the card in his pocket and ran off.

11

"Who was that?" Agnes asked as we watched him run down the street.

"Manny."

"Manny who?" Good question.

"I don't know his last name come to think of it, but to answer your question, he's the nephew of Gene and Frankie Pronto."

Agnes looked down the street before turning back to me. "Aren't those the guys who almost killed you when you were even less street smart than you are now?" Clever.

"Yep."

"What did he want?"

A lot of possible answers came to mind. "Fool's gold." It was close enough.

"Fool's gold?"

"Yep."

Agnes rolled her eyes and motioned us towards the car. Jones, once again, pulled me aside. I motioned for the clan to keep going. "I'll be right there, go ahead." We watched as all but the two of us left.

"Should I be worried about this Manny?"

I shook my head. "No, he may be a burr in my saddle, but I don't consider him a threat if that's what you mean." I don't think he believed me.

"Uh huh. Well then, he's all yours, Tex. How about Jacob? Heard from him?"

"Just a short text. I have to take Emily home on Sunday. I'll see if he's gone home. Maybe he'll have calmed down. We'll see." I was surprised by the big man's concern. He had that serious furrow in his brow that told me this interest wasn't simply a part of the act.

"I hope so. We better go, our families are waiting."

Yes, they are.

. . . . .

The next day was no less hectic than the previous one. The gallery showings were to start at two in the afternoon; with multiple galleries participating, and it was expected that I make an appearance, however brief, at each one. Agnes was freaking out about whether it was a good idea for her to go, and how people would judge her. She whined she was no honey-bunny, an allusion to Natalya I assumed, and certain her deep ignorance of art would be clear for all to see.

"Are you done?" I was sitting on the bed enjoying the show.

"No, Mr. Smarty-pants, I am not!" She took a deep breath before continuing. "Maybe you're used to this kind of thing, but I'm not and it wouldn't kill you to be a little more supportive."

"Oh, I don't know, it might."

"Ha, ha. Seriously, Monk, I don't want to come off like some out-of-place yahoo." Two dresses were in her hands and she was vacillating over which one to wear. She held each out for me to see. "This one or this one?" One was a purple number with just enough cut to display her ample bosom without it being too much of a good thing, at least to me. The other was a fairly prim design, off white with a high neckline that reminded me of the dresses women wore to church when I lived in Virginia.

"The purple one."

Agnes crinkled her surgically repaired nose. "You don't think it's a little too showy?"

A salacious grin came to me. "I would hope so! Showy is a common theme at these kinds of events, so you'd fit right in. As for this irrational fear you have about being an art ignoramus..."

"Ignoramus?" She acted shocked. I laughed.

"Yes, ignoramus. Most people are, but I've found that many of the artists and curators are more than happy to explain their art, and the few that don't aren't that great, anyway. Besides, as a major sponsor of these events, I, and anyone with me are given a great deal of carte blanche when it comes to our knowledge of modern art. So long as you don't act like a complete ass, it should be a truly delightful affair."

She was unconvinced. "Really? Then why do you complain every time you're asked to go?"

"Because I miss you so terribly when we're apart, my love."

"Good. It's about time you owned up to that." I reached out and pulled her down next to me. She let the dresses fall on the other side of the bed. "Something on your mind, Sunshine?"

"Now that you mention it, there is..." I leaned in and began lightly kissing her intoxicating breasts. Agnes lifted my chin and kissed me.

"It'll have to be later; I don't have time to get cleaned up again, ok?" Her hand was softly stroking the erection beneath my pants.

"Fine..."

We dressed and moved on.

Agnes fished about, hoping her children were interested in spending the day looking at various permutations of paintings, sculptures, drawings, and performance pieces. To her dismay, she found no takers. Anna had things to do at her kitchen, it was now fully operational, and she wanted to be open for business. Barron and Gerta had other plans in and around greater Los Angeles. Fidel and Rebekah just wanted to stay home with the kids. Emily, aware that this was her last day before she had to go home, wanted to stay back and spend the day in the pool with Zach.

"It's just the two of us," I consoled her. "Besides, this'll give you a chance to meet all my various entanglements."

"What does that mean?" Always so suspicious.

"You'll see." Personally, I found the entanglements quite vexing, but that was my problem. We offered our goodbyes to the mob surrounding the pool.

Agnes said little on the drive to the galleries. The nervousness there in her eyes.

"Don't be worried about this. I got it all worked out." I was tired of the quiet. My worries about Jacob were seeping through the poorly constructed walls I had put up to keep them out.

"Worked out how? You're not ditching me, are you?"

"Not entirely, but I may be unavoidably detained from time to time, and I don't want you to be bored," I reassured her.

"Uh huh. What does that mean?"

I patted her hand. "I've arranged for Natalya to go along with us. She's far more knowledgeable than I am about the art and the artists, and I mentioned to her and Brigitte that you were concerned about looking out of place, so they agreed to act as your tutor."

"I have to hang out with your girlfriend?" Agnes groaned.

"That's another thing. We need to get that idiotic notion out of your head! I think once you spend a little time with Natalya, and you can be as blunt as a hammer if you want, you'll see she has no interest in me."

"No? Don't you have desires for *her*?" It was my turn to groan.

"No! However, if you feel the need to obsess about these kinds of things, it might be better if you transfer that obsession to Monika—"

"Monika? Who she?" Agnes seemed intrigued.

"You'll see. The woman stands out." I patted her hand again.

Agnes smacked me on the arm. "You're a jerk, Buttman!"

"Really? I hadn't noticed." I parked the car as she huffed dramatically. Good times.

Natalya met us at the first gallery with the appropriate name of Talon. The art inside was stark, sharp, monochromatic and dreary.

Natalya didn't share my assessment.

"You are too harsh sometimes; too quick to judge. I'm so happy you came, Agnes, can I get you something to drink? Something to eat?" Agnes, caught off guard by Natalya's kindness, mumbled a drink would be nice. "And you, Mr. Monk?"

I smiled. "A bottle of water, thank you." We watched as she retrieved our drinks.

"Why don't we start in the next room?" she said when she returned. "If you have any questions, please let me know."

"Ok," Agnes said, and with that, we were off.

It was at the third gallery that Monika moved alongside me. Agnes and Natalya were examining two sculptures best described as a diaspora of female reproductive anatomy in a cove on the other side of the room. I didn't notice Monika at first, but her scent drifted ever so softly to my olfactory senses and I turned just as she ran her fingers along the sleeve of my suit.

"It's good to see you, Monk," she spoke in a soft lilt that instantly put me on the defensive.

"Monika..." She smiled as I looked her over, something she invited and seemed to revel in. "You're looking lovely this evening." It was still light out, but that didn't matter. She and her smile were dressed for the evening, and it was hard not to take stock of the woman in full. Monika Danalek was a voluptuary, a delightful and decadent luxury of sexual indulgences. She possessed fulsome lips, breasts, and hips artfully displayed by clothing that accentuated her sexuality. Her face, framed by jet black hair that shimmered, held eyes radiating an insouciance that was fearless and provocative. I found it deeply erotic and deeply unnerving. We'd met at previous showings and she allowed that she was open to any number of amorous activities.

"Have you thought about any of my propositions, Monk?" Where do these women come from and where were they when I was a broke-assed nobody?

"Which ones, you mentioned several?" I should just walk away, right?

"You like it when I say it out loud, don't you?" She made an O with her lips, then broke into a wide smile. "Should I say I'm sure you have a wonderful cock, just as I'm sure you'd love to put it in my mouth. You'd like that, wouldn't you?" I was, by now, used to her fairly blunt manner, and yes, I should have walked away!

"If I weren't presently taken, yes, but—"

"We don't have to be exclusive; I understand that."

I was getting light-headed. "I see. And the terms?"

She took my hand and held it in hers. "I take care of you, you take care of me, simple enough. One rule though, I don't get passed around." Her colorful green eyes tightened a bit. "I love to fuck and I'm clean, what more could you want?"

"That is the question, isn't it?"

Monika laughed, then looked over at the two women staring at us. "Is that your woman, there with your *assistant*?"

I shook my head as I removed my hand from hers. "I get enough of that already, and yes, that is my woman."

Monika shrugged her shoulders slightly and turned. "You have my number and terms." With that she moved on.

I watched her hips sway. I imagined every straight man in the place did. Natalya had a knowing grin on her face, which I dismissed. It bothered me that a woman that young would be that sanguine about fucking around. Agnes came over as I continued to watch Monika as she worked the crowd. Agnes turned to me with a certain amount of wonder in her eyes.

"I assume that's the one I should worry about?"

"Yes. Unlike my dear assistant here, she is in fact open to a sexual liaison. However, I don't see that as a good thing. Tempting perhaps, but not a good idea."

"That's your answer?" She seemed annoyed.

"It is. I have enough on my plate already. The last thing I need is to get tangled up with someone like Monika."

She looked at me, then at Monika. "I'm holding you to that, Buttman."

I winked at Natalya, who frowned. "I would expect nothing less. Are we through here? On to the next gallery?"

Natalya led us to a few more exhibits before we left. I noticed Monika smile and wave as I left.

At the end of our conga line of galleries was a large converted garage, tastefully remodeled, and for this event set up for casual dining. Xavier Dunkle II greeted us as we came in. This part of the soirée was underwritten by his family's formidable foundation, and it allowed him to be more unctuous than usual. Not that he believed any of the flattery he was handing out like candy in a dish. He was, in private, something of a Marxist and dismissive of the very people whose asses he feigned to kiss, but he got a perverse pleasure out of courting the vanity of people he detested. Some were in on the joke while other were oblivious to it; some people just can't receive enough praise. Dunkle, having decided I was a kindred spirit, was more than happy to share his disdain for most of the other art aficionados joining us.

"More money than sense or brains!" was a common refrain.

He cared little for modern art, preferring the classics, but with excessive wealth came the need to "giveback" and foundations were, in his words, a wonderful tax dodge. He didn't care much for government either.

"Got to feed the beast!" was another.

Xavier offered his hand. "Monk, as always, it's good to have you here, and I see you talked Agnes into joining us. I hope it hasn't been too overwhelming, and, of course, the lovely Miss Constantinescu; it's always a pleasure." Dunkle had an intense crush on Natalya, something she was well aware of, but not totally dismissive of.

"Mr. Dunkle," she replied coolly.

"Xavier, please…" He was forever insisting she call him by his first name. She knew this but continued to play it coy with him. I was convinced they both were aware of the other's intentions and very much enjoyed their game of cat and mouse. "I have a table for us," he said as he lightly placed his hand on her shoulder, leading us on. Dunkle was older than Natalya by at least fifteen years, but she wasn't troubled by that. Sad to say, but most of her sexual interactions had been with significantly older men, and not consensual in any way. But now she had control of her life and was determined to exercise it. She was more concerned with what kind of man he was. As I knew them both superficially, it was decided that I would be a de facto intermediary whether I wanted to be or not.

"What do you think of this Mr. Dunkle?" she asked.

"He's a little odd. I can have him checked out if you'd like."

"I'd like."

So, I asked Bernie to check him out for anything untoward. He was hesitant. Dunkle occasionally used his services as well. I assured him it was strictly for Natalya's sake and nothing else. Besides, he'd checked *me* out for Dunkle. Fortunately, for all his eccentricities, Xavier Dunkle II was not a pervert or a creep as far as anyone could find out, with no evidence of scrubs or erasures or deletes.

"He's got a clean rap sheet," I told her.

"What does that mean?" She was unfamiliar with the term.

"As Josef would say, no worries."

Natalya was, in her own standoffish way, pleased to hear this.

Smitten the first time he laid eyes on her, Dunkle became more careful with his appearance and his health, determined to make sure that any possible rejection would not be tied to sloth on his part. He was also far more open to some forms of modern art in her presence than mine, but there were some things he couldn't stand, mainly interpretive pieces that mimicked normal life as a commentary on our fatuousness. One piece, a woman on a golden toilet, provided Natalya with endless opportunities to get under his skin.

"It's an essential expression of our unhealthy love of possessions, of our need to beautify our actions, even the elimination of waste."

I'm certain she got that line from Brigitte DuBare.

"It's disgusting. I'm mean really, it's a woman taking a shit!" he would exclaim.

"You have to look deeper," she would continue, knowing it bugged him. "Look at how beautiful she is. The toilet is an exquisite piece, and yet it cannot escape its elemental function. It is still a toilet. It speaks to the duality of our existence; our need to move beyond our coarser natures, to find beauty in all of our activities, and yet—"

"And yet it's a woman taking a dump." Natalya merely smiled, in a fashion I also noted in Ms. DuBare.

"The gallery is offering the piece for a mere hundred thousand dollars. A man of your means could certainly afford that, Xavier."

Xavier was having none of it. "Afford, yes. Acquire, no."

Natalya raised her eyebrows, nothing more.

Later, while Natalya was off talking to Ms. DuBare, Dunkle confided his trepidation in rejecting the piece.

"I hope my dislike didn't turn her off."

I laughed.

Agnes, alarmed at my lack of regard for the dear Mr. Dunkle, chimed in. "I'm sure she realizes that you won't like everything she does."

"There's no guarantee she even likes the thing. She might simply be jerking your chain," I added. "She's a bit of a troublemaker." I knew that would only make her more desirable to him.

Agnes had other ideas. "Well, she is young. What about that Monika woman? Isn't she looking for a nice man too?" I cracked a large grin at that, as did Dunkle.

"No, I find Ms. Danalek to be a very scary creature. While she's an attractive woman, I don't think I'd survive very long," he stammered, completely out of character.

"You hear that, Buttman!" Agnes was wagging her finger for emphasis.

"Yes, dear."

Dunkle excused himself to continue his courtship. Agnes and I had a little something to eat and wandered about the exhibits.

"Are you coming with me tomorrow?" I asked, knowing the answer.

"No, you're on your own this time. We're all going to the beach tomorrow, even Anna, and I don't want to miss that. Sorry."

"As am I. I'm hoping Jacob made it back. I haven't heard anything from him or Moses, so maybe everything's alright. I guess I'll find out." Anything to drown out the voices in my head.

"You never did say exactly what happened."

Didn't I? "He was upset by something Kurtis' aunt said."

Agnes was staring at me "What did she say?"

I thought about that. I didn't want to. I didn't want to say it out loud. Was it true? I looked at my feet and then the collage on the wall. It was a mix of action comics and numbers and splashes of paint.

"She accused him of being a rapist."

12

The morning was prime SoCal, warm and bright. Emily was ready, though not happy. She wanted to stay and go to the beach. There were commiserations, but no change in plans. She was due home, and I was the designated driver. It didn't help that as we charged north, the sun slid behind the spitting darkening clouds. By the time we got to San Francisco, the rain and the gloom matched our dispositions. Emily said little, preferring to stare out the window. There were no books or conversations this trip, just the whine of the engine and the pelting of the rain on the soft top of the Falcon. We stopped for lunch at In and Out, one last burger before it was back to farm food. I was alarmed that she was sounding more and more like Sunshine when he was that age.

"I don't want to live at the farm anymore," she said between mouthfuls of fries.

"I'm sure your mother wouldn't allow that, but if by chance she did, where would you live?"

"I'd like to come live with you and Agnes and Zach and Rebekah and Fidel. I like the city better. There's so much to see and do."

"What about your garden and your friends? What about your mother and Andrea? Wouldn't you miss them? The city has its charms, but it's loud and busy and it's easy to get lost in places like LA." I don't know why I added the last part other than to scare her. Realistically, if she lived with us, she'd stick pretty close to that part of town, but you never know. Plenty of bored kids in Beverly Hills wandered off in search of adventure and good times.

"I guess. The farm life isn't that great either. It's the same thing over and over again. That's what *you* said about being a farmer. Did you really like it and left because Lilith left you? Or were you happy to be doing something different? You know I remember the stuff you say!"

Apparently, you can't speak out of turn to anyone these days.

"Yes, it's true, I never particularly cared for farming. I did it for reasons beyond having the good earth crumble beneath my feet. But that's not the point here. You're only thirteen, and while I agree you're a mature thirteen, there are still, I don't know, lessons to be learned."

"What does that mean?" Yeah, what does that mean?

"Stuff!" I tried to think how I worked through this with Rebekah. Oh, I remember, we yelled at one another. A lot!

"Stuff?" Emily wasn't buying it, and I had no interest in yelling at her.

"Alright, maybe that's a little vague." I had to remind myself that like her mother, Emily was a bright little light and less apt to buy my bullshit. "But I don't think taking off or moving out is necessarily the answer. I think we should first ask what you're looking for in life." Yes, I actually said that to a thirteen-year-old girl.

"I want to go to a real school."

"You don't think the schooling at the farm is good?" Fair question.

"No," she said bluntly. "I want to go to school with kids my age, and I want to meet some boys. Real boys. I don't care what my mother says about them."

"I think she's just looking after your best interests—"

"I don't care!"

I tried not to laugh, but she sounded just like her mother. "Then what?"

Emily pointed at me. "I want you to help me talk to her; to let me go to school; to let me come stay with you." Yeah, that's not going to work.

"I don't know, she doesn't like it when you come down to visit, so the idea of you moving down probably won't go very far."

A nasty pout came to my thirteen-year-old companion. "I don't care!" She then softened a bit. "Please, Mr. Sunshine."

I sat there pondering my options. They were all bad. I knew Calista would not let Emily move to LA. Nor was I wasn't thrilled with the notion of having to care for Emily, along with all the other kids and grandkids presently residing in Judith's beautiful home, on the bizarre chance she did. Then there were the culture clashes between Moses' bucolic wonderland and LA's cesspool of glitzy excess. The thought of trying to justify any of it made my head ache. Why, oh why, did I sell my wonderful bungalow? I must have been out of my mind. I had a good life, a carefree life, the life of a broke-assed nobody and I was perfectly happy. I sighed. Agnes was right, my whining was wearing thin, even to me.

I took in the ever-hopeful Emily sitting across from me. "We'll see," was the best I could come up with.

Calista was not happy that Emily was not happy to see her. Calista glared at me. I knew the look. It was my fault for corrupting her little girl, turning her to the dark side. She wasn't the only one though. The whole vibe at the farm was bad. Moses and Sterling, who had reluctantly come up from Napa, were out looking for Jacob. Meredith's anxiety was all over her face, something I hadn't seen in her before. There was none of the peace or serenity I was used to, only a deep ugly knot tightening around everyone. Meredith was at a loss for words. Franco Mackinaw, one half of the Mackinaw brothers, came over and put his arm around Meredith.

"They had a nasty argument," he said. They, I assumed, were Jacob and Moses.

"Moses just wanted to know what was happening to him," added Meredith. "But it… it quickly turned into a shouting match about Jacob's leaving and Moses' anxieties. You know how he can get."

"We all know," Franco gave me a knowing look.

"I've never seen them so angry. Jacob was so different, so agitated…" She stared at me with tears streaming down her face. "What happened, Monk? What happened in LA?"

I just wanted to be at the beach.

"All I know is he was there to see his friends, but the wheels came off. It was nothing but bad news. I don't know all the details, but it was bad. Two were dead and one was missing, and—" I didn't want to say it, not to his mother. I just stood there. Both of them stared at me, waiting for the last of the sentence to exit my idiotic mouth.

"And?"

"There was an accusation that he participated in an assault on one of the guys he went to see, one of the ones who were dead."

"Like a fight?" asked Franco.

"No." I gave them a minute to take that in. "I was hoping to talk to Jacob about it before I said anymore."

"Who said this?" she asked. They were both shocked.

"Kurtis' aunt. The woman who raised him. She said it was in his journal, that it happened when they were in Afghanistan." What little color there was in Meredith's face drained away. Franco helped her to a bench just outside the entry to the dining hall. "I'm sorry. I don't know that it's true, but when she confronted Jacob, he didn't say she was wrong, and it was after that he took off, just jumped out of the car."

Franco sat down. He didn't look any better than Meredith. Jacob was their baby, and now their baby was a monster. Some of the others came by, trying to be upbeat.

That ended with the call.

I never asked how he knew my number. He gave no name, just a location. I knew the place. When I asked why, he hung up. Meredith and Franco were watching as I took the call. I said it might be nothing, but I should check it out.

"Let us know," they said.

· · · · ·

He was lying in a field by a service road that was rarely used. The grass was high, bleached by sunlight and time. The tracks were somewhat obscured, but it was evident one or two people had been this way. I followed a dry creek bed that wound down the hill. It was there I found him. The 9mm was still in his hand. His eyes were open. The hole in his chest visible, as was the dried blood around it. I stood there trying not to faint. I lost my balance and fell. I remember sitting up a few feet from him, wanting desperately to be somewhere, anywhere else. I pulled the phone from my pocket. My hands were shaking. I called 911. The next call was to Sterling.

"Are you with Moses?" I hoped he wasn't.

"Yes. What's going on?"

"It's bad. Do you remember the field past the Ottman farm? We used to have cows there."

"I remember... what's happened?"

I couldn't say it. "It's bad."

· · · · ·

Moses broke down. His beloved son was dead. Sterling fell to his knees, the tears falling freely. I stood there watching. The sheriff's men had cordoned off the immediate area and were conducting their investigation. I felt bad for Moses and Sterling. By the time they arrived, the authorities were already going through the motions, and while the sheriff's men gave them a few moments to see for themselves, Moses, Sterling, all of them, would have to wait till the county was finished. I, the one who knew him the least, had been the one to find him. My time away now felt distinct and vindictive. I was just a stranger, just a known face, nothing more. I called Franco, bearing nothing but terrible news. The sheriff, Lew Tallmadge, arrived. He knew Moses. He knew them all, but had only heard of me. He did what he could.

Through it all, I was just there, watching, waiting. In time they put Jacob in a bag, moved him to a gurney, and took him away. We followed them to the sheriff's office. There we were joined by Meredith and the Mackinaw brothers. The grief was overwhelming.

I had to go.

I thought for a moment of heading south to that big beautiful house, to the panic room, to the safety of the darkness, but I couldn't run. I could hardly move. I knew once I got to the farm I'd be swarmed, and I was. I told them what I could, absorbed as much of the grief as I could, before heading to my spot by the barn. I did what I could to embrace the light, the heat, the undeterred rhythms of life. I needed the quiet.

Later Emily found me.

She stood there with her own little crate. Her eyes were wet. She set the crate next to mine, wrapped herself in my arms, and sobbed. I realized that my eyes were dry, that they had been through all of this. Had I witnessed so much death that it didn't affect me anymore? I listened as Emily cried, talked of Jacob and then her mother. Evidently there had been an argument, of how unfair life was.

"Yes, it can seem that way sometimes."

"I want to go back with you," she wailed.

Just then, her mother and Andrea rounded the corner. I could see Calista had things to say, but I cut her off.

"Not now." She tried again, even Andrea thought to speak, but I said, "Please, not now." Andrea, a stranger like me, understood and walked Calista back. I let Emily hold on as long as she needed to, then I kissed her forehead and told her we had to go back.

Her mother, waiting by the door to the dining hall, told Emily it was her turn in the kitchen. I decided to join her. I had to do something. There were potatoes to peel, carrots too. I thanked them and got to work. As I was peeling, a little voice reminded me I could reverse the call that led to where Jacob was found. I thought about who would even know of such a place and that he'd be there. I took out the phone and looked up the number; it might be nothing, then again it might not.

He answered after the tenth ring.

"Lewis," I said, playing a hunch. He let me hang for a while.

"Did you find him?" he asked. A stupid question.

"What do you know about this?" Silence.

"I can't say. I'm sorry."

"People need to know what happened, man!" I was losing my cool, raising my voice. A few of the others, Emily included, looked over at me. I turned away.

"Find the sergeant, he can tell you." What?

"The sergeant? Sergeant who? And why can't you tell me?" Another long pause.

"MacMillan." That didn't help.

"Why can't you just tell me? You know they're looking for you?"

Lewis laughed, but it was far from lighthearted or even cruel given the circumstances. It was resignation. I knew it well. "I know. I'm sorry, but I made a promise, one I can't break."

That was that.

I put the phone away and got back to the potatoes and carrots.

·　　·　　·　　·　　·

Moses and Meredith were brought home by Franco and Brewster Mackinaw, sequestered in their small house, out of sight, to grieve. The sheriff came moments later to say that, while it seemed cut and dry, he still had to ask me a few questions. I told him what little I knew; choosing to omit Kurtis' mother's comments, and that the caller was the AWOL Lewis. I figured if something came up, I could suddenly recall certain germane facts. If Jacob had killed himself, and I agreed with the sheriff based on what I saw, there was no point in my bringing up whether or not he was a rapist. Maybe I should have asked Lewis, but I assumed it was part of the promise and he'd offer nothing.

I finally called Agnes and told her what had happened. There was shock and condolences, but life doesn't stop.

"What do I tell Rebekah and Fidel?" The wedding, three weeks off.

"I don't know. I'll ask, but it may have to wait." I had no desire to bring it up at all.

"When will you be home?"

"I don't know. It might not be for a couple of days. Maybe longer. If there's a service—"

"We'll come up. I'm so sorry, Monk." Yeah. "Please stay in touch."

"I will. Goodbye."

The next ordeal was the feud between Emily and her mother. Lewis wasn't the only one haunted by promises. I found the three of them in their living room, a pervasive silent oppressing them. There was no way Emily was moving to LA, and while I was sympathetic, I had to be careful not to cast Calista or Andrea as heartless ogres.

"I'm sorry, Em, but I don't think it's a good idea. I think it's better for you to stay here." Emily glared at me and then her mother.

"Can I go now?" was all she would say.

"I don't want you around Emily anymore," Calista said, after Emily left the room.

I half-smiled, which didn't help. "You can do as you like, but I'd be careful about pushing too hard."

"I'm not interested in what you think! You've been nothing but trouble, and I'm tired of competing with you and everything you stand for." Everything I stand for? "She's my daughter, not yours. I don't need your help, and I don't need you putting ideas into her head or making our relationship with her that much more difficult. She's not going to stay with you anymore, do you understand me, no more."

I had a headful of things to say, but there was no point. Not my battle, not my fight. "Then there's nothing left to say." She may have had more to say, but if she did, I didn't hear it. It was time to check on Moses and Meredith.

They were in the dining hall surrounded by friends and members of the farm. My sense of intrusion deepened. Meredith saw me and motioned that I come over. I apologized for being the bearer of bad news and offered condolences. There was nothing else to say. I didn't know Jacob and had no experiences with him outside of the last week. These were the people who knew him, loved him, watched him grow up. That was not me. Moses didn't speak. His eyes were glassy and his expression distant. I knew the look. To be anywhere but here; to be alone with one's sorrow, rather than among a crowd no matter how sympathetic.

"If you need anything, let me know," I told them. What did that even mean? I was useless, plain and simple.

I needed to do something and decided the thing to do was wander. I couldn't go too far, but I needed to breathe and that wasn't happening here. I headed into town.

There was sunshine and people going about their business. No pervasive sadness. I bought some candy at Ye Olde Confectionary and sat on a park bench in the town square. I let my mind wander and, in a fit of prurience, it began fixating on Monika Danalek and her propositions. It was fantasy, I rationalized. The imagined sex and nudity just that. It might not have been appropriate, but it was better than dwelling on why a twenty-four-year-old would put a bullet through his heart.

A voice filtered into my reverie.

"Can I talk to you?"

I came out of my stupor and saw Holly Pronto, her hands in her pockets, hunched over me. Her hair was blowing in her face, which was without makeup. She looked tired.

"Talk about what, Manny?"

She shook her head. "I already know about him. I want to know what really happened to my brothers. I'm asking if you'll tell me the truth."

The truth? Why should I say anything to this woman? Why shouldn't I?

"I can only tell you what I know. Why don't you sit down and tell what you were told?"

Holly Pronto looked around as if people were watching. I looked around and didn't see anything. She sat down at the other end of the bench.

"All I ever heard was they were killed by Mexican gangsters and there was money. Money that should have been ours, but between the Feds and the Mexicans it was all taken away. Momma believed there was a stash somewhere, and it was hidden so the Feds wouldn't take it like the other money. That's what I heard."

She was staring at her feet. I noticed how badly her shoes were worn.

"As far as I know, there was no money, as least on our side. I know James had big plans, and he did say that if the deal went through, we wouldn't be two-bit dealers anymore, but I thought he was full of shit, and to be honest, in those days I didn't exactly pay attention to details. I know there wasn't any money when we went to meet your brothers." Suddenly, I was back on that dusty road getting the shit kicked out of me.

"Momma said the Mexicans were the ones who killed Jimmy, that Frankie and Gene had nothing to do with it." I imagine she did.

"No, your brothers were there. Miguel and I were forced to kill James. Frankie and Gene had guns pointed at our heads and they put knives in our hands and told us to kill James or they'd kill us. Ironically, that's what got them killed. It would have been one thing if they'd just roughed us up and told us to get out of dealing, but it was another thing to make us kill our friend and then threaten to kill us unless we came up with money we didn't have.

"I split to the east coast and had no idea your brothers were dead till a few years ago. I heard Miguel went to his cousins who were in the trade. They took the threats personally, and maybe there were other things between them and your brothers. I don't know. As far as the money goes, it's possible James had a big deal lined up and maybe there was money, but I never saw it. I think it's more likely there was a misunderstanding about that and it got out of hand. Maybe James thought he could play your brothers, but I don't know what James was thinking. He didn't tell me. I just know it went bad for all of us."

That was the truth. It wasn't the whole truth and nothing but the truth, but it was factually correct at the time of the murders. The money I found was based on a hunch that came to me a year later when I was serious thinking about leaving Astral. But it was just a hunch. James never explicitly said anything. It was just dumb luck and the principals in the matter were dead.

Holly sat there playing with her hands. "Then what I heard others say was true. They were just bullies and drug dealers."

"That's who they were. It's doesn't mean that's what you are."

She raised her eyebrows, but just for a moment. "You don't know that. You're just guessing." I watched as she straightened up and brushed the hair out of her face.

"Perhaps." It was time to talk of something else. "I keep bumping into your son down in LA."

Holly Pronto shook her head. "I got no answers about Manfred. I thought being a Marine would do him good, but they threw him out and I don't know what he's doing, and frankly, I don't care. I tried. I tried real hard, but it didn't take. He's more like his goddamned grandfather than me." She stood up and then sat back down, "I'm tired of bein' here. I'm tired of failing and getting nowhere."

"I know how that goes—"

"I hear you got lots of money, so how would you know?" She wasn't angry; it was just unfair. How was I any different from this poor woman?

"Ah yes, the money everyone seems so interested in? I suppose if I was in your shoes, I'd be suspicious too, but the truth is it was all happenstance, the right place at the right time. When I left Virginia for California a decade ago, I had nothing besides an old car and a lot of anger. It's not my money; I simply ended up with it." I noted the incomprehension on her face. "I met a rich woman when I was working for a large law firm in LA. She took a liking to me and after she died she left me some money. I did nothing to earn it. I do, however, know what it's like to have nothing. I know what it's like to struggle."

"If it ain't your money then it's ok if you buy me lunch, right?" It was nice to see her smile.

"I don't think that makes sense, but you're right, I can afford to buy you lunch. Where would you like to go?"

She thought about it. "Denny's is good for me."

13

Her name was still Holly Pronto. There was no husband; never had been, only a boyfriend here and there. Manfred was a mistake, the product of a bad couple of weeks with a man she never saw again. Maybin was dead and Garla kept the memory of her deceased husband and sons alive by hectoring her only daughter about what should have been and how everyone was against them. Manny didn't care for either his mother or grandmother, preferring his grandfather and the punks he ran around with from an early age. Holly lived off her mother's disability and odd jobs.

"I'm sorry for boring you with all this. I don't really have anyone to talk to."

"That's alright, I don't mind."

A sheepish grin crossed her face. "Is it bad manners for me to say we didn't think much of you and your family after what happened to Frankie and Gene?"

"I didn't expect to be well thought of by anyone in this part of the world after what happened. It's ok if you hated me." She half smiled at that.

I sat back and pondered Holly Pronto.

Maybe once upon a time there was something there. She wasn't attractive by most measures, short and chubby with few of the curves we associate with women. Her hair, a sandy brown, was streaked with gray. She was younger than I was, but seemed older, worn down, misshapen by a life that went nowhere. Every now and again her beady eyes would sparkle, but only for a moment.

"I heard about Jacob. They say he killed himself... It's too bad."

"Yeah."

"He joined about the time Manny did," she said, trying to keep the conversation from flagging.

"I heard that too. There were some others. Cameron and Lewis. Mason. Did you know any of them?"

Holly Pronto shrugged. "Manny knew Seth and Al. Ran around with them for a while. He knew Mason, but I don't think they were friends. I was surprised they let him in, his being queer, but I guess it's ok now." She motioned to the waitress. "Do you mind if I have some dessert?"

"Not at all. Have you seen any of them around lately?"

"Them boys?" Holly curled her lips. "No!"

She'd ordered apple pie á la mode, and watched the waitress walk away after setting the dessert down. The waitress was a shapely young woman, blond, with green highlights in her hair. Holly turned back to me, all the while playing with her fingers. "I guess I'm not much to look at, am I?"

"We can't all be matinee idols or beauty queens."

"You don't have to be nice; I know I'm ugly, I always have been."

"I don't like the word ugly when applied to looks. To me, that's a word to describe someone's character. Our looks are what they are, and they can be managed. I once watched a Hollywood makeup team transform a woman from a sickly cancer victim to her former glory. What we see is merely presentation."

Holly Pronto shook her head. "I don't have any money for that."

"I do." She cocked her head slightly. "Is there a salon hereabouts?"

"You serious?"

I liked that she was surprised. "I am."

Holly Pronto was thinking, thinking about what I was up to. "Why would you do that?"

"Why not? Are you any less worthy than the other women here?"

Her beady eyes got beadier. "Are you expecting something in return?"

"No, it's nothing like that."

"Then why?"

"Because it's been a long sad day, and it makes me feel better if I can do something nice for someone. I get the feeling it's been a while since anyone's been nice to you, that's why. And besides, I got money to spend."

She pushed the last of her pie to the side. "Ok then!"

That made me laugh.

The salon, the best in town, had an opening. Holly was both excited and visibly embarrassed by her appearance. I told her not to worry. It was their job to make her beautiful. She could have the works. I went next door to the coffee shop.

I texted Agnes that I missed her and wished I was home. She sent me a picture of Zach and Lizzy waving to me. I told them I loved them.

I returned to the salon to find Holly Pronto looking much better. The streaks in her hair were gone and there was color in her face. She showed me her nails and lamented that her drab clothes no longer matched the rest of her.

"Then we'll get you something nice to wear."

"Really?"

"Really." I do this all the time.

A woman's boutique was two doors down and I let her splurge. Two dresses, three blouses, three pairs of slacks; even underwear.

"All you need now are shoes," I said. She found two pairs she liked.

It took four hours, but Holly Pronto looked pretty damned good. She was beaming in her new outfit, standing taller and smiling. I walked her to her car.

"It's probably too much to ask for a better car, huh?" We both gazed at the rusting brown hulk before us. It was the proverbial piece of shit. I would have asked too.

"Probably."

She laughed, then took my hand and kissed me. "This was the nicest day I've had in so long. Thank you. I don't know what I'm going to say to momma when she asks about all this."

"Tell her you deserve it and leave it at that." I watched as she got in her car.

"Goodbye, Monk."

"Goodbye, Holly." I watched her drive off.

Reluctantly, I returned to the farm. I was staying in the bunkhouse where I used to sleep as a kid. Sterling was staying with Moses and Meredith. The bunkhouse had changed little. It was used when there was no place else to put visitors or when the kids wanted a sleepover. The place was rustic, with ten roughhewn beds stacked in twos. This was the only bedroom I knew growing up. At one time there was six to ten of us in here, but in my later years the kids, more and more, slept in their parent's houses. Moses whined about it, but even he let Sterling, Isaac, and Jacob sleep in their house. There were communal showers and toilets at one end and dressers at the other. Three long windows at the top of the north and south walls let in the light. Chairs were scattered here and there.

Moses was sitting in one as I entered the bunkhouse.

"Do you want me to leave?" I asked. He might be hiding.

"No, I was waiting for you," he gestured to the chair next to him. I sat down. His eyes were red and his beard and hair were matted to his head and face. It was clear he hadn't been sleeping.

"What's on your mind?"

He put his hands to his lips and cried. He fell towards me and I cradled him as he wept. I'd never heard him cry before. All the other expressive emotions I knew of I had experienced with him, but not this one. He shook and heaved; he squeezed such that I could hardly breathe, and then he let go and sat up, wiping his eyes.

"I don't deserve this," he said a moment later.

What do you say to that?

"Nobody does." The bunkhouse was quiet. The only sounds were the creaking of the chairs as we shifted in them. "What's on your mind?"

"My failures and you boys."

Ah, us boys.

"Our failures, your failures, or a combination of the two?" I asked, not wanting to know. He didn't answer. "Why don't we start with your argument with Jacob."

He started then hesitated. Embarrassed.

"It was the same one we'd been having for the last four or five years..."

"About his leaving?"

He looked at me, shaking his head. "About all of you leaving. All of you have gone for one reason or another. I hoped, obviously in vain, that he would be the one to stay." He looked at me, "You were a lost cause. I'm sorry to say that, but it's true. Sterling comes and goes, but like you he has demons to contend with, and Isaac wanted adventure. And then Jacob went and joined the fucking Marines and they fucking killed him with their fucking wars." I knew what was coming. I knew it by heart. We are nothing more than the means to an end, cannon fodder for self-righteous *leaders* who see us as a mere commodity to be used up and thrown away. "I asked him to come home, but he said *that* Jacob was gone..." Moses grabbed my hand, squeezing it. "What happened to him down there? What the fuck happened to my boy?"

"I don't have the answers. All I can tell you is what I know, but that isn't the answer." I said squeezing back.

"Then who knows the fucking answers, the goddamned government?"

"I doubt it." I wanted to help, but the little voice in my head was against it. What did I know? Nothing! Just scraps and maybe a hunch; the only bet I ever played. "I think something happened to him, to those with him, during their last time in Afghanistan."

"Why do you think that?"

"Promises," I teased.

"Promises?" Moses lessened his grip.

"The call I got about where to find Jacob was from a man named Lewis. Lewis is in trouble. He's taken off from the Marines, gone AWOL. He was one of the guys Jacob went to LA to see, but he was gone by then. I believe he's up here somewhere. I asked what was going on, but he wouldn't answer, said he made a promise not to. That makes me think Jacob was looking for his buddies because of what happened to them in Afghanistan, and when two of them turned up dead in a murder-suicide and another had run off, he started to freak. He was very, I don't know, edgy, and then the whole thing with Kurtis and his aunt—"

"What thing?"

The little voice was kicking me. I shook my head. "You won't like it."

"WHAT?" You won't like it!

"She accused him of sexual assault."

Moses slumped back, his head in his chest. "I don't believe that; not Jacob. I didn't raise him to be that kind of man."

"Maybe not, but something happened; something bad, and it was obviously weighing on his conscience. I was hoping to, well, it doesn't matter now." My head was aching again. My good deeds vibe had skipped town. There were no sounds other than our breathing. The light was fading from the room of my foolish youth, from me, the lost cause. "We should get you back. Meredith will be worried," I said at last.

"I can't bury him, I can't."

"Then one of us will, but we can't stay here." I stood up and held out my hand. After a moment he let me help him up.

"Why did this happen?"

"I don't know. Maybe I can look into it. I know a guy. Maybe he can find out what happened over there. I can run down to the Marine base at Pendleton, talk to this Cameron—"

Moses took my arm. "I'm going with you. I want to talk to those people too—"

"No, you need to stay here with Meri, and I don't need you screaming at the Marines till I find something to scream about. Come on."

Moses stood there. "How much are you worth now? How rich are you?"

I checked his eyes. Was he still on this planet? They weren't glassy or fogged. "Where did that come from, and what does that have to do with Jacob?" I didn't want to talk about money. He ran his hand through his hair.

"Money makes people talk. How much did that woman leave you? I know it's a lot if you can live in fucking Beverly Hills."

Ah, how I wish I was in fucking Beverly Hills. "It isn't important."

"How much? What, are you embarrassed?" He pressed his finger into my chest, something I didn't like.

"The trust is valued at three hundred and forty million dollars, give or take a few million. And while I administer the trust, I don't consider it my money."

Moses laughed. "Don't try and bullshit me, boy, you could liquidate the trust tomorrow."

"I'm not liquidating anything! Let it go!"

"It'll destroy your soul, wealth always does..."

I pulled him out of the bunkhouse. "Well, when you're a lost cause, these things happen." I ignored him as we walked back to the dining room.

The evening meal was an exercise in futility. Calista and Andrea, and by extension Emily, had dinner at their house; best to avoid the problem with whatshisname. Moses wasn't hungry, moping back to his room. Meredith helped in the kitchen, but the other women took her back to Moses after she began crying. Franco and Brewster decided this was the time to engage me in the specifics of retrieving and interring Jacob to his final resting place.

"The sheriff called. We can claim Jacob's remains tomorrow. I called over to the mortuary and they can pick him up." Brewster nodded as Franco spoke.

"We have a place up on the old north pasture set aside for a graveyard. It was supposed to be for us old guys. Didn't expect Jacob to be the first we buried," Brewster said.

"Don't forget, we have to wait for the Marine rep before we can bury him," added Franco.

"No cremation?" I asked.

They shook their heads in near unison. "No, they don't want that. We might need you to go with us, Monk." I understood why Moses, or even Meredith, wouldn't want to go, but why me?

"What about Sterling?"

A sly grin crossed Brewster's face. "Sterling's a good kid, but he has to go home, get back to his wife, and I can't see him signing for his brother's body. I think you're it." They spoke as if this was just business. "I spose we'll have to mark off the boundaries if we start burying folks, probably need a headstone too. I don't suppose you could help with that?"

"I'll take care of it." The Mackinaw's were pleased to hear this.

"You're a good kid, Sunshine," said Franco.

I laughed. "If I remember correctly, I believe I'm a lost cause."

Brewster snickered. "Now don't let any of that talk get to you. Moses, right?" I nodded. "He's just upset, and maybe rightly so, but he doesn't mean it. Don't let it get to you. He loves you."

"It's true," added Franco.

"Good to know." This time they both laughed.

I finished the evening alone in the bunkhouse with a glass and the bottle of whiskey I kept in the car for just such an emergency.

14

Emily was waiting outside the door.

"You're not supposed to hang out with me anymore," I told her.

Emily scowled. "It's not fair!"

"Perhaps, but that's the way it is. You better go back before we both get in trouble." She mumbled something under her breath and walked off.

The Mackinaws were in the dining hall with Moses. He looked a little more composed. It was decided we would all go, mostly for moral support, to the mortuary to hash out the details of Jacob's burial. There was some concern about whether we could bury him on our land without a permit or some such from the county.

"I already called about that," Brewster informed me. "It has to be delineated, to use his term. I'm pretty sure that means we have to build a fence or have a recognized boundary, and the body has to be in an approved burial conveyance, again, to use his term. You alright with this, Moses?"

Moses nodded, "I'm ok."

"The Marine representative will be there. The sheriff's already spoken to him and we can talk to him when we sign—" Moses visibly stiffened when the word, Marine, was spoken. We all took note of it. "Now I know you have issues with them, but we need to keep this orderly. I don't like saying that, but that's how it's got to be. We have an understanding about that?"

Moses clinched his jaw and nodded. "I said I was ok!" None of us were buying it.

"Yes, you did," Brewster reminded him.

With nothing else to say, we piled into the car and headed to the county morgue.

Those representing officialdom were waiting for us. The sheriff, the coroner, and a Marine captain who had come up from Camp Pendleton. The captain showed no emotions when Moses refused to shake his hand. The

Mackinaws and I covered for that. Moses did what he could to keep his temper in check, and the Marine kept to the script. Having concurred with the coroner as to the cause of death, and with the sheriff that there were no extenuating circumstances, the captain informed us that the Marine Corps would let Jacob remain at the mortuary until there was an official release from the Department of Defense.

"Unfortunately, there's a certain amount of paperwork that needs to be completed. I apologize and hope you'll be patient with us. I promise we'll expedite the matter. If you have any questions, you can contact me here." He passed out several cards with his name, rank, and contact information. I thought he probably shouldn't ask if we had questions, but we did.

"How much time is this going to take?" asked Brewster.

"I've been told about a week, but I'll confirm that for you," he said. I don't know how practiced the captain was in these kinds of situations, but he seemed to take it in stride. It's just business; it's what you do.

We signed the papers the county and state required. We watched in silence as the man from Sunset Mortuary and his assistant put Jacob in their van and drove off. We followed. The next hour was spent deciding on caskets and arrangements. The mortuary guy would need time to come to the site; make sure the grave was dug to the proper specs, and there was the actual date of the burial, which was complicated by Jacob's being in the Marines.

"We'll do it in a week. Is that enough time?" Brewster asked. He was taking charge. Moses didn't object. Flowers were picked and once the arrangements were finished, the next stop was to Owens Marble Design for the headstone. Moses wanted nothing more than a simple headstone, name, dates, and beloved son.

"It doesn't need anything more," he said.

I made sure everyone was paid. We were assured that everything would be ready a week hence. With that completed, it was time to return to the farm. I said my goodbyes and promised to be back for the funeral. There was nothing more I could do.

* * * * *

I called Bernie outside of San Jose asking if he had a minute to spare.

"If it's only a minute I suppose I can make time." I could see him smiling.

"Only a minute," I said.

He was in his office when I arrived. Two glasses of whiskey were on the desk. "What can I do for you, Monk? Is this car related or is this about other things?"

Bernie was, ostensibly, the owner of an automotive repair shop, and it was that. I'd brought every car I ever owned to be serviced here, but his sideline was information. It might have been his primary vocation with the shop as a front. I didn't care. I'd known Bernie a long time, and he'd been more than a little helpful.

"Other things."

I filled him in on recent events centering on Jacob, but I threw in Monika just to see what he'd say.

"It's always interesting the things that happen to you, my friend." I nodded. What could I say? "If something happened to your brother in Afghanistan, then Art would be a better source. He has contacts in Washington and at the Pentagon who might be able to help. For me, it's not my area of expertise. But I would caution about expecting too much. War is fairly chaotic, much as we try to organize it, and facts can fall through the cracks whether through happenstance or by design. If you can talk to the people who were there, that'd be the way to go, but *people* also let things slip through the cracks." He was watching the ice swirl in his glass of whiskey. There was no more whiskey in mine.

"And Monika?"

Bernie smiled. "Are you shocked by her advances?" I nodded. "I'm surprised, but you've been somewhat sheltered when it comes to these things. Maybe that's just the nature of your character."

"That doesn't help," I said.

"No?" I noted his amusement.

"No."

"Well, it's up to you what you do. Given your newfound wealth, money isn't going to be a problem either way. The question is one of access and opportunity. If women like Monika are your weakness, then you either succumb or you don't put yourself in a position to be tempted. You know, this is old school stuff," he laughed.

"I know, but it's good to hear it now and again."

"There's also the misery you put your loved ones through when you give in to these weaknesses. Some of us are bothered by such things; others are not. Some may even revel in them."

"I know." Agnes was looming before me.

I thanked him and made a mental note to call Art Devaney the next day.

• • • • • •

Instead of heading to the house in the hills, I stopped at the small house in West Covina I shared with Agnes. No one was there. I parked the car and wandered through the quiet house checking each room. I found my fingers running along dressers, chairs, and the counter in the kitchen. I sat down and called Agnes.

"You're where?" she asked.

"At our other house," I couldn't tell if she was surprised or exasperated.

"Why are you there?"

"I don't know, it was closer, I miss the place. I noticed you didn't make the bed."

"Uh-huh. Are you alright? You don't sound alright?"

"I don't?" I think I sound just fine. "Are you sure?"

"Monk, are you coming back, and what's going on with Jacob?"

"Jacob's dead," I reminded her.

"You know what I mean. How is everyone doing, Moses, Meredith; you know?"

"Exactly how you would expect. They're overwhelmed with grief and disbelief. The Marines want us to keep him on ice for a week while they close out his file, so the funeral will be a week from today. The Mackinaw brothers are holding the place together. Oh, and I've been officially barred from doing anything with Emily. I think that about covers it." The city lights were dancing with the leaves on the neighbor's tree, the tree that shaded this quiet little house.

"It was the outfits, wasn't it?" I'd forgotten about that.

"It probably didn't help, but I think it was mostly Emily's desire to live with us. She wanted me to argue in her defense, but I never got the chance, and I wasn't big on the idea to begin with."

"Are you coming home?"

I laughed. "I am home."

"I mean here, smart guy. I miss my snuggle-buddy." I envisioned her pouting on the couch, ignoring the vistas just beyond the pool.

"I don't know. It's peaceful here—"

"We can talk about that. I miss it too, but we're all here for now. Come back, ok?"

"Alright."

She seemed pleased by that.

I turned off the phone. It took a while, but I finally got my butt out of the chair and made my way to Agnes and the house in Beverly Hills.

•　　•　　•　　•　　•

I was on the floor playing patty-cake with Lizzy. Zach was beside her, vacillating between helping her and feeling left out. Lizzy was feeling pretty good about her ability to sit up on her own and liked grabbing at my fingers while I held my hands palms out.

"Gamps!" cried Zach, tired of waiting his turn.

"Hold on, little dude, Gamps only has two hands." Lizzy looked at her brother. I turned and patty-caked with Zach. It was now Lizzy's turn to be miffed by my inattention. Agnes was watching and no doubt enjoying my conundrum. "Hey, no laughing. If you have time to laugh, you have time to clap." She shrugged and sat down next to me and reached out to Zach. The kids looked at each other and us before agreeing to the arrangement.

"The prenup paperwork is ready. I told Ms. Lagenfelder we'd be down to review it this afternoon." A nice conversational change of topic.

"Why do we need a prenup? We've been doing fine so far?" groused Agnes.

"You know why. We're no longer two people with a small house and a few hundred grand between us, and that's me being generous."

"I don't like the idea of a prenup. It assumes the demise of our relationship."

I smiled at her turn of phrase, a rather lawyerly one. "True, but that's the nature of modern relationships these days." Lizzy was pulling on my middle fingers. Zach, noticing this, did the same to Agnes.

"What if I don't sign? What if I don't want to?"

"Then you don't. But if you don't, it means we won't get married, and we'll have to live apart, even if we're, you know, together." I moved my arm forward so Lizzy would have to hold on tight or fall backwards. Like her brother, she found this endlessly fascinating. God bless the giggling child absorbed in play.

"I don't like this, Buttman!"

"Neither do I, but that's life in the fast lane."

Zach decided he wanted to play the finger game with Lizzy, so we turned them to face one another. Their coordination left something to be desired, but they marshaled on, mostly to their own amusement.

"If I sign, how much am I getting?" she asked, no doubt curious.

"If I remember, it's somewhere between five and ten million dollars."

"That's all? Isn't the trust worth a lot more than that?" I could see her staring at me out of the corner of my eye. I kept my focus on the kids.

"Quite a bit more, but that doesn't mean you're entitled to more simply because you know me biblically." Agnes frowned. "How much money did you have when you met me?"

More frowning. "I don't know, maybe ten grand."

"Ten grand, plus a house payment, and five million wouldn't be enough now?" I asked.

"You don't need all that money either, Sunshine!"

That made laugh, so much so that the kids stopped grabbing at each other's hands and stared at me. "That's absolutely true. I don't need any of it and I don't know what I'm going to do with it. I have more than enough from what I realized when the bungalows were sold. That's not the point, however." The kids turned their attention to Agnes.

"Maybe I should get a lawyer then," she huffed.

"That's fine. You're more than welcome to have an attorney advise you on what it says."

"Maybe I will, Buttman, maybe I will." Agnes reached for my hand, still staring at me, "I don't like this. It makes me feel like I can be easily discarded with a little money thrown in."

I looked at her cute nose. "I have no interest in discarding you. It's simply common practice when this amount of money is involved." I leaned in and kissed her. The kids seemed fascinated by this, too. "I'm also thinking of kicking everyone out of this house."

Her expression of disbelief was worth my blurting it out.

"What? Why?"

"Because I think they're more than capable of finding their own places and supporting themselves. They've shown that already, and I'm not suggesting it'll happen right this minute. I'd give them six months or so..."

The frown was back. "Wow, Mister Generous!" I noted her forehead tightening. "See, you say all these good things about not worrying and everything's ok, but wanting everyone out says the exact opposite!" Always suspicious.

"It's not that," I said. "I want to go back to our simple life and I can't do that with everyone coming and going up here. We can still use it for get-togethers when there's a lot of us in town, or we can sell it, but that's what I want to do, and since it belongs to me, I can. I'm not doing this to get *rid* of anyone!" Not that I didn't give her a valid reason to be suspicious. "Besides, you yourself suggested it not long ago."

"Uh-huh." Agnes let go of my hand and got up. "I don't like this, Buttman, not one bit."

Lunch and the trip to Aeschylus and Associates were quiet affairs. Agnes was angry or fearful or worried or all of the above, and the kids were picking up on our unhappy vibe. I had no intention of dumping her or our kids, but I was more and more restless and willing to weather an early storm rather than a long drawn-out atmospheric event. Ms. Lagenfelder set out the agreement, went over what it said, and answered Agnes' few questions.

"It's probably bad form to ask your boyfriend's lawyer whether it's ok to have someone else look at it?"

Taylor, in her very controlled lawyerly voice, assured her it was not only ok, but a prudent thing to do. "Having another attorney review it is well within your rights and something we recommend." She did however note that as *my* attorney, offering references was problematic when Agnes asked if she knew anyone.

"Talk to Johnny, I'm sure he knows lots of capable lawyers." Agnes ignored me. She excused herself and walked off to the restroom. Ms. Lagenfelder noted Agnes' unhappiness. "She's convinced herself that I'm doing this so I can get rid of her quickly if I meet someone younger or better or something—"

"Are you?" asked the equally suspicious lawyer.

"No, nothing like that." I was surprised by the question. It was Ms. Lagenfelder who strongly suggested the prenup to begin with. "The truth is, I don't like having all this money, and I'm just not comfortable pretending to be a 'I've got it all together rich guy' who fucks around, and screws with people, and thinks he's perfectly justified in doing so simply because he has a lot of money. I want my simple life back. And *you're* the one who said I had to do this."

"I simply recommended it. I'm not forcing you to do this. You can if you wish forgo it," my lawyer corrected me.

"I know. I apologize. I just don't like it."

Ms. Lagenfelder nodded in that reassuring way that lawyers do.

Agnes returned in no better a mood than when she left. We retrieved the kids from Ms. Lagenfelder's assistant, who was reluctant to let them go, but had to get back to whatever she had to do. Agnes stayed withdrawn on the drive back. The kids fell asleep in their car seats.

"Why is this so hard now? All I want is for us to be together, to be married," she said to the car window.

"It just seems that way right now, but we'll get there, I promise." Agnes stared at me for what was more than a few seconds.

"I don't want any more promises, Monk." She went back to staring at the world beyond the tinted windows of the car.

15

The next delightful enterprise was to call Art Devaney, the former intelligence operative, or CIA man, or whatever he was before he sort of retired to grow tobacco in the idles of rural Virginia. He was jovial as ever, no matter the subject; maybe it's an intelligence-gathering thing or a sociopathic trait. Whichever, he listened to my tale, such as it was, before asking questions.

"I see. What regiment was he in?"

No lights went off. "I haven't the slightest idea."

Art Devaney laughed at my ignorance. "So, it's probably pointless to ask about his battalion, company, or platoon?"

"Yeah. I can find out," I said.

"I assume you believe all these events are connected. The death of your brother, the murder-suicide, and the deaths of the two marines in Afghanistan, is that correct?" A not so small amount of foolishness crept into my consciousness.

"That's my hunch." More laughter.

"Those are always my favorites," he said. "I should probably say that anytime you stick your nose into the affairs of the military; the Marine Corps in this instance, a certain amount of resistance should be expected, particularly where death is a component in the overall composition of the event. Any number of circumstances may have occurred that will not be in the official review, and there's no guarantee we'll get anything beyond that through backdoor channels, and, though I assume you've considered this, it's possible that nothing more than the obvious happened, meaning the deaths were just as they were described; the result of war and these individual's responses to their participation in it." Art Devaney let that linger a minute.

"That sounds terribly clinical. They were people, flesh and blood and all that," I protested.

"Yes, they were, but they were also active participants. They enlisted of their own free will, they were not drafted or coerced, correct?"

"I assume so."

He must have noted my misgivings. "I'm not saying these things to sound heartless, simply as a reminder of the forces in play. I do appreciate the human element, that these were, or are, real human beings who were subjected to situations you and I probably never will be. But we have to remember that we're talking about a very large, very bureaucratic organization that by its very nature has to, in many respects, reduce its members to something other than fragile human beings while also not losing sight of that. It naturally creates tensions when everything doesn't go according to plan, or even when it does. Official reports are just that, reports. A lot depends on who does the reporting and how it's received up the chain of command. Have I made that confusing enough?"

"For the time being..." It was already confusing.

"Excellent. I'll see what I can find on this end. In the meantime, I need you to find out where he was in the grand scheme of the Marine Expeditionary Forces in Afghanistan. Again, sorry to hear about your brother. Take care, Monk."

"Thanks, Art." He hung up. My brother. Words I rarely spoke or considered were now bandied about as if they had been that way from the beginning. More fraud perpetrated by Sunshine Bohrman.

Agnes was asleep with Lizzy in our room. Zach, whose desire for naps was diminishing, was in the living room with me. He stood in his pen eyeing Gamps in hopes of liberation.

"You want out, little dude?" He began jumping up and down.

"Out!" he cried.

"We have to be quiet. Your sister is sleeping." He stopped jumping and spun around to see if I was telling the truth. I put my index finger to my mouth. He did the same. I pointed to the pool. Zachary Bohrman banged on the rail of the pen, his way of agreeing. I pulled him out and he trotted to the cabana where the swim diapers were kept. I helped him put them on and we moved to the shallow end where he eagerly wadded in.

After a moment he turned to me and said, "Em?"

"Sorry, no Emily for a while. Her mom wants her to stay at the farm from now on. We'll see her when we go up for Jacob's funeral next week." Zach just stared for a moment before pointing to one of his pool toys. I grabbed it and tossed it his way. I eased over to the bar and poured a little whiskey into a glass, all the while keeping an eye on the water rat. He seemed pretty bright when it came to that part of the shallow end where his balance became more tenuous and his footing unsure. As a general rule, he would shout to whoever he was with if he wanted to go further; a sturdy hand to keep him safe. I returned to the edge and watched, sipping here and there.

Agnes and Lizzy wandered out, and I changed into a suit so I could swim with Lizzy. Nudity was no longer an option in Judith's pool, once a haven for swimming in the buff. I knew Agnes would be too embarrassed, certain we'd be "discovered" and just as certain that no one, apart from me, wanted to see her naked butt in the pool.

"Why the interest?" she would ask.

"Just a thought," I'd reply.

Rebekah returned in the early afternoon, sans Fidel. A solemn look upon her face, attention directed at me. I glanced at Agnes, who promptly crossed her arms and frowned. The word was out. Lovely. Rebekah wasted no time in voicing her displeasure with me.

"Agnes tells me you're planning on kicking us out. Where the hell are we supposed to go? You know we just started this business, which you invested in, and now we're going to be homeless?!"

I continued playing with my grandkids.

"Agnes said that? That's terrible, and I come off like such an ogre. I suppose she also mentioned that I'm going to leave her a pauper as well after I force her to sign that awful prenup!" I winked at Agnes, who continued frowning. "Just so I can leave her for some hot young money-grubbing babe. Yep, Gamps is a real jerk, isn't he kids?"

Lizzy and Zach laughed. Agnes and Rebekah did not.

"Am I kicking you out? No. Will you need to find another place to raise your brood? Yes. Does it have to be this minute? No. But in the next few months you should seriously start looking. And if you find something you like and can afford, I'd be willing to consider helping with the down payment or something to that effect."

Rebekah stood there dumbfounded. "Why are you doing this? It makes no sense."

"Actually, it makes all the sense in the world. Think about it. Do you really see yourself in this house, the house of my dead girlfriend, shared with all of us, as the place you plan on spending the rest of your life?"

"No, but that's not the point—"

"Then what is the point?"

"Don't interrupt me!" she shouted. This caused Zach and Lizzy to start crying. "Are you happy now?" Evidently this was my fault.

"Hey, I'm not the one who's upset and yelling. If you'd calm down for a minute, I'll explain my reasoning. You may not like it, but I think you'll understand. Then again, maybe not."

"Monk, this isn't the time to be a smartass." Agnes was wagging her finger at me.

"You're the one who brought this up. I wasn't going to say anything—"

"So, you were just going to one day say, get out?" Rebekah had not calmed down. The kids continued crying, their wails ringing in my ears.

"Please sit down and stop yelling," I handed Lizzy to her. Zach, always the partisan, saddled up to Gamps. Rebekah, cradling Lizzy, finally sat down at the edge of the pool. Lizzy and Zach calmed down as well, and I drained the last of my whiskey.

Agnes continued to scowl at me. "Alright, Buttman, tell her why."

I shook my head. "It was your idea, remember?"

"I was joking," she insisted.

I was undeterred. "It's simple. I never intended for this to be everyone's home, and after Judith died, it seemed a waste to not use it. But now that everyone is finding their way; you and Fidel with your business, and Anna with hers, it's my preference that all of us have our own place. It doesn't mean we can't still use this house, but we want to go back to our house," I motioned at Agnes, "and I know you'll want your own place—"

"If you don't want this place why not let us have it?" Rebekah huffed.

"I didn't say I didn't want it, but there's no way you could afford this house. The property taxes alone are as much as most regular houses cost. Then there are the maintenance costs and the upkeep. Do you have the time and money for that?" My daughter said nothing. "I didn't think so."

Agnes piped up, "I like having everyone here; you know that!" Agnes' dismay was morphing into tears.

"I'm aware of that, and I like having them here too, but there are other things that are tied to this house that I can't get away from, whether it's Judith or the money or the idea that I need to take care of everyone. And it's not like we won't be seeing each other if the kids have their own places. Let's be honest, you and Fidel have said you want your own place and Anna has as well, and, I think we should all live within our means."

Agnes poked me in the ribs. "Except you're worth a fortune now, Sunshine."

"Yeah, I get that everyone sees me that way, but I didn't ask for any of this, and as far as I'm concerned it's not my fortune. I've been more than generous in helping you and Fidel and Anna get your businesses off the ground, but—"

"But what?" demanded Rebekah.

"But I don't like being the guarantor of everyone's financial wellbeing, and all things considered, there are plenty of people out there who need the help more than you do."

"So, you don't think we're important enough?"

My turn to frown. "I don't want to be responsible for creating a lot of entitled pricks who think they're better than everyone else simply because a pile of money fell in their lap. I can live with you being angry for however long it takes, and you may not like my reasoning, but that's how I feel and that's what I'm going to do."

Rebekah didn't like being referred to as an entitled prick. "So, you're just going to change everything all of a sudden?"

"You can't do that, Monk," added Agnes.

"Oh yes, I can!"

"Then fuck you." Rebekah stood up. "Come on, Zach," Zach started crying again. She came over and pulled him out of the pool and marched off to her room.

Agnes was fuming. "How could you say that?" She got up.

"Agnes."

"WHAT?"

I put out my hand. "Will you please sit down for a minute?" She stood there scowling. "Please?"

"Just say what you want to say!"

I needed more whiskey. "Please sit down." I moved my hand so she would sit by me. She hesitated before coming over.

"What?"

I put my arm around her. "Did I say I was kicking them out? No. Did I say I was cutting them off? No. What I'm saying is it's better for all of us if their success is of their own making, not just me throwing money at them. Like I said, if anyone was listening, I'll help with financing if they need it. I'm already invested in their businesses, and if it makes sense to invest more, I will. If they need help buying a home, I'll help, but if they want this kind of home, then they need to earn the kind of money it takes to support it. It's not my responsibility to give them that. I think that's more than enough." I kissed her forehead after wiping her eyes.

"You're a jerk, Buttman."

"That's better than being an enabler."

Agnes put her hand on my face. "What about us?"

"Were you unhappy when we were living in *our* house?"

"No," she sheepishly admitted.

"We fixed it up just like we wanted, didn't we?"

"Yes, we did."

"We can set up a little pool in the backyard and have the kids over, and we can be married and have a happy life together. That's what I want. I don't want to be mister moneybags responsible for everyone's happiness. I just want to be Gamps."

Agnes kissed me and then got up. "You make it sound nice, like everything is ok, but our life has changed. I'd like to go back to the way we were, but I don't know if I can believe in your promises anymore." She turned around and walked away.

My head was aching. I looked at the clock on the wall. Maybe not too late, six o'clock.

Captain August Sinnons answered on the third ring. I asked if he had time the next day to speak to me.

"Can you be here at ten? I have an hour available from ten to eleven," he said.

"I can do that."

"I'll let the gate commander know."

I had a thought, "Would it be possible to talk to a Marine named Seth Cameron?" The captain paused. "Jacob mentioned he spoke to Cameron the day before he killed himself. I was hoping to have a word with him, maybe find out what he knows, if anything."

"I'll ask, Mr. Buttman."

I thanked him and hung up.

．　　　．　　　．　　　．　　　．

Fidel found me in the kitchen making spaghetti and sausages. For all the turmoil, there was still the need for food, so I was preparing dinner and wanted something comforting and easy to make, and store, if certain elements of our happy little band were uninterested in sharing a table with me. I grabbed a beer out of the fridge and handed it to Fidel.

"I assume you got the good word?"

Fidel laughed. "And then some."

"Are you here to get to the bottom of things and talk some sense into me?"

He took a swig and placed the bottle on the counter. "Let me check." He pulled out his phone and revisited the text from Rebekah. "Yeah, that sounds about right."

I reiterated my demands and my reasoning, allowing for a judicious amount of editing so I didn't seem like such an unfeeling ogre.

"Seems fair," was his appraisal.

"So why all the hysterics?" I asked.

"Beats me, although I think Jacob's death is a part of it. It's always shocking when you meet someone and you want to get to know them and you can see that something is wrong and then all this happens...and..." A curious little grin came to Lizzy's father.

"Yes?"

"I probably shouldn't say, but I also think some of this is Becky's concern about you and Agnes, and based on what she's said to me, she thinks you're on your way out. I apologize if I sound like I'm sticking my nose into your business. Becky really likes Agnes, and I think she doesn't want to see that end or find herself between the two of you." Fidel noted my sigh. "Sorry."

"No need to be. Would you be so kind as to tell the others that dinner is ready if they want it?"

Fidel got up and smiled. "Sure."

After what I assumed was some cajoling, Fidel convinced Rebekah they should come eat with us. Agnes came out as well. There were a few brief attempts at conversation; mostly Fidel recounting the day's adventures setting up for a car chase to be filmed early the next morning, but beyond that the mood was sullen. Fidel and Rebekah took the kids and went to bed early; they had to get up early. Agnes retreated to the cabana, staring at the city. I waited for Anna. I presumed that Agnes had warned her of my insidious plans.

Surprisingly, her reaction was much like Fidel's, though she was more conversant.

"Actually, that works for me because I've been looking around and, to be perfectly honest, I'd like to have my own place. And I appreciate all the financial help you've given me. I mean you didn't have to, and we need to make it on our own. Dad said the same thing when I came down here. It's ok."

"There's one other thing, if you don't mind," Anna sat there, her eyes watching mine. "Do you think I'm doing all this so I can leave your mother?"

"I don't know. I like that you're with her and I believe that you love her, so I hope you stay together, but things change. Just look at Mikal and Joanie." That made me smile. Joanie. "Goodnight Monk."

"Goodnight."

Agnes was still in the cabana; still watching the lights of greater LA.

I sat down next to her. "It's late. We should go to bed."

"I suppose." She was looking at me just as her daughter had only moments before. I held out my hand and lifted up the both of us. I put my arms around her and she put hers around me.

"I know you don't believe it, but I know what I'm doing, Beautiful." She smiled before kissing me.

"I don't believe that for a minute, Buttman."

It was worth a try.

16

The guards at Camp Pendleton gave me the once over before checking my ID and the car for bad intent. It'd been a while since dogs and mirrors were introduced to the Falcon. The guards themselves may have been amused by the guy dressed to the time when the car was manufactured; a probable parody of early sixties chic, but if they were, they kept it to themselves. They provided directions and sent me on my way.

The camp was not what I expected, which on reflection was based on the idiotic idea that the entertainment industry presented an accurate view of military life. Instead of lines of barracks and parade grounds, and to be fair there were those, the camp struck me as mostly a small town with all the amenities you would expect, along with firearms, tanks, artillery, and aircraft. I followed the map and did my best not to appear completely out of place, but as a poster boy for a bygone era, that might have been asking a little too much. I found the building with the number given by the guards, and made my way to the captain's office. A sergeant led the way. Captain Sinnons greeted me along with a Lt. Colonel named Jaron.

"This is my commanding officer, Mr. Buttman. I asked him to join us in case there were questions you had that I might not be able to answer." The captain turned to the colonel.

"Please have a seat, Mr. Buttman." It was possible the term 'Mr. Buttman' would be uttered more times during our talk than at any other time in the history of Monk Buttman. "What can we do for you?"

"I have a few questions to ask about my brother Jacob's time in the Marines. I was also hoping to talk to Seth Cameron, but I get the impression that isn't going to happen."

The colonel smiled in a way I did not find reassuring. "Corporal Cameron did not feel he could be of assistance in this matter. What questions did you have, Mr. Buttman?"

"I was curious about a number of things. One, what Jacob was doing when he was in Afghanistan? Two, what happened that might have changed him after his last tour? This was passed on to me by those that knew him better. And three, whether you were aware of the deaths surrounding some of the men he served with. Recent deaths."

The captain spoke first.

"What your brother was doing during his last deployment involved our engagement with the local Afghans. We were there to support their security forces and to build a network that allowed them to better interact with the government and with us. We acted as liaisons and worked to build trust between the people and the regional administrations. We also provided combat support as necessary."

The colonel went next.

"Obviously, the Marine Corps is deeply concerned about what happened to Corporal Bohrman and what may have led him to that decision—"

"Are you aware of the deaths of Santos and Saunders in LA? Jacob came down from Ukiah to talk to them and was quite upset about their deaths."

The captain glanced at the colonel. "We were made aware of it when the LAPD asked for information concerning their service."

"Did detective Mallory also inform you he found a newspaper clipping that referred to the deaths of two Marines, I believe their names were Dezi and Lambert, who were killed in Afghanistan?"

The captain started to speak but stopped.

"No, I was unaware of that," the colonel admitted.

"Were they in the same group or platoon as Jacob and Seth Cameron?"

"Yes, they were all in theater together. Your brother, along with the others, were on patrol with Privates Dezi and Lambert when they were killed." This from the captain.

"Can I ask what happened?"

The captain again deferred to the colonel.

"They were ambushed. If I remember correctly, they were hindered by a sandstorm, and had become separated. It was during this time the two Marines were killed. Fortunately, members of a small village came to the aid of the others and helped them fight off the attackers." The colonel looked out the window. "I don't mean to assume too much, but often times the men become very attached to one another, to take responsibility for each other's safety. My personal belief is that the deaths of the two men impacted the others. It's my understanding they were a very tight group who had been together since enlistment."

"Yes, that's true," I said.

"That may also explain why they held on to the newspaper clipping," added the captain.

"Yes, I suppose that answers that. Mallory was surprised to find it, so I was curious what you thought."

"Are you associated with the LAPD, Mr. Buttman?" The colonel had his own curiosities.

"No. I know Detective Mallory through other matters. When we learned from Santos' aunt that he was dead from a murder-suicide with Saunders, I called Mallory about it and he mentioned the clipping." The Marines struck me as just as interested in what I might know. "Were you aware of the relationship between Kurtis and Saunders?"

After a moment, the captain answered.

"Officially, there was no known relationship between them other than as fellow Marines, but I learned later that they were," he looked at Jaron, "involved with one other. It's quite possible that this was known by the others in their platoon."

"Do you think his sergeant knew, Sergeant MacMillan?"

The two men didn't blink.

"If he did, he didn't share it with me," the captain answered.

"Would it be possible to talk to the sergeant?"

The colonel stood. "Sergeant MacMillan is no longer active. He retired some months ago, and if I may anticipate your next question, we're not allowed to divulge the whereabouts of former Marines without permission." I got the impression our meeting was coming to a close. It was my turn to stand.

"Well then, my only other question is whether there are any complications that might keep us from burying Jacob next week."

"None that I know of, Mr. Buttman."

The Marines escorted me to my car and again offered condolences for the brother I barely knew. The captain gave me the information that Devaney needed, though I couched the need as simply for the benefit of my own edification. I didn't really know any more than when I arrived.

Stupidity or desire drive men to attempt foolish things; to return to places where they are unwanted and unloved, looking for redemption or forgiveness; for a kind of grace so they can sleep at night. I thought of that as I returned to the house in Watts. I was, in some ways, a proxy for Moses, and maybe even Jacob, and I wanted to know what Kurtis had written; to see the proof; to find the truth in the words of dead men.

Ms. Harvin came to the door with the same foul expression she had the last time we'd encountered one another. "What do you want!" She looked around to see if anyone else was with me. "I see you ain't got your protection with you."

"With your permission, I'd like to read what Kurtis wrote."

"Why, so you can tell me it ain't true," she demanded.

"No. I'd simply like to read what he wrote so I can understand what's happened."

Ms. Harvin was unmoved. "Why don't you find out from your Jacob Bohrman? You don't need to see what Kurtis wrote."

"I wish I could, but Jacob is dead. He killed himself a few days ago." Her expression of anger lessened, but only a little. "I just want to understand, that's all. I'm not here to question whether what Kurtis wrote is true or not. I just want to know what he said."

Ms. Harvin stood there behind the screen, trying to decide. Her forehead crinkled and her eyes softened before she slowly opened the door. I followed her in and she pointed to a chair in the living room.

"Sit there and don't you dare move." I assured her I'd stay put.

There were photographs of who I assumed was Kurtis, both in and out of uniform; of him with Ms. Harvin, and with another woman when he was very young. The house was small, like the one I shared with Agnes in West Covina. A modest living room led into a kitchen with a place for a small table. Down the hall were bedrooms and a bath. The house had seen better days. The paint had faded, and the carpet was worn. The furniture was comfortable, but the fabric was fraying from too many years of use. Ms. Harvin returned and handed me a diary.

"I marked the part where he talks about it" Her expression was one of worry.

I opened the book as she sat on the couch and watched. The page she earmarked began with a complaint about the lack of privacy and a lament that this was what he deserved for stupidly joining the Marines. The next entry was what she based her accusations on and it was both blunt and vague. Blunt in what the two had done to him, and vague about the others' participation in it. There were also references to other incidents that I tried to find in the diary to no avail. He spoke of Jacob sparingly, but there was no doubt that Jacob had been there when the assault occurred.

"How could he do this to me? How could he be a part of it? I had trusted him. I had believed in him!" were the words that stuck.

I read on to see if there was anything else about it. Nothing. I noticed that a number of pages had been removed here and there in the diary. After what happened that night, the entries revolved around his wanting out, wanting to go back to the states; to be somewhere and someone else. In places he wrote of his feelings for Mason, and it was in these entries I found what I was really looking for.

The pact. The promise; what Lewis had alluded to.

"We're going to make things right! Some things you can stand, but some things have to be answered for," he wrote. *"And this time we make good on our promises to one another."* There were no specifics, and more pages had been removed. That was the last of the entries. I thumbed through the book, looking for more, but that was it. I handed the diary back to Aretha Harvin.

"I appreciate you're doing this," I told her.

"Kurtis was a good man," she said.

"I didn't doubt that, Ms. Harvin." She held the diary to her chest as I left her. I sat in the car trying to understand. The only thing I understood was that my phone was ringing. It was Natalya. She wanted to talk.

"I'll be there in a little while," I assured her.

·   ·   ·   ·   ·

It became apparent that the foolishness of the day would not be limited to expecting answers from the Marines or to wandering into Watts unannounced. I called Agnes to let her know I'd be a little late. She was neither happy nor annoyed. Instead, she was deep into resignation that I was once again fucking around on her.

"It's just a meeting, out in the open, that's all," I protested.

"Then I guess we'll see you whenever you decide to show up. Goodbye, Monk."

I groaned and banged my head on the steering wheel.

For the first time, in a long time, I was tired of Agnes and tired of her whining at me for my supposed lack of faith. I had no interest in talking art with Natalya. I had no interest in why Jacob killed himself, or why I didn't care more. All I really wanted was to go back to my cheap lawn chair in front of my tiny bungalow and sit in the sun while drinking a cold beer. I was even willing to drive back to West Covina, but that's not where I was going. No, I was putzing down Wilshire to talk to a twenty-year-old about God knows what.

Forty minutes later, and maybe fifteen miles, I was far from the working-class neighborhoods of Watts and into the rarified air of Hollywood and its trendy art scene. That only deepened my discontent. Natalya and Brigitte were waiting for me in their office in the back of Brigitte's gallery. Both seemed happy to see me.

"Why the foul mood, Mr. Buttman?" In Brigitte's elocution Buttman sounded like boot-mon. I'd forgotten they were unaware of recent events.

"I'm tired, my brother's dead, and I'm struggling through an existential crisis. Other than that, I'm good." I could see that Brigitte understood just as Natalya did not. I didn't care either way. "What did you want to talk about?"

"Mr. Dunkle," replied Brigitte.

"Natalya and Dunkle or just Dunkle?" I needed clarification. I noted a slight peevishness in Natalya's expression indicating this was more Brigitte's idea than hers.

"His attentions toward Natalya." She gave Natalya a brief glace before returning to her concerns. "While Natalya believes she's quite capable of deciding for herself, she is still a young woman with little experience in the world of romance, and, unfortunately, too much experience in the world of malicious predators for whom young women are merely to be used and discarded."

Natalya harrumphed, which made me laugh.

Brigitte did not appreciate my laughter.

"My apologies. So, if I may, the concern here is a number of things, predominately whether Mr. Dunkle is preying on Ms. Constantinescu, or is too old, or is both. Correct?"

"Correct," stated Ms. DuBare.

Ms. Constantinescu rolled her eyes. "I'm no child. I know how the world is!"

"Precisely, you are steeped in the ugly degeneration of what men do to women and conversely ignorant of the beauty of love and romance; of being desired for more than how well you perform a sex act. My concern is that Mr. Dunkle is taking advantage of your naiveté, and is infatuated with your youth and not your mind, and to be frank; not worthy of your affections."

I found it affecting that Brigitte cared for Natalya such that she cared not just for her empirical and professional development, but for her personal experiences as well.

"It seems to me that the two of you have already sparred over this, which raises the question of what you want from me?" I was hoping nothing was the answer.

"I would ask that you try to dissuade Natalya from engaging with Mr. Dunkle, but no doubt she will rebuff you as she has me. Therefore, I would instead ask that you act as a chaperone in this matter and engage Mr. Dunkle such that he understands that I will not allow him to trifle with her affections simply to satisfy his prurience."

I, too, had no doubt Natalya would resist my meddling, just as I didn't doubt Ms. DuBare's seriousness despite the florid language. Nothing would not do. I was, to Ms. DuBare, Natalya's father figure, and it was expected that I would honor that responsibility. My longing for my former life continued to intensify. Both women were waiting for my answer.

"I am in full agreement that life without love, and by that, I mean the opportunity for love to flourish on its own merits rather than by coercion, is a life not fully lived. But philosophy aside, I believe you only learn by doing and that includes screwing up. I'm well versed in that. However, I will determine the depths of Mr. Dunkle's affections and advise him that trifling with our Natalya is not acceptable." Ms. Constantinescu harrumphed again, which I, again, found entertaining.

Ms. DuBare did not, but like me, she recognized the limits the two of us would have on a very determined and headstrong young woman. Natalya got up, informed us she had more pressing things to do than be treated like an idiot, and stomped out as only a young woman in heels can.

"I know she finds my ideas as old-fashioned as I do, but I find great value in them, and since she is adamant to live this kind of life with the kinds of characters I've had to deal with for far too many years, I feel a sense of duty to at least proffer something other than the retrograde profligacy that passes for romance these days. To fuck is not to love is not to live. It is merely to fuck and be fucked. It is all deeply appalling. There is nothing more beautiful than to be loved, truly loved." The inestimable Ms. DuBare was actually wistful and bearing a small portion of her soul to a cad.

"I'm not the one you have to convince."

Ms. DuBare simply nodded.

Natalya caught me at the door. "I'm not a fool or a child," she insisted.

"I didn't say you were." I leaned in and kissed her cheek. "We just want you to be a happy young woman, that's all." Natalya touched her cheek where I kissed her and frowned. I impulsively kissed her other cheek. She stood there shaking her head. I smiled. "You don't want to be happy?"

"I want to be happy..." She seemed unsure.

"I'll see you later."

My good humor lasted until I got to the car and called Agnes.

17

She didn't answer. Three separate tries; three separate disconnects. Old resentments intruded on my willingness to be responsible. To anyone. The card was in my pocket. Monika answered on the third ring.

"What's on your mind, Monk?"

"Just a drink. Where would you like to meet?" Just a drink.

"Why don't you come over here. I live on Fountain. Are you close?" I could hear her breathing.

"Hollywood." My heart was pounding.

"I'll leave the door open." She stated a number, which I assumed to be where on Fountain.

The door was open. She was wearing a light blue chiffon dress that caressed her shoulders and breasts, then snugged at her waist before stopping just above her knees. She closed the door behind me. Her lips were soft and wet. With the lightest touch, she pulled the straps down along her shoulders, and the dress away from her breasts. She placed my hands on them. Monika's fingers then moved to the buttons on my jacket and the belt around my waist. She undid the clasp on my slacks and slid her hand between the skin and the fabric.

"I didn't come here for that," I said as her lips left mine.

"Yes, you did." The other hand loosened the zipper.

I worried I wouldn't to be able to perform or finish. I was wrong on both counts. Instead, I watched, as if disembodied, as if I were someone else. There was no struggle to become aroused or to orgasm. A glorious ache thrilled me as I ejaculated, my hands still caressing her breasts. Monika leaned back after assuring herself I was done and smiled.

"Did you enjoy that?" Her eyes were sparkling in the fading light of the day.

"I believe the reaction and result speak for themselves."

"Good." I made a mental note of her expression of a job well done. "And thanks for saving the theatrics..." She carefully put my spent cock back where it belonged and zipped up my pants.

"Theatrics?"

She stood up, adjusted the belt and buttoned the jacket. "The bizarre desire men have these days to shoot their cum all over our faces and tits, not to mention our hair and clothes, as if we were in some kind of porn film. Maybe that's why I like older men who learned about sex someplace other than the internet." She finished by adjusting my tie. "What would you like to drink?"

"Whiskey is fine."

It was impossible not to watch the woman move. A quick trip to the cabinet containing alcohol and glasses; to the refrigerator for the ice. The apartment glowed as the evening light danced about the polished steel of the tables, chairs, and couch. The sheer drapes acted like a filter to diffuse its color. Monika turned on a small lamp before handing me my drink.

"You seem surprised." She tapped the edge of her glass to mine. "I don't know why. I did, after all, explicitly offer to suck your cock." I watched her lift the glass to her lips and draw in the liquor.

"I haven't forgotten." We sat on the couch.

"Just for the record, and despite what you may have heard, I don't spend my time offering blowjobs to any man I meet."

"No?"

"No." That only heightened my concern.

"Then why me?"

"Why not you?" She leaned back.

"Because not long ago I was a nobody, and if I may protest too much, a relatively happy one; one you'd have passed by without so much as a glance." I put my hand back on her now clothed breast. Monika smiled and put her hand on mine, directing the caress.

"Oh, I glance a lot more than you think. And yes, your recent good fortune is alluring in its own way, and I won't deny it's part of why I approached you. But you are not of value to me simply because you have money. I may be calculating, but I like to think I'm not so driven that other factors such as appearance and manners, and even a certain amount of self-deprecation isn't attractive in and of itself." She pulled the dress away, exposing her breast. "You like them, don't you?"

"I do."

"I felt a minor enhancement was in order, but I wanted to avoid the obvious look of over-plasticized tits. I think they turned out well." She was once again directing my hand.

"I won't argue that."

"What will you argue, Monk? You'll forgive me if I avoid the Buttman part—"

"You don't like the name Monk Buttman?"

Monika Danalek laughed. "I think it's a terrible name, but on to our argument. I may be wrong, but I get the feeling you didn't just drop by to cum in my mouth and play with my tits." I tried to remove my hand, but Monika's hand said no.

"I didn't actually come here to avail myself of your hospitality, but I'd be lying if it wasn't in the back of my mind. To be honest, I'm not having the best of days, I'm angry at... at a lot of people. I'm tired of the responsibilities I find dumped in my lap... and there's this whole thing with Jacob. Anyway, in a moment of weakness, I found the card you gave me and here I am."

"I don't mind being your weakness. And who is this Jacob?" Exactly what I wanted to know.

"No need to talk of that. It'll only sour the mood..."

She cocked her head slightly. "A lover?"

"No, nothing like that. It's a family matter."

She released my hand only to then start fondling herself. "What?" She was obviously enjoying it.

"Nothing." Because this happens to me every day. "Before I came over, I was talking to Brigitte about Natalya—"

"Yes, your ingénue. May I ask what you discussed?" I was losing my train of thought and was experiencing more arousal.

"Only if you stop that and behave yourself."

She reached over and stroked my erection. "Perhaps I should. I hadn't planned on letting you undress me, but I'm warming to the idea." She stopped caressing her breast and covered it. She sat up and crossed her legs. "Better?" Reluctantly, I nodded. "So, what's going on with Miss Constantinescu?"

To my chagrin, the erection continued to make itself plain. I thought of what to say, of what would take my mind off wanting to fuck this woman.

"Our friend, Xavier Dunkle, has developed a rather intense interest in Natalya, which Ms. DuBare finds alarming for a variety of reasons, centering mostly on the difference in their ages and their sexual-romantic experiences. She believes it's important for the young to experience romance with others their own age. Natalya, however, is not amused that we're butting into her personal business. I, personally, think she's more than capable of taking care of herself, but given that Dunkle is quite wealthy, and you have a yen for wealthy men, I'm curious what you think about it and, for my own interest, what drives you to approach men like me. Oh, and do you believe in the idea of romance and love?"

Monika took my hand and caressed it as she had her breast.

"I'm not opposed to the idea of love or romance. I think there's nothing better than being in love, but love isn't always the answer, is it? The better question is whether Mr. Dunkle and Miss Constantinescu find common ground, common interests. Love, assuming it's not simply infatuation or sexual desire, tends to come and go. My preference is to find compatibility first. There's always time for love to blossom later."

"Very practical."

"Practical makes more sense," she said.

"Does it?" Monika Danalek continued to caress my hand, running her fingers along the knuckles and fingertips. "Seems rather impersonal..."

"Not at all. If anything, it's more personal because you're looking beyond simple attraction. The world is full of attractive people that are otherwise completely incompatible with one another. It's far better to find someone you share common interests with, rather than whether you think they're hot or sexy."

"Uh-huh, and where does approaching them in an art gallery and whispering how much you'd like to suck their cock fit into that?"

Monika Danalek feigned shock. "If you remember, I asked you other things before that, such as what you thought of the art and the atmosphere of the gallery. I remember complimenting you on your choice of clothing, and remarking that you had a healthy skepticism when it came to the apparent value of the art we were viewing. And I'll admit it was probably poor manners to say what I said, but I was curious how you'd react, and I must say, you didn't act shocked, and you didn't suggest we find someplace quick to do it. I felt you were intrigued, if nothing else, and maybe open to something like it further down the road." Monika let go of my hand and leaned against the back of the couch. "I can see you're looking for the why—"

"Why what?"

Monika laughed. "There's no need for games between us. I'm interested in you and you're interested in me, if not, then why are you here?" Good question.

"Maybe I just came for the blowjob?"

"If you did, then you got what you wanted, but there's no guarantee the door will be open the next time." Her eyes continued to sparkle. "What are you worried about, Mr. *Buttman*?" Her laughter increased. "You know I didn't ask before, but are you an ass man?" Apparently Ms. Danalek had a sense of humor.

"Depends on the ass." I let the laughter die down before answering her real question. "My worry is that all that matters is the money, that you are only interested in me for that; that it's all a pretty act to flatter my ego. I mean, how do you know I'm not some pervert or abuser who just likes to fuck with people while on some power trip?"

Monika looked me up and down. A different sparkle began dancing in her light brown eyes. "I don't, but I'm not some foolish girl who goes and gets drunk at some frat house and is shocked to find she's been gang-banged. It's important to understand the world as it is, not as it ought to be. That's why I don't get all googly-eyed about love. As I said, I'm not averse to being in love, but there's more to being with someone than love. And yes, the money is important, and yes, I understand the cynicism you have that this is only about the money, but I do find you an attractive man, and I think we have many interests in common beyond sex. Believe it or not, I do a little research before I proposition a man. Besides, you've probably noticed I'm not embarrassed that men are drawn to me because of the way I look, and I'm not embarrassed or ashamed to use that to my advantage. It's the world we live in and a part of how this town works. People have to take care of themselves and I'm no different."

I could feel myself slipping from the whiskey and the talk.

"So, I leave Agnes for you because we have common interests, and yes, you are an attractive woman with wonderful curves and there's lots of money. But why wouldn't I just replace you down the road?"

The light in her eyes sparkled on. "There's nothing to say you won't. But let me ask you this. Is Agnes the only woman you've ever known? Have you never stopped being with someone for whatever reason, including money?" She saw the answer in my face. "People move on, Monk. This isn't the old days of my grandparents who rarely spoke to each other and considered divorce a sin." She sighed. "Or my parents, who thought being swingers was the answer to keeping their marriage alive."

"Apparently it wasn't. And the money?"

"That's what prenups are for, aren't they? I'm not terribly greedy, Monk. As you can see, I don't live beyond my means, but I like to be comfortable. I'm sure we could work something out that was equitable to us both. I like to think I'm a reasonable gold-digger," she said with a smile.

"Yes, we've established that you're a reasoned woman." I checked my watch. I should have been home hours ago.

"Time to go?" Monika was still smiling.

"Time to go." Monika rose with me, and walked me to the door. Her lips were still soft and wet.

"I'll leave my door open if you call. Goodbye, Monk."

•   •   •   •   •

Anna and Rebekah were waiting for me in the living room.

"Agnes go to bed?" I asked. Nothing else came to mind.

"No, mom's at your other house. She has to go in early tomorrow. Johnny's has some things going on and he needs her and she didn't want to fight the traffic in the morning,"

Makes sense. "And what can I do for you two?"

"We're worried about you and Agnes, Dad, and we wanted to talk to you about it." Rebekah appeared more composed than she did the last time we "talked."

"Did she ask you to talk to me?"

"Not directly, but we're not blind, you know." I know.

I sat down and then got up. I was hungry and thirsty. I signaled for them to follow me to the kitchen and directed them to sit on the stools along the island.

"I'd like to say that everything is fine between me and Agnes, and in my heart of hearts, I want it to be, but I feel worn down by her insecurities and, I don't know, by my own insecurities as well."

"Where were you tonight?" asked Anna. Where was I again?

"With a woman named Monika," I said, as I put together a sandwich. I stood across from them. Anna seemed confused while Rebekah had the same look she had as a teenager when I'd question her actions.

"Are you fucking this woman?" Rebekah was curious.

"I was under the impression it was Natalya," Anna said, parroting her mother.

I just shook my head. "I was looking for answers. In fact, I spent the entire day trying to make sense of things, but unfortunately no such luck. To answer your questions directly, since I can see you don't care for my evasions; no, I'm not fucking her, but I can if I want to, and no, Anna, despite what Agnes believes, and no matter how many times I've had to say this, I have never had any interest in Natalya whatsoever!"

"But you are out there looking for someone to replace Agnes or Judith, aren't you?" This from a woman who fucked her coworker so she could become pregnant without his knowledge.

"So, what *is* going on?" Anna implored.

"Are you sleeping with Mikal?" I asked.

"What does that have to do with you and Agnes?" demanded Rebekah.

"Nothing. But it is what your mother believes, just as she believes I'm screwing around with Natalya, and is either true?" Rebekah remained irked, but I could see that Anna was caught off guard, and that maybe, just maybe, with Joanie out of the way, something was brewing between Anna and Mikal.

"It's true, I like Mikal," Anna admitted.

Rebekah rolled her eyes, refusing to be distracted. "You didn't answer the question, and if you add up all the other little moves you've been making or suggesting lately, like our moving out and prenups, it seems pretty obvious that you've got plans that don't include us or Agnes."

"And that adds up to me clearing out the house so it can once again be my playhouse with some hot young thing now that I'm growing tired of Agnes."

"So, you admit you're growing tired of Agnes?" Rebekah sat there with her arm crossed, her person swelled with indignation.

"Is that true, Monk?" Anna's eyes were tearing up.

"No. I don't know. Sometimes. But I'm not trying to replace her. If anything, I'm trying to get back to where we were before, and that's what all these little moves of mine are about."

"Bullshit, Dad!" Rebekah glared at me.

Anna wiped her eyes. "Then what?" she asked.

"I'm pretty sure I've gone over that already. All I want is to be with Agnes and that's what I'm working towards. Whether it works or not, I don't know, but I feel compelled to try."

"And that means spending the evening with some strange woman instead of being here?" More accusations from my cynical daughter.

"Sometimes it does. I called Agnes and she didn't answer, and I called more than once."

"That's your excuse?"

"I didn't say it was a good one..." I didn't like being put on the defensive.

"Oh, but you were able to find out that your new friend Monika was willing to fuck you, so it's all good, right?" Fuck!

"No, but if women like Monika think I'm no longer rich, then they'll go back to ignoring me, which, believe it or not, is what I find I prefer."

Rebekah exploded. "But you are rich, Goddammit! This is just a lot of bullshit arguing that shows you're saying one thing, but really planning on doing the other."

I stared at the two of them; angry Rebekah and teary Anna. The lying duplicitous Buttman just stood there. My legs were starting to weaken.

"I need to sit down. We can continue this on the couch unless you're done with me." I headed for the couch and the two of them followed after a fashion.

"I don't want you to keep stringing along Agnes if you're ready to fuck someone else. It's not fair and it's not right." Rebekah stomped off as she had the other night. Anna stood there wavering.

"I found a place to live," she said at last.

"Sit down, Anna." She thought about it before sitting down.

"It's close to the Manifesto. It's not very big, but I don't need a lot of room—"

"Is this the same place where Mikal lives?" I knew he had moved to a place not far from the Manifesto after Joanie left and the bungalows had to be cleared out.

"He said there was an apartment open in his building and I checked it out, and while it's a little pricy, I think I can manage."

"I can help while business picks up."

She smiled just a little. "I didn't mean it like that."

I smiled back. "Then why don't we see how it goes and if you need a little help, you'll know it's available. How about that?"

"Ok." She stood and then sat back down. "You're not going to ask me about Mikal?"

"No. Like Natalya, I think you can make your own decisions about your life. If you want to talk to me about Mikal, I know you'll ask." She raised her eyebrows at Natalya's name.

"Ok," Anna stood up, "I know it's not up to me, but I hope you and mom work things out."

I stood up and hugged her. "So do I."

18

I expected Rebekah to head off to work with Fidel, but found her feeding her kids as I rolled into the kitchen after forcing myself out of bed.

"Gamps!" exclaimed Zach.

"Little dude. How's everybody this morning?" Lizzy waved her hands amid small bites of baby food.

"Everybody's fine, Dad."

I was surprised. "I thought you were mad at me?"

She shrugged. "I am mad at you, but Fidel reminded me that yelling at you is pointless." Probably. "I want to know where you met this woman, Monika, if you don't mind my asking?" Still on point.

"At an art gallery about six, seven months ago." I poured a cup of coffee and sat down by Zach. He was working through a bowl of Cheerios and blueberries.

"Is she an artist?"

"I don't think so. She just likes art."

"Uh-huh. How old is she?" I hadn't thought of that.

"I don't know. If I had to guess, I say she's in her early or mid-thirties."

"Huh…" Rebekah didn't seem too impressed. Maybe if I explained that we had common interests, and that she was adept at oral sex… "Is she worth all the heartache this would cause?"

"Only if I was actually leaving Agnes, but as I'm not, the heartache will have to wait."

Rebekah just shook her head. "I don't understand, I mean there must be something, otherwise why even admit you were with her?"

"I wasn't interested in lying to you." Simple enough.

"My, how noble, and this idiotic talk about being poor again?"

"Yeah, that didn't come out right. What I meant was I'm going to limit my activities with the trust and turn all of its administration over to

Macklgrew's firm. I don't need the money. As for the house, I can sell it, or rent it, or keep it, but not a place to live, or as a place for trysts with Monika or anybody else. I'd rather go back to our place in West Covina. Maybe that's not realistic; maybe there's too much water under the bridge, but that's the plan, and that's what I'm going to do." Zach had lost interest in eating, and was playing with his food. I took the bowl, noted his disapproval, and wiped his face. "And if that's not enough, there's Jacob's death and all this stuff with Natalya and Anna..." I remembered I hadn't sent Art Devaney the information on Jacob.

"What about Jacob and Natalya and Anna?" she asked. Exactly.

"Agnes is worried that Anna is involved with Mikal, which I thought was nonsense but apparently isn't. Brigitte DuBare is worried that Natalya is getting involved with Xavier Dunkle, but Dunkle's no lothario, and Natalya's probably more than he can handle."

"And Jacob?"

"I don't know, but something's not right. I found out some things concerning him and the guys he was serving with; some of whom also killed themselves and... I don't know. Maybe Moses is right, maybe something terrible did happen while they were in Afghanistan... I don't know. Maybe it's just war. Maybe that's all it is, simple as that."

Rebekah looked at me, not knowing whether to believe me or not. Either way, she cleaned up Lizzy and stood up from the table. She came over and kissed my forehead before smacking my shoulder and sighing, "I'm still mad at you."

.   .   .   .   .

Art Devaney, on the other hand, was delighted to hear from me. I gave him the information Captain Sinnons had given me.

"Yeah, that jibs with what I found," he chuckled.

"Then why did I have to get it?"

"Corroboration is essential in this business, Monk."

I took a deep cleansing breath. Zach, who was supposed to be napping, was watching from his pen. He, too, took a deep breath or tried to. "Does that mean you found something?"

"First, tell me what you heard from the colonel."

I passed on what Sinnons and Jaron had said, which boiled down to shit happens, and that they, too, were concerned with the deaths surrounding the guys in Jacob's company.

"And the sergeant?" I was surprised that Devaney remembered a passing reference to Sergeant MacMillan.

"I was told he retired and they weren't allowed to say any more. Why do you ask?"

"Because it turns out your boys and the sergeant sent up a red flag when I inquired about them." I could tell he found all this very exciting.

"What do you mean red flag?"

"Most military reporting is fairly dry stuff and the official record of the deaths of Privates Dezi and Lambert hewed to what was reported in the papers, but I have a friend at the Pentagon and when I asked about it, he said it was a wash—"

"A wash?"

"Just something we say. It refers to an incident that ended up being scrubbed or cleaned for any number of reasons. That implies the deaths of the two marines were more problematic than just a patrol gone bad. My friend will see what he can find, but it's possible whatever happened was scrubbed locally before the official report was submitted. If that's true and the higher ups Ok'd it with prior consent, then who knows. That brings us to the sergeant. He was a trained relations specialist there to deal with the Marine's interactions with local Afghan communities. However, prior to that, his specialty was unit cohesion restoration, a fancy term for dealing with troubled units, and apparently Jacob's platoon was one of them."

I knew the answer but had to ask. "What kind of conflict?"

He hesitated. "There were reports of hazing, sexual intimidation, violence, but none had moved past the immediate commander, who deemed the complaints more smoke than fire, and whatever initiated the complaints were handled locally. There were no NJP's handed out."

"What are those?"

More chuckling. "Non-Judicial Punishments. It's what commanders are allowed to hand out if the offense doesn't merit a court-martial." Like we all know military jargon.

"Oh. Well thanks."

"No problem. If I hear anything more, I'll let you know." He paused. "I assume you'd like to find this Sergeant MacMillan?"

"I would. He seems to be the key to all this."

"He may very well be. Goodbye, Monk."

Zach was still staring at me.

Rebekah had run off to talk with a consultant about their company's books and the state of their finances. She promised it wouldn't take too long. I kept Zach quiet while Lizzy slept and handed back control when Rebekah returned.

"I assume you'll be back tomorrow? I don't have to leave till ten so it shouldn't be too bad of a drive."

"I don't know what you're talking about."

She thought that was cute. "You're supposed to meet Agnes at work and the expectation is you're staying on that side of town for the night." Both she and Zach had broad smiles across their smarmy faces.

"I see. And how was I to know this?"

"If you had been here last night instead of fucking around with your new girlfriend, you would have." And with that, she walked off with Zach, who was staring at me over his mother's shoulder.

•　　•　　•　　•　　•

Rey handed me a drink. I'd known the guy for four years now, and he hadn't changed at all. Wore the same white shirt and the same dark trousers; had the same haircut for the same shock of white covering his head. His weathered face did not appear to have aged any. How is that possible I asked myself; he has to be over eighty? I looked around, half expecting Agnes to come out guns blazing, but Agnes wasn't here. In truth, I didn't expect her to be, or Johnny, who was out of town. It was just me and Rey and two characters at the end of the bar. They were deep in conversation and far enough away that I didn't have to hear any of it. It's always good to count your blessings.

"Agnes mention when she'd be back?" Rey smiled; everybody was smiling today.

"Couldn't say." He wiped the counter before setting his forearms on the bar and leaning towards me. "When you gonna marry Agnes, Monk?"

"When she signs the prenup," I said with no emotion.

"Gotta happen?"

It was my turn to smile. "Gotta happen, Rey. No other choice. Otherwise, she risks getting nothing. Hopefully, the lawyer she's talking to will tell her that. Sad to say, but just because she knows me and we live together doesn't mean she's entitled to any of it. Besides, it's a good deal, whether I drop dead or she gets tired of me. And it's more money than she'd ever need unless she starts spending like crazy or gets ripped off."

"Yeah, sometimes bets don't pay off. You gotta be smart and take the for sure rather than the maybe," Rey reasoned.

"Exactly," I took a long swig of the whiskey and winced as it burned my throat. "It's a smart move because it provides a legal claim that guarantees her stake. No fighting with me or relatives or anything like that. It's bankable."

Rey stood up. The characters were thirsty. "Agnes worries this is a buyout, Monk." Concern had replaced the smile.

"Agnes is wrong, Rey. Thanks for the drink."

If I was supposed to wait, I preferred to wait at home.

The house, not far from the bar, was quiet and dark. The bed was unmade; some things never change, but other than that it was the same as when I'd been by a few days before. I made the bed and checked the kitchen to see if there was any food. For some bizarre reason, I thought maybe Agnes had gone shopping.

The answer was no.

We'd all gotten lazy with Theresa doing the shopping and keeping the house clean in Beverly. If I was serious about being back here full time, I'd have to get back in the shopping groove. Turns out it wasn't too bad and oddly therapeutic to be wandering the aisles, dealing with morons, and having to do all the work myself.

"It's all too much!" I said out loud, laughing. I don't think the stock boy in produce got the joke. There was no Agnes when I got back, so I put away the groceries, turned the radio to the jazz station, and went out back to mingle with the rhythms of life. I had a cold beer and Mingus to keep me company. I fell asleep.

Agnes was sitting across from me when I woke up.

"What'd the lawyer say?"

She had a drink in her hands. "That it was a good deal." She didn't seem particularly happy to be the recipient of a good deal.

"I told you it was."

"That's not what worries me." I wondered if it was too late to go back to sleep.

"I'm aware of that and, for the record, the prenup isn't intended as a buyout or a kiss-off or anything like that. It's simply to afford you some financial stability in the unlikely event I don't last too long. There's nothing sinister behind it." I raised my bottle to her and took a drink.

"Why don't I believe that?"

"I don't know, because it's easy not to, because it's in your nature to worry and find problems even if they don't exist. Whatever it is, is your problem."

"And the woman you were with last night?" God bless Rebekah.

"All part of the plan, and, I was only there a few hours, but you wouldn't know that because you'd left by the time I got back." Agnes got up and threw her drink at me. Unfortunately, or fortunately, depending on which side of the toss you were on, the drink sailed wide right. It was my turn to get up. "Are you hungry?" Agnes just stood there. "Come on, you can help. I hear you're quite handy in the kitchen now." I reached for her hand and after a moment she took it.

I had Agnes clean the vegetables while I prepared the chops. I poured her a fresh glass of wine when she finished, and joined her at the table while the chops cooked.

"I want to know what you were doing with that woman last night."

"Running around naked." Agnes didn't see the humor in that.

"I'm not interested in your stupid smartassed jokes right now."

"Alright, alright. I hadn't planned on seeing her, but you were blowing me off and I was having bad day, so I figured what the fuck. I called her and asked if she wanted to have a drink. She said yes, so we had a drink. That's what we did."

Agnes started to say something, but instead reached into her purse and tossed a manila envelope onto the table. "There's your goddamned prenup."

I opened the envelope and out came the prenup. Signed, notarized, and ready to go.

"Excellent. Now we can finally get this show rolling." I put the prenup back in the envelope. "Tomorrow we can drop it off at A and A on the way to the courthouse."

There was confusion on Agnes' face. "Why do we have to take it to the courthouse, can't Taylor do that?"

"We're not going to the courthouse to deliver the prenup. That's a separate issue. We're going to the courthouse to get married," I said nonchalantly.

"Get married?"

"Yes, get married. As far as a celebration or wedding goes, we can work that out, and if you want to hold off telling people till we have a wedding, that's fine too, but this is a onetime offer, for you, Agnes Duquesne, you and only you. I'm not offering this deal to anyone else, just you, so if you seriously want to marry me then I recommend you take it."

Agnes sat there with her mouth open. "You're serious..."

"I'm serious."

"Don't we have to make an appointment?"

"My lawyer is tight with a number of judges and she said she could get us in."

"Seriously?"

That made me laugh. "Seriously," I said.

"What about this other woman?"

I thought about it. "Naw, I don't think I can be married to two people; too much work." Oddly, Agnes didn't find that funny.

"You know what I mean."

"You mean am I going to see her? Am I going to make her my Judith replacement? Go back to having my little fantasy up in that beautiful house while you wait for me to come home at the end of the day?"

"That's what I mean." I could see all the damage and the hurt settling in her eyes.

"No."

"Then why go see her? Why let her think that you're available?"

The timer for the chops started buzzing. I rose and turned the timer off, took out the chops and set them on the trivet. I took two plates out of the cupboard and set them on the table. Agnes got the salad she'd made, and I divided up the chops.

"I wanted to see her because I needed to know, wanted to know, and I wasn't disappointed. This isn't about replacing Judith or having a good thing on the side. This is about what I'm capable of; what I'm willing to do. I don't have any interest in trying to find another Judith, and Monika is not Judith. That said, she's not the answer to my problems because having someone else isn't the answer to my problems. It's just an easy way out."

Agnes was shaking her head. "Is it possible for you to speak in good old plain English for once?"

I raised my wineglass to her. She raised hers while rolling her eyes. "Fine. The simple answer is, it's not what I want. I'm sure Monika would be a lot of fun, and a lot of work, but I already have that with you. Maybe she stroked my ego—"

"What else did she stroke?" snarked Agnes.

"May I please finish?" She groused a bit before letting me continue. "Like I said, she played to my ego and said a lot of nice things, and after having a bad day with the Jacob stuff, and…" I thought about implying that Agnes was somehow complicit in my going to Monika's because she ignored my calls, but I was already on thin ice. "Anyway, at the end of our talk I realized what I already knew; I can't be that guy. I can't be a rich prick who preens from one place to the next and does whatever he wants. It's why I'm turning over control of the trust. It's why I want everyone out of the Beverly Hills house. I want my life back and that doesn't include anyone other than you, because I don't need anyone other than you, and goddamnit, you're the one I love, and if we're married and we're living in our nice little house then I can go back to being what I am, which is a lazy guy who occasionally takes his grandkids to the beach."

Agnes shook her head. "I think you're full of shit, Buttman."

It was worth a try.

19

Agnes continued to believe I was full of shit right up to the point where we were ushered into Judge Policy's chambers for the big to do.

She ignored me throughout the previous evening, but pulled me close once we were in bed. The *I'm not buying this, Buttman* expression followed us as we stopped at A and A to drop off the prenup. Ms. Lagenfelder had the decency to keep her skepticism in check while phoning the courthouse to find an available justice. It wasn't till Rachel, the judge's assistant, set out the license and had us stand before him that it dawned on Agnes that this was for real.

"Do you even have a ring, Buttman?"

I feigned shock. "You already have an engagement ring, but I have its companion and I have one for me." I pulled them out of my pocket.

I promised to love, honor, and cherish, and not fuck around with a woman named Monika. Agnes promised to love, honor, and cherish, and not obsess that one day I'd tire of her and run away with a woman named Monika.

At least she'd given up on me lusting after Natalya.

The ceremony concluded with a big sloppy kiss.

Agnes stared at me, and the ring on my finger, as we waited for our order at the In-N-Out on Sunset.

"Do you want to tell anyone or keep this our little secret?" I asked.

"I'm still trying to wrap my head around the fact that we're actually married. I mean, I'd pretty much given up on you ever going through with it and now..." She put our ring fingers together, which made me groan. "Oh, grow up, Sunshine."

"Ok, it's nice I don't have to hear about it anymore."

Agnes ignored that. "I love you, Sunshine."

"I love you, Beautiful." Finally, there was that smile that made me sure I wasn't making a big mistake. It was also the moment our burgers were ready. On the way home, she sat close to me and put her head on my shoulder; God bless bench seats and classic convertibles. She kissed me for a long time after we pulled into the garage at the house on the hill.

"It's just me from now on, right Monk?"

"It's been just you for some time, but yes, it's just you from now on." Agnes smiled and then pinched me.

"I'm holding you to that, Buttman."

Lovely, I thought, as I rubbed where she'd pinched me.

"You never said whether you wanted to say anything about our getting married..."

"Well, it's kinda hard to not say anything with both of us wearing wedding rings." She once again put our hands together. I'm pretty sure I groaned again. "But I still want a for real ceremony someday soon, ok?"

'Ok.' There was time for one last smooch before we went in.

. . . . .

The kids were thrilled, surprised, and in the case of my dear daughter, deeply suspicious. But she could hassle me later about whatever sneaky shit she thought I was up to. I made reservations for dinner and got Anna, Jones, Coretta, MaryAnn; even Johnny D, who had magically returned from parts unknown, to join us. I invited Rey, but apparently Rey never leaves the bar. Coretta and Johnny couldn't have been happier for us, and Mr. Jones told me it was about fucking time. He pulled me aside, away from the others.

"I expect you to be good to your woman, Buttman."

"Yeah, yeah, yeah," I teased.

"Don't you dare yeah, yeah, yeah me, motherfucker. I will be pissed if I hear you're playing around on her. You're married now, right?"

"As far as I know." I noted his sense of humor on the subject was right there with Agnes'.

"Then you do right by her!" He not so lightly patted me on the back. "How's Jacob? You talk to him?" I stared at my big black friend, wishing I had another joke.

"No. Jacob killed himself after he got home last week." Mr. Jones stood there. In all the years I'd known him, I'd never before seen the light go out of his eyes or sadness cross his face. I thought for a moment he might tear up.

"I'm sorry, man. Was it because of…what the woman in Watts said?"

"Possibly, but I think something else is going on. I went back to Watts yesterday and asked to read Kurtis' diary. I think something happened that involved all those guys, including the two who were killed on patrol. It had talk about making things right and pacts. I asked Art to see what he could find since he has contacts at the Pentagon. His guy says it smells a little odd, but right now there's nothing other than suspicion."

Jones pondered that. "You remember I told you shit happens, right?" I nodded. Mr. Jones was lost in thought. Coretta was calling us back to the table. "I tell you I saw your friend Manny hanging out across the street from the Manifesto the other day? I assume looking for you?"

"Did I tell you he went in at the same time Jacob did, along with Lewis and Cameron?"

Jones raised his left eyebrow. "I don't remember that. You ain't thinking of talking to that punk, are you?" He seemed alarmed at the prospect.

"He was there. He knew them. Maybe he knows something, heard something. It can't hurt to ask."

Jones was shaking his head "He stuck a gun in your ribs, man!" That little comment drew the attention of everyone at the table. All of them, minus Johnny, who smiled, seemed shocked.

"No problem," I assured them. Jones frowned while Johnny laughed.

The rest of the evening was mercifully free of any talk of dead brothers or unfaithful boyfriends. For the first time in my life, I was officially married, with a certificate from the state of California to back it up. No youthful vows in an empty church as I had done with Astral. Instead, I stood before the honorable Judge Policy and made plain my willingness to do the right thing by Agnes.

My wife.

Agnes. Agnes Duquesne. A nasty thought occurred to me. I turned to my beloved. "Does this mean I can call you Agnes Buttman now?"

Agnes smiled and patted my knee. "No, it does not," she said, to the delight of everyone at the table except Monk Buttman.

He said, "Suit yourself."

The party shifted to the beautiful house on the hill, for once used in its intended and future purpose. We toasted our getting this taken care of, which once again seemed predicated more on my reluctance than anything else. I nobly held my tongue rather than respond to the veracity of the accusation. That, and it was probably true. The city stayed lit up and the sky clear. A warm breeze kept us comfortable, and why not? People didn't live here to be miserable.

It was, if only to me, a curious moment. I'd had qualms about marrying Agnes, yet wanted nothing more than to be with her and grow old doing my SoCal thing. Floundering under the weight of my actions, whether foolish or not, I was under no illusions about my susceptibility to the charms of women like Monika Danalek. I wanted to believe that Agnes, and the ring around my finger, would keep me on the straight and narrow, but I hadn't been on the straight and narrow since the day I met Judith and Agnes.

I wanted to do the right thing.

Isn't that what Mr. Jones was demanding of me?

We said goodnight as, one by one, our guests headed home. They were happy for us and I wanted to believe them. I also wanted to believe that being rich was hard, that it was weighing me down, but curvy Monika Danalek cured me of that lie.

It was easy being rich.

Nobody cares when you're poor; an ugly fact of life. People ignore you. Doesn't matter if you wear fine clothes if they're second hand. Doesn't matter if you have a classic convertible; it's still an old car. Doesn't matter if it's an architectural representation of old LA; it's still a cheap little bungalow. It's easy to be a nobody when you have little. Agnes and Judith were anomalies. Agnes was lonely and broken; Judith angry and bored. I was Mr. Opportunity.

The three of us.

We just wanted to be loved.

I don't know what Judith was thinking when she decided to leave me her money. Maybe she thought I'd treat it as I did her, because I loved her. But Judith built a beautiful cage for herself, not me. I was not congenitally predisposed to the idle life of a rich man. I was predisposed to the idle life of a nobody. Women like Monika didn't offer oral sex to some dude in a used suit driving an old Ford, no matter how charming. But put a cool three hundred and forty million dollars in his pocket and the man quickly becomes interesting, maybe a little eccentric, and he can afford all the women he wants. If Agnes got pissed because he spent his day being pleasured by a woman in Hollywood, well, she got her settlement. Same with the woman in Hollywood. That's the way it works. Would it be the way I worked?

"What are you thinking about, Sunshine? Why so serious?" Agnes was watching me.

"Moses," I answered.

"Moses? It's a little late to call, you can tell them tomorrow."

That made me sigh. "It's not that, but you're right we should call tomorrow."

In my head were Moses and his sermons about the corrosive nature of wealth and its seductions, until you're reduced to a caricature of a human being sucking the life out of others for nothing more than your idle pleasures, turning yourself into a junkie, a cipher, a grotesquerie; a mockery of God's vision of man.

Agnes was unbuttoning my shirt.

"Something on your mind, Beautiful?"

"I believe it's customary that we consummate our marriage." She was gently tugging on my tie, leading me towards the bedroom.

"I believe you're right."

Some things you gotta do.

•   •   •   •   •

Zach and Lizzy were fascinated by Gamps' ring. Gamps rarely wears anything other than a watch; a second-hand watch, because Gamps has issues. Ag, who does not like to be called grammy or grandma or mee-maw, because she has issues, thought their fascination was cute.

"Gamps has a nice ring, doesn't he?" The kids nodded in agreement. "It means he has to be nice to me forever and ever, right, Sunshine?"

I just shook my head. "Did Anna tell you she's found a place?" The kids noticed the scowl on Grammy's face.

"Yes, she told me yesterday while you were talking to Mr. Jones, I mean Orville."

I snickered. "Orville? You've never called him Orville before!"

"Coretta doesn't care for Mr. Jones; it's his work name. She asked me to call him Orville, so I'm trying to remember to call him Orville. Is that alright with you?"

"I'm just curious, that's all. You don't like that Anna has found a place?"

"If you paid attention when I talk to you, you'd know the answer to that," she huffed.

I pretended to be shocked. "I always listen to you when you talk." Well, most of the time. "It's because it's in the same building as Mikal's isn't it?"

More scowling; "I don't like it. He's a lot older than she is." I laughed. "What's so funny, Buttman?"

"Oh, it's just that that seems to be a common theme here lately. Ms. DuBare is worried about Natalya getting involved with Dunkle. You're worried about Anna and Mikal—"

"And you and that Monika woman!"

"Yes, we can't forget about me and that Monika woman. But it's not that uncommon for women to be involved with older men. I'm older than you are," I reasoned.

"Twenty years is a lot more than three, Buttman." Lizzy wanted onto Grammy's lap.

"True, but Mikal's a good guy and it's possible Anna is seeing more in this than is actually there." Agnes wasn't buying.

"Really, Buttman?" She picked up Lizzy.

"I'm just throwing stuff against the wall to see if it sticks. Do you want me to put the screws to Mikal, see what he's up to? I have to go down there today."

Agnes thought about it. "Well, maybe in a nice way."

•   •   •   •   •

Mikal had carved out a small office for himself just off the food court. The idea was to minimize the space for administration to allow more space for instruction, practice, and performance. As I entered the building, I noticed someone lurking in an alleyway across the street. Manny, I assumed. I sent a text to Jones just in case he was still worried for my safety. Mikal, as always, was happy to see me.

"Monk," he got up and shook my hand, "I was going to call and let you know everything is copacetic. We got the last of the rooms finished, the scheduling app is working great; we're already filling up the rehearsal spaces, and there are concerts and shows booked for the next six months. It's very exciting."

It was hard not to get caught up in his excitement. Mikal was clearly in his element and loving every minute of it. From early on, he got the music community to join in and get the word out. The only point of concern was the compensation for his time. A salary? A percentage of the gross receipts? A grant? That in itself was contentious because the whole idea was to give aspiring artists and musicians a place to learn, rehearse, and perform. But most artists and musicians are, by the very nature of the business, broke, which limits income potential as Macklgrew warned me.

Having been through all of that, Mikal was wide-eyed about what to expect; not a lot, and he was upfront about this. He was also upfront about wanting to simplify his life, which I learned is code in the music business for not touring your ass off, fighting for money, and still being essentially broke regardless of how well known you were.

In other words, is there any possible way he could earn a reasonable income doing this?

Being the easy touch that I am, and not wanting to be the bad guy, I had money added to cover his time and energy.

I blamed Jones. When I first met him, he was a struggling promoter who made most of his money in the security business. He had dreams of being like the big shots his security company protected from the unwashed masses. But that didn't pan out, and he found he was more interested in helping struggling musicians find a place to perform than in becoming the next bigshot promoter.

"Aren't there plenty of those places in LA already?" I asked, not that I was particularly interested.

"Yeah, a lot of people come here trying to make it big, but most of them have stars in their eyes and want to make millions, and that ain't going to happen if you're into jazz or the blues or anything that ain't pop music. I want to help those people," he mused, not that he particularly cared whether I was interested or not.

That all changed when Judith Delashay decided I was the person to whom her fortune should be left.

"What you gonna do with all that money, Buttman?" Jones, after I informed him of Judith's duplicity, had a mischievous sparkle in his eyes. He noted the surprised look on my face. "People gonna be asking you for money, brother, and I'm willing to get in line." His broad smile was clear evidence I might not enjoy being wealthy.

"Does this mean I can call you brother, brother?" My turn to smile. Orville's smile disappeared into the character of Mr. Jones.

"We talked about this, Buttman; you ain't a brother, so no. That's the way it is." He was quite resolute in this matter.

"Doesn't sound very fair..."

"This from a white dude with more money than sense," he harrumphed.

"Meh," was all I could come up with.

This was all definitely his fault. Where was I again?

No sooner had I sat down in Mikal's little office than my wife's daughter sauntered in. She was, to coin a phrase; caught off guard. Mikal was not.

"Come in, Anna. I think Monk's here to find out what's going on between us," he said, rather whimsically.

20

"So, what *is* going on?" I asked.

Anna looked at Mikal, who looked at me. "I don't know that anything is going on—"

"We just went out a few times. It's no big deal. Mikal's just helping me out, that's all." Anna apparently felt the need to interrupt Mikal, which made me smile.

"Personally, I'm not worried either way, but your mother is, so all I ask is that you be forthcoming if this is more than what it appears."

Anna frowned in a way that reminded me of Agnes. "I'm a grown woman. I can make my own decisions. She needs to accept that." Now where have I heard that before? Mikal sat there smiling.

"I'm just saying..." I gave her my smarmiest grin. "Is your establishment of business open yet?"

"Couple more minutes. I had a few questions for Mikal. You don't mind, do you?" Anna returned the grin.

"Not at all." I got up. "See you in a few." I left the lovebirds, or whatever they were, to themselves.

Manny Pronto was still there on the other side of the street, slightly obscured by the brick of the building he was huddled against. I shook my head and waved him over. He acted like he didn't see me, or I was talking to someone else.

"Manny!" I shouted, "Get your ass over here."

He told me to go fuck myself, but soon enough he had crossed the street.

"Hungry?" He looked hungry.

"A little..."

"Then let's get something to eat." I directed him to follow me. Anna having returned to her kitchen, eyed the slovenly Manny before eyeing me, and took our order. Manny followed me to a small table by the front windows.

"I want my gun back," he mouthed while stuffing his face.

"When was the last time you had something to eat?" I ignored the request for the return of his property, assuming it was his in the first place.

"I don't know, a couple days maybe..." he finished his plate before I even started mine. I said it was ok if he went back for more. Anna motioned to me from afar as Manny stood there. I assured her it was ok. I was buying.

"Give him as much as he wants," I instructed. I figured a full Manny might be easier to pump for answers. Jones saw me as he walked in front of the building. Manny didn't see him; he had his back to the window. Jones came in and I told him to get himself something to eat if he was hungry. Manny watched as Jones walked by. "It'll be alright," I assured him, "no problems." Jones ordered a sandwich and joined us. His expression of concern had not changed.

"Where are you living?" I asked.

Manny looked at me, *like you're kidding, right?* "I live on the streets."

"You know Kurtis Santos and Mason Saunders from your days in the Marines? I heard they were homeless too."

He looked up between mouthfuls. "I heard they were dead."

"Did you know them?"

Manny Pronto fidgeted. "Why do you want to know?"

"For the same reason I want to know why you think I should hand over money you believe I stole from your long dead uncles. I'm curious that way." Jones also noticed our dirty little friend squirm. We waited for him to swallow.

"I knew 'em," he said at last. "I heard they were queer and living in a camp off the viaduct. Then I found out they were dead."

"Were you in Afghanistan when they were?" I asked.

"Which time? They were deployed twice. I was there the first time, but the last time I wasn't. I was in Iraq when I got injured."

"What part?" asked Jones.

"Mosul," he said, almost in a whisper.

"What happened?" I asked.

"What the fuck do you care?" His head was in his chest.

"Good question, but for the time being let's say we do."

He looked between me and Jones. "We were part of a caravan of trucks being delivered to the Iraqis when the truck in front of us hit an IED. The truck blew up and smashed into us. I ended up with a skull fracture and a broken arm." Manny pulled aside part of the mash of brown hair to expose a long scar. "Anyway, after that I had some problems with my sergeant, and the drugs for the pain didn't help. I got into a fight with him and they kicked me out. When I got back, I had a hard time getting straight and my fucking mother wouldn't leave me alone so I came down here."

"Are you still addicted to the painkillers?" I asked. "Is that what you want the money for?"

"I want the money to start over! I don't need any fucking drugs anymore!" He seemed put out by my question.

"And you thought sticking a gun in my ribs was the answer to your problems?"

Manny Pronto stared at us, his face tight with anger and loathing. Jones and I went back to our lunches. Manny relented after realizing we weren't intimidated.

"So maybe it wasn't a good idea. It was something to try, and how is jail any worse than being on the street?"

Jones shook his head. "Because you never get out from it, dumbass. It's one thing to be homeless. It's another to be an ex-con and you're already down one strike because of your discharge, huh?"

Manny didn't like that either, but knew it was true. "What the fuck does it matter anyway?" he pouted.

"Ain't you kinda young to not give a shit?" Jones was getting angry. "You got your whole life ahead of you; anything could happen, and you're sitting here acting like it's all over. You gonna shoot yourself like the others? You gonna just give up? I don't get that. You think God don't give a shit? Makes me crazy listening to this kinda shit." Jones leaned forward towards Manny. "You say you kicked the drugs?"

Manny didn't know quite what to say. "Yeah?" he muttered.

"Yes or no?" Jones demanded.

"I kicked 'em, ok!"

Jones sat back, still shaking his head. "You get yourself clean and then you say what the fuck? You see the problem here? Why are you still on the street? Don't you know how to work on trucks? You know a trade, right?"

"I'm tired of that." He didn't seem convinced.

"Tired of that? Goddamn. Then what you gonna do other than believe some pipedream that Buttman here's gonna throw some money at you?" Manny looked at me. I shrugged.

"I'm curious, just how much money do you think I stole from your uncles?" I asked.

"Grandma was sure it was at least fifty grand—"

"Well, get over that. I'm not giving you fifty grand. I asked you before, but what else you got? Like Jones says, what's the plan if there's no money?"

A sheepish half grin on his face said it all. "I don't really have a plan. It's hard, man."

Jones wasn't having it. "Have you tried to get any help? I know the VA's tough because of your discharge. You tried the city or the county, any of the veteran outreach programs? They're out there. We got one at our church, but you got to be clean or you got to be honest about getting clean. Ain't nobody gonna help you if you ain't willing to help yourself."

Manny's sheepish grin was gone. "Not really..."

"Not really?" Jones was on a roll. "Motherfucker, get off your dead ass, stop feeling sorry for yourself, get cleaned up, and goddamnit, be a man. Didn't you learn nothing being a Marine?"

Manny seemed offended by that. "What do *you* know about being a Marine?"

"Nothing, motherfucker. I'm Army green through and through, but I did my time and been to war so you can't bullshit me. And I know how different the world looks when you get back, but that's how it is and you got to organize yourself and move on. You're a mechanic, right?"

"I worked on diesels."

"You any good?"

Manny didn't like that either. "I know what I'm doing."

Jones crossed his arms. "Yeah, we noticed. I know a number of garages looking for good mechanics, but you got to get cleaned up."

"I'm homeless, remember?"

Jones and I looked at one another. "I'm gonna ignore the stupidity of that remark. I'll get a hold of my pastor." Jones leaned in. "You ain't got a problem with black folks, do you?"

"No. I worked with lots of black guys," he said.

"If you want help, we can help, but no bullshit and no drugs. Got that?" Manny Pronto nodded yes, but he looked confused by what was happening. I still wanted to know what he knew about Jacob and the others who all enlisted together.

"Your mother says you knew Mason and the others from school."

Like his mother, once comfortable, Manny was a chatterbox. He knew all of them, some better than others. Seth Cameron, Al Lewis, Jacob, Mason Saunders, and Mallon Dezi were all northern California boys. Kurtis Santos and Raphael Lambert were from different parts of LA. They got along well. After boot camp and infantry training; SOI he called it, they split off to their separate schools. Most went to advanced infantry, Manny to vehicle maintenance. He saw them periodically, both at Pendleton and in Afghanistan. I asked if he noticed any changes in them.

"I think the biggest change was in Dez. He was kind of a quiet guy, you know, but when I saw him later, I thought he was a bit of a dick, mouthed off a lot and pushy. He was big, so he was intimidating. He got into weights and that kind of thing. You should ask Jacob; he knew him better than I did."

"Jacob is dead. He killed himself last week."

Manny's face fell. "Like Santos and Saunders," he said.

"You ever hear anything about them; maybe from Lewis?" I asked. That surprised him.

"What about Lewis?" I could tell he knew something.

"Lewis is AWOL, but I think you already knew that. He told me where to find Jacob's body. Somehow knew my number, so he was there or knew what Jacob was planning. What do you know about this, Manny?"

He stared between me and Jones. Jones put his sunglasses back on and sat there with his arms crossed, more implied intimidation. "I don't know anything about that. I know Lewis lit out, and I think he's back home. I heard there'd been some trouble during their last time in country, but I don't know what happened. Lewis just said it was bad."

"When was the last time you heard from him?" I asked.

"Just before he split. It was after he found out Santos and Saunders were dead. I haven't heard from him since." I watched his eyes dart between me and Jones. I was sure he was lying but decided not to push for more. I knew he'd blow me off.

I paid Anna, and reluctantly Mr. Jones agreed to take our slovenly ex-Marine to his church. He phoned ahead so they wouldn't be shocked by his white companion. Manny protested about getting his stuff. Jones assured him they'd take care of that.

Anna quietly moved next to me as I watched them drive off.

"Who is that guy?"

"It's a long story better told when there's nothing else to talk about." I motioned for her to sit down. "What's on your mind?"

"I don't want you to get the wrong idea about me and Mikal."

I laughed. "We wouldn't want that. So, why don't you give me the right idea I should have about you and Mikal."

Anna sat there collecting her thoughts. Apparently, there was no pre-rehearsed explanation. "It's not like there's any big thing going on," she stammered. "I mean, we've gone out a few times—"

"You mentioned that already," I helpfully added.

"Ok, so he's older than me. Maybe by a lot, but neither of us see this as some kind of hookup or a long-term relationship. It's just that... he knows what it's like to have dreams and that it's a lot of work. He isn't constantly trying to get into my pants. He listens and he's good about not telling me what to do or when I'm fucking up." She already had her mother on her case about that. "Which is nice, I mean he offers suggestions, but doesn't get upset if I do something else."

"I get all that. Like I said, I'm not worried about it. But I know that no big deals can change. I think that's what your mother is worried about. I also think that sometimes when it comes to your mother, I might not know what I'm talking about."

Anna smiled. "She does mention that occasionally."

"Hey, everyone needs a shtick. I don't know what to tell you. If you're having a good time and are reasonably open eyed about its prospects, you'll be fine, but if you start seeing it differently... you got to be honest about what you want."

"Like you and Joanie?" Joanie?

"Yeah, or maybe like Mikal and Joanie." She was amused by that. "They *were* together a long time," I said, knowing he'd been more important to Joanie than I ever was.

"He talked about that. I can tell he was hurt by her ditching him for the guy she's marrying, but he wasn't surprised. He said she'd worked herself up, wanting to get out of her dead-end life, and evidently believes her salvation is in this new guy—"

"Brian." That was his name, Brian.

"Sounds about right," she snorted. "I saw her talking to Mikal, telling him she wasn't coming back." Anna, it appeared, was happy that Joanie was out of the picture, "And to be truthful, I don't mind if he's using me to move on." Anna smiled again. "Are you still seeing that woman from the gallery?" Evidently, we were done talking about Joanie.

"Who told you that?"

"Rebekah."

I shook my head. "I'm not seeing her. I wasn't before and I'm not planning on doing so now. I met her once for drinks and that was it." I was sticking with that. "Rebekah is wrong. I'm not fooling around on your mother. I know the whole thing with Judith is still out there, but all that died with her. It's just your mom now." She seemed satisfied with that. We both noticed that people were coming in. "Well, I better get back home. See ya."

"See ya." Anna patted my head as she went back to her kitchen.

Mikal was still in his office. He smiled when I came in.

"Anna, tell you it was ok?"

I smiled back. "Yes, she did. Is it ok?"

He sat back. The smile went to wherever predisposed smiles go when they're not needed. "Anna's an interesting woman and we enjoy each other's company, but I've been straight with her about the fact that I'm not looking for anything long-term right now. Besides, while she doesn't think the age difference is a big deal, I do, so I'm trying to be careful not to raise her expectations, assuming that's possible." The smile was back.

"That's the variable."

The smile faded a bit. "That it is," he said mostly to himself. "Interested in checking things out now that we're a fully functional musical center?"

"Might as well."

The slogan for all of us.

21

Brewster called to remind me the funeral would be Saturday. They'd gotten whatever they needed from the Marine Corps and had been busy prepping the burial site. I thanked them, informed them that Agnes and I had tied the knot, and promised to help with whatever I could.

"Thanks, man, wish the circumstances were better," he said before ending the call.

We were in the pool. Zach had waded a few feet from me as Lizzy, who was between my legs on the upper step, splashed the water with her feet. Agnes, after grousing about my lack of outrage at her daughter's dating habits, was taking a nap on one of the lounge chairs just out of the sun. There are no greater satisfactions in life than sharing the simplicities of life with children. No worries or fear; no problems or mysteries to solve. All that matters is the warmth of the water and how daring to be. Zach was slowly inching his way towards the deeper water. For the longest time, he would go where the water came up to his waist. He would either accept his self-imposed limit or try to get one of us to ferry him further, but today the adventurer within was boldly propelling him into unknown waters. He stopped when the water got above his navel and loudly proclaimed his victory, waking the sleeping newlywed.

"What?" she exclaimed. The three of us looked at her.

"Zach has reached a new level in the pool," I informed her.

"Sure. Maybe a little quieter, ok?" Ag fell back into her stupor. I put my finger to my lips.

"We have to be quiet. The old lady is sleeping," I told Zach.

"I heard that, Buttman!" Evidently, it was a light stupor. She groaned as my phone began chirping. "Your damn phone's ringing again."

That's what happens when you're an in-demand sort of fellow.

I got up and put Lizzy in her pen. The call was from Art Devaney. I sighed. Could be worse, I thought. What if it was Monika Danalek, now interested in moving our "relationship" beyond a casual introductory blowjob? You've got to think before you act, Buttman!

"Art, what's up?"

"I've got news, my friend. Interesting news." I waited for him to continue, but Art likes to drag things out.

"Then lay it on me, man."

"As I told you before, the official report was that the two Marines were killed in an ambush after being separated from the rest of their squad during a sandstorm. There's nothing in the report to refute that. Also, while there was some disharmony within the company, officially, there's nothing to indicate that what was going on was any different from what you'd expect to find in any of the other Marine units assigned to that area at that time." I could hear the giddiness in his voice. "However, my contact met one of his classmates from Annapolis, who happened to be with the Expeditionary Forces at that time..."

"And?" It was like pulling teeth.

"While talking, my contact referred to my inquiry. This, he said, lit up his friend. The answer the man said, was not in the two lost Marines, but in other events taking place at that time. Pressed, he directed my contact to news concerning the locals. As far as the Marines were concerned, he could say no more." Art paused, again, for dramatic effect.

"Turns out, the only event of any consequence was the murder of a family in a village not far from your Marines. It was alleged that the family was killed by the Taliban for dealing with the Americans. The head of the murdered family was a relative of a powerful warlord whom the U.S. was courting for support. Since I knew some folks working on such matters, I asked them about it. More red flags. The warlord, a man named Abdullah Musa, had been holding out for a particular type of weapon which we were reluctant to provide."

"What does this have to do with Jacob?" I asked, bored by the interesting story.

"Patience, my friend. The interesting part is in the details. While the warlord publicly lamented the death of his cousin, the two men had, in fact, been feuding about how to interact with the Americans. The slain man was working directly with, surprise surprise, your Sergeant MacMillan, which prompted members of our intelligence team to believe that Musa had his cousin killed. That can't just be coincidence."

"Uh-huh." I think he picked up on my disinterest.

"Stick with me, Monk. The problem with that is Musa would have understood that killing his direct contact with us would not advance his ambitions. The other problem is there were no elements of the Taliban in the area, hadn't been for some time. To add to the intrigue, the weather on the day the two Marines were killed was uneventful. No storms of any kind. So, what really happened? Are you with me now?"

"I don't understand?" I was lying.

"I know you do. Something out of the ordinary happened. The question is what? This Sergeant MacMillan, are you still interested in talking to him?"

"Assuming he's willing to talk, yeah. But if he's like the others, it's probably a waste of time. I don't even know where he is."

Art chuckled. "Monk, do you really think I wouldn't look into that as well?" He didn't wait for the answer. "It turns out the sergeant has a home here in Virginia. If you're amenable to the idea, I'd be willing to go talk to the man." I imagine he was.

"I'm amenable to that, Art." This time he laughed.

"Then I'll keep in touch. Adios." The kids and Ag were watching as I put the phone down.

"No problems," I assured them.

I got up to make lunch, presuming that lunch would be the four of us, but life, or more precisely, the life of others, intrudes. The intrusion was in the form of one Xavier Dunkle II. He wanted to talk to me. How about lunch, he asks? Agnes was dubious that the caller was actually Xavier Dunkle II, more likely a shapely woman looking for a rendezvous.

"Have your *friend* come over here for lunch?" I put the phone on speaker as Agnes was accusing me.

"You like kids?" I asked Dunkle. I thought it important he knows what he was in for.

"You mean like all the time?" I hoped he was making a joke. "I got like a thousand nieces and nephews. I'm good. I assume you're at the big house?"

"Yep." And he was on his way. He lived a mile away in his grandfather's old mansion. Agnes grumbled for no apparent reason, and I continued making lunch.

"What does he want?" she asked at last.

"He didn't say, but in keeping with prevailing trends, I believe it concerns his crush on Natalya Constantinescu and Ms. DuBare's disapproval, much like your disapproval of your daughter's affairs."

Agnes frowned, crinkling her surgically repaired nose. "You're a jerk, Buttman."

"Merely playing the hand I'm dealt, my love. Would you like chips with your sandwich?"

"How long have you known me?"

"Evidently not long enough," I handed her the bag.

Dunkle appeared at the door ready, willing, and able to convince me, and the more disinclined Agnes, that his intentions were both good and honorable towards the young woman who had manipulated me into being my liaison in the art world. He was somewhat shocked by what passed for lunch; PBJs, chips, and mac and cheese, and not the highfalutin gourmet mac and cheese either.

"My wife demands that once a week we have what she calls an all-American kind of lunch. Like the kind she used to have as a kid—"

"Your wife? You got married?" He seemed surprised.

"Is that so shocking? I never said I didn't want to." I feigned surprise at his surprise.

"Behave, Buttman," my surly wife demanded.

"Yes, dear. But on to more pertinent matters. What is it you wish to discuss with me and my better half, and, of course, our delightful grandchildren?" Zach let out a whoop while Lizzy was still trying to decide if she liked this stranger.

"It's a little embarrassing, to be honest..." Dunkle stammered.

"Is this about Natalya or something else?" I handed him a bowl of our steaming orange goo. He sat next to Agnes, looking both at me and what passed for lunch. I assured him it was edible, perhaps even addicting.

"Natalya."

Agnes, already angry about her daughter's flirtations with Mikal, grumbled, "Aren't you too old for that girl? What are you, like forty?"

"Agnes, behave," I chided. "What about Natalya, and I must say if you're looking for me to persuade her as to your charms, then I'll have to demure, partly because she's more than capable of taking care of this herself, but mostly because I don't want to. That's how I feel about Anna and Mikal as well, my dear." My dear wife continued to grumble while the normally indefatigable Mr. Dunkle was at a loss as to what to say.

"No, I don't... well, I wouldn't mind your speaking highly of me, or even of me, but I don't expect you to, and maybe if you did, I'd come off looking like a weasel. No, I was hoping for a little coaching, I mean you seem to do reasonably well with women and to be frank, I... well, I don't know how to talk to women when it comes to, well, relationships."

"I know you've had girlfriends. I've heard that." I found it oddly delightful to needle my erstwhile wealthy compadre.

"True, but most of them either approached me or were introduced to me by my family whether I wanted that or not, but Natalya is different, and I know how that sounds..." He directed that comment to Agnes, who continued to eye him with suspicion. "Anyway, I thought I'd ask you what you think about how I should approach her." I waited for Agnes to bark at him, but she was staring at me.

"Yeah, let's hear those pearls of wisdom, Buttman?"

"Wow, not even a day later and the romance is dead. I am depressed." That made Agnes laugh, which made me laugh. "Alright, my pearls of wisdom are these: be yourself, take an interest in what she likes and listen. I mean, actually listen. Be honest about how you feel, but don't be creepy about it. That means give her whatever room she needs. Also, if it ain't happening after a reasonable amount of time, it ain't happening."

Dunkle seemed unsure.

I could see Agnes smiling at me for reasons unknown.

"I would add this. She's knows you like her and she hasn't said she doesn't like that, so make a date for lunch or dinner and see how it goes. Just be aware that Ms. DuBare is not happy about this."

"Oh, I'm well aware of that," he admitted. "She gave me an earful the other day, but then Natalya called and told me not to worry, but didn't say anything else, so I don't quite know what to do."

Agnes shot Dunkle a look while wiping Zach's orange-tinged lips. "Oh, for christsakes, she obviously wants you to pursue her." Agnes continued looking the uncomfortable Mr. Dunkle up and down. "You never said how old you are?"

"I'm thirty-five."

Agnes pondered that. "I still don't like it, but these girls do what they want." I burst out laughing at that. Agnes frowned and wagged her finger at me, "Don't you dare say a word, Monk Buttman," which made me laugh more, which made the grandkids laugh. Agnes tried to be mad or serious, even stating that, "I'm serious here, Buttman!" which didn't help. She finally smiled at Dunkle. "You're on your own, slick," and got up to clean and change Lizzy.

I finished cleaning Zach while Dunkle sat there.

Zach was in the mood to roam, so I motioned for Dunkle to join me on the couch for a better view of the wandering.

"It's ok to have fun with romance, and I'm assuming that's your interest versus I just wanna fuck that young piece of ass." He acted embarrassed again which made me smile. "Natalya is all too familiar with the dark side of sex. Did you know that?"

"I'd heard some rumors, yes."

"Well, they're true, so be good to her. Here's my last piece of unwanted advice. Stay away from idiotic notions that love is some great cure-all. Not that I'm saying love is a bad thing or not worth pursuing, only that it's never perfect. If you're looking for that, you're going to be disappointed. But if you're willing to allow for a certain amount of craziness, you'll be ok." I tilted my head towards Agnes who was returning to the room sans Lizzy.

"I put her down for her nap," she informed us.

Dunkle nodded, not knowing what exactly he should say.

"I'm thinking of getting out of the rich guy business and going back to being a nobody," I said just to say.

"I'm happy for you," he smirked. Finally, the Dunkle I know and love. "You realize that's impossible unless you actually give the money away. And if you do that, you'll have to put up with ridicule for the rest of your life."

"Ridicule?"

Agnes laughed. "He means everyone will think you're an idiot or a dumbass."

I looked at my wife, aghast. "I'm shocked that my family and friends would be so shallow and money obsessed."

"Oh stop," chided Agnes, "no one's buying the poor pitiful rich guy shtick anymore. It's getting old."

"Old?"

"Old."

"Wow, I'm so incredibly disappointed to hear that, but I've made up my mind, and that's that." Dunkle laughed, while Agnes shook her head. "Is there anything else I can help you two with?"

"No, I think that's plenty." Dunkle got up. "Thanks for lunch and the words of advice. If I may be so bold as to offer some in return, I've always liked irony, if it helps, or you can take pride in being a pompous weasel. Just a few options to consider."

I assured him I appreciated the humor, and wished him the best in his courtship of the young Romanian woman. We escorted him to his car.

"You have some interesting friends, Buttman." Agnes put her arm around me as we returned to the living room, taking care not to step on Zach, who thought it fun to weave in and out of our moving legs.

"I've noticed that too, but to be fair, he was very well behaved. Usually, he's much more antagonistic, but in a nice kind of jerk way. Maybe it was because you were here and the topic was Natalya." Agnes picked up Zach after one too many close calls.

"Is it possible for you to behave too, Zach?" she demanded.

Zach just squirmed and shouted, "No!"

She handed him to me. Zach and I stood there as Agnes judged us. "I still think he's too old for her."

"What about him?" I held up Zach. Agnes groaned and walked away.

22

"You can be as involved with the trust as you like." Mr. Macklgrew, amused by my unwillingness to get my head wrapped around this money thing, stayed just on the edge of condescension as he listened to my tale of woe. "I apologize if I didn't make that clear when we first discussed this or in our subsequent conversations." He knew full well he had pointed this out many times. "How you choose to participate is up to you from complete control all the way to divestiture."

"What I'd really like is to give the impression that I'm no longer in control while leaving it, as it is, in your capable hands."

"Isn't that the same thing?" he again pointed out.

"I suppose."

The affable Mr. Macklgrew tapped his fingers on the edge of the table. "Perhaps what's necessary is a change in ownership, if in name only. Right now, the trust bears the name given to it by the late Ms. Delashay, and you are associated with it by that name. If I'm assuming your motives correctly, you'd like to redirect prying eyes elsewhere. We can change the way the trust is organized. I assume you want it to remain philanthropic, correct?"

"Yes."

"Then in the reorganization, we can essentially remove your name, but you will still retain ultimate control over the trust. If someone wants to find you, they'd have to dig pretty deep. Is that something you'd be willing to consider?" I could see the delight in his face.

"Sure. So, we'd have to create a whole new place to put it?" I wasn't exactly familiar with such practices. Fortunately, Macklgrew was.

"We can. However, I noted in your accounts an LLC by the name of Sunshine Holdings, where you have the monies you brought in on your own. It's nice and obscure and because you already own it, it makes the process easier. So rather than create a new entity, we can transfer the trust to

Sunshine as a parent company and bury your ownership in the fine print. If anyone has dealings with the trust, they'll deal with us. It would also erase you from certain registries which would allow you a certain amount of anonymity, not completely mind you, but enough so you're not directly identifiable."

"And our relationship..." A sly smile came to the man of the moment.

"Our relationship remains the same. We'll act as the conduit to you and we can be as open or as closed as you like. As far as reporting and any of the decisions that need to be made concerning disbursements, taxes, etc., that won't change." It was all perfectly logical and orderly.

"Alright then, I can't think of anything else to bother you with," I said.

"No bother at all, Monk. It's what I'm here for."

Such joy. Why didn't I feel the same way?

· · · · ·

We spent the rest of the day preparing for our trip north. Because Agnes had to go to work and I had my appointment with Macklgrew, Rebekah was left with no alternative but to care for her children. She didn't seem to mind.

"Are you free now? Ready to kick us out?" were her first words as I walked in the door. I couldn't tell if she was serious or not.

"Soon enough, soon enough. The plan is in the works and the plan is the thing. Besides, you'll be much happier on your own. If you stay here, you'll only grow resentful and feel stunted and angry, whereas if you have your own place, you'll feel stuck and ruled by your possessions and I think you'll agree that's much, much better." I winked in case she missed the sarcasm.

She was not amused. "What does Agnes say when you're like this?"

"You're the best, Buttman."

"That's not it." She was trying to get Lizzy to frown at me, but Lizzy was tired and not interested in the smartassed old dude.

"Oh, I think it is."

"Goddamnit, Dad, this isn't a joke." Lizzy, noting the alarm in her mother's voice, started to cry. "Are you happy now?"

"Hey, I'm not the one who's making her cry, and before you start tearing into me, take a deep cleansing breath..." I felt the need to illustrate by taking one of my own. Rebekah just growled. "Excellent! Now what are you worried about? What do you think is going to happen?" I was surprised to see her tear up.

"I don't want to go back to living in some horrible dump again, struggling to get by, that's what." I shook my head and sat down next to my excitable daughter and put my arm around her. I wiped her eyes, then Lizzy's eyes; she had calmed down a little, and kissed each of them on the forehead.

"Seems unlikely. I'm sure Chess has rented it out by now." Chess was Farrell's father, and a known moron.

Rebekah continued frowning. "That's not funny."

"Oh, come on, that's comedic gold and you know it," I admonished.

"You know what I mean." I could see the cracks in her frown beginning to show.

"Uh-huh. Does Fidel share this irrational fear too?" I knew the answer. So did she.

"That's not a fair question, Fidel's an eternal sunshine kind of guy..."

"Isn't that part of the reason you like him?" I didn't let her answer, "So what does our man in Havana think?" She tried to pull an Agnes, but Lizzy impeded her fingers, which I grabbed at the last second.

"You shouldn't call him that," she huffed.

"Nonsense, you know he says it himself and we all get the joke. It's one of the reasons I like him and am thankful you're done with clods like Farrell."

"Farrell had his moments..." Yeah like when that crazy fucker Roger Peterson was ordering Farrell to shoot us after he'd stabbed Ashton Cox.

"Don't remind me. So, let's think this through. First off, while you've been more than willing to rag on me about Judith, without her money you and Fidel would be in much worse shape, right?" She glared at me. "Without it you'd still be working for Johnny D and Fidel would be out hustling gigs cuz there's no guarantee he'd still have a job after his old company was sold. Plus, where would you live? It wouldn't be here. The bungalows? Maybe for a while, but we know what happened there, and before you say a thing, I don't want to hear how I stuck it to the old folks—"

"Well, didn't you?"

Well, Buttman? "Everyone still living ended up at a nice place, even Rosalyn, god bless her cantankerous old soul, so no, I did not!" Lizzy had fallen asleep in her mother's arm. My voice has that quality.

"Is there a point to all this?"

"Who knows, but as I was willing to invest in your business—"

"You said you did because Mr. Macklgrew told you it was a good deal," she huffed again.

"Don't interrupt. If I was willing to invest in the business, why wouldn't I help when it comes to where you end up living, other than here."

"Because you're a jerk?" she smirked.

"That's Agnes talking."

"The point, Buttman?" I leaned in and kissed her forehead again.

"There is no point, only love, so be grateful for a change." Rebekah smiled and kissed my cheek.

"Yes, Dad."

"That's more like it." She put her head on my shoulder. "You've been kinda moody lately. You're not pregnant again, are you?"

"We'll see," Rebekah snorted.

Makes you wonder how many kids she'd have if Farrell wasn't shooting blanks.

•　　　•　　　•　　　•　　　•

No one was remotely thrilled about our impending trip. Nor did the mood improve as we piled into the car and drove north. Little was said, save for whether to bring up Rebekah and Fidel's wedding ceremony now only a month off. The somber mood, as expected, enveloped the farm even as Mother Nature was incongruently throwing a warm sunny day at us. The Mackinaw brothers directed the proceedings having made the arrangements, for which I was given the bill; another reason to get out of the rich guy business. We stood as the casket was lowered into the ground. A few words were said; a wake was to be held later at the farm, and I think most people were saving their remembrances for then.

Moses was lost, weeping over the casket. Meredith stood behind him, more composed, her hands on his shoulders. Sterling, his eyes wet, was obviously unsure how to be there for his parents as they grieved over his youngest brother. The middle brother, Isaac, was nowhere to be found. I later learned it was inconvenient for him to leave Africa. It allowed me to take comfort in the fact that, for this singular moment, I was not the most disappointing son. I didn't know what to make of Isaac, but I knew no more of him than I did of Jacob. I assumed it was a dodge, much like the ones I once employed.

My little group, Agnes, Rebekah holding Lizzy, Fidel holding Zach, were off to the side. The more immediate members of the farm were behind Moses and Meredith. Emily came over for just a moment to give me a hug before returning to her mother who, despite the circumstances, continued to glower at me. I rolled my eyes. As the invocation was given; odd, I thought, to invoke God, my attention wandered, and it was then I noticed the young man standing by the road. I excused myself and walked towards the young man. He hesitated before walking away.

"Lewis," I did my best to speak firmly without shouting.

The young man stopped. "Who are you?"

"I'm the one you called, to tell where Jacob could be found after he killed himself. My name is Monk, I'm Jacob's older brother."

A knowing look crossed his face. "What do you want?"

"I want to know why he killed himself? I read Kurtis' notebook, so I know a little about what happened. I also know about him and Mason. I want to know what happened in Afghanistan. What really happened when Dezi and Lambert were killed in the so-called ambush?" I expected surprise from Lewis; that I knew what I knew, but he just smiled.

"I promised not to say anything. I have to honor that. Talk to the sergeant, if you can find him. He's the only one I'd trust or believe."

"MacMillan? Where is he?"

His eyes darkened. "I don't know. Maybe that's a good thing." He turned his head back to the burial party.

"Doesn't that bother you?" I pointed to the funeral.

"I'm sorry that Jacob did what he did, but I've learned that life isn't really that precious or hopeful. Death is what we all come to..." He turned to me. "All of us."

"Isn't that a little depressing for someone your age?"

He shook his head. "Not after what I've seen."

"You don't seem too worried about being here. Don't you think they'll be looking for you?"

"They know where I am. I'll go back soon." He came over and hugged me. "I have to go." He smiled at the shock on my face.

"Who was that?" Agnes asked after I got back.

"That was Lewis."

She craned her neck trying to find him, but he was gone. "The AWOL guy?"

"Yes, the AWOL guy," I could see the confusion.

"Shouldn't we tell someone?"

"Apparently, they already know." I motioned to the others. "It looks like it's time to go back." With the casket in the ground and the symbolic shovel of dirt tossed on it, the assemblage broke up. We collected our brood and got in the car, following the others back to the farm.

I thought about mentioning that wakes technically should be held before the body is interred, but Agnes told me to zip it.

"Behave, Buttman."

"What?" All of them were staring at me. I expected as much from Rebekah and Agnes, but I was disappointed in Fidel. I thought we had a connection.

"For once behave!" It appeared Agnes would have the last word.

The wake was held in the dining hall and the adjacent courtyard; the doors turned open, and Mother Nature blessing us with sunlight and a soft breeze. The somber mood from the burial carried forth during the wake. Moses was more composed but chose not to speak. Instead, he sat with Meredith and Sterling as, one by one, members of the farm got up and said a little something in memory of Jacob. All were of his childhood and adolescence; once he joined the Marines, they only saw him when he returned on leave and it was always too brief. Emily got the only laugh when she admitted she thought Jacob was a cute guy. I noted Calista's ambivalence. At the end, Sterling spoke quietly of his younger brother, stopping now and again to wipe his eyes. Meredith rose and thanked everyone for their help and support. The three of them left for their house, just beyond the closed doors on the other side of the dining hall.

The rest of us helped with the evening meal.

I hadn't planned on saying anything either to Moses or Meredith about Jacob other than offering condolences. I hadn't planned on saying anything to anyone, but Emily, in clear defiance of her mother, sat next to me and Agnes with Zach across from her. Zach was ecstatic; he missed Emily, and Emily missed him.

"Aren't you worried about getting in trouble?" I asked.

"I don't care," was her response. Agnes smiled at that, as did I while staring at my daughter. Rebekah frowned at my unwelcome comparison. I was thoroughly enjoying my moment when Sterling tapped me on the back.

"Dad wants to talk to you." Dad? It took me a minute to realize he meant Moses. I almost said something stupid, but the wife pinched me in advance. I shot her the same look Rebekah shot me, which made Fidel laugh. We all looked at him.

"Sorry," he sheepishly said. I left them to their merriment.

Moses was on the couch. In his hand was Jacob's good conduct medal. On the table was a bag returned by the police. I sat down next to him. He turned to me before returning to the medal in his hands. I absent-mindedly took the bag from the table. In it were Jacob's wallet, keys, phone, and the 9mm he killed himself with. Moses glanced over but said nothing. I examined the pistol. I don't know why. I popped out the magazine. It was empty. I watched as Moses fingered the medal.

"Did you look at this?" I held out the 9mm.

"What's to look at?"

"There are no rounds in the magazine," I informed him.

"That's what the sheriff said." I thought he'd be more animated.

"That doesn't make sense. You can't kill yourself without bullets?"

Moses put the medal down. "Yeah, but the shell found at the scene matched the gun, so there was at least one."

"What else did Lew say?"

Moses took the 9mm. "What does it matter now?"

"Humor me." I saw a glimmer of life in the old man's eyes.

"He said the only other thing they noticed was that there were more than one set of tracks, but they assumed that was you when you found him." He was wondering what the lost cause was getting at. "Why?"

"I don't know, but something isn't right here."

"Like what? What did you find?" His eyes grew brighter.

"It's the little things that involve not just Jacob, but all the guys he was with on their last tour in Afghanistan. Five of them are dead. According to official records, two were killed after getting separated from the others in a sandstorm. But a guy I know did some checking, and found that there was no storm and that the Taliban hadn't been active in the area for months. The other three died by murder or suicide. Then there's Kurtis' journal. It mentions Jacob, but only says he and the others were there when Kurtis was assaulted by Dezi. Then there's Lewis, who knows what's going on, or pretends to, but will only say I need to ask the sergeant, that the sergeant has the answers."

"Sergeant who?"

"A Sergeant MacMillan. When I asked Captain Sinnons about him, all he would tell me was that he had retired and they weren't allowed to tell me where he was. However, Art found out he lives in Virginia and was going to feel him out as it were." I didn't know if it was a smart move to pull Moses into this. He was already deeply suspicious of government and big business and all that old hippie shit.

"Anything else?"

"Oh, some stuff about the murder of a family around the time the two Marines were killed. Apparently, they were working with Jacob's company and were related to an important warlord. Art's guy thought it was fishy that it happened when there was a lot of hesitation about giving this warlord more weapons."

Moses snorted, "Isn't that how the whole business of war works? Make a show for the public, but do the deals quietly later?"

"Probably, I'm just throwing that out there." Moses put the 9mm back in the bag.

"So, what do we do now?" We?

"That depends on what Art comes up with. I have to add these other things might be nothing, just coincidences. It could be exactly what they say it is."

He furrowed his brow. "I don't believe that, I just don't. I don't believe any of it. I want to know what this Art has to say. You'll let me know?"

"Sure."

A moment for the lost cause.

23

Meredith came in, followed by Agnes, Rebekah, and Fidel. The kids were with Emily. Moses acted confused, but I knew what they were here for, the upcoming wedding.

"I didn't get a chance to congratulate you and Agnes, Monk." Meredith offered her hand and after I got off the couch, she hugged me. She then hugged Agnes. Moses, somewhat out of his fog of depression, rose and hugged Agnes and me. I found it extremely awkward. The six of us stood there. Again awkward. Finally, Rebekah spoke up.

"We were talking about the wedding with Brewster and wondered if it was still a good idea, or whether we should postpone it, and then Meri came over and we talked a little more, so we're wondering what you think, Grandpa?" Grandpa looked at his wife who slightly raised her eyebrows.

"I don't know, this has all been very hard to deal with," he said.

"It has, but I think it'll be good to have some happy moments to look forward to. With all this sadness lately, it's easy to forget that so many other things have to go on. And it's not like it's happening tomorrow or the next day. Then there's Monk and Agnes' good news; we should celebrate that too." Meredith wrapped her arms around the old man. She put his head on her shoulder. "As much as we miss Jacob, we can't forget those who are still here, who are important to us. We need some joy, Moses; we still need to love and believe."

Moses, attempted composure but failed, only nodded as the tears fell into his beard. We gathered around them, all of us teary-eyed. The only sounds were the sobs from the old man. At length we let go and left them in their room. Agnes had an unusually firm grasp of my hand. We ended up back in the dining hall where Emily was amusing Zach with stories from one of her books. Lizzy was fast asleep in her car seat. I vainly tried to convince Emily that she was digging herself a deeper hole with her mother, but Emily was having none of it. The stubbornness that got her from Philly to Virginia, on her own two years earlier, was clear to see in her resistance to her mother's demand that she stay away from us.

As often happens in these situations, Calista and Andrea entered at the other end of the dining hall as I was giving up on persuading Emily.

"Emily!" Calista shouted.

Emily ignored her mother while the rest of us turned towards Andrea and Calista. Andrea took Calista's arm and said something to her.

"Why should I do that?" Calista demanded, but Andrea persisted and Calista stormed off, leaving Andrea to approach us.

Andrea sat down on the other side of Emily, much to Emily's displeasure. She was, oddly, rather cheerful. "I think we need to figure out how we can make our home life less crazy, Em."

"I didn't start this!" Em fired back.

I tried to help. "Emily—"

"I didn't do anything wrong!" Emily looked at Rebekah, who looked at me. I looked at Andrea, who cocked her head and raised her eyebrows.

"It's not about being wrong," I started, "it's about respecting boundaries."

Emily glared at me. "What does that mean?"

Like I know.

"It means your mom has the right to make decisions for you; decisions you may not like or understand, but that are made with your best interests at heart." Pure unadulterated pablum, I thought. The same crap I hated hearing at that age.

"What about what I think? Don't I have a say?"

Andrea put her arm around Emily. "It's not that, Em. Of course, you have a say, but you're asking for too much. This is your home, not Los Angeles."

"I don't like it here anymore! I like it in LA," Emily huffed.

"Are you going to tell her, Buttman?" Agnes, good old Agnes.

"What does that mean?" implored Emily.

I gave Agnes the evil eye. "I've decided we're not going to live in the big house anymore. We're going to move back to our house in West Covina."

"Why?"

"Yeah, why Dad?" My dear Rebekah right on time. Will no one stand up for good old Monk?

"Because I'm the dad and I get to decide." Oddly, no one appreciated that. "Look, I'm well aware that no one is happy about me doing this, and yes, it might seem rather arbitrary, but the big house is never going to feel like home to me. It's always going to be a place with a lot of memories of Judith. I tried to live there, but in the end, I think it's in everybody's best interest if it's not our everyday home. We've already talked about options for you and Fidel, and Anna's already found a place. Agnes and I have a nice home and that's where we want to live." I could see Emily frowning. "It doesn't mean you can't ever come down and spend some time there, but it does mean your home is here."

It was a nice thought, but Emily wasn't buying. The anger burned in her eyes and on her face. I felt like a heel, but I'd made up my mind. Andrea told her it would be alright. Emily ignored her. For once, Agnes and Rebekah held their tongues. Fidel adroitly offered to go for a walk with Emily and Zach. I wish I'd thought of that, but I was the bad guy.

"Don't be gone too long, ok?" cautioned Andrea.

"We won't," responded the cheery Fidel. I turned to the three women opposite me.

"Are we done here?" I was tired.

"No, Sunshine," my delightful wife answered, "we are not. There's the wedding business."

"Ok, what about the wedding business?"

"Meri suggested that maybe it would be a good idea if we had the weddings at the same time," Agnes said.

I looked at Rebekah. "Uh-huh."

Rebekah leaned towards me. "The problem with that is mom and Judah and maybe grandma will be coming out, and it might be a little awkward for them to be a part of your wedding ceremony too."

"Uh-huh."

Agnes frowned "That's all you've got to say?"

I smiled. "Uh-huh."

Andrea, obviously not interesting in more drama, bowed out. "I'll see you guys tomorrow." We wished her well.

Rebekah turned to me after Andrea left. "Boy, it's a good thing I didn't upset the apple cart like that, huh?" Her big broad smile mocked me and our many years of adolescent battles.

"It certainly is." I rolled my eyes in response. "So, everyone is still coming out, huh? Well, if we're adding ourselves to the bill, maybe you should invite Car and Leslie? Might be short notice, but hey, I got money; at least for now, so I'll even pony up the dough. How about that?"

Agnes curled her nose. "I'm not in the mood for pranks, Buttman."

"No pranks. I'll leave it to you two to make the calls and find out what works."

About that time Fidel returned with Emily and Zach. Zach was out of gas. Fidel picked him up and Zach put his head on Fidel's shoulder. Emily came over and gave me a hug.

"I'm sorry for being mad at you, Mr. Sunshine."

I hugged her back. "No need to be sorry. I'm sorry for getting you into this mess."

She squeezed me tight before letting go. She said goodbye and headed home. Fidel noted the surprise on my face.

"We had a quick little talk, that's all. I had a similar situation when I was a kid, so I understand." Simple as that.

"Thanks." I gave a stern fatherly face to my daughter. "Don't ever let go of this man!" Rebekah shrugged. I looked at Fidel. "You know she might be pregnant again?"

Fidel shrugged. "I like kids." Simple as that.

"Yeah, I guess they're ok…" I looked at Rebekah. "So, you two aren't upset about sharing the wedding with us?"

"No, not really," Rebekah admitted. "Plus, it'll give Agnes a reason to drag Anna and Barron up here."

Agnes nodded in agreement. "It all works out, Sunshine."

"It certainly does, Beautiful. Anything else?" I was still tired.

"I want to know the real reason you're so eager to kick us all out of the 'big house', as you call it? It's a great house. Why would you want to leave it?" Rebekah wouldn't let go.

"Two reasons. One, because for me it's still Judith's house; it's where I watched her die. Maybe in time that memory will fade, but it's still very real to me." I took a moment to breathe. "Second, it's deeply corrupting, that's why. Yes, it's a great house and there's plenty of room and who wouldn't want to have everything at your beck and call? We don't have to clean or shop or mow the lawn, because there's always someone else to take care of it. And we lose our sensibilities. People stop being our peers and become lesser beings whose job is to serve us. We forget how much work life can be because we don't have to work, and we become precious and wonderful because who's going to tell us otherwise? And as you so rightly noted, it becomes very easy to cast people off once you're done with them." I paused in the hope that Agnes and Rebekah got my drift. "I don't want to become that person, and I don't want you to become those people. That's why."

"You sound like grandpa."

"Great minds, my dear, and with that, I bid you a good night." I stood up.

"You do realize we're all sleeping in the bunkhouse, don't you?" Agnes huffed.

"What's your point?"

"For a rich guy, you're a real cheapass, Buttman." She had to point that out.

"Then we'll get rooms down at the Comfort Inn. I have a membership card you know."

Agnes smiled at that. "Yes, how could we forget our time at the Comfort Inns of America?" Fidel didn't get the joke, so Rebekah told him it was part of our adventure tracking down Farrell. Fidel, having heard the story, nodded. We packed up the kids, said goodbye to Brewster, who had wandered in, and left for something better than a hard bunkhouse bed.

·　　·　　·　　·　　·

I liked our room. It had a king-sized bed and was two doors down from the kids. We could make as much noise as we wanted. Agnes was of a similar mind.

"I expect some affection, Mr. Sunshine..." I noticed lately she'd been using that appellation when certain desires were on her mind. She cozied up to me, making sure I got a close and personal view of her delightful breasts.

"I'm all yours, Beautiful." Agnes undid my pants and slid them down.

"Really?" She slid her hand down my shorts. "That's not what Monika told me in her own interesting way." I noticed her hand was cold.

"Oh? What *did* Monika tell you in her own interesting way?" I pulled the tank top away from her breasts. If I was in big trouble, I might as well get what I can.

"Well, if I understood her correctly, it was how wonderful sucking your cock was and how much you enjoyed coming in her mouth." Agnes gave me a fairly insistent tug as she said that. "Makes me wonder if I should even bother trying to be nice to you if you're getting such wonderful blowjobs from your *friend* Monika." She looked me in the eye while continuing to move her hand along my erection. She also leaned in as I fondled her breast.

I was confused.

"Ag—" She started kissing me. After a few minutes my curiosity got the better of me. "I don't understand? Do you believe her? Are you mad? I'm getting some mixed signals here."

Agnes pushed me down and sat on my chest. "You know I'm mad at you whether what she says is true or not." She didn't sound terribly mad. Then there was the matter of those glorious breasts being mere inches from my face. She noted the effect that was having on my erection, and began to squeeze. "You like fucking me? You seem to." A forceful tug.

"You know I do." Her grasp was starting to hurt.

"Then why am I getting calls from women telling me how much they like sucking your cock?" There was the anger, which oddly made me feel better.

"I don't know," I sputtered.

"Don't lie to me! I'm not going to put up with this, you understand?" I meekly nodded. "I'm not stupid." I reached around and grabbed her hand.

"I know you're not stupid, and I'm not screwing around. Why would I marry you if I wanted to be with someone else?" She loosened her grip. "There's nothing going on..." I moved her back off my chest and down to my hips.

"Then why did she call me?"

"To fuck with you. To make you mad. If you leave, I'm fair game; that's how it works. She was probably very congenial and nice; didn't raise her voice or say anything vulgar. It was all matter-of-fact kind of stuff, wasn't it? It's the way men are, aren't they? I just want you to know how it is, Agnes, that's all." Agnes let go of my cock and crossed her arms. "Right?"

"How do you know that?"

"Because she gave me the same spiel. Hey, it happens, it's the way people are, why fight it. You only live once. I won't be so possessive, and on and on."

Agnes didn't look convinced. "Kinda like your spiel." I opened my mouth, but she cut me off, "I have my own spiel, Monk Buttman, and it goes like this. I'm it, you understand? The only blowjobs you're getting are going to be from me; same with the other stuff, like the Judith thing. I don't care if she has nicer tits, or a firmer ass, or a flat stomach. You promised me you're going to be straight with me and you goddamned better be. I won't go through that again!"

"Agnes, nothing is going on, nothing is going to go on. I have no interest in Monika, period."

"You promise?"

I shook my head. "No."

Agnes leaned forward, resting her arms on my chest, "Why not?"

"I'm not going to promise. It's just you and me now, that's the way it's going to be. No more promises or anything like that. We're married, and that's that. Now either have your way with me or roll over cuz I'm having a hard time breathing."

She sat up allowing me to catch my breath. "For real?"

"For real." I put my hands on her hips.

"Then there's only one thing left to settle..." Her hand had warmed up.

"What's that?"

A sly smile from the missus clued me in. "You'll see."

Apparently, we were back on.

．　．　．　．　．

I gave up trying to figure people out a while back. Agnes had every reason to doubt me and probably should have left me, but we both knew it wouldn't happen. She had a thing for me and I had a thing for her. It was that simple. Call it love, call it lunacy; call it whatever you like. Whatever it was, it worked. Stop trying to figure it out, go with the flow, and be thankful it's not like the bad years with Astral.

"So?" she asked, as we lay there in the moonlight of our motel bed.

"So what?"

"So, who's the best?" She poked me for effect.

"I never said you weren't the best."

Agnes smiled and burrowed closer to me. "And don't you forget it!"

For once I kept my mouth shut and went to sleep.

·　　·　　·　　·　　·

Someone once said that no good deed goes unpunished. The next morning brought that home. Holly Pronto was at the door. I was surprised to see her. She had on one of the outfits I bought for her. Her hair was fixed up, as was her face. A smile was there to greet me when I opened the door.

"I heard about Jacob's funeral, and they said you were here when I asked..." Agnes was standing behind me. "I just wanted to stop and thank you again for what you did, that's all." Holly was looking over Agnes, who was returning the favor.

"You're more than welcome." I motioned towards Agnes, "This is my wife, Agnes." I turned to Agnes, "This is Holly Pronto." They both exchanged pleasantries. An uncomfortable silence followed.

"Well, I just came by to say thanks and how sorry I am about Jacob. Have a nice day."

Agnes leaned out the door, watching our visitor depart. She shook her head. "It's always something with you, isn't it, Buttman?"

"It sure looks that way," I said. I tried to explain what happened, and how it was just an impulse to help someone in the wake of Jacob's death, but Agnes didn't seem interested in my tale of doing good deeds. Rebekah stopped by with Lizzy.

"You just missed your father's other girlfriend," snarked Agnes.

I simply rolled my eyes.

"How disappointing, and on so many levels," Rebekah replied, with just a hint of condescension.

"Life is like that. Are we ready to go home?" I asked. Both walked off. I assumed we were.

After a brief stop at the farm, we were on the road heading home in a slightly better mood than when we arrived. Agnes couldn't resist asking about Holly, so I told what I knew. That only added to her vexation over the matter of Holly Pronto.

"I don't get it?"

"What's to get? We talked, I took pity on her and bought her a few things. I have no other interests in the woman or any ulterior motives. Nor did I intimate anything to her. If you feel the need to get worked up over Holly Pronto, knock yourself out," I added.

Agnes huffed, "I should knock *you* out."

"Shoulda, coulda, woulda," was my pithy rejoinder.

"You're a jerk, Buttman!"

I started to say something when Zach shouted out, "Gamps!"

For some reason we all laughed.

The plan was to stop at the house in West Covina. Fidel, Rebekah, and the kids would take the Mercedes and go back to Beverly Hills. Agnes' car was at the Covina house, as was the truck, so we had transportation at our disposal. The plan did not include checking out the house for sale down the street. I was tired and protested, but Agnes shot me down. Fidel and Rebekah were intrigued and willing to look.

"I noticed it the other day, and since Buttman is set on driving us out of his precious love nest, I thought it might be an option to consider, and you'd be close so we could watch the kids." *We* was Agnes speak for Monk watches the kids.

The house was a nice sized split level built in the late sixties. It had been renovated and made modern, which I thought robbed it of some of its idiosyncratic Sixties charm, but no one was interested in what I thought. It was priced at more than three-quarters of a million dollars.

"I don't think they can afford it," I said, as hands were run along countertops and bathroom fixtures.

"You've got money, Buttman, and you promised to help," was my wife's response.

"That's all I am to you now isn't it; a wallet?"

Agnes saddled up next to me. "It is now."

"I don't know that I like that," I huffed.

"But you're ok with putting this precious little face on the street?" Rebekah held up Zach, who thought this was all very funny.

"No, he can stay with me. His sister too!"

Rebekah mocked my huff. "No dice, old dude. We're a package deal, right Fidel?" Fidel just smiled. "He's on my side, you know."

"I know how the game works," I said.

"Let's hope you remember that when Monika or your new friend, *Holly*, comes by to play, Buttman!" I ignored that as I sashayed out of the way of Agnes' pinching fingers.

It was a nice place, big enough for four or more people. Both Agnes and Rebekah picked up a copy of the listing and we thanked the woman who was manning the door.

Once back at our house, I made dinner because everyone was hungry, and after dinner we said our goodbyes and sent the kids on their way.

"You were just kidding about the wallet thing, weren't you?" Agnes had her hand in my back pocket.

"Only if you were," I said.

We took our wine glasses and sat at our little patio, listening to the familiar sounds of our neighborhood.

"It is a nice little house, isn't it?"

"It is," I said.

And if they're just down the street, it wouldn't be so bad," she mused.

"I assume you expect me to buy them the house?"

"They could always pay us back." Us?

"Uh-huh, and what about Anna, or Barron? We wouldn't want to play favorites, now would we?"

Agnes reached out and squeezed my hand. "Probably not, but you're loaded, so it's not really a problem." She let that float into the ether.

"Uh-huh," I squeezed back. "I don't know that I want to buy Joanie's ex a house..." I let that float.

"Don't kill the mood, Sunshine."

"Yes, dear."

24

The next day, after rousing Agnes from her slumbers and getting her up and on her way, I cleaned the house, congratulated myself on having a normal person kind of morning, got in the truck, and headed to the big house.

Rebekah was waiting. She had things to do, and things to say... evidently before those things to do.

"It was a nice house, huh?"

I played dumb. "What, this house? Yeah, it's pretty nice. Kind of expensive, though. That reminds me I need to talk to Theresa."

Lizzy was on her hip, which allowed her mother to badmouth her grandfather indirectly. "Mr. Sunshine thinks he's funny, but we're not laughing, are we, Lizzy?" Lizzy looked at her mother quizzically before giving me the same look.

"Lizzy is well aware that her grandfather is a barrel of laughs, and yes, the house was nice. What's your point?" I crossed my arms and stood tall.

"The point is, I think it was nice, that's all," she demurred.

"Uh-huh, and?"

"And, I think it's kind of cruel to let us get our expectations up only to—"

"To what?" I tilted my head. Rebekah smiled and handed Elizabeth to me.

"I shouldn't be too long. Zach's in the pool with Anna. Bye."

Anna and Zach waved as Lizzy and I joined them by the pool. It was another languorous Southern California day, warm, sunny, a bit of haze, and no real demands on our time, or at least mine and the kids. Anna had to work.

"I hear you're buying everyone houses, is that true?" Anna asked this as Zach was splashing the water with the flats of his hands.

"Your mother seems to think so." The boy had some rhythm. Anna had other things on her mind. Things put there by Rebekah Bohrman.

"Does that include condos?"

"Depends..." I began aping the boy's percussive slaps with my own. Lizzy took hold of my forearms so she could participate.

"On..."

"Apparently, my mood at the time the proposition is proposed. Do you, like Rebekah, presuppose an opportunity?" Anna looked to the side for a moment.

"Well, to be honest, I hadn't thought about it, but I noticed a new condo building just down the street from the Manifesto." Lizzy was chortling as we played along with Zach.

"We can check it out if you'd like," I said to no one in particular.

"Maybe tomorrow?" She had the same stars in her eyes that Rebekah did.

"Sure." Anna excused herself and left me to tend to the wards of the house.

Lunch came and went, and the grandkids were shuttled to their pens for a momentary pause in their inexhaustible inexorable drive to wear out their grandfather. The afternoon now belonged to me. Iced tea sated my thirst, and the quiet of the living room allowed me to stretch out on the couch for my own nap.

Didn't last.

First up was the delightful Art Devaney. He had news.

"I found your sergeant," he stated with glee. I attempted to ask where but was stopped before the air left my lungs. "He's not where you would think!"

"And where would I think?"

"Why right here in the beautiful state of Virginia, my friend." Virginia? I don't want to go to Virginia. "Except that he's not."

I heaved a great sigh and waited for the story. "Alright, let me have it."

"Sergeant MacMillan, recently retired from the Marine Corps, returned to his ancestral home, and it is indeed ancestral; I learned it has been in his family since before the civil war, but as it turns out he's not there. His wife was somewhat reticent to receive my call, but soon became rather talkative, and as you've probably guessed this played right into my wily charms."

"Uh-huh."

Art chuckled. "I expect a little more enthusiasm, Monk, but no matter. Apparently, whatever happened in Afghanistan had a measurable impact on all of them. The sergeant, a man his wife described as nearly unflappable and as even-tempered as a warrior can be, was so unnerved by his recent experiences that he inexplicably canceled his reenlistment and retired. He was unusually moody and distant and then one day announced he was going to live out west and was she coming with him?" Art was clearly excited by what the sergeant's wife had told him.

"And?"

Like my family, he ignored my lack of enthusiasm. "And it was not a happy adventure. She returned here to Virginia convinced he'd lost his mind."

"And has he?"

Art Devaney laughed. "I'm not a trained psychiatrist, so I can't say one way or another."

"Nice, but you are interested in my finding out, right?"

"I'm not opposed to that." The phone reverberated with his excitement.

"Ok, so, where is he?"

"He lives just outside a small town in Idaho called Lautenberg on State Road Sixteen." I got up to find something to write on.

"Anything else?" I asked, hoping the answer was no.

"Tell him his wife wants him to come home."

"Sure." Art wished me good luck and told me to keep in touch. I told him I'd think about it.

He laughed, "Oh, where's the fun in that?" I let the question hang in the air. The call was over.

Second was Theresa.

She had the same seriously worried look I associated with my family during my periodic inclinations to drive the bus into the ditch. I knew business had been good with her having to shop and clean for us, and once we vacated the scene, there'd be little to do.

"Can I talk to you for a minute?" she asked.

"Sure." Word of the day.

"I only bring this up because Miss Agnes said I could." I smiled at the reference. It was Theresa's honorific for Agnes, and I realized I hadn't told her we'd gotten married.

"I imagine she did, and since we got married, I think she feels more emboldened when it comes to my affairs." A look of wonder momentarily replaced the look of worry. "What's on your mind?"

"I was wondering if you would be willing to sponsor me..." She paused and looked at her hands, "I mean, maybe that's not the right word, I heard that you're leaving the house and that's ok, in fact, I was going to talk to you about how much time you might need me to be here, but I have an opportunity to start my own business and it's hard to get money, I mean financing, and I was talking to Miss... to Agnes..." It was obvious she was embarrassed.

"What kind of business?"

"Flowers. When I was a teenager, I worked at a flower shop and it's for sale and I know it would be perfect for me, but I don't have the kind of credit I need for a loan and—"

"And you'd like me to front you the money?"

"I'm sorry, I know I probably shouldn't be asking, but I know I'd be good at it. I already do arrangements for my friends. It's a nice shop..." Theresa was babbling.

I sat up and motioned for her to sit down next to me. Her standing there was beginning to unnerve me.

"Well, regardless of what Agnes might think, I don't just hand out money. However, I will say you're one of the hardest working people I know, and it's obvious you're organized and detail oriented. My moneyman always chides me to be mindful of that when I'm approached for money. So, here's what I'll do, or what I need you to do. I need you to show me your business plan, which should include costs and projected sales; things like that. Obviously, I'll need to know where the shop is and what they're asking for the business. When you have that we'll go talk with Mr. Macklgrew, he's my moneyman, and if he thinks you're a good bet, then I'll finance. That's my offer."

Theresa turned and pulled a large envelope out of her bag. "Here is the information. Do you have time to look at it?" I looked at the package. You mean now?

"Sure. Do you want to wait while I go over it?"

"I have some work to do." She smiled and headed towards the south bedrooms.

There must be a sign I don't see that says "easy touch" floating just above my head. The envelope contained all the requisite information: price, location, sales for the last five years, operating costs, taxes and expenses; there was even a note from the owner indicating a willingness to help Theresa get going by assisting her two or three days a week. It was all there, everything a conscientious money guy would want to see. The problem was financing, pure and simple. Theresa needed it to make this work and her credit history was thin, and, while she didn't say it out loud, being young and Hispanic made it that much tougher to get.

I set it down and closed my eyes, hoping for a few moments to myself, but it turns out nap time was over and my young ward was yelping to be let out of his pen. His arms went straight up as I approached him, his face pinched and determined. I knew the look. I picked him up and hauled his soiled butt to the bathroom. Once that delightful task was complete, we went to the kitchen for a snack. Sliced grapes and mangoes hit the spot. I left the mess-making Zach to retrieve his awakened sister, cleaned her while Theresa kept an eye on Zach; she was going through her grocery list, and returned to feed child number two. She wasn't ready yet for sliced fruit, but the blender soon took care of that and my grandchildren were ready for more adventures.

Theresa quietly waited for me to say something. I noted that she had picked up her envelope and was holding it close to her chest.

"You have it all well in hand," I said, as I wiped Zach's face.

"Then it's ok?" Oh, to be young and hopeful.

"I think so. I'll give Mr. Macklgrew a call and we'll talk to him, hopefully in a day or so. How's that?"

A cautious smile came to the young woman. "Thank you for your interest and kindness."

It was my turn to smile. "Sure." No doubt Judith would approve.

Third was the curious call from the colonel. I was surprised, but not really. People talk and when they do, others take notice. The colonel did not mince words.

"I understand you've been asking questions about our operations, Mr. Buttman, and that concerns me." I didn't care for his tone, which darkened my mood.

"More so than the deaths of these men; men under your command?"

"That's an idiotic argument I won't get drawn into..." I noted his voice softened just a touch.

"I assume your friends in Washington alerted you that someone was asking questions, and you pegged me. If that's your concern, so be it, but my interest is what drove my brother to kill himself, and if that means questions need to get asked, then I'm going to ask."

"This is about our national security, Mr. Buttman." Isn't it always?

"It's also about lost lives and the value of those lives, not just the investment in notions of security, whether real or imagined, Colonel." Moses would be proud.

"This isn't an easy job, and I don't need to be lectured about its aims and purposes. Safety and security matter most to those that have to provide it; more so than those that sit back and reap its rewards—"

"Then what do you want, Colonel?"

"I want to know what you're up to, Mr. Buttman."

"You *know* what I'm up to. You want to know if I've found out about stories that don't add up, like the one about Marines ambushed on a clear day by insurgents who weren't there; about sexual assault and bullying, and AWOL Marines hiding in plain sight!" The line went silent. As I stood there, a thought occurred to me now that I'd opened my big mouth. What if his source wasn't anyone in Washington? "Sergeant MacMillan's wife called you, didn't she?"

"Who called is immaterial. That they had to call at all is disturbing, and what do you mean AWOL Marines hiding in plain sight?" he demanded.

"Your man, Lewis," I explained.

"Lewis? You spoke to him?" He seemed surprised.

"Yes. He said you're aware of what's going on..." I paused, wondering whether to say anything more. "He said, as I told you before, that the sergeant has the answers."

"Yes, you did. Are you planning to speak to Sergeant MacMillan; to find these answers?"

"Assuming he's there, yes."

"I see. And when are you going on this little adventure of yours?" Somewhere in the recesses of my brain I recognized the change in his demeanor; the angry demanding Marine was gone, replaced by the far more unnerving one who sounded almost gleeful.

"Soon," I said. "Are you going to alert him first?"

"No need," the colonel said, "he'll know before you do. Goodbye, Mr. Buttman."

I wondered what he meant as I put the phone down. Zach was staring at me. I picked him up and put him on my knee. He reached down and handed me the phone. They learn so early. I called Macklgrew. He was more than happy to stop by the next day. Theresa, who was listening, was more than happy to stop by as well.

"Then it's all set," I said to the both of them, and no one in particular. Both wished me a good day before saying goodbye. Zach took the phone and put it in my coat pocket. He found this amusing.

I wasn't so sure.

The afternoon merged into evening. I handed the kids to the woman who gave them life and headed to the wife patiently waiting, I assumed, for her knight in gleaming 1964 automotive sheet metal to make her dinner. Traffic was thick and clotted as it always was this time of day. I turned on the radio and listened as it serenaded me with mariachi music. I inched my way to West Covina.

The fucking phone was chirping again.

I almost shouted an obscenity as I answered, but the purr on the other end was not who I thought it was.

"You haven't called me, Monk, I was worried," Monika worried about me; how sweet.

"Yes, you were so worried that you called Agnes and allowed how much you enjoyed sucking my cock."

She laughed. "Well, I did enjoy it. You did too, as I recall."

"What's on your mind, Monika?" There had to be a point to this.

"You." More purring from the woman with the glorious hips.

"I'm flattered, but I can only see ruin and rueful remembrance if I allow myself to wade too deep into your waters."

"Sounds like I'm the one who should be flattered."

"No doubt, but I'm in need of quiet and I don't see that happening if I start dropping by and taking advantage of your hospitality." Resolve, Buttman; find your resolve!

"Are you sure? I can be quiet if that's what you like." The purring and laughter were making my head spin.

"I'm sure. Goodbye, Monika."

"Goodbye, Monk." If only it were.

·　　·　　·　　·　　·

The good wife was standing in the doorway to the kitchen wearing only a white-collared shirt, unbuttoned, and a pair of high cut cotton panties. In her hands were two wineglasses, and on her face a suggestive smile. Whatever aggrieved feelings I was having with either Monika, or the sea of bad drivers I was forced to deal with, evaporated as I took in the beautiful woman before me. Agnes handed me one of the glasses.

"Penny for your thoughts, love?" she asked in a voice that matched her outfit.

I thought I was worth more than that? "I'm sorry. What was that? Your choice of outfits is causing me to lose my train of thought, or, more correctly, to move in other directions."

"Really?" she saddled up to me, her breasts pressed delightfully against my chest. The hand not holding the wineglass began unbuttoning my suit jacket.

"Really," I brushed the hair away from her neck, which she helpfully tilted, exposing more of it to my waiting lips. "I thought you'd be hungry by now..." This between kisses.

"But I am hungry." I pulled her hips in close.

"Evidently, the question is hungry for what?" I put my wineglass down on the coffee table.

"I would think that was self-evident." She put hers down.

Dinner could wait.

25

Agnes sat at the kitchen table watching as I prepared dinner. It was impossible not to notice the positive effect marriage was having on our love life. Her outfit hadn't changed, but now that our desires had been satisfied, she demurely buttoned her shirt, which was technically mine. I probably shouldn't talk, all I had on was underwear and an apron to ward off stray oil coming from the frying pan before it went in the oven.

"It's kinda nice to revisit some of our more adventurous moments," I said, as I put the steaks in the oven. "I can't remember the last time we did something like that."

Agnes smiled in her knowing way. "It was just before you heard Judith was dying..." She let that linger in the air. More than a year. Long enough for Lizzy to be conceived and brought into this world. A lifetime ago when everything seemed right; an equilibrium felt only by the dumbass in the apron. I poured more wine into our glasses and sat down.

"It has been that long, hasn't it?" I knew the answer but wanted to say it out loud.

"Nearly a year and a half and you're still complaining about this terrible situation it put you in." Agnes looked around the kitchen, past me, and out to the backyard. "You're right about this place. It is our home, and I feel a lot more comfortable here. I can indulge my fantasies and not wonder if they're a repeat of what might have gone on between you and Judith like I would at her house."

"Yeah, but the truth is I spent far more time with you than I ever did with Judith, and I'm not saying that to minimize what happened, and believe it or not, it wasn't just sex, although I'm pretty sure that may have bothered you more..." Agnes was frowning at me. "What I'm trying to say in a particularly poor way, is that I always gave you more time, and I wanted it that way..." Now she was shaking her head. "I'm just making it worse, right?"

"Yes, you are."

"I guess some things never change," I held up my glass.

"We can always hope." She raised hers.

"Then we'll move on to more prosaic subjects. Thank you for telling Theresa she could hit me up for money."

"Oh, come on, Buttman, you're loaded. No, you're beyond loaded; you're filthy stinking rich as my father would say, but then he never knew anyone with real money. Why not support the people you know could use a little money? You won't miss it. You'll make more than enough in interest to cover every dollar you hand out or loan, and you know it." I started to state my... my what? She noted the confusion on my face. "Didn't Judith say you could do whatever you wanted with the money? And how is Theresa or Anna or Rebekah any less deserving than those rich brats we see acting like they own the place? Those are your words, darling; your words. So spend a little of it. Besides, it's not, as you so often like to say, your money. Was Judith so tight with her money that she wouldn't help a friend or a relative?"

I laughed at that. "Judith detested both her family and many of the people considered her friends, but you're right, she told me I could do whatever I wanted with the money."

"Then what's the problem?"

"I don't want it to be wasted."

Agnes frowned again. "Oh, brother, a few dollars might be wasted."

I feigned shock. "It's the principle of the thing."

"I believe the principle of the things is you're a cheapass, and really, all of this is of your own making. You can't blame anyone but yourself."

I feigned more shock. "How do you figure?"

Agnes rolled her eyes. "Hey, I'm not the one who gave everyone a taste of the good life and money out the wazoo. That was you, Buttman. So, you can't be surprised when those very same people object as you pull the rug out from under them. It's human nature for them to believe you're a sneaky little cheapass. I was only trying to help soften that image."

"*You're* the one who wanted to live in the big house."

Agnes shrugged. "*That's* immaterial, as you say."

"I don't think it's fair that you keep throwing my own words back at me," I whined.

"I'm sure you don't, but if you feel aggrieved, tell it to your girlfriend."

I leaned in and grinned. "So, I can have a girlfriend?"

Agnes shook her head, "No."

"Wow! I don't know if I care for this marriage thing—"

"Too bad," she said resolutely.

As a coda, the timer on the stove went off.

"Probably just a well. I told Monika she'd have to find someone else, and if I went back on my word, she'd think I wasn't very decisive." I took the steaks out of the oven.

"So, you've been talking to *Mon-i-ka*?"

"She called to remind me she was still available, but I politely declined." I took the salad out of the fridge and handed it to Agnes, who was pouting.

"I don't like this, Buttman. Did you tell her we're married now?"

I handed her the bottles of dressing and took two plates out of the cupboard. "No, but I assumed you did, and I doubt she cares one way or the other." I divvied up the steaks and handed Agnes hers.

"So, what's the plan, and it better not include visits."

It was my turn to frown and shake my head. "There are no plans, or visits, and sooner or later she'll give up and find someone else to pin her fortunes on. This is LA; the place is loaded with rich guys. She'll be just fine without me."

Agnes shook her steak knife at me. "Uh-huh. Just remember the only loving you're getting is from your wonderful, charming wife and nobody else. Do I make myself perfectly clear, Sunshine?"

"Yes, dear."

Agnes smiled and put down the knife. "You can't complain because you said I needed to be more assertive in how I feel about these things." She was quite proud of herself, which only made me smile more.

"Yes, I remember."

"Good."

I said a small prayer for our marriage.

● ● ● ● ● ●

While our backyard is fairly private given the fence and the neighbor's mature trees, it was not like the house in the hills where you could parade around naked and not be noticed. With that in mind, I put on my pants and shirt, and Agnes put on the skirt she wore to work. It was another glorious suburban evening, and I didn't want to be anywhere else. Agnes set her chair close to mine and held my hand. I closed my eyes and listened to the world around me. I could hear Agnes taking a sip of wine, the neighbor's TV blaring, and the airplanes high above heading into LAX.

Agnes interrupted my reverie. "Are you going to give Theresa the money?"

"I don't see why not. Her business plan looks good and there's no reason not to unless I want to be a, how did you put it? Oh yeah, a sneaky little cheapass."

"Of course, but first you have to get the Macklgrew guy's ok, right?" Agnes snorted.

"He's merely looking after my interests. Apparently, people with money have to be careful of grifters, scam artists and the like. Also, entitled relatives, both by blood and marriage," I casually added.

"You're a real jerk, Buttman."

"I'll be in town all... actually no, I've got to go to Idaho in the next couple of days to see this Sergeant MacMillan and finish up this thing with Jacob." Agnes sat up and set down her glass.

"Idaho? We're going to Idaho?"

I opened my eyes and looked at her. "No, *we're* going to look at a condo with Anna, and meet with Theresa and Mr. Macklgrew. But after that *I'm* going to Idaho and you're going to hold down the fort till I get back."

"What if I say you can't go?"

"Then you'll say I can't go, but I'll go, anyway." Maybe I could just send Agnes? Unfortunately, she doesn't know everything that's going on. I could tell her and... give it up, Buttman.

"Why can't I go?" She wants to go to Idaho?

"Because someone has to be here to help the kids buy all these houses someone promised them. So, I'm putting you in charge." Agnes frowned. I thought we'd gotten past that.

"That doesn't make any sense," she said.

"In all the years you've known me, have I made any sense?" I crossed my arms for emphasis.

She thought about it. "No."

"Then problem solved," I said triumphantly.

"Again, no. Boy, it's a good thing you didn't say all this before we had sex."

"I'm not a complete idiot."

"I think the jury's still out on that," Agnes huffed.

Time for another prayer.

.   .   .   .   .

Trivialities abound in life, but what constitutes a triviality is dependent on one's perceptions and circumstances. The longer my association with Judith's fortune stretched, the more trivial certain aspects of life became. There was nothing I couldn't afford. I thought about that as I drove north. This was the first time I'd driven north, by myself, in decades. The last time being a drug run for Miguel's cousins just before our run-in with the Pronto brothers. Since my return to California, I was always accompanied on my drives by Agnes or Rebekah or some combination of our extended family, but this time, it was only me tooling up I-5. It was oddly exciting, yet laced with a kind of melancholy I couldn't quite define.

Is that right?

The previous day, spent running from one place to the next, was just as ethereal. There was our rendezvous with Anna at the condo she wanted to buy. That was preceded by Rebekah admitting she and Fidel had gone back to the house down the street in West Covina when we came to pick up the kids. Rather than fight a losing battle, I told them I'd have Macklgrew make a cash purchase, and we'd figure out the rest later. My daughter actually hugged me like she meant it. The condo Anna took us to was right out of the "You Should Live Here" magazines plastered by the checkout stands down at the market. All in all, I suppose, it was a nice place: not too big, not too small, and not too ostentatious. Anna, like Rebekah before her, had big eyes for the place.

"Oh," she exclaimed, "this is just the kind of place I want to have!" Those eyes turned to me. I noticed Agnes looking as well. What could I say? The same thing I said to Rebekah, "Are you sure you don't want to look at some other places?"

Apparently not. Such concerns were trivialities, mostly to me. They were sure, excited, nearly unable to contain their glee. Macklgrew had work to do.

Macklgrew played it straight, but I'd known him long enough to recognize his disingenuous glee at my awkwardness. It was at these times he reminded me of Art Devaney. They were both devious little pricks. He was businesslike with Theresa and impressed by her preparation and poise; qualities he held to be very important. He went over her plans and expectations; he pushed her on her goals, and peppered her with questions to see if he could get her to hem and haw. But Theresa was just as clever, and matched him as they parried. I was thankful I had nothing more to do than sign the check, or should I say checks.

It was only money. Everyone was happy, even Macklgrew, who left with a smile. What else was money for?

The rest of the day flew by and before I knew it, I was driving by myself to the old man's farm. I didn't call to say I was coming up; it was going to be a quick stop, a few words about what I'd found, a layover, and I'd be on my way.

"I'm going with you," he said.

"There's no guarantee he'll speak to us, or that he's even there." I was not predisposed to a road trip with the old man.

"I want answers and you say he's the one who knows."

"I *said* that Lewis *said* I should ask the sergeant, not that the sergeant has the answers."

"Why are you being like this? I deserve to know what happened."

"Because I don't know that you'll find what you're looking for; because no one is required to answer our questions, and because I know you, and getting pissed off and confrontational won't change that."

Moses drew close. "Then why are you going? You didn't even know him!" He was shaking. I stepped back and took a minute before I said something I'd regret. Meredith came over and got between the two of us.

"There will be no arguing over this; do you understand me?" She was right in the old man's face.

"I have a right to know," he shouted.

"We all want to know," she shouted right back. I had never heard Meredith raise her voice. It's possible that put a slight smile on my face.

Moses noticed. "What do you find so goddamned funny?"

I laughed, probably not the thing to do, but I couldn't help it. "I'm hitting the road at seven tomorrow. If you're going, you're going."

I think he said something as I left. It didn't matter if I missed it; it'd be on the agenda the next morning. Emily found out I was here, defied her mother, and followed me as I took a walk, mostly to escape the possibility of running into Moses or the Mackinaw brothers. I didn't want to talk, which made no sense because the only reason I was away from my comfortable life was to talk about what had driven Jacob to put a bullet through his heart. Emily took a hold of my hand. She didn't want to talk either. I held tight to her hand. The wind was blowing our hair and the sun was kept away by a series of clouds drifting across the sky. I waited for the rain, but it lingered in the distance.

"How come it's only you this time?" she said at last.

"I'm only stopping for the night. I'm going to Idaho to talk to a man about Jacob."

"Can I go with you?" I had a picture of Emily, Moses, and ME stuffed into the truck for hours on end.

"I think you know the answer to that."

Emily's face tightened. "It's not fair!"

"Sorry, it's the way it is. Besides, you'd be bored hanging out with me and Moses." Lame perhaps, but true.

"Moses is going? I heard he never leaves the farm unless he's dying or something." That made me laugh, which caused Emily to smile. "What?"

"Nothing, just that that sounds about right." I omitted the something was the unexpected death of his favorite son. "Things are still uptight at home?"

Emily shook her head. "People don't say uptight anymore, Mr. Sunshine."

I shook my head. "Then they should get with the program." Emily rolled her eyes.

"I don't know what's wrong. Andrea is nicer to me than my mom. Sometimes it gets so bad that I'm even looking forward to seeing my dad just so I can get out of here for a while."

"Wow!"

Emily squeezed my hand. "Exactly," she sighed.

For a moment I thought about bringing her along, but the idiocy of that thought and the outrage it would bring quickly pushed it away.

"Well, all I know is that parents can develop ideas, strong ideas of what their children should be and be like, and for some it's hard to accept that their kids are going to be different from what they wanted them to be. I had some of that with Rebekah, particularly when she was your age, and I'm certainly not what Moses thought I would be, but that's life. People got to be who they are otherwise they'll just be miserable and unhappy." I squeezed her hand back.

"I should tell her that."

"Yes, just don't say it came from me." We laughed at that.

I decided to sleep in the bunkhouse. I sat there wondering whether my hunger or intransigence would win out when it came to dinner. I could head into town, but laziness was overtaking me. The door opened as I was berating myself for being indecisive. I assumed it was Moses, but it was Meredith.

"Can I come in?"

"Sure. What's up?" I asked.

"I want to ask a favor of you." She sat down next to me.

"What kind of favor? Does it involve the disposal of a particular individual?" I regretted the stab at comedy as soon as I said it, but Meredith just smiled.

"It's tempting, I'll give you that, especially these last few weeks, but no, I'm not asking you to dispose of him, at least not yet. The favor I would like is for you to open up and talk to him." I'm pretty sure I frowned at that.

"I talk to him," I said defensively.

Meredith patted me on the knee. "We both know that's bullshit, Monk." Her expression reminded me of the one Agnes gives me far too often. "I'm not asking you to reveal your soul to him, but it's important. None of you boys ever really opened up to him, and now with Jacob gone he feels even more isolated from you, Sterling, Isaac—"

"Well, if we're calling bullshit, then you know why that is."

She smiled and continued. "Yes, I'm aware of why, but you're older now and he's not the firebrand he was all those years ago. I don't want you to be strangers anymore. I realize I can't force you, but as a favor to me will you try?"

I put my hand on hers, mostly to stop the patronizing patting.

"Alright, I promise I'll try." Meredith leaned in and kissed my cheek. I watched as she walked away, after which I decided to avoid dinner.

26

The next morning, I found the old man waiting by the truck, breakfast sandwiches in hand, and coffee resting on the hood of the Chevy. I shrugged and unlocked the doors.

"I don't know why you persist in locking your car doors here."

I tried to smile while opening the canopy. "Habit."

I loaded his suitcase and took my sandwich. Meredith came out to wish us well. Emily was watching from the kitchen window. I waved; she waved back. The plan was to take Interstate-80 to US-95 and head north. We'd stop whenever we got tired. Little was said the first hour or so.

I couldn't stand the silence. Apparently, neither could he.

"Where are we going exactly?" he asked. Good question.

"Lautenberg. Supposedly, he lives around there. I have an address."

"How far is that?"

"I don't know, about six hundred miles." A long six hundred miles.

"What do you know about this guy?" I was beginning to deeply regret stopping at the farm.

"Name, rank, and serial number," I offered. Moses was not amused.

"We got a lot of miles to cover. Is this how you're going to act? If it is, it's going to be a long trip." Funny, I was just thinking that.

"You mean it's not already?"

"Why are you like this? It doesn't help. I don't understand you, I really don't. Maybe I never did." He sunk down into the bench seat.

"Life is absurd that way, and you have to admit mine's been that in spades. As far as understanding me, why bother?" Moses shook his head.

Meredith was between us, frowning at me. The apparition was unhappy, her voice was ringing through my thick skull. "You promised, Monk." Damn!

"Fine, I only know a little about the guy. I know he was a sergeant in the Marines. I know they were having problems in Jacob's company, that's one of the reasons he was assigned to them. I know he abruptly retired, and I know he has a wife in Virginia who wants him to come home. Other than that, it's whether Lewis was bullshitting me or not. Art found that there were discrepancies concerning an incident in Afghanistan that cost two Marines their lives, but I don't know if that involved Jacob, or if it was one of those things that makes the military look bad so they covered it up. I don't know that he'll talk to us, or allow us onto his property. Just playing it by ear at this point."

Moses mulled that over. "Do you think he knows anything about the abuse accusations?"

"My guess is he would. The question is whether he'll talk about it." I looked over and saw that his head was down.

"Do you believe it?"

"Believe what?" I asked. I heard him sigh.

"That he... that he assaulted that man." The pain radiated as he spoke. What did I believe?

"I honestly don't know. I hope it's not true, maybe a misunderstanding. I mean Kurtis' journal entry wasn't explicit that Jacob had sexually assaulted him, as the other two, Dezi and Lambert had; only that he was there. So, I don't know if that means he was a passive participant, or that he could have stopped it but didn't, or was unwilling to report it or support Kurtis if he had. I know you want to believe it's all lies, but we both know in certain circumstances our moral landscapes fail us. I don't pretend to know what war is like, but I've read enough books by people who've been through it to know what we consider normal behavior doesn't apply. The truth is, Jacob could have."

Moses simply shook his head, "I refuse to believe that."

I saw no good reason to argue with him.

We stopped for the night in Winnemucca, Nevada, known as an oasis in the high desert. I noted the greenery as we came into town. The Holiday Inn Express welcomed us and we found ourselves in our room staring at one another.

"We could've gone at least another hundred miles," he grumbled.

"Perhaps, but I'm in no big hurry and in no mood to be stuck in the middle of nowhere. This isn't exactly the most populated part of the country.

Besides, I'm hungry and need a drink." I got up and motioned that he should do the same.

The hostess at the restaurant raised her eyebrows as we entered. I hadn't given it much thought, but we made an odd-looking pair. I was wearing a light tan sport coat over a buttoned-up polo that was just a shade darker than the coat. My trousers were a light blue, and my shoes were brown loafers. I looked like something out of a late fifties Hollywood rag extolling the good life movie stars enjoyed in places like Palm Springs. Moses, on the other hand, appeared to have just stepped out of a barn. His usual attire of cambric shirts and faded jeans had given way to the more distant appearance he had when I was a kid of worn overalls and work shirts. Today's color was red, blood red.

The hipster and the hillbilly.

"Monica will be your server," the hostess said, as she handed us the menus. That made me smile.

"What?" inquired Moses.

"It's nothing."

I perused the menu, preferring not to discuss the woman who desired me for no other reason than I had plenty of disposable income to spend on her. I looked around the room out of habit. With all the excitement of the last few years, I found I was becoming more attuned to similarities, patterns, especially faces and vehicles; certain reoccurrences of the same type of car, like the mid-nineties dark green Mustang with the California plates in the corner of the parking lot. Had I seen that car before? It was something to be mindful of, just in case someone was watching. Agnes cautioned it might not be a bad idea to have Josef or Anton tag along, but having them with me on an extended road trip didn't excite me as I imagined it wouldn't excite them. I told her not to worry. What could happen?

Moses was grousing over the menu. He wasn't much of a traveler, hadn't been since he and the Mackinaw brothers settled on the farm as their final destination. Whatever his more modern trappings of late, Moses' distaste for modern life and modern convenience, like roadside diners, had not appreciably abated.

"There's not a thing here that looks even remotely healthy."

"It's one meal, you'll survive. Have a salad." I tried to ignore the years of Moses-isms bouncing around in my head.

"How do I know the produce hasn't been inundated with pesticides?" Oh, brother!

"Then have something really bad, like the chicken fried steak and the mashed potatoes. It comes up better than salad."

Moses didn't care for that. "Do you always have to be like that?"

"Like what?" I asked innocently.

"Like a smartass!"

That made me grin. "I've been a smartass all my life. Why change?" I reasoned.

"Because people would appreciate it, that's why."

"Perhaps, but I've been given a certain carte blanche by those who've tolerated me over the years, and because of that I feel no need to alter my personality. I believe I'd become way too bland if I did. Besides, if I changed, what would we argue about? It would take all the fun out of our relationship." I figured that would get him going.

"Our relationship?" He wanted to say more, but Monica was here to take our order. While she shared the same name with the nymph in LA, this Monica bore no resemblance to the other. She was easily in her late fifties, a little heavy with weary eyes, and a smile honed for two such as me and the old man. Her hair was graying and tied up in a bun. The notion that she would regale me with the quality of her sexual prowess seemed remote. I took that as a good sign. Moses continued to grouse, which Monica ignored. I ordered the chicken fried steak just because and Moses ended up ordering the fried chicken dinner. He didn't care for the wide grin on my face. Monica smiled too, but I assumed for a different reason.

Moses didn't care for the quality of the water either. Every time he took a sip, he made a face. He turned his attention to the others in the diner. Most were middle-aged, although there were a few younger couples, either with the oldsters or by themselves. I counted twenty-two of us all together.

"Do you think about life, about what it means?" he asked after looking over the crowd.

"Sometimes."

"I'll probably regret asking, but what does it mean to you?"

I rolled my eyes at that. "Normally I'd be glib and say it doesn't mean anything, that life is an absurdism foisted on us by a mischievous god, but given your previous remarks concerning my propensity towards smartassery, I'll try to be serious."

"I'm honored." Moses couldn't help himself, which made me smile.

"If I may be so bold, I think what you're looking for is whether any of your words of wisdom have sunk in, whether I've absorbed any of it." I noted the disdain in his expression.

"Is there anything wrong with that?" He was dead serious, which I always found amusing. It was one of the things about me that infuriated him. I'm like that.

"No. But to answer your question, yes, much of what you have imparted has stayed with me, for good or for bad. As an example, I blame my deep unease in having to deal with Judith's money to your railings against the corruptions of wealth. Rather than luxuriate, which I've found is the preferred response, I prevaricate and whine, much to the dismay of everyone around me."

"Then give it away. Give it to the poor."

"I can't do that. The poor are undeserving, that's why they're poor." I was pricking at his outrage, but he'd known me long enough to know better.

"And life?"

"Life is absurd and illusory. I offer myself as a prime example. But even if we move beyond the last couple of years, if we discount the odd turns of those years, there's still the beginning and the middle, and while few grow up on communes and end up farmers in Virginia because of drug deals gone bad, how is anyone else's life any less absurd?"

"So, life has no meaning?" He took another drink and shook his head at the glass.

"Turn the question around, after all you asked for the meaning of life. For me, at its most basic, life is simply an experience that we one day pass out of. Once done, it's over. You don't return, there are no retries, any of that. You go back into the universe. Biologically, our only true purpose is to procreate and beget the next generation, no different from any other species other than we've evolved to obsess over the meaning of life."

Moses shrugged. "You sound like a kid I used to know in college. He, too, thought there was no point to life."

I looked at the Mustang.

"I didn't say there was no point to life, simply that it was absurd. The point is to experience, and to revel in that experience, whether it's good or bad. Yet somewhere along the line our ancestors decided we were much too important and profound, that our lives should be projections into infinity. That we were, as you well know, created in God's image; therefore we must be inferior gods and that inferiority would ease as we progressed toward the one true god whoever that might be." I was on a roll.

Monica brought our dinners and a couple of beers. The perfect historical compliment to brackish local water. Moses took a moment to appraise his meal. I, on the other hand, dug in. It was a perfectly decent chicken fried steak. Not too dry, not too bready, reasonably seasoned, and not sized to feed a family of four. The mashed potatoes and the brown gravy were equally edible. Moses, after inspecting his fare, grudgingly ate everything on the plate.

"Was it as completely unsatisfying as you had expected?" I couldn't help myself.

"It was actually pretty tasty, but I was hungry." Yes, the only plausible explanation.

"Well good, and the meaning of life?"

Moses finished the last of his beer. "From what I've heard, it sounds more like the meaninglessness of life."

"In a sense, it is. Everything we know and will experience; the earth, the solar system, the stars beyond, are finite and will at some point burn up, taking all of our collective experiences with them. Nothing will be left. It will all be consumed." Moses shook his head, but I detected a slight smile and more light in his eyes.

"Maybe you're right. Sunshine really doesn't fit you anymore, certainly not with that attitude. You must be the life of the party," he mused.

"Most of the people who know me, know better than to let me to speak of such things, but I find it a liberating viewpoint."

He chuckled. "I imagine you do." Monica brought us two more beers and cleared the table.

"Dessert?" she asked.

"Why not?" Her well-honed smile left us a pair of dessert menus. "And your meaning of life?"

"It hasn't changed. The meaning of life is in the soil and in the earth. We are our most connected when we ply the fields and till the land. The joy of life is in our communion with one another. It's as simple as that." He seemed quite satisfied as he said this.

"Sounds like the same thing I said."

"Perhaps, but it is far more appealing and poetic than life is essentially pointless because it all ends in flames and disintegration." He tilted his head for effect.

"Perhaps," was all I was willing to concede.

The dessert was apple pie á la mode, the evening was quiet, and the night was listening to Moses snore on and off for seven hours. We hit the road early with one of us more refreshed than the other. I made him drive while I slept through the last of Nevada and into Idaho. Our meals were at stops along the way with Moses whining about the food, and it being hardly in our best interest to consume it. I threatened to take him to McDonald's if he didn't stop complaining. It was early evening when we rolled into Lautenberg.

Lautenberg had seen better days. Main Street went for a mile or so, possessing the bones of the past that held up the facades of worn brick buildings before returning to the state road it was technically part of. The town was buttressed by a few forlorn motels at the south end, near a manmade lake, and a sawmill to the north that was closed. The town resided next to the national forest, which I assumed had fed the mill and had been the principal source of income for the town before it closed. Many of the storefronts were empty. There was a tavern not far from the mill and next to that, a small grocery and gas station. The homes, such as they were, framed the road through town and dotted the hills on both sides. We chose forlorn motel number one.

The woman who came to the counter was nice enough until I asked her a question about how to get to the sergeant's place. The address was on the state road and I assumed there was a turnoff onto his property. I didn't think it a problem to ask.

"I couldn't tell you," she informed me, but it was clear she could have. "Maybe Dahl down at the tavern might know. Most folks up along the road like their privacy so they don't mark their driveways. How long were you thinking of staying?"

"A couple of nights," I replied.

She wrote that down and set a pair of keys on the counter. "That'll be a hundred dollars, please." I handed her the money. A smile found her as she took the five twenties in her hand. "Your room's down at the end, number 12."

"Thanks. Is there a good place to eat around here?" The woman at the counter rubbed her chin.

"Well, I usually go to Millie's. You passed it if you came through town. It's nothing special, just regular food, but she's got a garden so the food's fresh if you like that kind of thing." I assured her I did, and left for our room.

The motel was what you might call log cabin rustic, though the rooms weren't actually log cabins, and as far as I could tell, the place hadn't been upgraded or remodeled in some time. Room 12 was reasonably clean and brought to mind the Seventies in the prints on the wall and the small table and two chairs that complimented the twin beds. The heater worked, as did the plumbing fixtures. The light in the bathroom was sallow, and it took more than a minute for the hot water to arrive. I looked out the window. There were no other vehicles in the parking lot.

"We might be the only ones here," I said.

Moses didn't respond. He sat on the edge of his twin, lost in thought. I took out my phone and was surprised to see we had decent reception. On a whim, I Googled the history of the place known as Lautenberg. It was, I learned, a company town owned and named for one Franklin Lautenberg who had come west in search of gold, but instead made a fortune in timber. A succession of Lautenbergs kept claim to the town through good times and bad. The site blamed environmentalists and cheap Canadian lumber for the demise of the mill. I turned to Moses.

"Hungry?"

He looked at me for a moment before returning his gaze to the floor. "I'm not hungry. Go eat if you want. I can survive without a meal or two."

"Then I'll run down to the store and pick up a little something. Be back soon." He motioned me off with his hand. I sat in the truck wondering if I should leave him. It wouldn't take long, I thought.

The woman at the store, like the woman at the motel, was friendly at first, but she, too, darkened when I asked about finding the address I was given. A man in a state's rights tee shirt with a week's worth of beard wandered over.

"Who ya looking for if ya don't mind my asking?" I wondered if he thought I was easy prey out here wearing a coat and tie and looking out of place. The 45 was tucked into my waistband. Just in case.

"I'm looking for a man named MacMillan. He served in the Marines with my brother. You know him?" The man looked at the woman before returning to me.

"Don't think I do. Dahl might know him. He was in the military. He keeps up with that sort of thing." I nodded in appreciation.

"Dahl's down at the tavern?" I enjoyed the shock on his face. "The woman at the motel said the same thing." I handed the woman three twenties for the groceries. She opened the till and handed me five dollars and six cents in change. I thanked them and headed to the tavern.

There were three cars and four trucks in the lot. The bar appeared to be a converted house. It had a porch and two large windows on either side of the front door. Both were covered in plywood. The word Tavern, in faded neon, adorned the ridgeline. The interior was simple enough. A long bar took up the right side of the room; whatever original walls there were had been removed and replaced with a metal beam crossing the ceiling. Two pool tables and three pinball machines were in the back off to the left. The rest of the place was filled with unremarkable tables and chairs. Most of the patrons were towards the back, playing pool and talking among themselves. They all took a gander at the guy in the suit. I nodded in their direction and moved towards the bar and the man behind it. He took a moment to consider the town dude standing in front of him. To the side I noticed an older man with wild white hair tucked in at the end of the bar, almost out of sight.

"Are you Dahl?"

"Who's asking?" The man was of considerable size, most of which appeared to be muscle. He had dark hair that was pulled back in a ponytail. Tattoos covered his forearms and a close-cropped graying beard adorned his face.

"My name's Monk. I'm looking for a man who served in the Marines with my brother. I have an address, but when I asked about it, I was told to ask Dahl." A few of the other patrons were working their way over, but the man behind the bar waved them off.

"I'm Dahl. What's this man's name you're looking for?"

"MacMillan." The wild-haired man turned to Dahl, but Dahl's expression kept the man's tongue quiet.

"Damn," was all the big man said.

Whatever thoughts I had were interrupted by the commotion as the door burst open and three men walked in. The one in the middle was short, maybe five-foot-four, and had a pinched red face topped with wispy blond hair. He was not athletically built like the two towering over him. They reminded me of all-American versions of Josef and Anton. The dink was not in a good mood, which deteriorated upon seeing the wild-haired man tucked in at the end of the bar.

"What the fuck is he doing in here, Dahlgren? I specifically told you I didn't want that drunken piece of shit in my place."

"It's not your place yet, Jay." The muscles in Dahlgren's forearms visibly tightened.

"Soon enough, goddammit, and I can break the lease anytime, you understand that! The old man ain't long for this world and you do not want to be on my bad side." The man, Jay, then pointed at the wild-haired man who had begun inching towards to door. "Throw him the fuck out a here." The goon to the left grabbed the quivering man by the scruff of his frayed jacket.

"Let him go, Bill. His legs work. Take off Jasper." Dahlgren had his hand on something just underneath the bar. Bill apparently understood the threat and let go of Jasper, who stumbled out the door. The trio turned to me. Jay stood directly in front of me while Bill and the other goon stood on either side. I put my hand on the stool next to me. My legs were shaking. Jay looked me up and down while the other two scowled. If they thought this would intimidate me, they were right. I began hoping I would get the same opportunity Jasper got to get the hell out of here. MacMillan wasn't worth this.

"I hear you're asking about that fucking jarhead," he said at last.

"I'm looking for a man named MacMillan, served with my brother. I was told he lives around here. That's all." The man, Jay, snarled and grabbed my tie, yanking down on it.

"I don't fucking believe that. Who are you? What's your name?"

"Monk Buttman," I said. The bar erupted in laughter. I ignored it. "I'm exactly what I said I was. I'm just stopping by."

Jay didn't laugh.

"Stopping by? Nobody just stops by, jerkoff." He yanked again on the tie. "Now you're going to tell me what the fuck you and that fucking jarhead are up to, or I'm going to let these two go to town on your ass. You understand me?"

Jay was beginning to piss me off. He was close enough that I could pull the 45 and blow a hole through his gut before the goons could do anything to stop it. "I'm sorry, but you didn't tell me your name?"

A quizzical smirk crossed the man's face.

"I'm Jayson Lautenberg and this is my fucking town." And with that, he punched me in the stomach. Unfortunately for both of us, his hand struck the 45. I groaned as he let out a howl. The goons were surprised and stepped back momentarily, which gave me enough room to pull out the 45. The room got quiet. Lautenberg was holding his hand. "What the fuck you think you're going to do with that, you sonofabitch?"

"I'm going to use it to get myself to the door. I don't know what kind of bullshit you got going on with Sergeant MacMillan, but it isn't my bullshit. Now why don't you give me a wide enough berth and I'll get my sorry ass out of here."

Lautenberg's face reddened. "You ain't telling me what to do in my place, motherfucker." He moved towards me and I pulled back the hammer on the 45.

"This place is worth your life, brother?"

"What?" He stepped back.

The rest of the bar moved in. They might enjoy the sight of me killing this man. I could hear myself breathing. The door to the tavern opened. An old man with a walker and a middle-aged woman came into the bar. Every patron in the bar moved back, allowing the old man some room.

"Jay!" he shouted, "what in God's name are you doing? Step back from that man." Jayson Lautenberg grimaced before moving back. "You sir, put that firearm away." I did as the man asked. "What the hell's happening and what business do have in our town?"

"I came here to speak to a man about a personal matter concerning my brother; they served together in the Marines. I have an address and was told

I might get the directions here at the tavern from a man named Dahl." The old man's expression didn't change.

"What's your name, sir, and the name of this man you're looking for?"

"My name is Buttman, Monk Buttman. The man I'm looking for is named MacMillan. And may I ask your name, sir?" I assumed he was Lautenberg's father, but you never know.

"I, sir, am Franklin Lautenberg IV, and as I'm sure you've found out, this is my nephew, Jayson. Unfortunately, your man, MacMillan, and my nephew have been unable to resolve their differences. I apologize for his conduct. However, I am not pleased with the conduct of Mr. MacMillan either. It has caused a lot of unnecessary tension here in town—" The old man wobbled and the middle-aged woman took his arm. "Goddamnit, Lorna, I'm alright."

Lorna wasn't buying it. "Let's sit down, Mr. Lautenberg."

The elder Lautenberg huffed and waited as a patron moved a chair under him and then sat down. "What's your name again?"

"Buttman, Monk Buttman," I repeated.

"Buttman, that's a terrible name." He waved his hand at the man behind the bar. "Dahlgren, is this man telling me the truth?"

"Yes, sir."

"And do you know where Mr. MacMillan's place is?"

Dahlgren shook his head. "No, sir."

Franklin Lautenberg IV waved his hand at me. "Then unless you plan to have a drink, I think it might be time for you to move along. And I would also suggest that you not dawdle too long in town." The old man pointed to the door.

I thanked him and left with my skin.

27

The wild-haired man rapped on the truck window just as I was about to leave the parking lot. The door was unlocked. Jasper opened it.

"Interested in a deal, mister?"

"Depends..."

Jasper grinned, exposing his rotting teeth. "You're looking for Angus, right?" I didn't know MacMillan's first name.

"I only know him as Sergeant MacMillan."

"That's him." Jasper's hand was shaking, and he periodically turned to check the entrance to the tavern.

"What's the deal?"

Jasper eased into the truck. "Think of it as a service. I know where he lives; I could guide you... Hundred bucks?" I smiled to myself. It's a good thing I brought along a fair amount of cash.

"How far?"

"About ten miles," Jasper needed a bath. "Deal?"

"Hop in." I noticed a gathering at the tavern door, "Aren't you worried they might follow us?" Jasper shook his head.

"They been warned. The money?" He stretched out his hand. I retrieved the bills from my wallet.

I looked back. We had company, and not just the truck from the tavern. Jasper was unconcerned. He had money.

"So, what's the problem with everyone if you don't mind my asking?"

"Town's dying," he said, fingering the twenties. "Once the mill closed, the work dried up. I have to admit it was a nice gig, but then I didn't do as much as the others; didn't need to." I looked at all the trees lining the road.

"Can't be for a lack of trees?"

Jasper grinned and looked out at the forest. "No, there's plenty of timber. The truth is the times have changed. Canadian lumber is cheaper.

There isn't any reason to buy local, and the people and builders who might prefer local aren't going to buy enough to support the mill. That's hard for folks around here to understand. Most of them have been here all their lives, sometimes generations like the Lautenbergs." I was surprised at the answers coming from the town drunk. Jasper must have seen that in my face. "You probably think its work for me to complete a sentence, but I'm not stupid, I just have trouble sleeping and the drinking helps with that."

"I don't see how that explains Jay Lautenberg's hatred for Sergeant MacMillan."

"Maybe not, but it plays into it. The town and the mill are all the Lautenbergs have; their fortune *is* the town. If the town goes broke, so do they. Jay's problems with Angus are more about me and his dead cousin, Frank. Frank and I were friends. After I got my draft notice, I went down to join the Navy. My father fought in World War II, and he told me if I had any brains, I should spend my time learning something useful other than how to get killed, but the Marine recruiter got to me first and when Frank learned I was going into the Marines, he wanted to join too. But his father, Franklin Lautenberg IV, forbade him from joining, telling him he had to go to college. So, he went to college, finished in three years, and received a commission in the Corps. The old man wasn't happy about that and tried to keep him out of Vietnam, but Frank wanted to go. I was already there. I tried to warn him, but he was a big boy and he was going no matter what. He didn't come back. The family needed someone to blame, and me and my undue influence were it. Imagine that."

I was about to ask a question, but Jasper kept talking.

"That left Jay. When he was younger, Jay bore the brunt of his uncle's anger after Frank was killed. During the war Jay took a deferment and never had to serve, and he didn't like being reminded time and time again about his smarter, better-looking cousin who was a fallen war hero. So, he would lash out at people like me." He took ahold of his pants to keep his hands from shaking.

"And Sergeant MacMillan?"

"Angus is Corps through and through; you need to understand that. His family's been serving since the Civil War. When he first came out with his wife there was concern he was a carpetbagger looking to take advantage of the town's collective miseries. They talked about transforming the town into an arts colony or some such nonsense. Not that I'm against that, but soon enough they found that even if people liked the idea, the Lautenbergs did not. They remain chained to the past and the idea that with the right people in office, the mill and the profits will come back. And since they own most of the town, they still get to decide."

"Uh-huh." Get to the point.

"I'm getting too talky. Sorry. The big blowup came at the tavern. I like to stop by and Dahl's always been accommodating even though he thinks I drink too much. But as you saw, Jay doesn't want me at the tavern. I met Angus early when he was talking with Dahl about Dahl's time in Iraq, and Jay came in and started thrashing on me and Angus told him to stop. Jay told him to butt out and mind his own business. Angus didn't listen. Jay knocked me down and Angus did something no one in this town has ever done before or since. He kicked Jay's ass. That caused a lot of bad blood. Jay tried to retaliate using Bill and Donny, but Angus is no fool, and he's been careful not to get himself in a situation where the three of them might jump him. The turnoff's coming up." He pointed to an almost indistinguishable marker off the road.

The sun was setting.

"How far?" The light through the trees was thinning and my sense of unease was growing.

"About a mile. He'll know we're here. Don't be surprised by that, and do what he tells you; that way you won't get shot." Lovely.

The driveway snaked through the forest, before it opened onto a meadow with a medium-sized cabin on one side and a barn on the other. There was no one to greet us, and nothing but the sounds of the wind and the birds circling above the trees. Jasper didn't seem worried as he got out of the truck.

"We should wait on the step," he said. I got out and followed. We waited for ten minutes. Nothing.

Jay Lautenberg and his goons, Bill and Donny, drove up. After a minute or two they got out. I thought about getting off the step, but Jasper put his hand out in front of me.

"Don't take out the gun either."

Jay and the boys approached us spinning around to see if anyone else was coming up on them. When they got close to the house, Jay waved Bill and Donny back so they were perhaps ten paces behind him. His face was still red.

"Where is he, Jasper?" Jasper was playing with his shoelaces. "Look at me when I talk to you, motherfucker!"

"I don't think you should be here, Jay. You know what he said."

Jasper looked up at the livid Jayson Lautenberg. It was then that I noticed a shadow behind the truck and the two goons. Neither Bill nor Donny knew what hit them. The Marine was efficient; two strikes, two men down. Jay turned when he heard the two men fall. Sergeant Angus MacMillan stood there with a nasty-looking shotgun in his hands.

"I'm right here. Is there a reason you're on my property? And don't spout that 'this is my town' shit to me. This is my land, free and clear, Lautenberg, and you're trespassing."

Lautenberg, for once, was speechless. MacMillan moved towards him, which prompted Lautenberg to step back and lose his balance. As he fell, he stuck out his hand, which twisted and cracked when he landed on it. He screamed, rolling on his back, holding his injured hand. MacMillan stood over him with the shotgun cradled in his arms.

I got up and offered to help Lautenberg off the ground.

"Leave me the fuck alone!" he cried.

"Then just lay there," I said.

The two goons were moaning. MacMillan went over and pointed towards the side of Lautenberg's truck. "Over there." Bill and Donny, having no interest in fucking with the sergeant, crawled over and leaned against the large front tire. MacMillan returned to where Lautenberg was, just in front of the porch. "Why are you here, Lautenberg?"

"I," was all that came out.

MacMillan was clearly disgusted. "I'm not interested in whatever's troubling you and your family, and I can't stop you from shooting off your mouth to every soul in town. But these thirty acres are by invitation only, and I won't tolerate you not respecting my rights. I don't like resorting to violence, but I won't be intimidated. I don't care who the fuck you are. If you try this again, I won't be so understanding, you got that?"

"You can't hold me here. I need medical attention," Lautenberg mumbled.

"Nobody's holding you here. There's your truck. Get going!"

Lautenberg lay there trying to get up and failing. MacMillan signaled for the goons to get their boss. Gingerly, the two wobbled over and helped Lautenberg to the truck. We watched the three get in and drive off. Jay stuck his middle finger out the window. MacMillan didn't seem too concerned. What he *was* concerned with was me, and why Jasper led me up here.

"What business do you have with me, mister?"

"My name is Monk Buttman. Jacob Bohrman was my brother. He killed himself recently, and I want to know why. The people who knew him told me you had the answers."

"And who would these people be, Mr. Buttman?"

"Lewis said to find you," I said.

"Lewis?" He acted surprised.

"Yes, Lewis. You did hear me say that Jacob killed himself?"

MacMillan put the shotgun over his shoulder. "I'm sorry to hear that, but I don't see how I can help you."

I was aghast.

"How about explaining what the hell happened in Afghanistan when Kurtis Santos was sexually assaulted? Or how Dezi and Lambert were ambushed during a sandstorm that didn't happen, by the Taliban who weren't in the area. Weren't you running the show, taking charge, all that kind of crap?"

MacMillan looked first at Jasper before looking back at me.

"You're rather well informed, Mr. Buttman. How did you come across this information?" He directed Jasper and me to follow him into the cabin.

"I know a guy who knows a guy at the Pentagon." Jasper and I sat in a couple of chairs placed in front of the fireplace.

"I see." MacMillan set the shotgun above the mantle. "I appreciate that you think I have the answers to your questions, but there's nothing I can tell you either about the allegations of sexual assault, or what happened to the two on patrol."

"Can't or won't?" MacMillan sat down.

"A little of both," he said. "Are you staying, Jasper?"

Jasper grinned. "I'm gonna head back. I'm a little thirsty."

I stood up "You sure that's a wise move?"

Jasper shook his head. "Doesn't matter. My time's up when my time's up." He got out of his chair and went with me to the door. MacMillan stayed in his chair, "Take care, Angus."

I closed the door.

.   .   .   .   .

Moses was sitting on the bed watching the TV.

"Where the hell have you been? You've been gone nearly five hours. I thought you were making a quick trip to the store?"

I flopped onto the other bed. "Yeah, I thought so too, but I hit a detour instead. On the plus side, I found MacMillan. On the downside, I nearly got my ass kicked. This town has more issues than I do."

Moses moved to the edge of the bed. "What did he say?"

"He said he had nothing to say. Sorry." I sat up. Moses got up and went to where the groceries were.

"Maybe that's for the best. I don't know that I want my worst fears confirmed. I sat here wondering if I could go through the rest of my life knowing my son was a rapist, and the truth is I can't." He set the contents of the bags on the table. "This is what you got?"

"Unfortunately, the Whole Foods was closed."

"Yes, what was I thinking? I assume you ate while you were on your little adventure?"

"I wouldn't assume that. Are you hungry now?" I realized I was hungry.

"A little something, assuming any of this is edible, might be nice. Would you like me to make you a sandwich?"

"I'd like that."

I got off the bed and opened two beers. They were warm, but it was what we had. I set out a bag of chips I bought to annoy Moses. He considered processed junk food to be anathema to the human spirit. He noticed the chips and chucked them across the room. I tried to act shocked, but laughed instead.

"Good Christ, Monk, are you ever going to grow up?" he chided.

"I don't think there's any money in it."

"At this point isn't money the least of your worries, assuming you have any?"

I shrugged. "Money or worries?"

Moses handed me my sandwich, turkey and Swiss on rye. "I consider the question to be self-evident," he said.

The room was quiet aside from the TV, which was turned down to where any dialogue was indecipherable. "Are you going to tell me what happened?" he asked between bites of sandwich and gulps of beer.

"Not much to tell," I said, before revisiting the store, the bar, the drunk, the Lautenbergs, the sergeant's cabin, and the sergeant himself. Moses nodded occasionally, but asked no questions while I talked. After recounting my adventure, I put the beer and the groceries in the small refrigerator by the table. The two of us retreated to our twins and stared at the boobtube. It was couples looking for houses, searching for perfection on a limited budget.

"Do you think it's worth my trying to talk to this Sergeant MacMillan?" Moses asked during an interminable series of commercials.

"I don't think we should even stick around this burg, let alone try to go back up there. Did I point out his aversion to people just showing up uninvited?"

Moses thought about this. "Maybe Jasper, that was his name, wasn't it? Maybe he could ask if we could come out for a talk."

I shrugged. "Assuming he isn't wasted. I think it might be time to sleep on it; consider our options in the morning."

"Alright." He turned off the TV, and we got ready for bed.

We never made it.

28

The knock came as we were getting into bed. I was tired and gave no thought to asking who it was, if it was anyone at all. The clock was emphatic that it was midnight and I was worn out by my adventures here in funsville. Moses had already turned out his light. Whoever was out there continued to knock.

It was Lewis. He pointed a 9mm at my head when I opened the door.

I just stared at him. The green Mustang was next to the Chevy. He pushed past me; the gun maintaining my forehead as its target, and closed the door.

"What's going on?" groused Moses, before turning and seeing exactly what was going on. "I know you, don't I?" Lewis didn't answer.

"Both of you get dressed. Now! You're taking me to see the sergeant," he demanded.

"Go yourself, you followed us; you know where he lives," I uttered. Lewis, in green fatigues and war paint, his eyes darting around the room, seemed perplexed by my answer. "Is there a reason why you're pointing that gun at us?" I asked after a tense couple of minutes.

"I can drop you right here, you understand that?" I sat down on the edge of the bed. Moses was still standing by his.

My head was beginning to ache; just what I needed. "If that was your plan, you would have done that straight away. Put the gun down." Lewis, ever mindful, slowly pulled the gun back, so it was pointing at the ceiling rather than my head. "Why do you need us?"

"I missed the turn. I was too far behind the truck that was following you. You know where the turn is. Let's go." He pointed the 9mm at Moses. "Get up or I'll kill him. You want that on your conscious?"

I looked at Moses. He wasn't used to having people pointing guns and threatening to kill him. I was surprised it didn't really bother me, and that I felt the need to banter with Lewis over whether he'd kill my father if I refused to go with him. Moses was still standing in the same spot.

"What do you want to do, Dad?" I'd never called him that before.

"I don't know that we have a choice," he stuttered.

"Then I guess we are going to see Sergeant MacMillan."

Lewis had something planned beyond going to see MacMillan. If it were simply that, we could have gone in the morning, out in the light, without guns pointed. My stomach began to knot in coordination with my aching head. Once outside, Lewis had us stand by the truck as he retrieved an assault rifle and a backpack from the Mustang. He ordered me to open the canopy and the tailgate of the truck and to open the slider on the truck so he could keep an eye on us, but, I presumed, not be seen in the front seat. It would have been tight up front, but not impossible to make sure Moses and I kept to the program if he had. No, Lewis had something more dangerous in mind and it appeared Moses and I were the bait.

I tried to think. It was possible to get out of this when he went into the bed of the truck. There would be a moment where we could run before he had time to get out. But Moses and I weren't exactly sprinters, and was I willing to take the chance that we could get away before Lewis hunted us down and shot us dead?

The other options rested under the driver's side and behind the bench seat. The 45 was tucked away in its holster and the shotgun was on its rack; both were loaded. The 45 I could easily retrieve. The shotgun would be trickier. The seat would have to be moved forward. I was ordered to get in the truck, while Lewis kept the 9mm pointed at Moses. Once I was in, Moses closed the canopy and got in the truck. All the while, Lewis pointed the gun at Moses. I moved the seat, grabbed the 45 and put it in my coat. I began picturing MacMillan's cabin and calculating Lewis' plan. My heart was racing and my hands were shaking. I knew were we dead men, and I was driving us to that end. I had to think of something other than taking a bullet to the head.

Lewis took his position in the back with the 9mm pointed at Moses' head.

Moses did not look good. I took his hand after he got in the truck.

"Let's go," commanded Lewis.

We crawled through town and past the sheriff's deputy who was talking up the woman at the convenience store. As we snaked along the state road, what had been a fairly dark sky brightened considerably as the clouds gave way to the moon. Lewis noticed it too. If nothing else and for no good reason, the moonlight eased the panic settling in my chest and allowed me to work through the questions banging around my head. I wondered if he actually had been to MacMillan's cabin earlier, and knew that getting the jump on the sergeant would take some work; no dropping by and having him answer the door. Why else would he need the fatigues and face paint? And why at night? Other thoughts festered; thoughts about dead Marines presumed to have killed themselves. Had they, or had they been helped along the way, willingly or not? I tried to remember exactly where to turn, focusing my attention on finding a nearly indistinguishable post with a green reflector by a bent cedar.

Moses turned to Lewis. "Why are you doing this?"

"Loose ends," he said.

"Was Jacob a loose end?" I asked.

Moses turned to me. "Are you saying he killed Jacob?"

"Did you?" I asked.

Moses turned back to Lewis, who was focused on what was coming. "Did you kill my son?" he demanded.

"We're all loose ends," he repeated.

"What does that mean, Lewis?" Moses looked at me quizzically. I noticed his expression. "What?"

"Why are you calling him Lewis?" I looked at the face in the rear-view mirror. It was grinning at me. I had it all wrong. Lewis was hiding at Pendleton or in Ukiah, not Cameron. Cameron was on his way to kill another Marine. The hipster and the hippie would be collateral damage.

I remembered the mile marker Jasper had pointed to. The cedar and the post were just past the marker. I made the turn onto the dirt driveway.

"Turn off the headlights," Cameron demanded.

The moonlight, filtered through the trees, gave just enough light to allow us to weave our way to the pasture and the cabin in the distance. There were no lights on.

"Stop," he said. I stopped the truck at the edge of the forest. He moved back and opened the canopy door. "Drive up to the house and knock on the door. Try anything stupid and I kill you both. Got that?"

I nodded.

He climbed out, closed the canopy door, and knelt behind the truck. I started slowly towards the cabin. Cameron stayed on the bumper of the truck.

"We should do something," whispered Moses.

"Like what?"

"Drive away, run him over; something. He plans to kill us!"

I pulled the 45 out of my coat. "Yes, he does, but we're no match for any of that. The truck's not fast enough if he starts shooting, and he's not directly behind the truck, so running him over would be tricky." Moses noticed the 45.

"So, you're going to shoot him?"

I shook my head. "We're going to play it safe and pray the sergeant is with us. This," I patted the 45 in my lap, "is our last resort."

I drove to within ten feet of the porch and turned off the truck. I put the 45 back in my pocket. We got out of the truck and went up to the door. I knocked three times for good luck.

No answer.

I knocked again.

No answer.

"What now?" Moses whispered.

"I want you to look to where Cameron is and look at me and then turn back to the door."

He didn't get it. "Why?"

"So, *he'll* know, that's why." If this wasn't so serious, I might have laughed at Moses' uncomprehending expression.

"Who?"

"MacMillan," I told him. Moses looked to where Cameron was, then to me.

The wind spoke next.

"Put the weapon down!" the voice called. I grabbed Moses, and we ducked behind the porch rail. I took out the 45. Cameron stood there looking for where the voice was coming from. I noticed the goggles for night vision strapped to his face. He crouched lower and took a few steps away from the truck. "Put the weapon down, Marine."

"I can't do that. I have work to finish," the Marine shouted back.

"I'm not going to argue with you. Put the weapon down." Looking to his left, the Marine took a chance and fired a burst into a stand of tall grass.

A single shot answered, striking him in the leg. He groaned and dropped to his knees, firing a second burst.

The second shot struck him in the chest, but it sounded odd; Cameron was wearing body armor.

"Put the weapon down," MacMillan cried. "For christsakes, put the goddamned weapon down!"

"I can't do that. Loose ends." Cameron fired a third burst.

The last shot blew the top of his head off. The Marine toppled over onto his side. Moses fell back and threw up. A figure arose out of the tree line and approached the dead Marine. I put the 45 back in my pocket and went to meet him there. MacMillan kneeled down and put his hand on Cameron's shoulder.

"You were expecting him, weren't you? Colonel Jaron alerted you, didn't he?" It was time for answers.

"Call the sheriff, Mr. Buttman," was his answer.

•   •   •   •   •

The sheriff, a man named Belsen, arrived with a bevy of personnel, whose vehicles lit up the area, obscuring the moonlight with white beams and throbbing red flashes. Moses and I were sitting on the porch steps. MacMillan sat next to the dead Marine. Belsen wandered over to the sergeant. It was apparent they knew each other.

"I didn't expect to be up here till morning," the sheriff said, as he knelt down to look at the carnage. "Mr. Lautenberg filed a complaint, but I figured it could wait." Other members of the sheriff's department crowded in, "Got a name for me?"

"Seth Cameron," MacMillan told him.

"Apparently it wasn't a friendly visit." Belsen got up and MacMillan followed.

The other's in the crowd set up a perimeter and waited for the forensics team. They had to come up from Boise. The sheriff took a gander at me and Moses and introduced himself. That preceded a lot of questions. Who are you; why are you here; did you know the dead man; how do you know MacMillan, and what's your story? We told what we knew, and he responded by saying "I see" and "interesting." At the end we were exhausted and needed to lie down, sit down, something. I could barely stand and Moses was leaning hard against a porch post. They had roped off the truck, so we couldn't leave.

"You can rest inside," MacMillan offered. We quickly found two chairs and passed out.

Moses woke me up sometime later. I knew it was morning; there was sunlight streaming into the cabin. My neck and back were stiff, and it hurt to move. I sat up and tried to orient myself. Where the hell was I? I looked at the old man. He looked terrible.

"You get any sleep?" he asked.

"Some. You?" I didn't like the way he was shaking.

"No. I need to get out of here." I pushed myself up and gave the man a hug. He grabbed me and began to sob. It took all my strength to keep us both from falling over. MacMillan must have heard, and came in from the porch. He helped me lead Moses to the porch. There was a long bench with cushions on it. I hadn't noticed it before. Moses was shaking and crying. I held on to him as MacMillan left to get some water. He returned with water and some medication.

"This'll help you relax and get some rest."

"I don't want that. I want to leave," he protested.

"I understand, but they're not finished and the deputy there is charged with keeping us here." I spotted the guy standing next to the Chevy. The body was still there, as were most of the forensics people. Moses reluctantly took the water and pills. He was too exhausted to put up a fight. He laid back. "Take a series of slow measured breaths," the sergeant told him, "four counts in; five counts out. Concentrate on breathing and nothing else." Moses followed his instructions and began to calm down. He closed his eyes and let go of my hand. Angus MacMillan sat down on the top step of the porch. Moses was soon asleep. I moved down and sat next to MacMillan. We watched as the forensics team went about their work.

"It's beautiful country, isn't it?" He cast his hand towards the mountains to the east. "Quiet and peaceful. I bought this property years ago, sight unseen. A man my father served with in Vietnam recommended it. I own thirty acres. There are trees and meadows, mountains and streams. I've been dreaming of my time here for years. I got through every tour and deployment because I knew I had this when I was done. Now it's all coming apart."

"It's still beautiful, even if the town is owned by a miserable little prick."

MacMillan tried to smile. "True, but it's hard to go it alone. There are times when you have to go into town, and it belongs to them. Maybe Karen is right. It's not a welcoming place and that's not going to change. I can't hide up here. That wasn't the plan, but I know if I leave, Lautenberg will come up here and burn everything and no one will stop him."

"There's no one who can look after the place when you're gone? Jasper?"

He shook his head. "Jasper has a good soul, but he's unreliable. The others are too afraid or too intimidated. Besides, I have a reputation and not a good one." He did smile at that.

"Jasper told me you kicked Jay's ass."

MacMillan again shook his head. "No, Lautenberg built up that story to justify his hatred. I didn't know who he was when it happened. All I knew was that he was beating on Jasper, calling him names, and disparaging the Corps. I told him to stop and when he didn't, I knocked him to the ground. I don't consider that kicking his ass. After that, the word got out that anyone helping me or Karen would be on his shit list. It worked. Karen went back to Virginia and Lautenberg's been dogging me every chance he gets, telling anyone who'll listen that I'm nothing but trouble."

"And then this happens..."

MacMillan looked away. "I told him to put the weapon down."

"But he wouldn't, would he? It's like he expected this. When I talked to him at Jacob's funeral, he..." I stopped. I couldn't say it, that he expected to be killed.

"People do foolish things; commit foolish acts..."

The question popped back into my head. "You knew he was coming. Jaron warned you, didn't he? He called me before I left, but I didn't get what he was saying. I didn't understand, but something was wrong. Too many men from the same company were killing themselves. And now it looks like one of their own was systematically killing them off. Lewis, I mean Cameron, told me to talk to you; that you had the answers."

"And you believed that, didn't you?" MacMillan stood.

"I believe you're part of the puzzle and you know what started all this." I stood.

"You realize I'm under no obligation to talk to you." He moved to where Moses was sleeping.

"I'm aware of that." The sergeant looked at the mountains. A Golden Eagle was circling above us; watching.

"We'll talk when your father wakes up." He left me standing on the porch.

29

Moses was trying to shake off the effects of the drug MacMillan had given him; he felt better, which was something. MacMillan brewed a pot of coffee and handed out cups, which were labeled USMC.

I picked up mine. "Jasper told me your family's military service goes back to the Civil War."

MacMillan poured the coffee into our cups.

"That's true. My namesake, Angus MacMillan, and his brother, Declan, fought on opposite sides during the war. They'd come to America to get away from the highland clearances that were decimating their clan. Angus settled in Virginia while Declan ended up in Ohio. They grew tobacco before Declan departed, or so the story goes. Years later, when Angus was in arrears to the carpetbaggers, Declan came down and helped save the family farm."

That made me laugh. MacMillan didn't get the joke. "I know a number of tobacco farmers in Virginia," I explained.

"My son was a farmer for many years in Virginia," added Moses.

"Whereabouts?"

"Outside Bedford," I could see Car's tobacco fields in the distance.

"I know Bedford well," he said.

After an uncomfortable silence, Moses spoke up. "I want to know what happened to my son. I want to know what you know."

"What I know..." Sergeant MacMillan, the USMC cup in his hand, ran his fingers along the embossed letters. "What I know is complicated by who I am, what I do, and where I come from. I don't expect you to understand that for the simple reason you're unfamiliar with military life, with military institutions and the way they work. But more important to me is the honor of military service, and the honor of military institutions like the Marine Corps—"

"Honor? You just killed a fellow Marine. Where's the honor in that?" Moses was shaking. His antagonisms towards corruptive powers of the state, of militarism, were personified by the sergeant, by Cameron, by Jacob. "What's honorable about institutions that train men to kill each other? My son is dead! That man you killed; I knew him as a boy! What kind of institution changes him to the point where he ends up in a field with the top of his head blown off by someone he served under?"

MacMillan put down his cup. I half expected him to abort our talk, but in a measured voice he sought to calm my angry father.

"There is no honor, if that's the right word, in what's happened to the men in your son's squad. It is, as I understand it, tragedy. I realize you're angry that your son is dead, and maybe more so if it's true that Cameron played a part in it. It's also true that the Corps is not removed from its responsibility for what's happened. But to me, and I don't expect you understand this, the institutions, the foundations are what keep us anchored to our ideals no matter how poorly we may live up to them." He leaned in towards Moses. "I can't describe the sorrow I feel after what happened, by what I had to do. I do not enjoy killing people, and certainly not my fellow Marines. Would you have preferred he'd killed us?"

Moses was undeterred. "That's an excuse.... It shouldn't have to come to this." I could see him searching for the words to convince MacMillan that he was wrong or wrong-headed.

"But it did," I said.

"And that's what, ok? That's acceptable? What have we gained by any of this? Anything? How is there any benefit at all?" He looked at me. "How many of these boys are dead now?"

"Six," I answered.

Moses buried his face in his hands. "Six lives gone, and for what? I don't get it. I don't understand. It's fucking pointless. Why be a puppet to institutions that would throw your life away?" he moaned.

MacMillan seemed to be searching as hard as Moses. "Because it's important, that's why. And I'm no puppet! It's important because it's a part of my heritage, a part that I treasure. Because I love this country, and because it's in the service of something bigger and more important than whether everything we do is noble and right."

"Then what happened that wasn't right or noble?" I asked. "Your wife said you had planned to stay in and then abruptly retired—"

MacMillan didn't like that. "How do you know what my wife said?"

I tried to answer as Art Devaney would. "It was passed on to me by a man with a talent for gathering information, in reading people, and in knowing how to get them to talk. That's how. And it only strengthens my belief that what happened over there is part and parcel to what's happened here with Jacob and Cameron; with Kurtis and Mason, and what really happened to Dezi and Lambert on the patrol that got them killed."

A rueful half-smile found the sergeant. "So, you don't believe the official report?"

"I know it's bullshit. Did the rape allegations by Kurtis have a part in what happened?"

MacMillan was back to cradling the USMC cup in his hands. "First of all, there were no rape allegations, at least nothing formal," he said.

"Then what do you know about it? I need to know if my son was a rapist." Moses had let go of his face and sat back in his chair.

MacMillan looked at him briefly before returning his gaze to the cup. "I don't know what happened, none of them were eager to talk about it. From what little they said, and what I pieced together, what had begun as horseplay degenerated into something that wasn't explicitly stated. I know they'd been drinking. As for Santos, his biggest concern was getting Dezi and Lambert off his back."

"So, it's possible there was no rape?" Moses was clutching at straws MacMillan wasn't willing to hand out.

"Like I said, I don't know what happened. But in this day and age, sexual assault in the military is no longer an unspoken evil. Mostly it centers on female Marines. Men, at least in my experience, and in the experience of others—"

"Whose experience?" Moses demanded.

MacMillan looked at the two of us.

"I asked my father about it once. He served in Vietnam. I asked if there was ever talk about that kind of thing. Maybe my service isn't representative, but I hadn't come across it before they came to talk to me. Dad said in those days something like that would never be talked about. It was bad news. You'd be branded a fag or a pussy and you'd never hear the end of it. I asked him if he thought it happened. He said he was sure it happened during all the wars MacMillan's had fought in. He said it was human nature. My grandfather served in World War II and my great grandfather in the First World War. I had a hard time believing there was any time for something like that. He was surprised by my naiveté. He reminded me that war is terror and boredom."

"Lewis brought it up?"

MacMillan shook his head. "No, Saunders. I learned that he had been there. He admitted that maybe things got out of hand, but wasn't willing to go beyond that. Your son said the same thing when I talked to him. Command had no interest in pursuing it, so it was dropped."

Moses was crestfallen. We were getting nowhere. I tried to remember everything Devaney had told me. The murdered villager!

"What about Dezi and Lambert? I also heard it might have involved an important warlord in the area?"

MacMillan frowned. "Your source talks too much."

"What about it?"

MacMillan put down the cup and stood up. "We need to come to an understanding about this conversation..." He was pacing.

"If you're worried we'll be blabbing to the media, don't be. I don't know that anyone would care, anyway. Our interest is in Jacob and how this involved him, that's all. We're not here to besmirch the Marine Corps or make you look unpatriotic."

MacMillan laughed at that. "There was nothing patriotic about it, Mr. Buttman. We were there to buttress the government in nation building at the local level; a way to make something out of a seemingly endless conflict. Believe it or not, I wasn't there to kill. My mission was to forge partnerships between the villages and the local state security forces we were supporting. Places like Afghanistan are riddled with corruption and regular people, people like you and me, are wary of government types making promises and then pocketing the money for themselves. The villagers, especially, were suspicious of people like me and our support for the central government. It was my job to overcome that. I was not there to straighten out your son's squad. That was thrown in my lap."

I played my ace. "Is what happened to the man in the village, the cousin of this warlord Musa, a part of what happened to Dezi and Lambert?"

Moses was confused by the question, but MacMillan was not. It was whether he would answer it.

"What are we talking about?" Moses asked.

"You seem to be well informed, Mr. Buttman, why don't you fill us in."

"I was told this warlord was trying to get certain military hardware we didn't want him to have. Then his cousin, who I was told worked directly with you, was killed along with his family, and those deaths were blamed on the Taliban. But the Taliban hadn't been operational in the area for some time. He also said the cousin and the warlord were fighting over how to deal with us, and after his death we quietly gave the warlord the weapons he wanted. Sounds like a quid quo pro was worked out, which makes me think whoever killed the man and his family had American ties, whether it was our people or the government's people."

The mid-day light was filling the room, warming it. MacMillan wandered to the large window facing the Bitterroot Mountains. He stood there saying nothing. Moses was looking back and forth between us.

"Well?" he asked, either to me or MacMillan.

"Who killed the man and his family?" I asked.

"I don't know. The people in the village said it was us, the Marines..." He was speaking to the window.

"All of them?" Moses asked.

MacMillan shook his head. "I don't know. I don't think so."

I was getting frustrated. "You do know! The Marine Corps knew because Musa knew, and the villagers knew, and he used that as blackmail to get his weapons as a form of payment."

MacMillan continued staring out at the mountains.

"The man's name was Alam. He had a wife and four children. He was the spokesman for the village; our contact. We worked through him. His disagreements with Abdullah were about how cooperative they should be. Alam was more open to working with us while Abdullah was not. Feuds were not uncommon, and Abdullah had many with individuals in the Afghan government. So, Alam's working with me put him in conflict with Abdullah.

"I considered Alam a good friend, and his death hit me hard. Initially, it was thought that Abdullah was responsible, but that was quickly shot down. Whatever their disagreements, he and Abdullah were not in direct conflict with one other, and Abdullah wasn't stupid. Even if he didn't like Alam working with me, it gave him a means of talking to us without looking like he was. It was because of Alam that we were able to drive the Taliban out of the area. Through him we had excellent intel, and I took care to nurture our relationship."

"So, what happened?"

"I don't know, but in Afghan society they are very conservative when it comes to relations between the sexes. Apparently, one of our Marines had developed a fondness for one of Alam's daughters. I didn't encourage those kinds of interactions and the daughter was spoken for. After explaining the situation, I made it plain that he was not to see her or engage with her in any fashion. As far as I knew he followed my instructions."

"Who was it?" asked Moses.

"Lambert," he said.

"And the murders?" I asked.

"At first there was a lot of confusion. Alam and his family's home was far enough away from the other villagers that no one saw or heard anything. They were found in the morning after they failed to meet up with others in the village. They had all been shot in the head execution style. I later learned the daughter had been separated from the others. It was later that rumors began to spread that the deaths were caused by Americans; that the villagers knew who was responsible; that there was a witness. The witness, however, was not the most reliable, and that was used against him. At the same time, discipline in your son's squad was becoming a problem. It was in dealing with that, that information came to me about the murder of Alam and his family."

MacMillan looked at us, anticipating the question. "It was Lewis who first broached the subject. He told me Santos was being threatened and the threat was explicit. If he didn't keep his mouth shut, he'd end up like Alam's family. I asked who was threatening him. He said I already knew."

"Dezi?" I asked.

He nodded. "The idea that Alam had been murdered by Marines caused a great deal of concern. Abdullah learned of the rumors too, and was making his own threats to go to the media, to rile up his people. He knew they wanted revenge; that they wanted the men who did this. But there was no proof, no physical evidence that could directly tie any Marine to the crime. There were no shell casings found, and the rounds were what Afghan forces used as well. There were no reliable witnesses, save the man who had been asleep in the field, and he changed his story based on who he was telling it to. The village was up in arms. All my work was wasted and now there were these problems with this group of Marines."

"Then the two Marines were killed, which conveniently took out a pair of possible suspects," I said. MacMillan winced at that. "What really happened to them?"

He picked up his empty cup. "I don't know. The people who know or knew are dead now. I wasn't with them, and it wasn't supposed to be anything more than a routine patrol. But it's a big deal when our people are killed. They were reported missing and subsequently found dead. Their hands were tied behind their backs and their throats cut. Their weapons were found beside them unfired. Like the murder of Alam's family, nobody knew or saw anything. All the men on patrol said the same thing. Dezi and Lambert went to check out a building, and missed the rendezvous. The others searched for them, and found them where they were killed. They all told the same story with no deviations. None."

"Then why the phony-baloney report?"

"Because a week later, a video was sent to us. On it, Dezi is shown laughing and admitting that he and Lambert got away with murder; that they killed Alam and his family. Lambert protested that he didn't actually shoot them, but Dezi said it didn't matter who fired the shots. He was there, and a part of it. Apparently, everyone in your son's squad knew about it. Somehow Abdullah got a hold of it too. Given the situation, and given the individuals involved, it was decided that the incident would be smoothed over. The killers were dead; there was nothing to be gained by turning it into a media circus. To keep Abdullah quiet, we gave him what he wanted. No one was interested in any moral or ethical questions, or in pursuing how Dezi and Lambert came to be in that field."

"But you know, don't you?" Moses inquired.

"That is something I won't talk about. I've told you what I can. The rest you can figure out for yourselves."

Moses continued to press, "Because it might damage your precious Corps?"

Macmillan shook his head. "Because it serves no purpose. The Corps isn't immune from human folly. Its strength is in its ideals and those who strive to uphold them, even if they sometimes fall short. And before you get too self-righteous, remember that Jacob Bohrman was a part of this." MacMillan looked towards the front door, "I see the sheriff is back, maybe he'll release your truck and you can move on."

He was right. We were free to go. I turned to Sergeant MacMillan, who was standing on the porch. "Thanks for the talk." I paused. "Oh, there's one other thing."

"Yes?" The sergeant was tired of questions.

"It's a message from your wife. She wants you to come home."

It was the only time he smiled.

30

Moses was staring at me.

"What?"

We were back in the motel room, exhausted from a very long night and day. I'd finished my check-in with Agnes, who scolded me for not calling sooner. Moses watched as I lied through my teeth, telling her that our trip had been mostly non-eventful, other than a person died, which we weren't a party to and, yes, it was a bad thing. I told her we were heading back to the farm in the morning.

"Do you miss me?" she asked in her baby voice.

"Absolutely and without a doubt the time I'm away from you is truly beyond lonely. I'm lost without you and can't wait to see your beautiful smile again." I heard her snort at my facetiousness.

"Just get your butt back here, Sunshine."

I laughed, "Yes, dear."

Moses was shaking his head.

"What?"

"After everything that's happened, and you tell Agnes it's nothing. We very easily could be dead now!"

"But we're not and I don't want her to worry because she's a worrier. Besides, I'd have to listen to her berate me for doing stupid things and I have you for that. I'll flesh out our adventure when I get back." I waited for his response, mostly to validate my predilection for doing stupid things, but he appeared deep in thought. Of course, it might simply have been exhaustion.

"I don't understand you boys. At one time I thought I did, but not anymore."

I shrugged. "What's to understand, and didn't we already go over this?"

"Still doesn't change how it makes me feel," he grumbled.

"That's the beauty of parenthood. Bitter disappointment. I'm disappointed in Rebekah, you're disappointed in me, and Ezekiel was disappointed in you. It's the circle of life."

Moses seemed shocked. "How would you know your grandfather was disappointed in me?"

"He told me." Moses still seemed shocked. "What, you didn't know I talked to him? Mom didn't tell you? He was in Virginia; I was in Virginia. He'd reconnected with mom after she'd gone back, and she thought it would do me some good to get to know him."

My grandfather, Ezekiel Bohrman, had been a preacher all his life, which made me think of Lucian DeBerry, who wanted that life too. Ezekiel's father, Josiah, had been a preacher, and it was assumed that all four of Ezekiel's children; Moses, Isaiah, Elijah, and Miriam would follow in the family tradition, but it didn't quite work out that way.

They were devastated when Elijah suddenly died, Elijah being the epitome of a god-fearing soul. The story told was he had gotten sick, and they had prayed and believed and, as I understand it, he appeared to recover before abruptly dying in Moses' arms. Feeling mocked by a frivolous god, Moses took his anger out on the system, religious and secular. Miriam, radicalized as well, but within the church, became a feminist organizer. Isaiah wandered in and out of faith before becoming a beer distributer in Milwaukee.

"Disappointment is the wrong word," he mused. "Frustration is more accurate." I rolled my eyes. He sighed. "Maybe Meri is right. Instead of seeing what's before me, I keep looking for what's not there. Look at you and how you handled what's happened over the last twenty-four hours. I don't know that person, or to put it another way, I don't recognize that person, probably because I decided you were a certain kind of man long ago, and I've refused to see you for who you are. Thinking about that, I realize I've done the same thing to all you boys..."

"You're tired. Get some sleep. If you're so inclined, we can talk about this tomorrow." Moses nodded and got into bed. I turned out the light and prayed he was not so inclined.

•   •   •   •   •

The motel owner took the keys, a disapproving look on her face. Word of what happened had filtered down to her and the others. She did not wish us a safe trip or encourage us to come back. I bought coffee and a couple Danish at the convenience store on the way out of town. I half-expected to find the deputy still there. The woman behind the counter registered the same look as the motel owner.

Moses took the coffee but had no interest in the sweet roll. He didn't appear to have slept very well, the bags under his eyes were as pronounced as they had been the previous day. I don't know why I assumed he wouldn't be badly traumatized by what happened at MacMillan's cabin. Other than finding James, and I don't know for a fact that he was there when James was found, this might have been the first killing he'd been a party to or had witnessed firsthand.

I noticed him nodding off. The coffee wasn't strong enough to overcome his fatigue. I pulled the blanket from behind the seat and told him to rest. The rumble of the truck knocked him out, and he slept until it was time for lunch.

"Where are we?" he asked, somewhat confused.

"Roadkill Café," I answered.

"Roadkill Café?"

"I didn't name the place." He shook his head as we got out of the truck and entered the diner. "Hungry?"

"No!"

I opened the café door. "You still gotta eat."

A spritely young woman with a silver nose ring pointed to an open table. She eyed the town dude and the hick entering her place of business. I don't know if it was odd to find an offbeat diner in the northeast corner of California, but it was a nice distraction from the last few days. Whoever decorated the place had been to San Fran and LA, and had brought back that goofy hippie vibe or its modern equivalent. Moses looked around and smiled. He'd seen it all before.

"It's cleaner and more organized," he said, when I asked him about it. I was hoping the retro groove would cheer him up.

This was the longest I'd ever seen him sad and bummed out.

Some of that was my doing. I had consciously avoided the farm, and consequently Moses, even after returning from Virginia, believing if I returned to northern California dead men would come after me. I don't know why I thought the Pronto brothers, twenty years on, would still be around given their propensity for violence and thuggery; most guys like that end up dead or in prison, which is exactly what happened. Deep down I knew I stayed away because I was embarrassed to be known as a fuckup and a goof.

Moses hadn't exactly been quiescent on my character flaws, and I had no interest in reliving them every time I came around.

That was the Moses I knew.

The Moses of my youth was strong and vigorous and contemptuous of failure. He was optimistic that what he believed was the truth, and those around him would come to see the light. He would shake his head when I'd throw questions at him.

"The day will come," he'd thunder, "when you'll understand; when you'll see I'm right."

I wasn't so sure.

The man across from me, looking around, taking in the paraphernalia and memorabilia, his beard and hair unkempt, didn't strike me as anything like the man I once knew. This one was fragile and soft, more human to me.

"You alright?"

"No." He was looking out the window at the weathered building next to us and the brown hills beyond. "What did you think of Ezekiel?"

Ezekiel? I had to think. "He reminded me of you."

"I don't look anything like my father," he said, somewhat defensively, which made me smile.

"I'm well aware that you take after your mother, but in temperament you are your father's son."

He smiled back. "True. It was Elijah who was Ezekiel's spitting image. Miriam and I were heir to Dot's side, and Isaiah was somewhere in the middle."

Dot was Dorothea Bohrman, my grandmother, and the quiet iron that held the clan together when Ezekiel was on the road spreading the gospel. Elijah's death struck her as hard as it did Moses, but she was from a different time, one closer to mortality, one more accepting of God's imperceptible habit of calling home his flock without any outward reason. A reminder of our frailty and our duty to the Lord's will. She carried on, rallying her children, but God called her and the three of them fled. Moses, then Miriam, and finally Isaiah. Ezekiel, though grieving, was ever practical, staying the course and waiting for the prodigal's return. In the meantime, he married a widow named Margaret. I never knew Dorothea.

"So, you think I'm like Ezekiel in temperament? Maybe so," he mused.

"How are you not? I find that doubly true now."

Moses turned his blue eyes on me. Those fierce blue eyes I avoided as a fuckup and a goof. "In what way?"

"In your demeanor; in your certitude. Whether it's the word of the Lord or the sanctity of the good earth, which is what God is minus the theology. Then there's all the issues the two of you share when it comes to your progeny. Ezekiel was no less angry or disappointed about the paths his surviving children took any more than you are, though I think he was more, what's a good word, accepting of where the three of you ended up. There's also the matter of both of you losing your favorite sons at such a young age." He opened his mouth, but I cut him off. "There's no need to deny it. Jacob was your favorite, just as Elijah was Ezekiel's."

Moses' eyes misted up. "He told you that?"

"He did. He also said his biggest regret was the distance between the two of you. He understood your need to go and was content to hear you were well and succeeding. But unlike your brother and sister, you never came back to see him, and by that time he was too frail to travel. So, I regaled him with stories of the farm and your thundering away about this and that. He'd always laugh and say you'd have made a fine preacher if you'd forgiven the world its sin, and made peace with God. His preaching never left him."

"I had my reasons," he whispered, wiping away the tears.

"I know, just as he knew. He loved you all the same." Moses put his head in his hands to hide his tears. I reached over and put my hand on his. He wove my fingers in with his. I looked up to see the embarrassed young woman with the nose ring standing there, not knowing what to do. "Bring us your two favorite dishes and two glasses of iced tea," I told her. She nodded and left.

"I'm sorry," he said after a moment. He then let go of my hand and wiped his eyes.

"Why?"

"For misjudging you."

"Misjudging me?"

Those blue eyes were there again.

"Yes. Since Jacob died, I've been doing a lot of soul searching, rethinking some of my beliefs and opinions, especially about you boys. To be honest, I never thought of you as a serious person. You were someone who did what they had to, to get through whatever work they had, or as your grandfather would say, a lazy man with a lack of respect for the Lord and the good graces so given. I guess that's why I was surprised when Becky told me you were a good farmer. You weren't exactly interested when you were working with us."

"I was seventeen! Who wants to farm at seventeen?" I said.

"You were an irresponsible seventeen; poor work habits, no account friends, and a baby you had no business fathering," he went on.

"I was there, remember?"

Moses sat back and crossed his arms. "You were and are an inveterate smartass."

I sat back as well. "It's in the contract."

Moses shook his head, but there was a hint of a smile. "Yes, and yet a person I didn't recognize kept his head and got the both of us through a very scary situation. I was certain Seth Cameron was going to kill us and MacMillan. All I could think of was how much I missed Meri and my friends and the farm and how badly I didn't want to die. And of all people, my son, Sunshine Bohrman—"

"Please don't call me that—"

"Don't interrupt." He leaned forward, placing his elbows on the table. "Alright, my son, with the god-awful name of *Monk Buttman*, remained calm and resourceful. You were nothing like that terrified teenager I sent packing years ago." Moses looked up. Our server with the nose ring was back. She held the dishes so we could see. I motioned for her to put one plate in front of Moses and one in front of me.

"You asked for my favorites, so I picked the blacken trout with couscous and seasoned Brussels sprouts, and our venison burger with baked sweet potato fries. I hope you like them," she said with a hint of pride.

"They look and smell wonderful, thank you." The young woman smiled and left. The old man picked at his, before taking a tentative bite. Upon realizing it was not crap; that it was quite good, he consumed the contents of his plate. He noticed my glee as I watched him devour his meal.

"I guess I was hungrier than I thought," he mumbled.

"Apparently."

"Décor doesn't always equal quality fare," he continued.

"True," I agreed, though he may not have cared for my tone. "This venison burger is tasty." I held up the burger to highlight my point.

"How should I know that. I've never been here before."

I shook my head. "Yeah, you need to get out more."

Moses harrumphed. A fine slice of peach pie ended our time at the Roadkill Café. I thanked the woman with the nose ring, something Moses echoed and we were soon back on the road.

"So, what did I miss?" he asked a few miles down the road.

"Miss what?" I didn't know what he was talking about.

"About you?" Moses and his never-ending need to know. I was tempted to say something snarky, but assumed he was continuing our table talk.

"I was just as frightened as you. The nice thing about these loose-fitting slacks is they hide how badly your legs are shaking. As to the rest, I learned a long time ago to have a plan, mostly from farming."

"Farming?"

"Yeah, farming. I didn't care for it and felt boxed in, but at the time I didn't want to lose Astral or Rebekah, and I'd developed an irrational fear that if I left, I'd be found out and gruesomely murdered. Anyway, it became pretty obvious that you had to have a plan to be successful as a farmer, and it had to include variables such as whether it was a wet or dry planting season; in dealing with pests, soils conditions, and on and on. I merely applied that principle to other situations. If you have a plan, you have something to focus on rather than when the bullet's going to be put through your head." Moses winced at that. "That's why they train solders for combat, so they don't break ranks and flee when all hell breaks loose."

"And you figured this out by farming? Sunshine out on his tractor?"

I smiled at that.

"I did a lot of reading as well. Amends for blowing off so many of my formative years. Turns out you can learn a lot by reading up on things, history being one of them. However, since you're curious about who I am or have become, I'll say that these last ten years working in LA, have allowed me the opportunity to keenly observe the human condition, and I've become good at noticing tics in people."

Moses was intrigued. "So, you knew what was going to happen up there? How?"

"Know is the wrong word. Suspect is better. I notice when odd or out of the ordinary things happen around me because I'm ordinary, unremarkable. It struck me as odd that Colonel Jaron would call me out of the blue concerned about what I might know, but he'd heard from MacMillan's wife and then I mentioned Lewis—"

"But really it was Cameron?"

"I think Jaron found my confusion humorous. I assume Lewis is hiding in Ukiah, probably in fear that Cameron will find him, but we're getting off track. Jaron told me MacMillan would know I was coming before I got there, and sure enough when I went up with Jasper he was hiding in the weeds, waiting. So, I expected the same thing when Cameron forced us up there. I figured all we had to do was get out of the way."

"Simple as that?" he asked, amazed.

"Simple as that." Why not, I told myself.

Our trip was winding down.

Thank God!

31

The visit didn't help.

After another sleepless night in another anonymous motel; a mere three miles from the farm, the bleary-eyed Moses Bohrman motioned towards a turnoff just outside of Ukiah.

"I want to talk to her," he blurted out.

"Who?"

"Mallon Dezi's mother." He pointed to the turnoff. "She lives here."

I drove the truck along the dirt driveway. The house reminded me of Kurtis' home in Watts, small and worn. The place was quiet, so quiet we could hear the crickets in the grass. Once on the stoop, Moses stared at me. Apparently, it was my job to knock. A rustling followed and a middle-aged woman answered the door. Save for her expression, Mallon's mother, Deidre, was the opposite of Aretha Harvin. She was a tall woman with dusty black hair, a thick frame, and large round glasses that obscured the circles under her eyes. She opened the door and took us in and was at first uncomprehending of the hipster and the hick standing before her. But a light went off as she looked us over.

"Come in, Moses. I'm so sorry to hear about Jacob."

"Thank you. This is Monk, my oldest boy, he lives down in LA." Moses patted me on the shoulder. "I apologize for barging in, but I wondered if I could talk to you about Mallon and the other boys. I don't understand what's happened, and thought maybe you might share whatever you could about... about what changed them." His voice was low, he was rambling, and it cracked as he spoke.

Deidre put her arm around him and gave him a hug. "It's so hard some days to accept that they're gone."

I stood there, once again reminded of my status as an outsider. After a few moments, she let him go and we crossed the small living room and entered the equally small kitchen. On the way I noted the large photo of the unsmiling Mallon Dezi in his dress blues, flanked on both sides by displays. To the right was his flag, to the left his medals and a letter from the Commandant of the Marine Corps.

Deidre Dezi offered us coffee and we sat at the dining table across from the kitchen. Sunlight filtered through the thin drapes. I was curious how he knew her; how she knew him. During my youth, Moses had no need or desire to interact with the locals beyond what was necessary, which was little. He preferred his oasis away from the maddening crowd, those who saw no problem with the capitalist/consumerist/militarist autocracy that ruled the land and put us all in bondage. Yet here he was, with me in tow, to talk with the mother of a dead marine of whom we, or maybe just I, had heard nothing good. I noticed Moses concentrating on his hands, lost in thought.

"I remember them as kids, these boys, running around. I wasn't thrilled when Jacob wanted to join the Marines, but there was nothing I could do to stop him. He was old enough to decide for himself, and he didn't seem to be any different the few times he came home, but this last time he was so upset and distant and unwilling to talk..."

"They wanted to go together," Deidre answered. She was staring out the window, "Mal told me they decided one day to go, that it was important, and it was the right thing to do. At the time, I was quite proud of him. Young people don't seem to be very patriotic anymore, but it changed him. I don't know why I thought it wouldn't," she said, running her fingers along the edge of the table. "He was such a sweet child, shy, even though he was good sized. When I asked him about it, he said Marines aren't shy sweet little boys, they're hardened men who have a job to do." She absent-mindedly took a sip of coffee.

"Did he say much about his time overseas?" I asked.

Deidre shook her head. "He was very restless the last time he was home, angry and short-tempered. I'm ashamed to say I told him it might be better if he went back early because he was clearly unhappy being here with me. I guess I thought he'd figure things out and come back a little more like he used to be, but he never came back. They came to tell me on a Friday that my Mal was gone. He's buried at the national cemetery in the Sacramento Valley." She put her hand on Moses'. "I hear you buried Jacob on your land. I think that's a beautiful thing to have him so close. It hard for me to go see

Mal sometimes. I get so angry and there's nothing to make it go away. It feels like such a long drive and the last time I could barely get up to leave." Moses was crying, which brought tears to Deidre, and then to me.

"It's such a waste," Moses said through the tears.

Deidre mouthed the word, yes, but couldn't bring sound to it.

"I thought Mal was a fine young man. I can't believe they're all gone." Moses sat up and wiped his eyes.

"There's Lewis," I reminded him.

"Lewis? Oh, yeah..." Moses had forgotten.

Deidre turned to me. "Audrey told me he was in town."

"Who's Audrey?" I asked.

Deidre smiled. "Just a friend."

Moses was unconcerned. "Doesn't matter now," he stood. "It was nice of you to talk to us on such short notice, Dee." Deidre and I rose and she walked us to the door.

"When did Audrey till you Lewis was in town?"

Deidre tilted her head. "Yesterday. Is it important?"

I tried to smile. "Just curious."

Another hug sent us back to the farm. Moses said little as Meredith and the Mackinaw brothers came out to greet us. To say they were disturbed by his appearance and demeanor would be an understatement. Meredith looked at me and I promised to fill her in after she got Moses to bed. He needed to rest.

I watched as they took him into the house.

I had to think. Something was out of place, not right, and it revolved around Lewis. Had I spoken to Lewis at all? Were all my interactions with the man I thought was Lewis really Cameron every time? I wandered to my spot behind the barn, grabbing my crate along the way. Something didn't fit, and that *something* I knew I had come across but couldn't remember. Lewis was here, but the guy I thought was Lewis at the funeral was Cameron. Had they been together? If Audrey told Deidre that Lewis was here yesterday, did that mean he was still alive? It had to. This place was too small for a dead man to go unnoticed or not spoken of. If Lewis were dead, Deidre would have said something.

"Are you alright, Mr. Sunshine?" I looked up; Emily was standing over me. She was taller.

"As far as I know. You?"

"I came to check my garden, and I saw you sitting here. I called your name, but you didn't answer." She was pouting at my lack of awareness.

"Sorry, I was deep in thought." Emily nodded and walked to the back door of the barn, opened it and pulled out her crate. She set it carefully next to mine and sat down. I felt her hand on mine as we looked at the high clouds moving lackadaisically above us.

"When are you going back to LA?"

"Tomorrow. There's someone I have to talk to before I go."

"Who?"

"Man named Al Lewis. He knew Jacob."

"Oh. Can I go back to LA with you?" I looked at her to see if she was serious. A sheepish smile answered that.

"Maybe another time. How's the garden going, I haven't had a chance to see it lately."

Emily shrugged. "It's ok. I'm not growing anything new this year."

"I'd still like to see it." Another shrug. We got up and made our way to the garden.

I was saddened to see the great care she had given it over the years was no longer there, but not surprised. It wasn't that the garden was threadbare or overgrown, only that it didn't have that characteristic look of formality and order I associated with Emily's gardens. She must have noticed my disappointment as she began pulling the stray weeds and fumbling for her trimmer. I helped with the weeds as she pruned back the plants. I noticed Calista out of the corner of my eye. Emily saw her too.

"What? He's just helping me with the garden, ok!"

Calista shrank at her daughter's continued belligerence. "Please don't yell at me, Emily," she replied in a strangely quiet tone. "I'd like to talk with Monk for a few minutes, that's all. Please, no more fighting."

Emily looked at me.

"No worries," I said.

Emily glowered at her mother as I walked away.

Calista looked at Emily. "As you can see, my relationship with Emily is difficult to say the least."

"I hadn't noticed." Moses was right, forever and always a smartass. To my delight, Calista smiled at that. I tried to remember the last time I saw her smile. The wedding, I'm pretty sure she smiled then.

"I wanted... I came to apologize for being so angry with you about Emily going to Las Angeles and all that. That doesn't mean that Emily can do wherever she wants, but it didn't help matters, if anything it made everything worse with Emily, and now Andrea..." That made me wince.

"Please don't apologize. I should have put more thought into the invitations, and I sometimes forget that kids need rules and boundaries. I didn't intend to cause trouble between you and Emily, or with Andrea, but obviously I did."

"Yeah." Evidently there was little to say beyond our admissions of guilt.

"I'm ok with making peace so things can get back to normal. I promise not to let Emily talk me into letting her do things without your permission, and just so you know, I've decided not to live in Beverly Hills anymore, so maybe with that enticement gone, it won't be you who's keeping her from living the good life; it'll be me."

Calista shifted and crossed her arms. "Ok." She looked at Emily before turning and walking back towards the courtyard.

Emily came to where I was standing. "Am I in trouble again?"

I put my arm around her shoulder. "No. It was your mother and I coming to an understanding about you and me."

Emily looked confused. "What does that mean?"

"It means were ok again." Emily smiled and put her arms around me. I kissed her forehead. "We need to finish the garden," I said. Emily nodded, and we went back to work.

• • • • •

Moses was sitting in his living room. He still looked exhausted, but Meredith had cleaned him up and he was back where he belonged. I sat down across from him on the couch.

"Where can I find Al Lewis' family? I want to talk to him."

"There's only his mother. She lives on Rutherford, just past the high school," he said, after thinking about it.

"No father? Like Mallon Dezi?" I was guessing about the father.

"Yeah, they took off years ago." His tone indicated old news. No big deal.

I still didn't get it. "I'm curious, how do you know these people? When I was a kid, you were fairly contemptuous of every soul in town. You called them morons and sheep."

He smiled at that. "Yes, I did..." He drifted off. I wondered if this was a sign of things to come. "Well, to answer your question, Jacob is to blame for that. He wanted to play baseball and because he was the youngest, and because I had played when I was a kid, I decided it would be ok."

Uh-huh. "I assume with some prodding from Meri?"

"Some. He and the other boys were together through Legion ball."

Uh-huh. "Yet when I wanted to play, it was corporatist and reactionary and would only make me more pliable in the evil external matrix!"

Moses waved his hand defensively. "Now don't be so resentful."

"I'm running the gamut these days. First, I was a thoughtless clod, then resourceful, and now resentful," I harrumphed. "Seems to me you're the one who's been made more pliable, hmmm?"

Moses shook his head. "Maybe, but you're still a smartass, plain and simple."

"Man's got to have a stock in trade." It was my turn to wave a hand. "Do you want to come along?"

Moses looked out the window. "No, I don't want to know anymore."

I left him in his chair.

•   •   •   •   •

Al Lewis' home looked remarkably like Mallon Dezi's home. Lewis' mother, however, was nothing like Deidre. I don't know why I thought she would be. Rather, she was lithe, made up, and somewhat amused by the well-dressed stranger at her door. Her green eyes sparkled, surrounded by a fair amount of like colored shadow which complimented the highlights in her auburn hair. The white satin-y blouse was just loose enough to define her bosom but not burden it, and her lower half was accentuated by black form-fitting yoga pants. Her smile was quite welcoming.

"And what might you be looking for, stranger?" What was I looking for again?

"I want to talk to your son, Al. I heard he's in town."

The grin faded away. "I haven't heard from Al, mister."

I raised my eyebrows at that. "I know he's AWOL from the Marines, and I know he's here somewhere. I need to talk to him. He can meet me where Jacob Bohrman died. He knows where that is."

The lithe woman leaned again the door jamb. "I'm sorry, but I didn't catch your name…"

"Monk. Jacob was my younger brother. And your name? Mrs. Lewis sounds awfully formal?"

The woman continued to ponder my presence. "If you need a name, it's Connie." Connie struck me as a more attractive version of Molly Pronto.

"Please tell him it's important, Connie. Just talk." I stepped back and turned before turning around again. "Also, let him know that MacMillan killed Cameron. He'll know what that means. Have a nice day."

The surprise on her face made my day.

32

The field was empty. Whether Lewis would show, I didn't know. I sent Agnes a text telling her I was back at the farm and would head home the next day. She replied it was about time, and a madhouse there with everyone trying to get organized to leave, move, etc. I hope you're happy about all this, she texted. I texted back; I was not unhappy about it. I could see her standing there with her hands on her hips, shaking her head. The image produced an incredible erection I didn't need. To my right was a stand of oaks. I glanced at the place I'd found Jacob and climbed the short rise to the trees. I sat between two of the oaks and waited for Corporal Alvin Lewis.

A lone car approached, slowed down, and drove down the road before turning around. A second pass by the man in the car confirmed, I assumed, my being there. I was visible to see if the effort was made. The man, I further assumed, was Lewis. He got out slowly, continuing to look around.

"No one else is here," I shouted. I put my hand in my pocket to reassure myself that the 45 was there. He closed the car door and walked my way.

"What do you want?" he asked, stating the obvious.

"Well, unless you were assisting Cameron in the killings..." I pulled out the 45, which caused him to step back. "What I want are some answers, and spare me that pact bullshit because as last man standing, there's no one left to protect. You're it, Lewis; all the others are dead. Cameron. Santos. Saunders. Jacob. And of course, Dezi and Lambert. Something happened, something bad enough that it led to murder, and you're the last one left. The irony is you started this, didn't you? Kurtis mentioned it in his journal; the pact, the pact you started."

Lewis stood there unsure. "What did Jake say?"

Yes, Jacob, my conflicted, foolish younger brother.

"He didn't say anything," I answered. "It was Kurtis and Saunders that started all this coming apart with their murder-suicide. But it makes me wonder if it wasn't a straight up double murder. I learned the cops found a newspaper clipping in Saunders' pocket about Dezi and Lambert being killed in Afghanistan. Then there was Kurtis' journal and his aunt's belief he'd been sexually assaulted by the rest of you. From there, I found out that the official report on Dezi and Lambert's deaths was made up, and MacMillan added a few of his own admissions about what may or may not have happened; not only to Kurtis, Dezi and Lambert, but also the family that was murdered in the village near the ill-fated patrol when Dezi and Lambert were killed. All that begs a lot of questions." My hand tightened around the 45. "Why would Cameron take on the role of executioner? What happened that would cause him to kill his friends and fellow Marines? Even in war that's unusual. So, I want some fucking answers, man!"

I realized I was shouting.

Lewis was oblivious to it. He kept looking around the field.

I pointed to the spot where I found Jacob. "Over there. Were you here when Cameron killed Jacob?"

Lewis nodded. I put the 45 back in my pocket.

"I was behind the trees. Cam's mom was worried about him and heard I was around, so she talked to my mom, who told me. I came around, and heard Cam and Jake talking. They were playing a game we played when we were bored and drinking; it was a kind of Russian roulette, but not really—"

"What do you mean, not really?"

Lewis sat down below the oak. "It was a way to, I don't know, get rid of bad feelings, that sort of thing. It was... symbolic. That's what Mason used to call it. A symbolic death."

I sat down.

"But what happened wasn't symbolic, was it?"

He shook his head. "Cam handed him the gun and told him it was alright. It was all taken care of, he said. Cam put the gun against Jake's chest. Jake pulled the trigger, but it fired instead. Usually, it just clicks. Cam got up and walked away. I couldn't believe it. I didn't know what to do. I just left. When I heard people were looking for Jake, I remembered he'd given me your number, so I called so you could find him." Lewis closed his eyes.

"Why would Cameron do that? Tell me."

Lewis shut his eyes closer. "What does it matter now?"

I thought about it. "Because it's the only way I'll know anything about my brother."

Lewis looked over at me. "I don't know what to say…"

I knew. "Start with what happened to Kurtis. Was he raped?"

Lewis blushed. "I don't know. I wasn't there. I was sick and had to spend the night in the infirmary. But I know it caused a lot of bad feelings. Before that, we'd all been pretty tight. Close, you know? But after that, it was bad."

"Was Jacob a part of it?"

He shrugged. "Not really. From what Cam told me, they'd been drinking and things got a little crazy. Mal was fucking with Kurt about being gay, which wasn't unusual, but he thought it'd be funny if he made Kurtis pretend to suck his dick; suck all their dicks. Cam said Lamb told Mal he was a fag too, and Mal went ballistic and, like I said, things got out of hand. I don't know exactly what happened, but Mason said that Mal forced Kurt to suck his dick while Lamb jerked off to it. Mal said they were just having a little fun and we were all a bunch of pussies the few times it came up."

"Then why did Kurtis make it seem that Jacob was a part of it?"

"He was mad at them for not stopping it, for not standing up to Mal, but Mal was a lot of trouble by then."

"What do you mean?"

"He was always quiet growing up, easygoing, even though he was a big guy. But the war changed him. He got mean and angry, took it out on everybody. He was a scary guy when he got mad. And then—" he stopped, looked at me as if hoping I'd let it go.

"And then?" I wasn't going to.

"Alam and his family were killed. At first no one knew what happened. The quadrant had been quiet for months. Our patrols were nothing more than backing up the locals when they needed it. We were just waiting to rotate back to Pendleton, to go home. It was Kurt who said we were in trouble; that they'd been killed by Mal and Lamb. It was… I mean we all knew Alam and his family, especially his kids; the two little boys and their sisters. But I noticed Mal and Lamb were quiet after that, which was strange after what had been going on." Lewis began pulling at the grass at his feet.

"Sergeant MacMillan told me a villager came forward to say he'd seen the two of them at the house where the family was killed."

Lewis didn't look up. "Yeah, we heard that too, but the word came down from command that it might have been a Taliban assassination. I asked the sergeant about that. It seemed odd that all of a sudden, the Taliban would kill a low-level guy like Alam rather than Musa, who was fighting them. He wouldn't say. I could tell he didn't like it, but we were told it wasn't our concern."

"But that wasn't the end of it, was it?"

He got up. "No. A few days later we learned the truth. I heard the guys talking among themselves and Mason showed us a video he'd had on his phone. He got it from Kurt. Mal was drunk and didn't realize Kurt was recording him. On it he was hassling Kurt and Lamb told him to stop. Mal blew up and called him a fag who couldn't get it up to fuck that stupid bitch he liked. We all knew Lamb liked Alam's oldest daughter. Kurt confronted them, 'you were there? It was you two?' and Mal started laughing, admitted it was true, and when Kurt asked why, Mal said they deserved it; that there was nothing we could do, and if Kurt said a word to anyone, Mal would do the same thing to him he'd done to that fucking bitch and her family."

He let the grass in his hand fall to the ground.

"It was like getting kicked in the stomach. We didn't know what to do. Jake wanted to tell Sergeant MacMillan, but Kurt said it wouldn't change anything. They had their bad guys, and it wouldn't help our cause admitting it was Marines that did it. He said it was up to us if any justice was going to happen. We knew the villagers pretty well, and we knew the tension after the killings was bad, so I said we should turn Mal and Lamb over to them, but Cam objected. Marines don't turn on Marines."

"But you did turn them over, didn't you?" He didn't want to admit it. That was the pact. That was what Kurtis was referring to, not the rape, bad as that was. "Didn't you?"

Lewis looked me in the eye. The anger bright and shining.

"We couldn't just let them walk away. It wasn't right. We talked and decided it was the Afghan's right to judge them. I made contact with one of the villagers, told them what we knew and where we'd be. On that day, Jake went off with Cam because we knew he wouldn't go along with it. When we got close to the village, we took a break and the villagers who were waiting confronted Mal and Lamb. Kurt, Mason, and me grabbed Mal and Lamb's rifles before they could get them. Several men from the village grabbed them and tied them up. Mal was screaming at us and Lamb was crying, begging us not to go, but we left. Later we went back and found them dead. We put their firearms next to them and called in that we had two men down."

He reached for the oak next to him, but seemed reluctant to touch it.

"As we waited, we made a pact. No one knows or says anything. We knew Cam would be angry, but we couldn't let this go. Like I said, we knew and respected Alam, and we were the only ones willing to hold Mal and Lamb accountable for what they did."

"And Seth Cameron? What about him?"

Lewis stared at where Jacob was killed.

"I don't know. After it was over, he really didn't say anything. I thought he'd blow up, but he didn't. It was done, and that was that. Sergeant MacMillan asked a lot of questions. He talked to all of us as a group and individually, but there was nothing to say. Colonel Jaron came down and said that he didn't believe the stories floating around about what happened to Mal and Lamb, but he didn't press it and it was time to rotate stateside. Kurt and Mason got out, and the rest of us were being moved to other companies."

"I thought it was over." He looked at me. "I remember sitting on my bunk and Cam sat next to me and poked me in the chest, hard, and when I said, 'what the fuck,' he said, 'I'm gonna finish this,' and then I heard Kurt and Mason were dead, so I took off. When I heard Cam was up here, I tried to warn Jake, but—"

I got up. There was nothing left to explain. "Are you going back?"

"Yeah, I already called."

"I'm heading to LA tomorrow, need a ride?"

He shook his head. "Nah, I already got a ride."

We walked down to his car. "You gonna tell Moses?" he asked.

I thought that was odd. "Only that Jake didn't rape Kurtis. The rest, as you say, is done. Thanks for talking."

That was that.

When I got back, Moses had been medicated and sent to bed. That was probably for the best. My mood had soured, and all I wanted was to go home and crawl into bed with Agnes. Playing nice with Moses didn't interest me. The only other person in the dining hall was Franco Mackinaw. He came over with a bottle of wine and a cheese plate.

"Did you find what you were looking for?" He set the plate down.

"Yeah."

He pulled two glasses from his pocket, popped the cork, and poured the wine.

"Care to share?"

I took a long drink and passed on what Lewis had told me. Franco leaned on the table as he listened. Didn't say a word till I finished. I asked if he was shocked.

"No, but I know what war is like. Brew and I were in Nam. That was early, 1965, before it got crazy, but we saw more than we wanted to." He noted the surprise on my face. "I thought you knew that?"

"No, the only talk I remember about Vietnam, or war, was you, Brewster, and Moses going on about militarists and the war machine eating the young. Stuff like that."

Franco laughed. "We were pretty single-minded back then, weren't we, and at the time Brew and I saw no reason to go on about it. We did our time and got out. That's the way it was. There was the draft back then, and we got called up. I ended up in the infantry and Brew, being the smarter one, ended up in supply. But we both got sent over. It was an eye opener to be sure."

Franco refilled my glass before continuing.

"I know it's easy when you hear these kinds of things to lose heart about the people who serve. But while I have some very strong opinions about the military, and the people running it, I feel I should remind you that a lot of good people go through the service and they come out better than when they went in. To be honest, the Army made me appreciate life a lot more than I would have otherwise, and it's the reason Brew's the organized pain-in-the-ass he is. If you think about it, you probably know more people who served than you realize."

"How does that make what Lewis and the others did ok?"

"It doesn't. But it's easy to judge from the sidelines. What would you have done in their boots?" Franco, like Brewster, had thick bushy eyebrows, which heightened his expression as he raised them. "Would you have preferred they did nothing? That they should have taken it up the chain of command? And if they had, and the brass did nothing, because they had a scapegoat, and no interest in going through the ugliness of owning up to the public that another of our strong American sons has slaughtered an innocent family, then what? War is an ugly business, Sunshine. It puts incredible stress on people and sometimes they fail. Would you feel better if they found out and didn't care? That they were ok with the slaughter? If nothing else, at least you can take heart that they sought some kind of justice."

"I get your point, it's just that this isn't what I expected to find."

Franco was unimpressed. "And what did you expect to find? Heroes? The heroic age is long dead, my friend. Presidents and generals don't lead the charge anymore, and you're as aware as I am that these kinds of wars, the kind where you go in trying to change centuries of beliefs, are messy and complicated and bad shit happens. That the warlord took advantage of the situation to further his own interests shouldn't be surprising, nor should you be shocked that the military will do what it feels it has to to maintain whatever bullshit mission it's forced into by the morons running the show in Washington. People get killed in wars, including a lot of innocent civilians. Nam wasn't any different. Think of all the civilians killed during the bombings. War is a terrible business." Franco looked hard into my eyes. "You wanted to find out what happened to Jacob, and you did. Leave it at that. None of us are happy about what happened, to Jacob, or to any of the others. Remember the good, mourn their loss, and move on."

"That's the answer? Move on?"

Franco got up.

"I lost some good friends in Nam; friends I remember to this day. I still miss them and mourn that they lost their lives for no good reason. And I'll do the same with Jacob. What's there to understand? Honor the good; honor his memory. Get some sleep, Monk. Go home and make love to Agnes, and thank the stars for your good fortune."

"Thanks."

Franco Mackinaw stopped at the door. "What are you going to tell Moses?"

"Only that Jacob wasn't a rapist," I said.

"Get some sleep, Monk."

33

Agnes wasn't kidding; the place was a madhouse. Anna, Fidel and Rebekah; even Theresa, were moving. Because I was fronting the money, there was no need for long drawn-out applications to determine if they had the income, work histories, or other qualifications to secure a loan. The starter pistol had been fired, and they were off to the races. Everyone was in motion, much to the distraction and dismay of my lovely wife, Agnes Duquesne.

"It's about time you showed up, Buttman!" She'd been in the library, I assumed, with the kids.

"It hasn't even been a week!"

"Yes, isn't it amazing how quickly you can make things crazy even when you're not here?"

"I prefer to think of it as a visionary management style," I said, as seriously as I could. Agnes thought of smacking me but gave me a hug, anyway.

"I'm sure you do. So how was the trip?" I was hoping she wouldn't ask.

On the long drive back to LA, I went round and round over whether there was any good reason to speak of what I'd learned, or even of the mayhem Moses and I witnessed. I imagined it made the papers, but had no idea if it made any real dent against the usual dross of Southern California mayhem. Still, a Marine killed by his sergeant would, I reasoned, be of interest since I considered it unusual.

"It had its moments, some of which may have made the news. Did you hear anything?"

Agnes merely squeezed me more firmly. "You know I don't pay attention to the news. It's the only thing that makes me crazier than you."

I grimaced. "Then I have work to do."

It was at that point that a light went off in my beloved's head. "What do you mean made the news? What happened, Monk?" She released me and was staring into my beady little eyes.

I shrugged. "It was nothing. Man got shot, that's all."

Agnes, as expected, overreacted. "Man got shot! That's not nothing. Who got shot?"

I shrugged again. I was getting good at it. "A young man named Seth Cameron."

Agnes' expression changed from overreaction to bewilderment. "Who?"

Providence saved me in the form on one Zachary Bohrman.

"GAMPS!" he shouted and bum-rushed me from the library. I picked him up and held him as tightly as I safely could. He felt and smelled wonderful. Zach pulled back after a second or two and brushed away the tears running down my face, a concerned look on his face. "Gamps?" Agnes was also concerned. I tried to shrug one more time, but Zach being in my arms made that difficult.

"I just miss you guys, that's all." Which was true.

"Uh-huh." Agnes moved closer. "What happened, Monk?" She put her hands over Zach's ears. "And don't lie or bullshit me." I thought about it. I could talk. Instead, I pulled her in and kissed her, which Zach thought was funny, so he started laughing. Agnes was startled.

"We'll talk about it some other time," I said, hoping we never would.

"Uh-huh. You worry me, Buttman, you really do."

"Thanks." I kissed her again. "Want to go swimming, Zach?"

A big beautiful grin covered his face. "YEP!" he bellowed. I let him down and followed him to the pool.

* * * * *

"They're going to miss this; you know that, right?"

We were sitting on the steps of the pool. Zach splashed in front of us, while Lizzy, who was up from her nap, sat between Agnes' legs and watched her brother make a lot of noise.

"I know, but it's not like we'll never be here again. As I've said, it's a good place for get-togethers and parties that are too big for anyone's home. Besides, given its history, I would think you'd be the happiest to go."

Agnes gave me a soft elbow to the ribs. "I suppose, but it is a beautiful house, and it does grow on you..." She was looking towards LA and the ocean beyond.

"Yes, it does." We sat there admiring Judith's view. The doorbell rang, but I ignored it. On the third ring, Agnes' elbow became more pronounced. "Fine." I reluctantly got out of the pool and went to the control panel connected to the camera aligned with the doorbell down at the gate.

It was Colonel Jaron!

"What's on your mind, Colonel?" A nearly imperceptible smile found the Marine.

"I'd like a few words with you, Mr. Buttman. I apologize for intruding. I was waiting for your response to my call and I was in town..." I didn't actually believe that.

"Come on up." I pushed the button that opened the gate. I dried myself and went to the front door. The colonel was getting out of his car. He took a moment to survey the surrounding greenery and the house before him.

"You have quite a home here." I appreciated that his admiration was genuine.

"Yes, it's a beautiful place. I haven't quite accepted that it belongs to me, but that's my problem. Please come in."

The colonel placed his hat; his cover in Marine parlance, on the front table. I introduced him to a surprised Agnes. Lizzy didn't care, and Zach was too busy amusing himself to notice. "We'll be in my office if you need me." She nodded as we walked away. I directed the colonel to a pair of seats by the desk, and excused myself long enough to find a shirt

"Would you like a drink?" I asked upon returning. I have some very fine whiskey."

"Thank you." I realized I had none here, so I excused myself a second time to retrieve two glasses, ice, and the whiskey. Agnes made a face at me. I shrugged; my preferred means of communicating on this fine sunny day.

I handed the colonel his glass, and sat in the chair next to him. The thought of sitting at the desk seemed overly formal.

"I assume you're here to talk about what happened at Sergeant MacMillan's cabin."

The colonel took a sip of his whiskey. "That and your conversation with Corporal Lewis," he said.

"He's back in the fold then?"

"Yes, he returned to the base last night." He said, as if it were no big thing.

"What did *he* say?" I asked, wondering.

"Only that he had talked to you. I didn't press him on the details."

I smiled at that. "Only to press me on the details?"

The colonel pondered the glass of whiskey. "No. As to what led to Corporal Cameron's actions, I know all that I need to know. My interest is in what you know, and what you plan to do with it. You're bright enough that I don't feel the need to lecture you on what spreading the information could do to our efforts, both in our ability to protect our image and to recruit. They may strike you as superficialities given what has occurred, but it is important."

"Yes, I picked up on that talking with Sergeant MacMillan. And while I have some rather profound concerns, I have no plans to spread the word." The colonel was unconvinced.

"And these profound concerns?"

I looked at him. "May I ask how long you've been a Marine?"

"Nearly twenty years." His voice softened. "I was floundering in my second year of college, wondering what I was doing there when I ran into the ROTC campus coordinator. At the time, I considered it merely an option; something to keep me focused on actually studying, and then we were attacked. From that day on I was all in. It was a singular moment, and it crystalized what it was I wanted to do." The colonel's demeanor was resolute. I wanted to admire that, but I wanted answers too.

"And after everything you know, no regrets?"

"A life without regret is a life without thought. I have my regrets like any man, but I do not regret becoming a Marine because of the actions of Corporal Cameron or Dezi or Lambert. Or for that matter, incidents you are unaware of."

"I see. I assume Sergeant MacMillan informed you that Dezi and Lambert were responsible for killing the Afghan family" Colonel Jaron shifted slightly in his chair and took another sip of whiskey.

"I was aware of it, yes."

"That's it?"

Jaron stared at his glass. "The decision not to pursue the matter was made based on a number of factors; factors that at this point appear coldly calculated based on what was learned, and whether there was anything to be gained by its dissemination. Our relations with the Afghans were predicated on our meeting certain objectives that involved the national government, the locals, and at the time, the probability of talks with the Taliban. Nothing would be gained by its disclosure, and outside of a small group of individuals, myself included, there was no interest in pursuing it. Musa and his people had what they wanted, the villagers the same. Whether the actions taken by your brother and his platoon were right or wrong are, at this point, inconsequential."

Jaron set his glass on the table between us.

"Would you feel better if an inquiry was opened to show the duplicity of the military generally and the Marine Corps specifically?" he asked. "And who would benefit if there were an inquiry? Because to do so may please that part of you that is angry at the decisions that were made, and whether those decisions were right or wrong, but it would also put your brother in the position of a vigilante orchestrating the killing of fellow Marines, and it would destroy the memories of people like Deidre Dezi by turning her dead son into a hateful savage murdering innocent children."

"But that's what they were, Colonel. That's what they turned into." It was my turn to set down my glass. I waited as the colonel collected his thoughts, but I was tired, tired of thinking about this. There was only one question left. "So here we are. Now what?"

Colonel Jaron picked up his glass and emptied it.

"I'm here to ascertain your state of mind. To find out, if I can, whether I should be alert to your going public with this, and whether I need to respond to that."

I finished the whiskey in my glass. "I'm not interested in dredging up what happened, but it's hard to let go. I wanted to know, for my father's sake, and for my own, what happened to my brother, and whether what I heard about him was true. In the end I got far more than I expected or wanted, and I'll be honest, if we were having this talk when I left Ukiah, I'd be much angrier." I put my hands together and stared at them. "But I had a long drive and a lot of time to think; about Jacob; about Cameron standing there searching for MacMillan, and knowing that every time I close my eyes,

I see the top of his head coming off. I hear Lewis' words rolling through my head; I hear yours; I hear MacMillan's, and I hear Franco—" Jaron didn't recognize the name. "Franco Mackinaw, he and his brother, Brewster, started the commune with my father. The place where I grew up. He served in Vietnam, something I didn't know, and he reminded me of the people I know who served. People I respect and care a great deal for."

Jaron sat back. "And where did all this thinking lead you?"

I picked up my glass.

"Not long ago, a police officer was killed while responding to a domestic dispute. It was all over the news. We learned his name; his time as an officer; his service to the community; his family life; the people he left behind. The mayor gave a speech and a great number of police officers from around the state, and some from out of state, were part of the procession and the funeral which was carried live on local TV. He was given a hero's farewell for doing his job. On the same day, two soldiers were killed in Iraq. I read about it in the paper on a back-page. It wasn't mentioned on the nightly news. The article consisted of three paragraphs which informed me they were assisting the Iraqi army when they were killed, and it was their third and seventh deployments, respectively. One man was twenty-eight and the other thirty-five. It didn't mention whether they were married, had families, or were heroes. They were simply two lives lost in a war no one cares about. There were no speeches, no processions. I assume their families buried them as we buried Jacob."

I tried to figure out where I was going with this.

"It's easy to forget how long we've been at war, but most people don't think of it, if they think of it at all. I'm no different. If it hadn't been that Jacob was my brother—" I had to stop to take a breath. "The people I know who are veterans, rarely talk about it. Life goes on as Mr. Jones would tell me..." I realized the tears had returned. I turned away.

Jaron waited for me to wipe my eyes.

"We live in a time when service is voluntary, Mr. Buttman, and as impactful as these wars are on people like me and your family, they are not existential threats to our country. We do what we're tasked to do, whether we agree with it or not. The rest of the country goes about its business. There are those who care deeply about us and those who do not. That's a fact of life for those of us who serve. There is nothing comparable to what our servicemen and women face in theater. That, too, is a fact of life. War changes you; it changes everyone who comes in contact with it; it is life altering.

"I'm not foolish enough to rationalize what happened to the men in your brother's platoon. Nor am I going to blithely say that these things happen, because anyone who studies war will already know that. But I know there is honor in service, and yes, given what you learned, that can sound deeply hypocritical. I won't argue that. Instead, I'll say this; people are good and bad, prone to acts of great courage and acts of cowardice. Always have been; always will be. As you said, there are those you respect, and they outnumber those you don't. The way we go on is to remember that they are the rule and worthy of our time. Let them be the big picture, Mr. Buttman."

Jaron stood. He was ready to go. I got up and led him to the front door. I handed him his cover.

"It must be quite the life living here," he said, as I opened the door.

"I suppose." I looked at the finery surrounding us. The colonel assumed this was my natural state of being. For a split second I thought to correct him, but what would that do? "What will happen to Lewis?"

"He'll have to come before me."

"And what will you do?"

He seemed surprised I would be concerned about Lewis, of all people.

"I'll do what I'm allowed to under the UCMJ, but most likely Lewis will be given a less than honorable discharge, which is too bad because outside of this he was a fine Marine. We'll see. Good day, Mr. Buttman."

"Good day, Colonel."

34

The big beautiful house was empty. I sat in Judith's library staring at her painting. I missed her. It was strange for the place to be so quiet, and yet that's the way it was before the family invaded; in that odd period after Judith died, before Agnes got it in her head we should live here, all of us. Theresa cleaned it top to bottom. The place was pristine. Her gift, she said. She refused every offer I made to pay her for her time. The baby stuff was gone. The adult stuff was gone. It was back to the way it had been a little more than a year and a half before. There were a few clothes in the closets on both sides of the house, and there were bathing suits in the cabana by the pool. Some things remain the same. LA and the ocean shimmered in the distance.

· · · · ·

In the two weeks since Jaron's visit, the sales for Fidel and Rebekah's house, Anna's condo, and Theresa's flower shop closed. Nothing talks faster than cold hard cash. There was also the matter of our children having no decent furniture. This did not suit Agnes. Having recently married a man of some means, she took it upon herself to make sure their new places were properly decorated with what she, and they, felt was appropriate.

"Don't be a cheapass, Buttman," was her comment the one time I brought it up. It became her go to response.

We were standing in the kitchen. "I was sure they had stuff when they first moved in together."

Agnes waved me off. "It was junk." Agnes then put her hands on her hips and cocked her head. "You're the one who dangled the good life in front of them." That again.

"So?"

"So, you're responsible obviously!"

I had no rebuttal for that kind of logic.

In addition, there was the little matter of the weddings on the horizon. I had forgotten that a lot people were coming; mothers, ex-wives, ex-husbands, family, Virginia tobacco farmers and the like. First for Barron and Gerta, then Fidel, Rebekah, Agnes and me.

And I was paying for it all. "I don't remember agreeing to any of this!"

Another wave from her imperial highness. "Don't start," she commanded.

I rolled my eyes and wandered to the backyard wondering what I was doing. Fortunately, the phone rang. The delightful Mr. Jones, my savior. I had forgotten about the show later that evening at the Manifesto; fusion jazz, one of Orville's favorites.

"Haven't heard from you, man, are you coming down?" It was good to hear his voice.

"Yeah."

"How'd the trip up north go? I heard some rumblings, *and* you've been unusually quiet." He was being stern with me.

I sighed. "It's a long story," I said.

"Then come down early. In an hour. No excuses, Buttman." Agnes was standing there smiling at me.

"Yes sir." I hung up and stared at Agnes.

"You called him, didn't you?" She came over and kissed me.

"I don't know what you're talking about." I kissed her back. "Have a good time and remember you come back here tonight, got it?" She poked me in the ribs for effect.

"Yes, dear." You have a few bad nights and slink off to the bunker in your beautiful house on the hill and you never hear the end of it.

Everyone seemed happy to see me. The felonious lovebirds Anna and Mikal both gave me hugs. Mikal enthused about how well things were going. Good venue; good crowds; good vibe. Industry people were nosing around, and the word was getting out to musicians, composers, managers, and other musical types, that the place was worth their time and effort. The rehearsal rooms were booked, classes were full, and while we weren't making the big bucks, we weren't losing the big bucks either. It helped that I had no interest in the place making a profit. Macklgrew wasn't onboard with that, but it was my money so he didn't complain too loudly. Anna was coy about whatever was going on between her and Mikal. I chose not to worry since Agnes was taking care of that all on her own.

Jones walked in as Mikal was wrapping up the good news. Anna brought the two of us something to eat. I asked her how business was.

"So far it's ok. There's good traffic, as Eric would say, and I've gotten decent reviews." I didn't pester her further.

For a large room, the dining area felt constricted. I could feel Jones watching me through the lenses of his dark sunglasses. For reasons unknown, I'd avoided coming down here and had been vague about why, so I knew he was on to me. Anna set down the plates and returned to her kitchen. We sampled our fare. It was her latest creation, flatbread sandwiches loosely based on a blend of Greek and Thai. Mine was beef, Jones' was chicken.

"What do you think?" I asked him.

"It's not bad. The food's getting better, more focused," he said. After a few bites, he took off his sunglasses, leaned back in his chair, and crossed his arms. "You gonna tell me what happened up there in Idaho?"

I thought about weaseling out. "It's not a pretty story—"

"I don't expect it to be, but your wife ratted you out. She says you've been moody and on a couple of occasions you didn't come home. Now with your history, I might think you're screwing around again, but I heard about some bad shit going down in a small town called Lautenberg, where a Marine was killed by another Marine, and it mentioned a witness named Buttman. Sound familiar?"

"Vaguely."

"Talk to me, brother." That made me smile.

"Does that mean I can—"

"No! Now talk!" I got a glimmer of a grin out of him.

Sensing no way out, I sighed, and with some hesitation told him what happened with me and Moses and my talk with Lewis. It surprised me how hard it was to say out loud. I finished with what Jaron said concerning the official response to the whole affair. I couldn't tell what Jones was thinking. He had perfected his poker face, a useful ruse in the security business, and it was on full display as I spoke. At the end, I confessed to not understanding why I was so conflicted over the matter. I had no direct connection to what happened. The person I was most connected to, Jacob, I didn't really know. And while I could rationalize the decisions they made, I felt I couldn't justify them. Jones unfolded his arms and quietly tapped his fingers on the table.

"Well?" I asked.

"Well what?" Great, he's stealing my shtick.

"You wanted to know what happened," I pressed. "Now that you do, what do you think?"

Jones leaned forward and put his elbows on the table. He started to speak, but stopped. He rubbed his hands together and leaned back again. His eyes glazed over. He was somewhere else. They began to water and after a moment he took his napkin and wiped them.

"During the first gulf war, our unit followed the initial surge that pushed the Iraqis out of Kuwait. We were basically mopping up, providing security, that kind of thing. The Iraqis had turned and run along the highway heading back to Bagdad..."

Jones looked away.

"We found them spread across an area the size of two or three football fields; maybe bigger. They'd been pulverized, blown apart. I'd never seen anything like it. They were strewn all over, but they weren't whole. It was arms and legs and torsos and heads. I don't know how many were there. Someone told me later there were more than a hundred. I don't know what hit them. A-10's maybe or helicopter gunships. Whatever it was, it tore them apart. I didn't eat or sleep for a week. And to this day I can still see them, clear as I see you. I remember thinking that's what you get for fucking with America. Just a bunch of stupid bastards dying for nothing. But I also felt my Christian upbringing telling me that these were God's children too. Men led to their deaths by tyrants who couldn't care less whether they'd left children or families behind."

"You talk to anyone about it?"

He shook his head. "No reason to. The only people I'd be comfortable bringing it up to had been there with me. I wasn't going to say anything to Coretta or the kids. What would they think? Why would I give them nightmares too?"

"But you got over it..."

Jones smiled as sad a smile as can be called one.

"No, it'll always be there. What happens is you have to go on. Life won't let you be idle unless you give up and die. I wasn't ready to die, so I focused on other things; things I had control over; things I could do right there, right then. Time passes and the memories take a back seat to living, but they never go away. You never forget. It's no different than when we found those people killed at that house; the two in the car, and the two in the house. Remember?"

"I remember." Desiree Marshan and her idiots at the beach house believing they could outsmart cold-blooded killers. They were slumped in the car and splayed out in the bedroom, their faces looking out with that dumbfounded expression. "Are you saying that was the same as war?"

Jones put on his sunglasses. "No, but the shock is the same. I know it seems crazy what happened with Jacob and the others, and I thank God I never had to face something like that, but I know how raw emotions can become, and I can imagine their anger at what those two... what were their names?"

"Dezi and Lambert," I said.

"At what they did and then boasted of getting away with. War has its own rules, and at times it has no rules. They made their choice. There's nothing you can do to change that."

"Yeah." My head hurt. I finished what Anna had put in front of me, but I wasn't hungry. Jones did the same. "How's Manny doing? Heard anything?"

Jones let out a snort. "You know that peckerhead was lying to us about being clean?"

"No, but I'm not surprised. Does that mean the job didn't work out?"

"No, he wasn't lying about that; he's a good mechanic. He's working for a man I know named Bunker, Hollis Bunker, Vietnam vet. Likes having a mixed crew. He's got Blacks, Hispanics, Filipinos, and now a white guy." Jones smiled at that.

"What?"

"Oh, it turns out Manny's got a thing for black culture, hip-hop. Holl says he fits right in. And I'll give him some credit, he is working on his addictions. He even goes to church now and again."

"Good." We looked around. The place was filling up.

Jones checked his watch. "About time for the show. You ready?" I could see he was starting to groove.

"Ready as I'll ever be."

.   .   .   .   .

Rebekah was in her new home; she had the day off, so she watched the kids instead of me. Agnes went to work; same as it ever was. I got in the car and ended up at the big house, staring at that long beautiful neck. I used to spent my free time at the beach, or in my cheap-assed lawn chair at the Moonlight Arms, shooting the breeze with the geezers, or Joanie, and glorying in that hazy SoCal sunshine.

Judith was staring at me. "Why aren't you happy, Monk?"

I didn't have an answer. I had no reason to be unhappy or dissatisfied or discontent. I had no problems. The people I loved had no problems. In truth, I'd had no real or existential problems from the day I left Virginia to my sitting here in this fine house. Only a few interesting joyrides along the way. I was as fortunate as a man could be. Everything I could want or need I had or could buy.

"So, what the fuck, Buttman?"

Yes, Mr. Jones, what the fuck!

The latest financial report from the ever reliable Mr. Macklgrew was on the table. The latest quarter had paid for the homes and businesses bought in the last two weeks, and threw more on the pile just because. I looked at Judith in all her glory. For once I didn't feel so overwhelmed with where to begin. Judith was smiling. So was I. Macklgrew might not approve, but it was my money. There were people to help. People like Manny Pronto and Al Lewis, Kurtis Santos and Mason Saunders. People like Jacob.

Finally, I had a plan.

I closed the front door and went to the Falcon. The top was down and I climbed in. One last look and I'd be on my way. I put the key in the ignition.

Damn phone started ringing.

Agnes, wondering what I was up to.

About the Author

An engineer for 40 years, David William Pearce, following open-heart surgery, decided to pursue his muse and write. He is the author of the *Monk Buttman Mystery* series. When not writing, David is the accomplished recording artist, Mr. Primitive. He and his wife live in Kenmore Washington.

Note from the Author

Word-of-mouth is crucial for any author to succeed. If you enjoyed *In the Service of Others*, please leave a review online—anywhere you are able. Even if it's just a sentence or two. It would make all the difference and would be very much appreciated.

Thanks!
David William Pearce

Thank you so much for reading one of **David William Pearce's** novels.
If you enjoyed the experience, please check out where it all began.

Where Fools Dare to Tread by David William Pearce

It's easy to be a nobody when you've got nothing to lose, but with his life and potential redemption on the line, can Monk be a somebody people will remember?

View other Black Rose Writing titles at
www.blackrosewriting.com/books and use promo code
PRINT to receive a **20% discount** when purchasing.